KNOT ON YOUR LIFE

RAELYNN ROSE

TRIGGER WARNINGS

Because your mental health is important to me, I wanted to alert you that there are elements of physical abuse in this book (NOT committed by the MCs).

There is also mild BDSM including Shibari, flogging, and spanking.

Voyeurism/exhibitionism (among the pack)

MM and MMFFMM

Explicit sex scenes

Predator and Prey play that ends in CNC (Consensual non-consent)

If I forgot anything, I apologize in advance.

If none of this has scared you off, enjoy!

Before you go, have you joined the party yet? Oops, I meant my newsletter. You can join here for a free short story within the Romegaverse world.

CHAPTER 1

<u>Kennedy</u>

My feet ached and my muscles were sore. It was my first night back since I'd taken time off during Spencer's heat. I probably should have taken off a few more days to recoup before going back to work at *Plumes et Fouets*. But since Rey tended to stay close to our omega, I was the sole bread winner.

And, hell, I made a lot of money as a performer. I didn't mind the fetish nights when I was tied to structures and tickled or whatever, but where I really shone was during burlesque month. That was where I could really put on a show, doing routines on aerial silks, dancing, or any other spot my boss needed me to fill.

Hitting the key fob, I yanked open the back door and tossed my bag into the backseat. It might be time for some new costumes. I'd already grown tired of the ones I'd had for the past year. Maybe something...sparkly. I had to keep it skimpy, sexy, but that didn't mean I couldn't find something with a little more bling.

"Raven?" Not my real name. Meaning whoever was approaching at a fast clip was a fan or a member of the audience.

With a sigh, I made sure all but the driver's side door was locked in case I needed to jump in quickly without this person attempting to climb in one of the other doors.

I didn't bother with a smile. It was best to keep from being too friendly with these guys; once I was off the clock, I no longer had to make them believe they had a chance in hell with me.

When I turned, my head tilted back until my neck was nearly strained to look into the face of the man who had managed to get within touching distance of me without me hearing his steps.

Shit.

"How can I help you?" I said, keeping my voice emotionless and my face a mask of neutrality with a touch of irritation. I'd perfected that look over the past three years as a performer.

"I just..." He reached out a hand, and I took a step back until my car hit my back. "I wanted to tell you that you put on an amazing show. You're my favorite. I've seen you on fetish nights, too. Very believable performances."

Believable? Of course they were believable. I enjoyed what I did, even when I was being teased or whipped by one of the other performers.

I never allowed anything that would leave welts or permanent marks of any kind due to the outfits I wore for burlesque. But I had never been opposed to a little spanking or paddling. We all knew our limits and knew how to hit the recipients without breaking skin.

"Thank you," I said with a short nod of my head.

Reaching behind me, I grabbed the handle and pulled.

Fuck. I'd managed to lock all the doors. Meaning I would have to hit the fob, alerting this asshole that I was opening the door when the horn beeped and the lock popped up.

"If you'll excuse me, it's been a long night. I need to get back to my alphas."

He didn't need to know there was only one, that my pack consisted of me – a beta – my rare female alpha and my even rarer male omega. As far as he knew, there was a slew of big, strong men waiting for me.

"Is there any way I could hire you for a private party?"

"Sorry. I'm part of a company. I don't do private contracts."

I thumbed the fob and hid the wince when all four locks popped. I would have to open the door to lock the other three. Stupid old car. Might as well have given him my back and unlocked the damn thing with a key like the old days while I was at it.

"We don't have to tell anyone. Just you and me. You can trust me. I'll…I won't touch you, if that's what you're worried about."

"I don't do private performances."

Although there was a room for VIPs who wished to be part of the show for quite an exorbitant sum of cash. But no way in hell would I tell him that.

When his hand reached forward this time, he didn't bother stopping himself as he wrapped his fingers around my bicep.

Out here, without the scent filtration system, I could detect his burnt beans smell. Which meant he would be able to tell I was a beta. If my body didn't give it away. At five-feet-seven-inches tall, I wasn't petite like an omega, but I did have big boobs, a round ass, and round hips. Those three attributes helped draw the eye to me. My performance skills kept those eyes on me and made me one of the most highly requested performers for the VIP room.

"I need you to release my arm and step back."

Shit. The one night I refused an escort to my car. It was late, we'd been closed long enough that the parking lot had emptied. I'd stupidly assumed there would be no threat of anyone lingering. Why would I? Two years at *Plumes et Fouets* and this was my first official overzealous fan.

"I'll pay you twice what they pay you here. I know how often you disappear into the backroom. I'll pay you more."

Fuck. He knew about the VIP room. "Why don't you simply wait until tomorrow night and reserve private time with me?"

His grip tightened to the point of uncomfortable and something passed through his eyes, something that made my stomach turn.

He didn't reserve private time in the club with me because he had no intention of letting me walk back out of his house after we were done. I highly doubted he would heed my safe word and stop when things went too far.

"I'm not an omega," I said, hoping that would be enough to deter him.

Omegas were the coveted designation. They were the ones alphas sought, the ones who were more on the side of subservient, the ones who could carry pups.

"Is that supposed to make a difference?" he asked. Even his voice sounded different. It was no longer friendly, as though he'd grown tired of trying to put me at ease.

No. This asshole had every intention of forcing my hand, of making me bend to his will. He would do whatever was necessary to ensure I was in his custody. Permanently.

Opening my mouth to scream, hoping there was someone close enough to the doors to hear me, I jumped when his hand slammed over my mouth hard enough to force the tender flesh of my lips into my teeth.

The coppery taste of blood teased my tongue.

This mother fucker had the balls to touch me? To manhandle me?

Without a second thought, I shifted enough to bite down on his fingers then threw my knee up, slamming against his balls. Maybe I got lucky and got the entire package with one hit and his dick wouldn't work for a few days.

The moment he released me, I turned and tried to wrench my door open, jerking my hand away to keep it from getting broken when he reached over my shoulder to slam it shut, yanking me around by my arm.

Shit. I should have pushed past him and ran for the back door. He couldn't have been stupid enough to follow me, not with the enormous and highly trained alphas kept on staff as bouncers and security.

"You fucking bitch!" he roared in my face, spit hitting my cheek.

Well, shit.

When his hand wrapped around my throat, I had a moment to

wonder why the hell I hadn't simply played along, pretended I was interested in hopes of disarming him.

Instead, I would be found dead on a dirty, glass and gravel covered parking lot of my place of employment. I would be found by the people I'd called friends for the past two years.

Raking my nails down the backs of his hands, I struggled to get any release from his death grip. He'd fully cut off my air supply and black dots began to shimmer at the corners of my vision.

"Hey," a man said calmly from behind my attacker.

He glanced over his shoulder, his grip loosening enough for me to pull in a little air.

And as I watched, a knife drug across his throat, opening a gash and spraying my face with blood as it gushed from him, staining his shirt and the ground around us.

His hand left me and slapped over the wound as though he could stem the loss of his life's force. But that cut...his head was held on only by his spine at this point.

Gasping in air and coughing, I fought the urge to puke as he finally dropped to his knees, then fell backward at a weird angle, his eyes wide and staring unseeing up at the night sky.

Behind him stood a man with hair nearly as dark as mine. His eyes were shadowed, and his body was backlit, but I swore I could feel his eyes locked on mine.

"Sorry I was late. He should have already been dead," the man said, a slight Russian accent coloring his words.

Unable to form a sentence – or coherent thought – I shook my head.

The Russian nodded at the corpse. "He should never have been able to lay a finger on you. He should have been dead hours ago. I was held up...with something else."

Either I was losing my mind or this man actually sounded apologetic.

And then he turned on his heel and walked away, practically disappearing into the shadows at the edge of the parking lot.

The moment I was able to pull enough air into my lungs, I

screamed and ran for the back entrance. I wouldn't be blamed for this. I could have easily gone home, but he was lying right where I was parked. Someone would connect the dots. Even if the cameras recorded every moment of the past few minutes, that man had never turned toward them and had kept his face in the shadows.

I could be accused of murder. They would lock me up and I would never see Rey or Spence again.

The door flew open before I could reach it and those who remained poured out.

"What the fuck happened?" my favorite bouncer, Milo, said, grabbing me by my shoulders and bending to look into my face. "What happened? Where is he?"

"Not my blood," I managed to squeak out.

This wasn't my first dance with violence. This wasn't the first time I'd seen someone murdered. But I had never come so close to losing my own life, nor had I ever been covered in someone else's gore.

Three more bouncers ran past us and straight to the alpha in the parking lot.

"Holy shit," my boss said as she stumbled down the stairs, her eyes going from me to the body then back. "What the fuck happened?"

Anais had opened and run this club for close to ten years. Not once in all that time had there ever been a single incident the bouncers weren't able to handle before it got out of control. Not once had any of her performers been so at risk, so up close with such violence.

She ran a high-end club with a dress code and strict rules in place. No nudity. No sex of any form. Everyone was trained to not only watch out for ourselves, but to keep an eye on our coworkers, as well.

"Why the fuck were you out here alone?"

And we were trained to never leave the building without an escort.

"I—" Trembles had started in my hands and spread to every inch of my body. No matter what I'd seen in my life, seeing a man's throat opened inches from my face, literally tasting his blood on my lips and feeling it on my skin was something I wasn't sure I would be able to forget. "The parking lot was empty. And everyone was busy."

Milo drew me into his arms, even as I pushed him away.

"You're going to get blood on your clothes," I protested weakly, but finally melted into his embrace.

At no point had either of us pursued anything romantic or sexual. He was like a big brother…well, maybe just a best friend. Pretty sure a big brother wouldn't want to watch his sister perform in the dress or manner I did.

"Did anyone call the police yet?" Anais questioned, turning me in Milo's arms so she could check me over.

"Told you. It's not my blood."

"Your neck looks bruised." Her fingers raised as though to touch it but drew back.

I didn't blame her. Her fingers would have come away sticky and coated in crimson.

"He was strangling me."

"Girl…" Milo growled out. He didn't release his hold on me, but he did turn me so he could look into my face. "Tell me everything."

I told him everything my fuzzy brain could remember up until the moment they'd come outside when I ran screaming.

Sirens wailed in the background. I was with my friends. The police were on the way. I was safe.

So why couldn't I shake the sensation that there was a pair of eyes watching my every move from the shadows?

CHAPTER 2

$\mathcal{M}$ ilo had called Rey while I spoke with the police. I would have rather he not. The moment I pulled into the garage, she and Spence were both waiting for me, panic all over their sleep deprived faces.

"Holy shit," Spence breathed out, rushing forward, then almost skidding to a stop when he got a full view of my appearance. "Are you hurt? Are you okay?"

"I need a shower. And I need to be held," I said as tears welled in my eyes.

Rey rushed past Spence and, regardless of the blood, pulled me into her arms, resting her cheek against mine. She stood a few inches taller than me but had all the power and authority of her male counterparts. Spence was only five-foot-nine and had a slight, but toned build, unlike female omegas who tended to barely stand taller than five feet and were soft and curvy.

I knew if Rey was a little taller or I was a little smaller, she would have scooped me in her arms and carried me into the house.

But I could walk just fine. Spence was the one who liked all the attention. Hell, our omega thrived on cuddles, compliments, and gifts. And he had zero issues with being a stereotype of his designation.

That had actually worked out well for Rey and me – both of us loved to dote on our omega, loved to shower him with affection of any form.

"Go get washed up and we'll meet in the pack bed," Rey said, leading me through the house with an arm wrapped around my shoulders. She would need a shower and change of clothes, too, after touching me so much.

"Hell no. I'm not letting you out of my sight," Spence said, tugging his clothes off as we walked through my room.

He turned the spigot and stepped in ahead of me, holding his arms open in invitation.

Rey followed me in, and I couldn't stop the tears from falling as my packmates gently cleaned the blood from my hair, my face, and every exposed inch of my body. Even with their hands smoothing over my naked flesh, there was absolutely nothing sexual about it. It was simply packmates caring for each other.

Spencer ran a towel all over my body, drying me from head to toe while Rey focused on brushing out my long, inky black hair. I was their beta, but they doted on me as much as Rey and I doted on our beautiful omega.

"Guilty pleasure, comfort, or background noise?" Spencer asked as he crawled onto the bed first, lifting the remote to bring the TV to life.

"Comfort," Rey and I said at the same time.

I loved these two so much. Rey and I were in love but were rarely together in a sexual manner; except for when the three of us were locked together for a week in the nest. That time was usually spent helping Spence, though.

I climbed in after Spencer, snuggling against his chest, and sighed when Rey wrapped around my back, her arm draped over me to rest on Spencer's stomach. We were a small and unconventional pack, but we were happy. We kept each other safe. We loved each other.

The opening credits to *Steel Magnolias* started and I let my body relax, focusing my mind on nothing but the screen and the sounds of Spencer's heartbeat below my ear.

It wasn't long before I drifted off, but, unfortunately, woke far too often with nightmares filled with blood.

Only it was mine that coated my skin in my nightmares. The knife cut across my throat each time. And a soundless scream tore my lips apart, waking me at least four times before the sun finally rose and I was tired of lying in bed and not getting any real sleep.

I had all day before I had to get ready for my shift tonight. I was sure Anais would demand I take time off, but not only did I need to make sure I made enough to keep my pack in comfort – especially when my omega adored anything with a designer label – but, honestly, I loved my job. I had always loved dancing, always loved performing.

Hell, I even loved the fetish months.

Besides, I would get plenty of time off when we rolled over to drag shows. I could take a few shifts waiting tables, but I wouldn't be straining my body the way I did when I swung from the silk ropes or when I was tied down and pleasantly dominated and tortured.

Rey scooted until she could snuggle Spence when I climbed from my spot between them and made my way to the bathroom to go through my morning routine.

After that…coffee. I would need copious amounts of caffeine if I was going to stay on my feet for the next few hours. Oh, I planned on taking a nap before my shift, but my body had grown achy from lying in bed, squished between my packmates.

As the fragrant brown gold dripped into the pot, I pulled my arms over my head and stretched, shivering a little at the cool air on my naked body. We rarely wore clothes to bed – there was just something so comforting about skin on skin, especially when any of us had had a shit day.

And that had been one hell of a shit day. Or rather night.

Who the hell had that second guy been? And what had he meant? *He'd been late. That wouldn't have happened had he not been held up.*

Did that mean he knew my attacker? And did he mean he'd meant to kill him earlier?

Another shiver wracked my body, but this one had nothing to do with the chilly air and everything to do with the fact I had been so close to a possible murderer.

For the moment, what he'd done had been in defense of me, even if he had taken off immediately after.

Once my coffee was poured and doctored with enough sugar and creamer to be just this side of too sweet, I carried it to the table and lowered my butt to the cool chair.

There were so many questions about last night that I very well might never get the answers to. I highly doubted the mystery man would show up at my door with an explanation. And being as he'd hightailed it out of there, there was no way he would turn himself over to the police.

Sorry I was late. He should have already been dead.

What the hell did that mean?

I jumped when something soft was draped around my shoulders, but eased when the sweet, tart scent of red wine wrapped around me and soothed my growing anxiety.

"You realize all the curtains and blinds are open," she grumbled as she made her way to the coffee pot.

My alpha wasn't a morning person.

"I'm sure the neighbors have seen more than just my boobs," I retorted.

Not like we ran around and shut everything down when Spencer got horny. Or…you know, when *any of us* got horny.

It didn't take his heat for Spence to be needy. I swore that omega constantly wanted to be touched, licked, sucked, and fucked. And Rey and I were always more than happy to oblige.

She sat beside me with her coffee and turned to stare at me. Her fingers were gentle and firm as she tilted my chin up and hissed.

"Fucking asshole."

"*Dead* asshole," I reminded her.

"And you don't know who it was? Who either of them was?"

Shaking my head, I pulled her hand from my chin and squeezed it before releasing it. "No. I couldn't really see the guy who…the other one. The one who killed the asshole. He said…" I took a sip of my coffee. "He said 'Sorry I was late. He should have already been dead.'"

"What the fuck is that supposed to mean?"

"No idea. Maybe he was looking for him? But why would he be dead? I keep thinking he was hunting that first guy or something. But he didn't look or act like a cop. And he had a Russian accent. It was light, but it was there."

Rey hummed and nodded, but said nothing else, her focus on the wall across from her as she sipped at her coffee.

Pipes squeaked down the hall. Spencer was up now, too.

"Did I wake you guys up?" I asked. I'd thought I'd been quiet, and it was still too early for the house to be up and moving around.

"Nah. He wants to go shopping."

A snort escaped me. Part of the reason I loved my job was the fact I made enough money to spoil the shit out of my omega.

"Which designer released a new line?" I teased.

Her head shook as she swallowed her sip. "Grocery store, *Nesters*, and he said he wants to look at some new costumes for you."

It wasn't uncommon for my pack to attend my performances. And it was absolutely foreplay for when I returned home, although my alpha and omega often started before I joined them.

"I was actually thinking I wanted something new. Maybe something a little more eye catching."

Rey's eyes dipped to my chest before raising to my face. "Pretty sure you're eye catching enough."

"Flirt," I teased. "I'm just ready for something new. Been rotating through the same few costumes for a year. And fetish month is in a week, so maybe something new for that, too."

Not that I wore a whole lot during that month. But all the staff wore some degree of fetish wear or another, whether chain mesh, partially see through, leather, or the like.

Looked like we were doing a group outing. Although I really had no desire to go to the grocery store. I'd simply drive separately and split off when they went to *Nesters* and grocery shopping so I could take a nap and then start getting ready for my shift tonight.

"What does he need at *Nesters*?" His little nest was stock full of every texture of pillow and blanket possible.

"He said he wants some twinkle lights and black out curtains. And there's a new product that he can add our scents to then wear it all day," Rey explained.

She stood and started rifling through the fridge for something to make for breakfast.

"He's with you all day."

"But he's not with *you* all day. Believe it or not, your omega misses you when you're gone."

I swore my heart did a little pitter patter. I fucking adored my tiny pack. I was so in love with both of them and missed them when they didn't make an appearance during my shifts.

As Rey mixed up the batter for pancakes, I mentally counted in my mind to Spencer's next heat. We should have a few more months. And then I would have to take a week off to help Rey see him through it. Oh, such a hardship to spend days on end getting licked and fucked to the point of exhaustion.

Rey took the brunt of it, though, being as she had a lock and I didn't; the best I could offer was my mouth, hands, ass, and pussy. And the silicon lock I'd procured to give Rey a break when she looked as though she was ready to pass out from exhaustion, hunger, and dehydration.

Without bothering to wait for my omega, I dove into the stack of pancakes my alpha sat in front of me, pressed a quick kiss to her lips, then headed off to change and get ready for our outing.

I wore quite a bit of makeup during my shifts, but always worried someone might recognize me in public. And it had nothing to do with being ashamed of my job, but fear of something like last night happening. Nothing worse than some fan of my work thinking he could flirt with me or, like what happened last night, try to force me to be with him.

By the time I'd changed, pulled my waist length black hair into a bun, and shoved my feet into a pair of sneakers, Spencer was done eating and waiting not so patiently for me.

"I was thinking," he started as I rounded the corner. "You could really use some new clothes. New costumes. Something–"

"Sparkly," I finished. "Yeah. I was thinking the same thing. Oh. And I have an idea for a new routine for the next burlesque month I want to show you two later." Later as in either before I left for work or my next day off. Because when I got home, it was rare to have enough energy to make love to my omega, let alone dangle from silk or a hoop.

"Oooh. Color me intrigued," Spencer teased. "You ready?"

"Yep."

Rey grabbed her keys and she and Spence piled into the small SUV parked in the garage while I climbed behind the wheel of my crappy little sedan. I had more than enough money to upgrade to something nicer, but Betsy had done just fine for me for the past eight years. No reason to dump her just because she was no longer the newest car on the lot.

Rolling down my window, I waited for Spence to do the same. "I'll meet you at *Latex and Lace*. I'm going to head home after for a nap before I get ready for work tonight."

"I still can't believe Anais is making you–"

I held up a hand to cut Spence off. "She's not making me do anything. I'm going because I love my job. And because I have a spoiled rotten omega who has expensive taste," I said, then rolled up the window before he could reply.

Didn't stop him from sticking out his tongue at me. Not like he could argue – he was spoiled rotten and did have expensive taste. But Rey and I also had a tendency toward bending to his every whim.

Except for the child thing. We would have to add a male alpha for that, and the two of us were completely happy with our life. Another alpha in the house could end up throwing off the beautiful balance.

CHAPTER 3

<u>Alexei</u>

*P*erhaps I was glutton for punishment. Or I could simply tell myself I was here to check on the woman from last night.

The woman who'd appeared in my dreams, causing me to have to palm my cock and jerk off in hopes of purging her from my thoughts.

It hadn't worked. Neither had jerking off in the shower after completing another contract and taking the life of a habitual pedophile. He'd molested and raped too many children and the court still refused to lock him up. So...I'd been contracted to end the line of misery.

That kind of contract was always my favorite.

And now...

I was at a table as close to the stage as I could get without being obvious. Not that she'd seen my face. I'd made damn sure of it.

The lights were dim, even between performers, but each of the tables had candles flickering for those who wanted to eat while being entertained.

A glass of vodka sat in front of me completely untouched. Had to keep up the illusion of being there for any other reason than stalking the woman from last night. Shiny black hair. Blue eyes the color of sapphires. Creamy, soft, pale skin.

So I didn't technically know if it was soft. I hadn't touched her.

Yet.

But I would.

I should have told Wolf where I was going, what I was planning. He would demand I share her. For now, I wanted her all to myself. I wanted to hold on to this little fantasy a little longer before she laid eyes on Wolfram and decided she would rather have my broody, sexy packmate over me.

Unless…

Maybe she wouldn't mind two alphas in her life. It was far from unheard of. I had seen packs with close to a dozen members before.

Yet…it had always been Wolf and me. Only the two of us. We didn't want a pack. We didn't want the responsibility of caring for and doting on a needy omega.

My raven-haired beauty wasn't an omega, though. And, up until that asshole had grabbed her by the throat and nearly strangled her unconscious, she'd done a damn good job at holding her own. A smile had split my face when she'd slammed her knee into his balls.

That moment of distraction hadn't lasted long enough. So I'd had to step in.

Had I been on time, she would have never had that interaction, wouldn't have been accosted.

And I wouldn't have laid eyes on her.

She was mine. She would be mine. And I would spend every free moment making her moan and cry out with pleasure. I would shower her with gifts, buy her a better, *safer* car, and build her a fucking house if she wanted.

And then she would never have to walk into this place again. She would never have to perform for people, would never have to…what did she do here?

I hadn't seen her walking around with any trays, hadn't seen her behind the bar. Fuck. She could be off tonight after what she'd gone through last night. I tended to forget the average person wasn't accustomed to being coated in blood the way she had been last night. She could have been traumatized. She could have asked for some time off to process what she'd witnessed.

A spotlight flashed onto the stage, highlighting blood red silk ropes hanging from the ceiling. At the base of those ropes was a woman on her knees, her arms stretched over her head as though she was being restrained by those ropes.

"Ladies and gentlemen…Raven," the emcee said over the PA.

Her head raised, and those piercing blue eyes seemed to find me in the darkness, as though she knew I was watching.

I knew, in reality, she was merely looking in the direction of the audience. Surely, every person in there thought she was looking at them.

Unlike last night, that dark as night hair was loose and hanging down her back and shoulders. Her eyes were coated in dark makeup, making the blue even more striking. Her lips were slathered in the same shiny red as the silk ropes.

She looked as though she was restrained and waiting…for me.

The music started, a slow, sexy tempo, and the ropes began to rise, dragging her to her feet as her head rolled on her shoulders and finally giving me a better peek of her body.

She wore a black, see-through one-piece deal. Her nipples would have been exposed had she not donned something underneath. There was a shimmer to the fabric that caught and sparkled in the spotlight as she rose higher and higher, her body moving to the beat as she twisted her hands and feet into the silk.

When she was high in the air, she dropped back, only hanging by her feet, her long hair swaying and shining like a fucking beacon, practically begging for my hands to be tangled in it as I took her from behind.

The song built as did her performance. She would twist and writhe, and then her legs would open wide in the splits, her head rolling on her shoulders as though she was being pleasured. And fuck me, I wanted to have my face buried between those muscular thighs.

For a beta, she was a little curvy. Small waist, full, heavy tits, round hips, and a nice fat ass that made me want to sink my teeth into the fleshy globes.

The longer she performed, the harder I grew. As tempted as I was to palm myself under the table, there were strict rules in *Plumes et Fouets*. No sex. No full nudity. No touching the staff in any way unless given explicit permission. And even then…no fucking sex.

I knew of the VIP room, the high cost of some private time with any of the performers. But that still wouldn't be enough. I wanted more than to watch her dance. I wanted to feel the weight of Raven's big tits in my hands, to pull away the costume and suck her nipples into my mouth. I wanted to plunge my fingers into her cunt, then lick and suck at her clit until she fell apart on my tongue.

I wanted to plunge my cock knot deep in her and see if she was daring enough to attempt to take the thickness, to enjoy the burning pleasure of being locked around an alpha.

As all these fantasies played through my mind, the song began to wind down and she was lowered to the ground, her wrists once more appearing bound, until she was on her back, arching as her legs scissored together, again, simulating being fucked, being pleasured.

The spotlight shut off and the crowd burst into applause and whistles.

Mine. That beta was mine. She didn't know it yet, but I would find a way to make her mine. I would show her that she could enjoy more than simply pretending to be restrained by silk ropes. I would show her…fuck. I would show her everything and give her the world for just one night with the unbelievable beauty.

For two weeks, I repeated the same pattern. If I had a contract, I'd fulfill the contract, ensure I had a reserved table close to the stage, then stare up at the woman who called herself Raven on stage. And I needed to know her real name. Needed to hear her voice.

After she was done, I would down my vodka, pay my tab, then rush home to jerk off until I spilled either on my stomach or on the shower floor.

Two weeks of fucking only my hand. This might have been the longest time I'd gone without burying my dick in another person since the day I'd lost my virginity to a sexy as hell beta. He'd thought we were in love. I was only in love with his mouth.

Hell. I had no idea what love was or how to define it. I supposed I loved Wolf, but I didn't have the desire to sink my dick in anything he had to offer. Ours was nothing more than pack love, brotherly love.

Now, I was at another table. I'd paid the hostess well to alert me to which table Raven would appear on now that they'd switched over to fetish nights. I wanted to be up close and personal with my fantasy woman.

And I'd made damn sure I wouldn't be sharing the table with anyone else. Just me and my beautiful beta.

In the hopes of not standing out too much, I'd ordered an appetizer and another vodka, although, just like every time before, they sat untouched. Tonight, I was there for one reason and one reason only – the VIP lounge at the end of her performance. I might not have been able to get what I truly wanted, but at least I would have a little more leeway, some way to actually touch her.

And fuck me…I sounded like some sick stalker, the same kind of fuckers I killed on a regular basis.

The performers began to file from a back room clothed in various degrees of not quite naked. But close enough.

Raven was helped onto the stand directly in front of me. A man stood behind her and gently pushed onto her shoulders, ordering her onto her knees. She wore a red leather corset that was open under her breasts. Only her nipples were covered with red pasties. Her lower half was hidden by a barely there red thong. And I would have paid any amount of money to have her turn around and bend over so I could run my hands along each cheek.

This time, when her eyes locked on my face, I knew she was seeing only me. There was no spotlight in her eyes, no one around me to snare her attention. Through everything that happened during her performance, she would have to focus solely on me as she received her punishment or pleasure.

Or both. To me, there was only the finest line between the two when it came to fucking.

The man raised her wrists and bound them with rope, then secured them at the top of the wood stand behind her.

And then, he began to expertly wrap her in the style of Shibari, crisscrossing her waist, her tits, her stomach. The rope lifted her tits, and her position caused her to arch her back and made them more prominent.

My dick was painfully hard and my mouth watered at the sight. She was like an erotic gift waiting to be unwrapped.

Decision made, I called over one of the attendants and immediately booked one of the VIP rooms before anyone else could get to my girl. She was mine. I would finally have a moment with her, private time with her. I would finally hear her voice.

And her moans. I might not have been able to fuck her, but there were more ways to bring a woman pleasure than simply stuffing her with my thick cock.

I watched her every physical nuance, noted the rapid rising and falling of her chest as the ropes dragged along her skin, as the man tightened or loosened the design he'd worked around her. If she was an omega, I knew her thong would be soaked with slick and the sweet liquid would be coating her upper thighs.

Even with the pasties securely in place, I could see the way her nipples pebbled with arousal.

By the time her performance was over and she was freed, my cock was weeping with precum, dampening the boxers I'd thankfully donned. Otherwise, the front of my slacks would have had a visible spot.

Raven was helped from the stage, her smile demure as her eyes stayed locked on mine, then she was led away from the dining room, and, hopefully, delivered to the room I had reserved.

The attendant bent and whispered the room number into my ear and then scampered away. Food and drink still sitting untouched on the table, I slowly unfolded myself from my seat and straightened my jacket.

Only two others were heading down the same dimly lit hallway as me, ducking through various doors.

And then I came upon room number four where my beta would be waiting for me.

She sat in a winged back chair, dressed exactly the same, her legs crossed, her arms relaxed on the rests.

"I suppose I should say thank you?"

Swinging the door shut behind me, I tilted my head.

"You saved my life that night."

So she did remember me.

"Your real name would be payment enough."

A sultry chuckle rumbled from her and made my dick twitch behind my slacks.

"You deserve far more than simply my name…but it's Kennedy."

"Alexei," I said, introducing myself with a light bow.

"So…Alexei. There are a few rules we need to go over. No penetration. I use a simple system: Green means we're good to continue, yellow means I'm growing uncomfortable but not quite ready to give in, red means you stop immediately. No questions asked. There are cameras there and there," she said, pointing to two corners of the room. "Both with audio, meaning we will have an audience if you're okay with that. But it's for my safety as much as yours. You can't pass my boundaries and I can't accuse you of anything you haven't done."

I nodded as she discussed our time together as though it was a business interaction. And I supposed it was.

"Are there any boundaries you wish to discuss?"

"None," I said. Honestly, because there wasn't much I wouldn't try other than anything to do with bodily fluids. Including blood. I had never been one who understood the need to slice into the flesh of someone I was pleasuring.

"While there is no penetration, I'm not opposed to you fondling yourself if the pressure grows to be too much, but you may not insert anything in any part of me. I'm a performer, not a prostitute."

A deep chuckle escaped me at that. "Not a hooker. Got it."

"You're not nervous," she said with a tilt of her own head.

Oh, I was nervous as fuck. I just wouldn't let her see it. I never let anyone see my emotions. Emotions were often perceived as weakness.

"No. Not nervous," I said, and let my eyes roam her, drinking her in.

"Is there something in particular you were interested in? Are you dominant or do you prefer to be dominated?"

With a slow shake of my head, I stalked toward her and held out my hand. She slid her tiny one into mine and let me pull her to her feet and lead her to the table.

Turning her, I pressed my front to her back, partially to feel her body heat and partially to let her feel the hard length being restrained behind my pants.

"Bend over," I said, pressing a hand between her shoulder blades and leading her forward until her chest was flat against the table. "Don't move."

Rounding slowly, smiling when I caught her eyes tracking my movements, I restrained her hands so she couldn't pull away.

"How often would you like me to check in?" I asked, crouching before her so we were eye to eye.

"I'll let you know if things move toward yellow or red. I want you to enjoy yourself."

I would absolutely enjoy myself. But I was going to make damn sure she got off, whether I could touch her pussy or not.

While she watched me, I perused the various tools hanging on display, glancing back at her each time my fingers ran over a crop, a whip, then finally settled on a wooden paddle. There was heat and curiosity in those bright blue depths and her breath was coming quickly again as though she was turned on in anticipation.

"If I strike too hard, tell me," I said, leaning so my lips grazed the shell of her ear and smiled to myself when she shivered the slightest bit.

For a moment, I stood behind her, admiring the roundness of her ass, the light red marks that had been left by the ropes softly chafing her skin. I stared at the sheer fabric separating her cunt from me, and noted the material was absolutely damp with her arousal.

"May I touch your ass with my hands?" I asked.

Yeah, I had paid more than a car payment for this hour with her, but I would never push her past her boundaries.

"Yes," she breathed out.

Smoothing my hands from her spine, I lingered slowly over each cheek before drawing one hand back and delivering a sharp slap.

The gasp that tore from her lips nearly made me blow my load then and there.

But I was far from done. An hour would never be enough, but I was going to take advantage of every moment we had together.

A couple more slaps with my hand and then I switched to the paddle. I would slap a cheek, the sound loud in the room, then smooth the red mark with the palm of my hand.

Then...I decided to take a chance. Tossing the paddle onto the table next to her hip, I returned to spanking her with only my hand, moving to the backs of her thighs, before kicking her feet wider.

Her breathing was coming in pants and, even with the filtration system, I could smell the beta's arousal, could smell cranberries and something savory in the air, could practically taste it on my tongue.

After another slap and caress of her thigh, I swatted her pussy through her thong and waited.

"You doing okay, lyubov'?"

"Green," she moaned out, her voice breathy.

Ohhh. She'd liked that. I wasn't supposed to touch her pussy.

Actually, what she'd said was no penetration.

Slapping her left thigh, I immediately moved to spank her pussy again, not giving her a chance to feel any relief between the stings.

A moan escaped her and her hips shifted the slightest bit.

I needed to be closer. I was going to lose my mind if I ever had the chance to feel that wet pussy wrapped around my cock. I would even settle for plunging my fingers into her until she screamed out my name.

For now, I would have to settle for teasing an orgasm out of her.

I became crazed, raking my nails lightly along her ass as though to soothe her before spanking her pussy again. And then I gave her three swift swats directly over her clit, one after the other, until she cried out and jerked, her legs shaking and her panties becoming transparent with her release.

Leaning as close as I dared, I inhaled deeply, memorizing her scent, searing it into my mind to use later.

Although she'd said I was permitted to fondle myself.

With my hands running along her ass, her spine, her thighs, I pulled my dick free and began to pull fast and hard.

"I want to come on your ass," I gritted out between clenched teeth.

"Yes. Please. I want to feel the heat," she begged as she writhed as though trying to pull from the restraints.

That was it. She had found the last of my control. My balls tightened, my knot swelled, and I shot my load across her lower back and her round ass, watching, mesmerized, as it began to trail down her skin.

It wasn't enough. I wanted her coated in my scent. I wanted anyone who came close enough to know I had branded her with my cum.

With shaky hands, I rubbed every drop into her skin like the most erotic lotion until her skin was only slightly tacky.

I'd thought feeling her, talking to her, making her come would purge her from my mind.

I couldn't have been more wrong. All I had done was cause an obsession unlike anything I'd ever known to begin.

Now, I had to find a way to spend time with her outside this place, away from the cameras, and without all the fucking rules.

CHAPTER 4

<u>Kennedy</u>

*A*lexei's hands were gentle as they caressed their way up my arms and undid the restraints around my wrists.

Not only had I gotten off, but I hadn't stopped him when he'd touched my pussy. And I'd begged him to spill on my bare skin. His hands were so warm and slightly calloused as he'd rubbed his cum into my skin as though searing his scent into my flesh.

Now, I stood in the shower, begrudgingly scrubbing every inch of my body in hopes of washing away his warm autumn scent. He'd smelled of juniper with crisp hints of snow, his signature reaching me past the scent filtration system.

What had I been thinking? Yeah, he'd saved my life. And hell yes, he was beyond sexy.

But he'd killed a man right in front of me. And made it sound as though that had been his purpose all along. The man was dangerous.

Yet...not once in the hour we'd spent behind the locked door had I felt a moment of fear. Although there were cameras and microphones for security to monitor for our safety.

Honestly, had the cameras been off, I still wouldn't have feared Alexei. Something about him just screamed protective alpha. And I wasn't even a freaking omega.

Spencer and Rey were dead asleep when I climbed into the pack bed, curling myself around my omega and turning my head to rest my cheek against his back.

They wouldn't have cared if I'd carried another alpha's scent, but for some reason I'd felt a twinge of guilt over the fact I'd let him cum on me, as though I'd betrayed Rey.

Closing my eyes, I ran every single moment of the night through my head, including the moment my eyes locked with his at the table and I knew without a doubt who sat there. I hadn't seen his face clearly, yet I'd known it was him, known it was my dark hero.

How had he ended up at the exact table where I would perform? Had he paid someone under the table? That was severely against the rules. Even my own pack had never attempted to gain that kind of special favor.

I really should mention it to Anais. But that would result in someone getting fired and I loved my coworkers too much to cause their unemployment. We had an amazing cast and crew. Every single one of us got along, a rarity in the workplace.

Anais and Milo had both been pissed that I'd returned to work so quickly, but I'd waved them off.

Wait…had Alexei seen my burlesque performances? Or had he waited for fetish month to begin so he could request the VIP room with me?

For some reason, the thought of him watching me work my aerial silks from the dark sent a new wave of heat and lust coursing through me to the point I was tempted to wake Spencer to help ease the growing pressure low in my belly.

But I wouldn't. It was way too late. Just because I had a wonky schedule didn't mean my pack needed to, especially being how quiet they were when I slept late into the day.

The day we'd all gone shopping together, Rey and Spence had helped me pick out a few new outfits for both my aerial burlesque performances and my fetish shows. I'd gone home after but had sat patiently the next morning while Spence showed me all his new goodies for the nest.

My omega loved gifts and being pampered, but he definitely wasn't feminine by any stretch of the imagination. His nest was painted in dark colors, the padded floor, blankets, and pillows were all in rich, earthy tones, and the blackout curtains he'd chosen were literally black. But the lights he'd chosen to string along the ceiling and walls cast a soft glow and allowed us to see each other even when he was uber sensitive to every one of his senses.

As my mind finally began to slow and my lids drooped, Alexei's intense gaze followed me into my dreams. Instead of replaying the events of the night, my mind decided to take it further. And we were no longer at the club but in a room with walls painted as black as my hair.

When I woke, the sun was creeping through a small gap in the blinds, and I was damn close to orgasm.

Holy shit. Simply dreaming about the alpha and my body had reacted.

No noise made it through the door, but my pack was no longer in bed with me. I was tempted to take another shower, just to make sure Alexei's scent was completely gone, but decided against it.

Tugging on a robe – it might be time to finally kick on the furnace for the season – I slipped my feet into some snuggly slippers and padded through the house in search of my two loves.

They sat snuggled on the couch, the TV on low as they watched something on Netflix.

"Morning," I croaked out.

Spencer looked over his shoulder and smiled. "Good *afternoon.* Who's the alpha?"

My feet froze on my way to the kitchen. I winced. How the hell had he smelled Alexei? I had scrubbed at my skin until it was pink.

Turning, I raised my brows.

He jerked his head toward a package sitting by the front door. Rey pulled her arm from around his shoulders and stood, lifting the box and setting it on the coffee table.

"Sorry. You're going to have to open it in front of us because my curiosity is getting the better of me."

They hadn't caught his scent. My sexy hero had sent a gift.

"How do you know it's an alpha?" I asked as I made my way to the box and began tugging at the ribbon.

"Who else would send a gift?" Spencer said with way too much *duh* inflection in his tone.

"Could be another stalker," I teased.

"Not fucking funny," Rey said.

The box was on the larger side. Lifting the lid, I ruffled through the tissue paper as my pack watched.

Inside sat another box.

"Holy shit. He sent you Chanel?" Spencer breathed out, his love of all things designer kicking in as he moved closer.

Inside the branded box was a tweed coat. As I pulled it out, I realized it would reach down to my knees. Small, gold buttons lined the front and leather piping ran along the collar.

"Excuse me, but that coat isn't even available to the public yet," Spence said, attempting to yank it from my hands for inspection.

"Mind if I try on my new gift," I said with a grin and a chuckle.

Rey swatted at his hands as though he were a toddler reaching for the stove.

Tossing my robe onto the couch, I wrapped the jacket around my shoulders and closed it around my naked body. The inside was lined with the softest, silkiest fabric and felt amazing against my nipples.

"You need to take a picture of you wearing it just like that and send it to him," Spence said, raising his phone and snapping a pic before I had a chance to stop him.

"One – don't have his number. Two – I look like shit."

"Wait...you don't have his number, but he has your address?" Rey said with narrowed eyes and a furrowed brow. "Do you at least know who sent it?"

I really did not want to have this conversation, but we had never kept secrets from each other. We shared everything from one-night-stands to some of our spicier fantasies – some of which we had repeatedly played out.

"Okay," I said, peeling the jacket off and redonning my robe. "Remember the night that guy tried to attack me and some mystery guy showed up and killed him?"

"No fucking way," Spence uttered as he dropped onto the couch, a grin bisecting his face.

"Yeah, so…he showed up last night. And somehow ended up at my table. And then, um…he reserved an hour with me in the VIP room. And he might have gotten me off with a little spanking…and I might have let him come on my ass and back."

"Shut the fuck up. This is sexy, gross, and romantic."

"How the hell is any of that romantic to you?" Rey asked our omega with a disgruntled frown. "Dude obviously bribed someone to be at her table. And marked our beta with his scent."

"And she let him," Spencer reminded our alpha.

"You said you didn't see his face that night. How did you know it was him last night?"

I shook my head and sat beside Spence, running my finger along the oddly soft tweed of the coat. "I don't know. I just…knew. Like, I could feel the way his eyes roamed my body and – fuck, I don't know. But it was him. And I thanked him for saving my life. Learned his name is Alexei."

"And then he special ordered a not yet available coat from Chanel that I doubt cost any less than ten grand and had it delivered to our door," Spencer said, completely unfazed by the fact Alexei knew my address.

"How the hell does he know where you live, Kennedy? Did he follow you home?"

I shrugged. "Either that or one of my coworkers is breaking a whole lot of rules and gave out my personal information."

"He slit a dude's throat in front of you, Kennedy. And you let him jizz on your bare skin? How is none of this freaking you out?"

Not much really freaked me out, honestly. And I had no idea how to explain to her that his presence lent me both a sense of peace and safety as well as made me feel as though I could combust with nothing more than a heated look from his pretty hazel eyes.

"I think you should let Anais and Milo know to watch for him. What if he shows up tonight? What if he thinks this buys you somehow?" Rey said, gesturing toward the designer coat.

"Just to be clear – you're worried about my safety and not that another alpha is interested in me, right?" I asked.

She made a dismissive sound in the back of her throat. "Any red-blooded human being who sees you and doesn't think you're the hottest woman on the planet would be fucking blind. So no, not jealous. Not even jealous that he got you off. What I am is worried that he's obviously a murderer who disappeared instead of calling the police. He didn't disable the dude who was trying to hurt you or whatever and wait for the authorities. He slit his throat. And you said he said something about he should already be dead which makes me think he's some kind of hit man or some shit. What happens if you piss him off?"

I opened my mouth then shut it. I didn't really have an argument to any of her points. She was right. I knew literally nothing about Alexei other than his name, his signature, and the fact he killed someone so close to me that I'd been covered in the man's blood.

"You are not returning this," Spencer said, pulling the coat free to examine it closer.

"She can't accept it," Rey said. "It's like saying she accepts him."

"And if I do?" I hadn't meant for those words to slip from my mouth, but now that they were out in the open, both packmates gaped at me.

"Are you…you want to leave?" Spencer asked.

There was nothing short of pain in Rey's eyes as she stared at me.

"Absolutely not." There wasn't a moment of hesitation. I couldn't let them think for a second the two of them weren't everything I wanted and needed. I carried Rey's mark on my shoulder, for fuck's sake, could feel them both through the threads that connected us through our bond.

"All I'm saying is…he did save my life. And he followed every single rule, listened to my boundaries, checked in with me every few minutes to make sure I was comfortable. Everything that happened last night was done with my permission," I admitted.

"We need to meet him," Spence said.

Rey's head whipped in his direction. "Excuse me?"

"I'm just saying if he's interested in our beta, he could be an amazing part of our family. He obviously has good taste in both women and fashion. And she's right – he saved her life. He could have easily killed her to avoid there being any witnesses. Instead, he took out some fucker who could have – and probably *would* have – hurt her in ways that I don't want to think about."

"He figured out where she lives, Spence. Where *you* live. My job is to protect you both."

"Your job is to love us and you do," I said, shifting so I could sit on her lap. "I'm not afraid of him. Maybe you're right and I should be, but there's something…like Spence said, he could have easily eliminated a witness to what he'd done. Instead, he'd made sure I was okay, then left. And, uh, might have tipped me two thousand dollars for our time in the VIP room."

"And sent her a coat that's–"

"We get it. It's an expensive coat," Rey said, cutting our omega off before he could dwell on the designer tag.

"Okay. Let's talk about this. He's obviously loaded. He kills people. And he either bribed someone for your address, followed you home, or has resources to get personal information. Could he be a member of ORE?" Spencer asked.

"No. ORE wouldn't cut some dude's throat then disappear," Rey said.

"Mercenary?" I suggested.

"I'm still leaning toward assassin or hitman."

"Oh. A morally gray sexpot."

"You know, life isn't exactly a romance novel," Rey said, but she couldn't suppress the smile that quirked up the corners of her lips.

"*My* life is, thank you very much. Think about it – I have my own tiny little harem, I'm showered with gifts, I buy anything I want…I'm practically a character in a rags-to-riches movie."

A rom com character who had the body of a professional swimmer and had beat a few asses when they'd become too aggressive with me while in public. My omega was such a beautiful mixture of soft and hard.

"What are you going to do if he shows up again tonight?" Spence asked as he set the coat gently back into the box.

I shrugged up my shoulders. "I'm on the rack tonight. I guess we'll see if he shows up, if he somehow manages to get my table, then go from there."

"We are so going out tonight," Spencer said with a grin. "I need to see this guy."

"We could reserve her table," Rey said, turning to look at him.

"You two are ridiculous," I said, standing and taking my box to my personal bedroom.

We each had our own rooms but hadn't slept separately in two years. Even in the rare occasion one of us entertained someone else, we still ended up climbing into the pack bed once the playmate for the night left.

That hadn't happened in a long time, though. We were perfectly content playing with each other, and I had my own supply of toys for when my pack was out or they were worn out.

"You going to follow into the back room, too?" I called out over my shoulder before stepping into my room.

Quick steps followed me as though Spence was running to catch up. "Are we allowed to do that?" he asked.

I turned to find a wide grin and wider eyes.

"Pervert," I accused, jabbing a finger in his direction.

Lowering his head, he began to stalk toward me, his hands stretched out in front of him like a movie villain. "Nothing wrong with watching my sexy ass beta get spanked then fucking the living shit out of her after."

He dove at me and I dodged to the side with a squeal. Oh, I would let him catch me. I always did. The hunt wasn't one of his kinks, but there was no reason I couldn't at least pretend to play hard to get.

CHAPTER 5

<u>Rey</u>

 $\mathcal{W}$ as I jealous my beta was flirting with another alpha?

I'd lied to Kennedy and said no. Although, jealousy might not have been the right word. I was scared. Scared she would find a man who could give her what I couldn't, scared of someone like this Alexei asshole who killed people then showered her with gifts.

I was the one who was supposed to be out there earning a buttload of money to dote on my pack. I was the one who was supposed to fill a bank account with money so the two of them could buy whatever their hearts desired.

Instead, my sweet Kennedy performed for strangers on a regular basis, danced half naked, even let them do things like spank her in the private rooms for tips.

I would never judge her for that. Kennedy was a strong, independent woman. She would never do anything she didn't want. But I think I had always been afraid of what was happening currently, that she would meet some big, sexy, wealthy alpha and decide Spencer and I weren't enough for her.

It was stupid. I knew it was. We were all in love. Kennedy and I might not make love often, but my love for her was as strong as it was for my omega.

Could Spencer be right? Should we check this guy out? If he made Kennedy happy, if he wasn't a danger to her, it wouldn't hurt to have another alpha in the pack, someone to help our omega through his cycle. My beta could fuck him, suck him, even jack him off, but a male omega only truly found full release with my lock.

Or a knot.

How the hell had the two rarest of our designations found each other? It was like fate had been watching over us and shoved us together.

Could that same fate have put this Alexei guy in the right place at the right time? In the two years since Kennedy had gone to work for *Plumes et Fouets*, she'd had fans and even repeat clients in the VIP room, but she'd never had anyone ballsy enough to not only wait for her after work, but actually put their fucking hands on her.

Had Alexei not shown up when he had…

I shuddered at the possibilities. I refused to give it too much thought or I might end up demanding she stay home with Spencer while I sought a job. Not that I would make even a portion of what she made in a single night.

Spencer tilted his head back and rinsed the shampoo from his hair, then glanced up at me, his dark auburn brows pinching together.

"What's got you in a funk?" he asked.

He grabbed my hand and pulled me closer so we shared the same shower head. His arms snaked around my back and he tilted his face up to look into my eyes. I was only a couple inches taller than he was, but I still always felt as though it was my job to protect him from the world. Fucking alpha hormones and shit.

"I think you're right," I said, draping my arms around him and running my hands along his wet back.

"About?"

"We should go tonight. See if we can't at least get a glimpse of this guy. And…maybe follow him home or something. See what we can find out about him."

"Or we do like he did and bribe someone to put us at the same table so we can actually talk to him," Spencer said.

His hands slowly moved down my back until he cupped my ass and pulled me closer, trapping his nearly chronically hard dick between us. The man was insatiable.

"If he sees us, if he sees her pack, it might scare him off," I said.

"Then he's not much of an alpha and not someone we want around our beta." His hands kneaded and massaged my ass as his hips began to thrust forward, rubbing himself against my stomach.

He had a good point. If this guy wanted to merely exist in the shadows, to merely visit our beta so he could have time with her in the back room of the club, he wasn't the type of alpha I wanted anywhere near my girl.

"Okay. We see if we can't get assigned to her table," I said as Spence's hands moved around my body to cup my tits.

"And bribe whoever the fuck needed to get into the security room so we can see what they do later." He gripped his cock and slid it between my thighs, pushing forward and rubbing his length between my folds and making me moan.

"That'll piss her off."

"I don't care." He reached down and hooked my thigh over his hip so he could push into me, moving us until my back hit the tiled wall so he could thrust into me harder, faster, until he tore cries from my lips.

I couldn't lock him, not standing here in the shower. He would have to lift me so I could wrap my legs around his waist and be carried from the shower if I let my body clamp around him and lock us together for the next twenty to thirty minutes.

Frankly, we needed to finish up, get ready, and get to the club before we lost our opportunity of being assigned directly in front of our beta and beside Alexei.

Spencer's kiss was deep, his tongue dancing and battling with mine. With a hand firmly holding my thigh up for deeper thrusts, he trailed the other up to cup one of my tits, rolling the nipple between his finger and thumb.

I tore my mouth from his as I fell apart with a cry, the sound echoing off the tiles. Spence only lasted a few more pumps before slamming hard into me and filling me with his hot cum. Male omegas came a lot, but even more during their cycle. And I'd never tasted anything as sweet as my omega's cum on my tongue.

"Fuck, I love you," he moaned, his head resting against my chest as he caught his breath and the steam continued to rise around us.

PLUMES et Fouets had a strict dress code. It wasn't technically black tie, but damn close enough.

There were quite a few patrons donning various styles of masks, and that included my omega and me. I wore a deep red silk gown that brushed the floor, even in my heels. I'd pulled my light brown hair away from my face and into a chignon and painted my lips to match the gown.

My omega...Spencer was a walking wet dream in his black slacks, dark blue shirt, and charcoal vest. The mask made his green eyes pop and made it hard for me to avoid staring into them every time he glanced in my direction.

Yep. Head over heels for my omega. The attraction I felt for the man went beyond simply alpha and omega; he was beautiful inside and out and made me feel as though I could take on the world simply because he'd chosen me. They had *both* chosen me.

All I wanted was for them both to be happy and safe. And if this alpha had intrigued Kennedy enough to actually allow him to mark her skin with his signature, he was worth meeting to make sure he was worthy of either of my packmates.

And safe enough to be around either of them.

My arm through Spencer's, we were welcomed inside by name and escorted down the hall to the hostess station. Spencer opened his mouth to request Kennedy's table, but I stopped him with a quick jab of my elbow.

He glanced up at me and I nodded toward the rack where Kennedy would be strapped later. There were two men sitting there, one who matched the description our beta had given us, and one neither of us recognized.

"Is Kennedy at table eight tonight?" I asked, turning back to the hostess.

"Yes, Alpha. I would seat you there, but the table was already reserved."

I smiled and waved off her apology. "It's fine. We can watch the other performers and check in on her after the show."

We were led to table seven where we could both see our beta and check out the two men. I assumed they were both alphas by their matching sizes but couldn't tell with the complete lack of scent through the filtration system cranking overhead.

As inconspicuously as possible, we seated ourselves so we could check out the possible competition, see the performer who would be on the small stage ahead of us, as well as ogle our beta when she took her place.

"She said Alexei has black hair," Spence said, avoiding the same urge I had to stare at them both. "They're both smoking hot, though."

That they were. The other man had dark brown hair that was a little on the longer side, but in a stylish manner and held sexy waves that made my fingers itch to tangle in them. When he turned his face in my direction as though checking out the room, my breath caught in my lungs. He had this broody, bad boy look about him, but there was something in his eyes, something dark and dangerous yet alluring, like a simple look was enough to draw me to the table and rub myself all over him to leave him covered in my scent.

If he was an alpha, he would bristle at that. He might see it as a challenge. And, while I might not be a small woman, I wasn't sure I could take on both men without enduring a few injuries. Or being completely bested.

His eyes locked on mine and for a brief moment, I felt frozen in place. Like a fucking omega being swamped by alpha pheromones.

Like prey being stalked by a predator.

And fuck me...I wanted to play with him. I wanted to lunge from my seat and run in hopes he would chase me, that he would tackle me and–

"She's up," Spence said, cutting into my inner fantasies.

Candles danced on every table, the flames shimmering with the system blowing chemically neutralized air and the movement of bodies throughout the room as performers climbed the few stairs up onto the stage where they would put on various fetish fantasies. I'd already seen nearly every performance, had seen my girl tickled, flogged, spanked, and tied up, among other things.

There was never full nudity, never any penetration. That didn't mean the performers didn't orgasm from the contact, from the mixture of pleasure and pain.

After our order was put in with our waitress, we settled back and split our attention between our personal performer, Kennedy, and the men at her table. Both of them were riveted to the beta, but I could practically *feel* each time the brown haired one glanced in my direction.

When this round was over, polite applause lifted and the performers were helped out of whatever contraption they were tied to then off their stage.

Spence and I watched out of the corners of our eyes as the two men dipped their heads together, then both turned in our direction.

Oops. We hadn't nearly been sneaky enough.

Alexei – I assumed it was him by the black hair – stood, straightened his tailored black jacket, and approached our table.

"We reserved an hour with Kennedy. My packmate would like for the two of you to join us."

Spencer pushed to his feet. I stood with him. My body was warm, my nipples strained against the strapless bra, but there was a fear of why exactly these men wanted us in the room with them while they were with Kennedy.

Did they hope to stake a claim on her? Did they hope to make us watch as they dominated her?

"We'll join," Spencer said, his chin raised defiantly as he wrapped a hand around one of mine.

We followed Alexei to where his buddy waited, both hands shoved into his pockets.

"I am Alexei Potrov. This is my packmate Wolfram Cillian."

"Wolf," my wet dream come to life said with a deep timbre that rubbed all the right places in my core.

"Rey," I said, offering my hand and gripping tight enough for them each to know I was an alpha.

"Spencer," he said, shaking hands with each man.

And then we followed them through the restaurant, down the dark hall, and stepped in behind them through a door marked Number Two.

Kennedy unfolded from her chair, a curious and somewhat suspicious look on her face. "What are you two doing here?"

CHAPTER 6

"What are you two doing here?" Kennedy asked, her gaze bouncing from Rey to me then back.

I nodded at the men. "They invited us."

Her eyes whipped to them, blatant suspicion bright in her beautiful blue eyes.

"What the fuck is this?"

"If they're your pack, I thought they might feel more comfortable being here instead of watching us disappear into a room with you alone," Alexei offered.

"I'm not alone," she said, pointing at the cameras as though reminding him they were under constant supervision.

"They were watching us. I felt they would feel better in here with you than out there waiting," Wolfram – Wolf – said.

His eyes darted to Rey, his pupils dilated a touch, before looking away.

"Are you comfortable being here?" she asked me, then glanced at Rey for confirmation.

"Nothing we haven't seen before," I said, hoping it came out as a tease.

Because yeah, we had taken her in one of these rooms as well as played out other fantasies at home.

There were various places to sit, including a couch long enough to fit all four of us. Rey led me there and sat, dragging me down to sit beside her. As much as I would prefer to join in, these men had paid at least a thousand dollars for one hour with our beta, and Alexei had tipped her extremely well last time.

As spoiled as I was by her wealth, I knew she took pride in the fact she could earn so much for the pack doing something she loved. Well, she loved burlesque, doing the aerial silks. She loved to perform.

We had never delved too far into how she felt about being hired by the hour like this.

"Fine. Wolf, since this is your first time with me, I have a few rules as does the club."

She ran down her boundaries, her color system for when she was fine with the activity, was growing uncomfortable, or needed everything to stop immediately. She reminded them both there was to be zero penetration, but they were welcome to masturbate themselves or fuck each other.

I couldn't help but notice she didn't tell either of them their body fluids were not allowed to touch her. And yep, my dick was hard, slick was coating the inner walls of my ass, and precum seeped from the slit of my cock and dampened the inside of my slacks.

"What did you two have planned for the evening?" Kennedy asked before her tongue darted out to moisten her pouty, red-painted lips.

These two would never know the wonders of that mouth, of how she could make me go cross eyed with what she could do with her tongue and lips.

"Alexei tells me you're not only quite...agile, but you enjoy a touch of pain."

I watched as my beta's lips parted, her chest began to rise and fall rapidly, and her pupils dilated.

"Same rules apply," she reminded them. "While you have the illusion of control, I can stop this at any time. The moment you hear the word red, all activity ceases. And there are no refunds."

I turned to look at my alpha. Did Kennedy's voice sound breathy? Huskier? Because it sure as hell did in my ears.

But Rey was watching Wolf closely, her eyes narrowed. She didn't trust him. And why should she? We didn't know either of these men. Were it not for the highly trained and well-armed security watching and listening to everything that happened in these rooms, I might have put a stop to the whole thing before they had a chance to step foot in this room.

"You are in complete control," Alexei said, hunger and lust burning bright in his eyes.

He motioned toward a raised bed where she hopped up. His hands looked gentle as he smoothed them up her leg and attached a cuff around the ankle, then did the same with the other until she was in the splits. She didn't look even remotely uncomfortable as she rolled her head to wink at me, a sexy smirk on her lips.

Shame we weren't at home. Because I would climb up on the side of the bed and feed her my cock one inch at a time.

The thong Kennedy wore stretched so much the edges of her pussy lips were exposed and, even from where I sat, I could see how wet she was in anticipation. I really didn't need to ask about this side of her job – it sure as hell looked as though she liked it.

Or perhaps it was the fact she was with someone she found attractive while her packmates watched.

Wolf smiled down at her with a predatory gleam to his eyes and attached her wrists to a cuff that would stretch her arms over her head, much the way she started her silk performances. "Too tight?" he asked.

Her head rolled side to side. "I'm fine," she said. And yep, I was right – her voice was absolutely filled with desire.

Wolf stepped back and leaned against the wall as Alexei perused the selection of toys on the wall. None were technically used to fuck another person, but the ends sure as hell could be used as a dildo. Yet another reason for the security cameras and mics.

"Green, yellow, or red?" Alexei asked as he held up a leather flogger.

"Green," Kennedy said as her breathing grew more rapid and her nipples strained against the silk pasties covering them.

These two would lose their ever-loving minds if they saw how perfect those tits looked, how beautifully her light pink nipples hardened, how delicious every inch of her tasted.

Alexei spun the straps in a slow circle then slapped the ends against her inner thigh. She hissed then moaned.

And my cock jerked.

"Fuck," I breathed out at the sight.

As much as we'd done together, it was a whole new thing to watch as someone else brought my beta this kind of pleasure.

The leather spun and hit her other thigh, pulling another moan from her. And then he began to focus his attention on her core, rotating from flogging her thighs, then her pussy.

She was writhing on the table now but couldn't move, not with her legs spread wide and her arms restrained over her head.

"Check in, lyubov," Alexei said.

"Green," she said, her whimper sounding so much like an omega in heat.

Rey's hand smoothed up my thigh to cup me through my slacks as Alexei returned his attention to Kennedy. He would drag the ends of the leather straps along her thighs, tickling her, then slap them against her, causing red marks to develop. Then he would swing it a few times, whipping her pussy over and over.

The sound of my zipper being pulled down was loud in the room as Rey freed my cock and began to stroke it to the sight of our beta moaning, whimpering, shifting her body as though trying to get closer to the alpha.

And all the while, Wolf merely watched, his fingers lightly grazing up and down the insides of her arms, coming close to the sides of her tits without actually touching them.

His eyes raised to where Rey's fist was wrapped around my shaft and he smirked. He was enjoying the show. Or perhaps he was gauging our reaction to our packmate being strapped down and teased.

"More," Kennedy breathed out when Alexei checked in again.

"I need the word, lyubov."

Wracking my brain, I tried to remember hearing the term he kept using in any of the movies I'd watched through the years and came up with nothing, but it was obviously a term of endearment by the gentleness of his tone.

"Green. Green," Kennedy said, raising her head from the padded table to look into his eyes.

And so, he went back to work, tickling, teasing, whipping. And then our beta cried out, her legs shaking as her body went taut.

"So perfect," Wolf cooed.

Rey's hands stroked me harder, faster, until I spilled on myself and her hand.

Pulling away, she cleaned me from her fist and fingers with her tongue, lapping up every drop, before gently tucking me away and seeking a towel to clean up any evidence of our play before we could leave the room.

Wolf carefully removed the cuffs from her wrists while Alexei pressed a kiss to each of Kennedy's inner thighs, removed her ankle straps, and slowly lowered her legs, rubbing the muscles to get the blood flowing again.

"Are you okay, lyubov?" he asked, bringing one of her hands to his lips to feather a kiss across her knuckles.

"You've used that word a few times," she said.

I could scent her cranberry sweet and tart release, as though the filtration system was unable to keep up. I could even detect hints of fallen leaves and juniper from the alphas. They were like winter and autumn, complimenting each other's signatures.

"It is like sweetheart–"

"Love. He's calling you his love," Wolf said, taking one of her hands and turning it over to inspect her wrists.

"After care isn't generally something people pay to do," Kennedy teased. "I'm fine."

"Only fine?" Alexei said.

The men stepped back, looked in our direction, then Alexei pulled a card from his wallet and set it on the bed beside Kennedy's hip.

"If you are ever in need of our assistance."

They stepped through the door. Before it was closed, I couldn't help myself when I called out to them, "And what kind of assistance is it you perform exactly?"

Alexei stopped and stood staring through the door a few seconds before he looked down at me. "The kind where we stop bad guys from hurting beautiful women." He winked at Kennedy, pulled the door shut, and left us all blinking at each other with his vague yet not so vague explanation of his line of work.

CHAPTER 7

<u>Kennedy</u>

My pack and I stayed in the VIP room long after the two alphas left. I'd been surprised to see the second guy sitting beside Alexei, but not surprised at all to see the Russian alpha at my table.

The biggest surprise, though, had been the men inviting my pack into the private room with us. I had wondered if it had been some show of dominance, as though they wanted to make sure my female alpha knew they were big and powerful men.

But Alexei was as gentle and attentive as he'd been the first time. Even the man named Wolf had been careful when he'd restrained my arms and ensured the cuffs weren't too tight, then checked for any burns from the leather chafing against my skin.

For alphas who apparently loved to dominate their lovers to release, they seemed just as pleased by the aftercare as they'd been by the attention they'd shown me. And neither had pulled out their own cocks, neither had sought their own release after I'd come.

Spencer crossed the room and picked up the card, looking down at the rectangular piece of cardboard with nothing but a phone number.

"What kind of assistance do you think he meant?" he asked.

But he wasn't stupid. Neither was Rey or I. Assistance as in another asshole needs to be put down. Assistance as in protection.

And, maybe, assistance in a different form. A more carnal form.

Rey stood in front of me, urging my knees apart so she could move closer, and cupped my face in both hands.

"Are you okay?"

A laugh huffed from me. Every part of my body still tingled from the explosive orgasm. It had built and built and then Alexei would stop teasing my clit and flog my thighs. Over and over, he'd edged me. And when he finally gave me what I wanted – needed – most, my body felt as though it had burst into flames.

Those flames still licked my nerve endings and my legs felt as though they were made of jelly. I wasn't even sure I could walk. Then again, I *had* just been restrained in wide splits.

"I'm perfectly fine."

"Are you going to call him?" she asked.

"For what? I have never found myself in the need of … an extermi-nator," I said, hoping she caught my meaning and remembered every single word and action was being monitored in the club and in this room.

"How much longer before you're off?"

"That was my last performance and no one else reserved any time with me tonight. I have next week off while they get ready for drag month and then I'm on waitress duty."

"Oohh. A whole week together? Whatever will we do with our time together?" Spencer teased, gripping my waist and helping me from the table.

It took a moment to get my legs steady on top of my heels. I opened the door and waved my pack out ahead of me. "I have a few more things to do before I head home."

"No, you don't," Anais said from the other direction. She'd come from one of the private rooms, an attractive man with silver dusting his temples on her heels. Apparently, my boss had enjoyed some time in the VIP area tonight, as well. "You should have taken off after…that night," she said, turning as though to glance over her shoulder.

"It was good to see you, Mistress," the man said, ducking his head and keeping his eyes lowered until he was well past us.

"You're good for the night. Cash out, collect your tips, and we'll see you in a week. Oh…and your new admirer asked for your address. Just a heads up."

"He already got it," Rey said.

Anais tilted her head and crossed her arms. "How did he get it? None of my…I better not find out anyone here divulged that information."

"Don't know how he got it, but a gift showed up at my door this morning."

"A not yet released Chanel coat that cost almost as much as a car," Spencer said.

I screwed up my face and shook my head. "It is *not* worth that much."

"If no one here gave it out, and they sure as fuck better not have," she said in her lilting French accent, "then you might have a problem. Do you want me to keep him from entering the club?"

"Hell no," I blurted out before I could stop myself. "I mean, so far he seems harmless, he follows the rules and my boundaries, and he tips extremely well." I had no intention of telling her Alexei had been the man who'd saved me by murdering that man in the parking lot.

"You orgasmed," she said, a smile pulling up one side of her mouth in a flirty smirk.

Heat flooded my cheeks, and I was having a hard time making eye contact with my boss.

"Good for you, Cherie. I love when we can enjoy ourselves while taking their money. Get changed and go home. Do not leave this building without an escort." Her dark brows slammed together at the warning.

"We'll wait for her," Rey said.

My boss pressed a quick kiss to my cheek and walked past me, squeezing Spencer's bicep and nonchalantly rubbing her cheek along Rey's shoulder.

I swore my boss tried to leave her scent on my alpha any time my pack visited. And no, I didn't mind. It was nothing more than flirting.

"I'll meet you two out front."

Spencer pressed his lips to mine, then wrapped his hand around Rey's and led her away while I headed into the locker room so I could remove my stage makeup and change into my streetwear. I even pulled my hair into a bun in hopes of camouflaging myself a little more.

None of that had helped that night. Not that I was a celebrity who needed to be incognito while in public. But I'd rather not have a conversation with someone who'd seen me tied down and tickled or flogged.

As the latter floated through my mind, my body grew warm. That was twice now that Alexei had finished me without actually physically touching me. Okay, so *technically* he had touched me, but he hadn't fucked me.

His buddy's name was Wolfram. Wolf. And damn, he was as appealing as Alexei, only where the Russian had a lightness to his appearance, Wolf was all broody and dark and sexy.

And he hadn't touched anything more than my wrists, my arms, my sides. He'd been content to watch, to praise me, to press sweet kisses to my wrists and hands after ensuring I hadn't endured any injuries while being restrained.

I wasn't sure why, but I'd worried Wolf would have been…maybe domineering. Controlling.

And, if it wasn't my imagination, he had definitely been into my alpha. I'd seen him watching her and there had been nothing short of hunger and want in his warm brown eyes.

I wasn't surprised when I'd heard the sound of Spencer's orgasm as they'd watched me during my time with the two sexy alphas; I had always been surprised my omega didn't walk around with his dick fisted in his own hand any time he wasn't making love to one of us. The man was insatiable.

Makeup removed, jeans and sweater donned, hair twisted into a bun, and I was ready to go. My outfit would need to be sent out to be cleaned, so I put it in one of my designated bags and tossed it into the hamper to be sent out with the rest of the laundry. One of the perks of working for Anais – she might be the owner, but she was the best house mom ever and made sure we were taken care of to the best of her ability, including laundry.

"You need me to walk you out?" Milo asked as I stepped into the main room, keeping my eyes averted from any patrons who might still be dining.

"No. My pack is waiting for me." I pointed to where they stood near the entryway.

"Didn't they park in the front?" he asked, raising a hand when Spencer smiled at him.

"Yeah. Actually, hold on. That's stupid to have them walk me around back then walk back to their SUV. If you don't mind waiting, I'll tell them to head out and walk out with you."

"Absolutely. It's my job."

Rushing over to where Rey was slipping her arms into her coat, I told them the new plan.

Rey looked over my shoulder at Milo and raised her shoulders, then smiled with a nod at my favorite bouncer and sometimes coworker. Yep. Milo had donned a mask more than once to act as my tickler. It had been so awkward the first few times, but then we'd learned to shove it out of our minds and see it as a show and we were nothing more than actors.

Pressing a kiss to both Rey's and Spencer's cheeks, I fast walked to where Milo was waiting, thick, tree trunk arms crossed over his chest.

"Ready?" he asked.

"More than ready."

Once we were out of ear shot of any paying customers, Milo turned to glance at me. "That's the second time that Russian has requested you in the VIP room. Everything good?"

My cheeks heated and I nodded. "Very good."

I could practically feel his eyes boring into the side of my head as he waited for more.

"What?" I asked without looking into his face.

"Are you two…"

With a sigh, I pulled him to a stop and looked down both ends of the hallway to make sure there were no eavesdroppers. "He's the guy."

Milo's brows dropped. "What guy? Are you trying to say he's the one, like you're in love or something?"

"What? Hell no! I barely know him. No…he's the *guy*. From that night. The one who–" I cut off and dragged a finger across my throat.

Milo frowned so deeply his eyes were shadowed. He dragged me outside then slammed the door shut behind me, crowding me against the door.

"What the fuck are you doing, Kennedy? Why wouldn't you tell one of us? Or call the fucking police?" His words were harsh but barely above a whisper.

I had seen Milo angry, but nothing like now.

As he nearly trembled with rage, I swore I could feel eyes on me. I knew who those eyes belonged to. Alexei was in the shadows watching me, watching over me. He hadn't left immediately after.

Did that mean Wolf was still here? Were they both watching my interaction with Milo?

And fuck me…they better not hurt my friend. I could only hope I hadn't misread Alexei.

"I…don't know why I didn't tell you. Or call the police. But he won't hurt me."

"How the fuck do you know that? He cut a mother fucker's throat right in front of you." His voice was rising. And I could have sworn I saw the slightest movement in the shadows.

Raising my hand, I placed my palm out where Milo couldn't see and hoped that I was right that it was Alexei and prayed that he would heed my warning to stay where he was. I didn't need protection from Milo. I would never need protection from my friend. While his rage appeared to be directed at me, it was *for* me. He feared for my safety.

Perhaps indulging that little secret wasn't the best idea. Especially since there was a good chance Milo would make sure Alexei was no longer welcome in the club. And I so wanted him back in the club, and, more specifically, back in the private room again.

"I…just know, Milo. I had a life before here. Trust me when I say I've seen a lot of bad people in my life. He isn't one of them."

Milo threw his hands up and paced away a couple steps before turning back to me again. "Do I need to remind you of how the two of you met?"

"Do I need to remind you that he more than likely saved my fucking life? I was a witness to…what happened. He could have easily killed me, too. Instead, he apologized for what happened as though it was his fault for not being there earlier."

Milo raked both hands through his hair and tugged a little as though trying to center himself or calm his rising anger.

"You have to be careful, Kennedy. These men – they see a beautiful woman on stage and think the fantasy is real life."

"Not him."

"Oh, and you know that from your two encounters with him."

"I know that because I can feel it deep in here," I said, placing a palm over my chest.

Milo stared at me a few seconds, blinking as the creases in his forehead slowly smoothed. "You think he's your mate. Have you told your pack? Do they know how you feel?"

Actually, I hadn't really thought any further than the pleasure he'd brought me or the fact he felt so familiar, as though I had been fated to be in that parking lot at that exact moment when we'd *met*.

"I don't know. I just know he feels…I don't know, Milo. It feels like he's supposed to be in my life. And yeah, that kind of scares me. And that night scared the shit out of me. And I can't prove it, but he's out there watching over me right now."

Milo whipped around and squinted his eyes, trying to see into the shadows. "Like a fucking stalker?"

"Like a guardian angel," I muttered as a wistful smile quirked up my lips.

My friend grunted in disapproval and turned his attention back to me. "He cut a dude's fucking throat right in front of you." He threw his hand up to stop me when I opened my mouth. "Yeah. He saved your life. But he killed someone. Violently. And then took off. Which means he's not exactly on the up and up."

Milo knew nothing about my past. Even my pack hadn't been privy to a few details of my unsavory upbringing or why I hadn't exactly suffered any long-lasting trauma from that night. Sure, I'd had nightmares. And it had been terrifying and disgusting. But I was no stranger to violence or violent men.

A few minutes passed of Milo looking around, roughly pushing his fingers through his hair, then glaring into my face. "The second you get a bad feeling, end it. Call me if you have to. You know any one of us would rush to your side in a second."

Wrapping my arms around his waist, I leaned in and smiled. "You're the best big brother ever."

He hugged me back but groaned dramatically. "You realize how fucked up that sounds being as I've spanked you on stage?"

I slapped Milo's chest when I pulled away and headed to my car, that feeling of being watched still there.

Maybe Milo was right and it was a touch stalkerish. But I wasn't afraid. I wasn't worried.

I had a sexy, scary guardian watching over me.

But I wanted more. I wanted more than our fleeting moments when I was on the clock and being observed by coworkers and security.

I wanted to know what exactly he meant when he'd offered his services.

And I really needed to know how my pack felt about spending more time with Alexei and possibly Wolf. Because no matter how much it felt as though the Russian sexpot was supposed to be in my life, Rey and Spence would always come first.

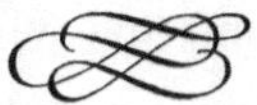

Wolf

lexei sauntered around the corner, his hands shoved into the pockets of his slacks while I waited in the car. His lips were quirked up at the corners and his eyes were focused on something I couldn't see. Memories of our short time with the raven-haired beauty, perhaps?

Everything in me had wanted the female alpha and her omega to join in the fun. But we'd paid for private time with the beta. And yeah, we could tell each of the designations even before their scents had exploded from them, surpassing the filtration systems that cleared the air of the club.

"Have you done this every night?" I asked as he climbed into the passenger seat of my Audi S-7.

"When I'm not working."

Pulling into highway traffic, I glanced in his direction as we passed under a streetlight and shook my head. "You're obsessed."

"You saw her. Do you blame me?"

With a dark chuckle, I shook my head. "She saw you cut a fucker's head off and still let you get her off."

"I didn't cut his head off."

"Doesn't it make you wonder about her state of mind?"

He threw his head back and barked a laugh. "Are you worried about me?"

I could see him look at me from my periphery. "I'm worried that you're getting too close to someone who might or might not either have some form of mental illness or who might end up turning you over to the police. Which would fuck us both over."

"She doesn't. And she won't."

"You sound awful confident for someone who has never spent a moment alone with her."

"I've been alone with her," he said, leaning and resting an arm on the rest between us.

"There were cameras and mics being monitored by the security team. That was not alone. And she has a pack. Good chance she's treating you like every other person who pays for VIP time with her."

At that, Alexei went quiet, and I knew he was now dwelling on my words.

"If you plan to pursue anything more than stalking her after work and playing with her in the back room, you might want to actually take her on a date." He'd also been stalking her during her shifts, even before fetish month had started. I knew damn well he'd attended every single one of her performances when he wasn't on a job.

He thought I didn't know, but he'd special ordered a coat and had it shipped to her after their first shared night together. And he hadn't even felt her cunt wrapped around his cock. What the hell would he buy her when he finally had her spread out below him?

Unless I was correct and she was simply doing her job, allowing him to tie her down and act out safe fantasies while under the close supervision of the staff of *Plumes et Fouets*. Just like the dancers at strip clubs, they had to make every single guy think they had a chance while keeping them at arm's length.

"The guy you killed, you said he followed her out?" I asked, pulling onto the exit ramp.

"He was out there waiting for her when I got there."

"Why did you wait so long to take him out?"

"I was hoping she would be able to dispel any notion he had of being with her, get in her car, and leave. Instead, he tried to hurt her."

A soft growl trickled from his chest and his scent carried a burnt edge to the normally sweeter juniper smell as his rage began to build.

"He wouldn't have stopped if someone hadn't stepped in. And I couldn't allow an innocent woman to be harmed by someone who was supposed to be dead."

Or at all.

Neither of us had a single qualm with snuffing out a life…as long as that person wasn't innocent or a child. We had even turned on those who'd hired us when we found out the person was simply trying to take out a packmate or rival out of selfishness or jealousy. Neither of us could stomach that kind of shit.

Even hitmen had to have some form of moral code.

"I understand stepping in. But you've grown obsessed with her to the point of being a stalker. Either walk away or take her out."

"What if she's content with our current arrangement?" he asked, scratching at the dark stubble dusting his chin.

I'd seen the way Kennedy had watched Alexei, the way her breathing increased, the way her shear thong had become practically see-through with her arousal. And there was no way to fake the way she'd acted when she'd orgasmed. The beta enjoyed the mixture of pain with pleasure. She might damn well be perfect for us both.

Although…there was something about her alpha that made me want to do exactly as Alexei was doing and stalk the woman. I wanted to dominate her, wanted to hunt her, to take her down, to fuck her into submission and feel her lock onto me. And yep, that shit would hurt so fucking good.

The mere concept of the alpha woman allowing another alpha to dominate was both laughable and erotic as fuck. Hell, I'd let her top me if she needed the same type of control I did in relationships. I wasn't opposed to a give and take.

Wait. Why the fuck had I just used the term relationship when I'd only meant to entertain a fantasy about the beautiful alpha?

Their omega was downright delicious, as well. Somehow, the little beta had found herself two of the sexiest examples of the human species possible.

As I pulled up to the secured garage, the door rumbled up with a push of the remote. I still had no idea why the hell they tried to pretend this place was secure. I'd rolled under plenty of garage doors as they'd closed behind a pizza delivery man or resident and taken out my mark without a single camera catching so much as a glimpse of me.

But neither of us worried. In the thirty-six years I'd been walking the planet, no one had yet to get the drop on me.

Oh, I'd had hit attempts on my life, even carried various scars from bullet holes, knives, and other various tools. But I was still walking and breathing while those who'd had the balls to try to kill me were either six feet under or missing.

After Alexei climbed from the passenger seat, I grabbed my backup Sig Sauer from the glove compartment, shoved it into the back of my pants, and stepped out, hitting the fob to lock the doors and set the alarm.

"We could court them," I offered before I had the chance to think about what I was suggesting.

"Court a fucking pack? An alpha?"

"Why the fuck not? You already sent a gift." I turned and looked at him and noticed the way he refused to look at me. "Shit. Did you send something else?"

The elevator doors opened. He shrugged as he stepped in, waved the keycard over the reader, and hit the button for the penthouse. Technically, we owned the top three floors to ensure absolute privacy but resided in the penthouse.

"Her car was shit."

"You bought her a fucking car? You really think she'll go for that?"

"I'll find out when it's delivered," he said as the doors slid closed.

Alexei was more than obsessed with the woman's sex appeal. Otherwise, he wouldn't hang around after every one of her shifts to make sure she got in her car and wasn't followed. And he sure as fuck wouldn't have put a fat sum of money down on a new ride for someone he simply wanted to fuck.

Looked like that one mark had opened a can neither of us had any desire to attempt to close.

CHAPTER 9

Kennedy

*H*olding the card in my hand, I held the phone firmly against my ear as my heart raced and my nerves stretched taut, my wide eyes glued to the SUV that had been delivered to our driveway.

"Yes?" a deep baritone rumbled. Alexei didn't identify himself, yet I knew it was him by that silky voice.

"Are you serious right now?" I all but screamed over the line.

A deep chuckle vibrated over the line and touched every damn erogenous zone in my body. "I take it your newest gift was delivered."

"This isn't a gift. This is…weird."

"I'll keep it if you don't want it," Spencer whispered with a wide grin.

"I can't accept this, Alexei. I barely know you. We've only seen each other twice."

"I've seen you more than that," he admitted, confirming my suspicion that he'd been watching me from the audience.

"Were you outside last night? When I left?"

Another of those deep chuckles.

"You realize how creepy that is, to skulk around in the shadows and watch me like a stalker?"

"I was just watching out for you. After what happened the first night we met."

I rolled my eyes and turned them up to Rey with a raised brow and a shake of my head. This man was fucking insufferable.

"We didn't exactly *meet* that night. You killed a man, apologized for not being there earlier, then disappeared like a horror movie monster." *Killed the man who obviously had nefarious plans for me had Alexei not scooped in when he had.*

"Monsters don't exist," he teased.

Oh, but they did. I'd seen plenty of them throughout my life. But they rarely looked like the burned up or masked figures portrayed in the movies.

"Then you send some ridiculously expensive designer coat. Show up to spank my...to enjoy my show again. And now this? This is next level creepy, Alexei."

"I told you she wouldn't like it," Wolf said from somewhere over the line. I didn't know the man, but even through the receiver, I could hear the amusement in his words.

"She didn't say she didn't like it," Alexei said, his voice muffled as though he was holding the phone away from his mouth.

"I didn't say I didn't like it. I'm saying it's entirely too much for a client to send to a performer."

There was a beat of silence where even my pack appeared to be holding their breath as they watched me.

"Is that all we are? Is that all you wish to remain?"

"I—" I couldn't finish the lie. Because no, I didn't want us to only remain client and performer. He felt important. He felt as though he was meant to be in my life in one way or another. So was Wolf, even after our brief time together.

But his life was obviously dangerous, and I couldn't drag that kind of violence into my pack's life. They hadn't grown up the same way I had.

However...they'd seen me covered in blood that night, had heard every detail, even sat in the room when Alexei and Wolf had played with me and neither of them had yet to voice a single complaint.

"I didn't say that," I admitted, turning my back on Rey and Spence when they both raised their brows and smiles began to bloom on their faces.

"Will you allow me to court you?"

"*Us*," Wolf said in the background. And I had a feeling it wasn't only me the other alpha wanted to court.

"Will you allow *us* to court you?"

"You know I'm not an omega."

"I'm fully aware," Alexei said. "Allow us to show you we are capable of taking care of and protecting not just you, but your pack, as well. Even the beautiful alpha. None of you would ever want for anything. I would never tell you to leave *Plumes et Fouets* unless you so choose."

"We aren't exactly looking for a sugar daddy or hurting for money, Alexei. I can't be bought."

"I would never assume otherwise. But it is in my nature to dote on those I care for. And believe it or not, I do care for you, lyubov. Whether you believe it is too early or not."

"No more ridiculously extravagant or expensive gifts," I said as I fought and failed to hide the growing smile stretching my lips.

"I can't promise anything of the such. I like to lavish my friends with beautiful things."

"A car is more than a beautiful thing, Alexei."

"It's gorgeous. What are you talking about?" Spencer whispered in the background.

I turned and shushed him with a finger to my lips.

"Is that a yes? May we court you? And your pack?" he asked.

"I would have to ask my pack. We're pretty happy the way–"

"Yes!" Spencer practically yelled in the background, cutting off any possible argument I might have had.

I snorted a chuckle when I tried to hold it in. Looking to Rey with raised brows, I waited to see whether she was amenable to being courted by two alphas when she, herself, was an alpha.

She shrugged up her shoulders and gave me a sexy crooked smile.

"Okay. Apparently, that conversation was a lot shorter than I thought it would be."

That sexy deep chuckle rumbled over the line again and tickled all the right places throughout my body.

If he could make me feel like this with nothing more than a chuckle, if he'd already brought me to such a strong orgasm without touching me with his fingers, tongue, or cock – twice – I couldn't help but wonder whether we would actually wait to get to know each other a little better before falling into bed in a sweaty tangle of arms and legs.

"Are you available this evening?" Alexei asked.

Actually, I was. Since we were switching over to drag show month, I had a week off while they switched everything out, then I'd be on a different schedule when I was called in to wait tables. I didn't make nearly as much money as I did when I performed or had private clients in the VIP room, but I still made money.

And Alexei and Wolf obviously made more than enough to make up for my tighter months.

Nope. Not thinking about our lives together in the future sense, not yet. Simple sexual attraction did not mean a comfortable and compatible pack. There had to be more than lust and hunger. I needed to know they would truly be good to my omega and my alpha. I needed to know we could hold a conversation that didn't consist of sex or my performances or even what happened that night.

And I needed some time with Wolf, to get to know him better, as well. He'd barely spoken to me that night, had merely praised me. And, sure, I strived on praise. I supposed it might have even been one of my kinks, or maybe my love language. But again, a lifelong relationship couldn't be built on that alone.

"I'm available for the next six days," I said, rolling my eyes when Spencer pumped a fist in the air.

"Excellent. Would you be amenable to dinner at our place tonight?

No dress code. No expectations. Simply our first official date," he said, and I swore I could hear a smile in his voice.

Pulling the receiver from my mouth, I turned to my pack. "Dinner at their place tonight?"

"Yep," Spencer said.

"I'm in," Rey said with a shrug.

"What time?" I asked.

"Would you like us to pick you up?"

"Nah. We'll drive." That way, we could leave if we didn't get along further than the back room at work.

"I'll text you the address."

"Send her my number, as well," Wolf said in the background.

"Wolf would like you three to program his number in your phones, as well. Is seven too late for dinner?"

"Nope. See you then."

"Do they want us to bring anything?" Spencer asked loud enough Alexei overheard him.

"Nothing but yourselves. This is a date, and we want to start our courtship the right way. See you tonight." And then the sexy Russian ended the call without another word.

"Well then," Rey said, throwing an arm around Spencer's shoulders as they began to circle the Cadillac Escalade. A freaking *Cadillac Escalade*. I could only imagine this thing was close to a hundred grand. And he'd had it delivered, a title in my name, plates already in place.

And that had been before I had agreed to let him court me and my pack. What would he have done if I'd told him I wanted nothing more than a professional relationship with him? Would he have demanded the coat and SUV back?

I would have gladly returned them. I wasn't lying when I'd said I couldn't be bought. I might have grown up a little rougher, surrounded by men who lived as under the radar as possible, but I'd been raised to never depend on anyone but myself.

"Holy shit," Spencer said, his phone in his hand. "The base model of this thing is over eighty thousand dollars. He spent more than eighty thousand dollars on a courting gift. What's the tally at this point between the SUV and the coat?" he asked, looking between me and Rey. "And why the hell don't you two spoil me like this?"

"Because I barely make eighty grand in a whole fucking year?" I pointed out.

We had a few hours before we would need to head into the city for dinner with the two alphas. And I needed that time to wrap my mind around everything that had happened in such a short period of time.

Stepping into my personal bedroom, I swung the door closed and pulled my phone out, hitting my dad's number and holding the phone to my ear.

"Hey, girly," his scratchy voice answered. He'd been the president of the MC that had pretty much raised me for so many years. Now that he'd stepped down due to his age and health, he'd grown bored and had actually found a legitimate job to keep himself busy.

"Are you at work?"

"Nah. Off for the week. Something about some wiring problems or some shit."

"Are they paying you for that time off?" I asked. "Do you need me to send some–"

"I dare you to finish that sentence, little girl. You're not too old for me to whip you."

Yeah right. I had never been spanked or hit by my dad in any way growing up. I'd always been the kid who needed nothing more than a stern word or look of disappointment to feel as though my world was crumbling around me.

Huh. Maybe that was why I enjoyed the sting of pain so much in the bedroom, because I'd lacked any form of corporal punishment as a child. And wasn't that fucked up.

"Got a conundrum," I said.

"A what now? Is that some kind of sickness?"

Barking out a laugh, I shook my head as I lowered onto my bed with my legs folded crisscross under me. "No. I've got a bit of a...I guess a moral dilemma. Although not really moral, I guess."

"Tell me."

And so I did. I told him everything from the night I'd met Alexei –

skipping over the parts of him paying for private time in the VIP room with me, of course – to his interest in courting me, my omega, and my alpha, and even the expensive gifts he'd sent.

"He showing off? Trying to buy your loyalty?" Dad asked.

"I mean, I don't really know him, but it doesn't seem like that. You remember that prospect…shit, what was his name? Cordell or Corden or something like that? He was always giving gifts to the omegas in the club, even though he knew he would never have a chance in hell with them. Alexei reminds me of him. Like he just enjoys giving gifts. Or like he has too much money and doesn't know what to do with it, so he throws it at people he cares about instead of letting the government get their hands on it."

"Smart man. And you said Alexei. Russian?"

"I believe so. Has a slight Russian accent. And his name sounds Russian. The other alpha is American, though. I think. I don't know him as well as Alexei."

"So what's the issue? What's got you calling your pops for advice?"

"I don't know. I guess I just needed you to tell me I'm not jumping into things too quickly."

Dad's rough chuckle turned into a cough before he answered. "I've never seen you jump into anything until you were a hundred percent sure it wouldn't be a cluster fuck. Trust your gut, kiddo. If you feel like this Russian is the real deal, let him spoil you. You deserve it. So does that pack of yours." Another of those rusty chuckles rattled over the line. "Spencer's eating it up, isn't he?"

"He's definitely not against another alpha spoiling him, that's for sure."

"Got yourself a brat of an omega." There was nothing short of affection in his tone. Dad had only met my pack a handful of times over the years, but he adored Rey and Spence. "If you have any problems, you know you can call me. I'll send in as many fuckers as you need to beat some sense into…what was his name?"

"Alexei. The other alpha's name is Wolfram but goes by Wolf."

"Sounds like a club name. Like him already."

"He's definitely not a biker, Dad." The man's suit looked as though it cost more than Dad's Harley.

"You said he killed that guy who was fucking with you? What do these alphas do?"

"I'm not positive. And I'd rather not discuss it over the phone."

"That's my girl. Make a trip out to see your old man soon and bring the whole gang. Including the two new guys. Got to get the old man's approval after all."

As a beta, I'd been conceived by my alpha father and my beta mother. My dad had never found any need to add an omega or anyone else to his love life but had formed a pack with the whole club. When he'd been the president, he'd run it like a family and had laid down strict laws that involved consent before fucking anyone's mate.

"We will. I don't know when, though. I have this week off, and then we're on drag schedule so I'll have a few days off here and there the rest of the month. We'll have to schedule a week so I can make the trip out and actually spend more than a few hours with you and the others."

"Wait 'til they find out my girl is being courted by rich fuckers."

"Maybe leave that part out," I said with a giggle. Talking to my dad always made me feel like a little girl again and somehow alleviated the stress I tended to carry on a daily basis. "I'm going to go start getting ready for our date. Love you, Dad."

"Love you, kiddo. Don't wait so long to call me again."

And then he ended the call without saying goodbye. He never said goodbye. Even when I'd moved two states away, he simply told me he'd see me later, as though he feared saying the word would make my departure too permanent.

I should have known my dad would have been on board with me dating someone who made enough money to buy a freaking Cadillac SUV. I'd also known he wouldn't bat an eye over the way we'd met. In Dad's eyes, Alexei had saved his daughter's life. And it didn't matter how that rescue had happened. I knew my dad, or at least members of his club, had done similar if not worse through the years. I'd even witnessed a few of those specific acts of violence when I got older.

It was time to start my pampering. I could easily shower and throw on some clothes and makeup, but I had the time to soak with a bath bomb, shave everything, and slather on some lotion. No reason I couldn't be smooth and soft for our first date, regardless of the fact I had zero intention of getting naked tonight. This was about getting to know each other on a more intellectual and emotional level. We'd already begun exploring the carnal side.

He'd said no dress code, but that didn't mean I wanted to show up in a pair of sweats. I would find something that was a mixture of casual and sexy. And then leave him and Wolf with something to think about after my pack left for the night.

CHAPTER 10

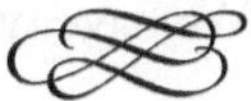

<u>Wolf</u>

"We could have just ordered something in. You're going to overwhelm them," I said as Alexei braised the lamb. "Should I have made something else?"

"Did you even ask if they eat meat? One of them could be a vegan or some shit."

His nose wrinkled as he looked over his shoulder at me. "Why the hell would anyone choose to be vegan?"

A chuckle rumbled from my chest. "There are a lot of vegetarians and vegans for a lot of different reasons. All I'm saying is you're making this big feast without knowing whether they'll be interested. Chinese takeout would have been fine for our first date."

"How the hell did I end up with the least romantic alpha in history as a packmate?" he muttered to himself.

"I'm not unromantic, I just think you're going overboard and you're going to chase Kennedy and her pack away before we have a chance to win them over. All I'm saying is reel it in."

He stopped and looked down at the food, at the table set with fine China and crystal goblets, then turned wide eyes on me. "Shit. They'll be here soon."

The Russian reminded me of a cartoon as he rushed around, gathering up the ridiculous dishware and stashing it in the closet before dumping the expensive cut of meat in the trash.

"I didn't mean to throw everything away. The fuck are you doing?"

"Order something. Hurry. We have twenty minutes before they get here. Unless they're early."

I should have kept my damn mouth shut. Alexei was nervous, something I rarely saw from the assassin, and it had everything to do with Kennedy. I would have thought my packmate would have been more interested in an omega, but he'd surprised me when he'd started obsessing over the raven-haired beauty.

I chuckled to myself at the fact her stage name was so damn appropriate.

Shit. Pulling my phone from the back pocket of my jeans, I pulled up our favorite takeout place and put in an order large enough for three alphas, an omega, and the pretty beta. Delivery time estimate was thirty-three minutes. Just something else to get Alexei all frantic about.

"Why don't you get some glasses out and make some cocktails. I'm sure they'll want a drink," I said, hoping to give him something new to do to occupy his mind.

"What if they prefer beer?"

"Then give them a fucking beer. Damn, Lex. This isn't the first time we've met these people. This isn't some blind date. And you bought the beta a fucking Caddy. Chill out. Relax."

He looked around the kitchen, then surveyed the open concept penthouse. We had a weekly housekeeper, so the place was impeccably clean. Had I actually spent more time here, the cleanliness might actually get on my nerves. The two of us were nearly polar opposites when it came to the whole organization thing. His room looked as though it was ready for inspection by a drill sergeant at any moment while mine looked as though my closet and dresser had exploded, leaving clothes lying on nearly every surface, including the floor.

"I didn't get the alpha or omega a gift," he said, that panic still on his face.

"Dude. Seriously. Make *yourself* a fucking cocktail and chill the fuck out. You're making *me* nervous."

He turned wide eyes on me again, then relaxed when I smiled at him.

"You're right. This is silly. I've made Kennedy come twice. The pretty alpha jacked off the omega right there in front of us. We've all been at our most vulnerable. I'm overreacting."

I held my hand up, putting my index finger and thumb an inch apart. "Just a bit. Reel it in. We're hanging out. Getting to know each other. That's it."

Ten minutes later, the ding of our personal elevator heralded our guests' arrival. And now it was my turn to get nervous.

It had nothing to do with the omega or even Kennedy. It was Rey. It was the beautiful, intense alpha who'd watched me with hunger and distrust in her eyes. Her heady red wine scent had made me feel drunk, as though her scent had contained the sweetest alcohol and flooded my system.

Not that I would let any of them see my nerves. It was dangerous to show an ounce of weakness, even if the three preparing to step from the opening doors and into our home weren't a threat.

Alexei took a deep breath, smoothed his button-down shirt, then sauntered to the doors as they slid open as though he hadn't been running around like a crazy man minutes earlier.

"It's so good to see you. Welcome." He leaned forward and pressed a kiss to Kennedy's cheek, then Rey's, then huffed a surprised laugh when Spence cupped his cheek so the kiss would be directly on the lips.

"I would say sorry, but I've wanted to do that since we met," Spencer said.

He made his way to me and did the same thing, pressing his soft lips to mine before stepping away. "Thank you for having us over."

Rey looked around the place, one brow raised before she glanced down at Kennedy and the two appeared to have some kind of silent conversation before they stepped fully into the apartment.

"Beautiful place," Kennedy said.

She turned her cheek and allowed me to press a kiss the way she had with Alexei. Why was it weird that she was being somewhat formal and cold when we'd seen her nearly naked and made her scream and moan as she came from our private play?

"Is this why you invited us here?" Rey asked, her gaze bouncing between me and Alexei. "To show off your wealth?"

Good thing I stopped Alexei from treating this date as though he was entertaining the fucking queen.

"Absolutely not. I simply wanted to cook for you. I wanted...I wanted to get to know you all better without interruptions of a restaurant."

The female alpha's eyes moved to the kitchen and the empty table.

"He made lamb. I made him throw it out. Chinese food is on its way," I blurted out before I could stop myself.

Shit. I had only meant to ease her suspicions, but telling her that Alexei had made her lamb and making it sound as though we made so much we could afford to throw out such expensive food...I was pretty sure I'd just made it worse.

"Why the hell would you throw out lamb?" Spencer said, breaking the ice.

"He was worried one of you might be a vegan. Or that you would think I was doing too much," Alexei said. And yep. My packmate looked close to wringing his hands.

"We all eat meat. And it *was* too much but I would never turn down fucking lambchops," Spencer said with confusion on his face.

"*He* likes to be spoiled," Kennedy said, nodding her head toward her omega with a growing smile. "So from here out, feel free to dote on him with ridiculous gifts."

"By all means, feel free to send me designer clothes and fancy cars. Unlike these two, I have good taste."

And just like that, the ice was broken.

"How about a tour?" Spencer suggested, wrapping his hand around Rey's and then looping an arm through my elbow.

"This place is huge," Kennedy said as we moved away from the foyer.

"We own the–"

"Thank you," I said, cutting off Alexei before he could ruin things when they were finally smoothing over. The pack didn't need to know all the nitty gritty until they were more comfortable with us. Especially when there would come a time when they'd have more questions about exactly how we made our income.

"Obviously, the kitchen and living room," I said, waving toward the open concept area. "When it's warmer, we can have our coffee on the balcony." I wanted to say when you move in but left that part out. That was a conversation for a later date. "Down here," I said, guiding the trio down the hall, "are the bedrooms. That one is Alexei's. I'm across the hall. There are four spare rooms down there and each has an ensuite bathroom."

"Why so many bedrooms?" Spencer asked. "Were you planning to add to your pack at some point?"

I shrugged my shoulders as I looked into his green eyes. "It had crossed my mind. When I was younger, I'd hoped for a large pack and a home filled with kids. But as I got older…I guess time just got away from me and it stayed Alexei and me."

"You still want kids?" Spencer asked as he turned the knob to Alexei's room and pushed it open without asking first.

"Really, Spence?" Kennedy admonished from behind me.

"What? Just because you don't want to have babies doesn't mean I don't. And I don't have to worry about keeping a hot body for performing."

He winked up at me and my dick twitched in my pants at the thought of taking the omega hard and fast and filling him with my seed, of his belly growing round with my pup.

And then I caught the glare Rey was shooting in my direction and quickly averted my eyes from the sexy auburn-haired omega.

"What about your room?" Kennedy asked from behind me.

I turned and glanced at her then did a double take. The pale beauty had nothing short of a shit eating grin on her face.

Great. Maybe I should have done like Alexei and had our house-keeper clean up my room, too.

"There's nothing special about it."

I didn't get the last word out of my mouth before she was pushing the door open and flipping on the light.

"My my my. You're a slob," Kennedy said with a wide grin.

"Why does this make you feel more human?" Spencer said as he stepped away from me and further into my room.

"I didn't feel human before?"

He waved a hand toward Alexei. "Your buddy acts like a character out of a book or movie, the romantic morally gray protagonist."

Kennedy huffed out a laugh. "You kind of do," she said, tilting her head to look into Alexei's face. And, for the first time since I'd met my packmate, the Russian blushed a bright pink and ducked his eyes.

I didn't think I would ever see anyone who could ruffle the man's feathers, who could cause him to act so unsettled. And all it took was a few words from this tiny pack.

Alexei could kill a man without losing a minute of sleep. He could seduce anyone. Could bring anyone to orgasm.

But the moment the fantasy world became real, Alexei acted as though he wasn't sure how to behave. Had this man never had a serious relationship? Had he never had a deep emotional romantic connection with anyone? Interesting.

A ding echoed through the house from the doorman. Rushing away from the group, I hit the button to allow the delivery person to enter the private elevator and bring our food up.

"If you're all done gawking at my messy room, dinner's here."

CHAPTER 11

<u>Alexei</u>

$\mathcal{W}$hat the hell was wrong with me? She was in my home. *They* were in my home. This was my domain. This was where I was able to be myself. Instead, I had become a bumbling fool and made one mistake after another.

Although I shouldn't have listened to Wolf about dinner. Spencer had appeared disappointed that I'd disposed of my original plan for dinner. And, yes, I wanted to win over the omega as much as I wanted to bond Kennedy to me, to make her a permanent part of my pack.

Rey...the female alpha watched Wolf and me as though we were snakes waiting to strike. She kept a close eye on us, stayed close to her omega, and constantly glared at Wolf.

Those two were either going to end up mortal enemies or having explosive and nearly violent sex. My vote was for the latter.

Issue with that was Wolf's tastes tended to be on the more...primal level. And I knew next to nothing about Rey.

Hell, I barely knew anything about Kennedy other than I would buy her a fucking building if it meant she would see me as more than a client. While I couldn't explain it, she was meant to be in my life. It was like fate had thrown obstacles in my way so I could be late that night simply so I could lay eyes on her, so I could meet her, so I would learn of her existence.

Wolf set the bags on the table and started pulling the containers out, arranging them on the table. He'd bought more than enough for the five of us, but at least he hadn't tried to set up a fine dining situation for what was supposed to be a casual first date.

My eyes strayed over to where Kennedy perused the selection, her back pressed against Rey's as though the alpha felt the need to watch over her two packmates while in our presence. We were the least of her concerns. Wolf and I both worked by the same code – no innocents were to be harmed. Ever.

The beta had worn her inky dark hair loose and it trailed down her back and brushed along the top of her ass. Her makeup was subtle and soft but brought attention to the surreal blue of her eyes that made me think of the finest sapphires. She'd chosen a soft pink sweater that hung off one shoulder and a pair of dark jeans. The outfit was completed with high heeled boots and simple jewelry.

Spencer was in a pair of jeans that looked as though he'd had them for years and were worn in. Not that they didn't hug his firm ass deliciously. A plaid button up shirt did nothing to hide his toned physique, his height and body quite different from the other smaller omega men I'd met in the past.

Rey had chosen a pair of black slacks, a silky cream-colored camisole looking top, with a black blazer over it. And I nearly chuckled when I realized how much she looked like their bodyguard instead of their lover.

Wait…*was* she their lover? She was obviously protective, obviously loved them, but just like with Wolf and me, they might not have been sexually involved with one another.

No. Not completely true. Rey had skillfully stroked Spencer's cock until he'd spilled on his stomach and her hand the night Wolf had insisted they be involved in our time with Kennedy.

"Can I make you a plate?" I offered.

Kennedy turned those pretty eyes on me and tilted her head. Turning, she whispered something to Rey then stepped away, wrapped her hand around mine, and dragged me away from the kitchen, down the hall, and into my bedroom.

The sight of her in my space, her sweet cranberry scent wrapping around me, made my dick instantly stand at attention.

"What's wrong with you?" she asked, keeping her voice low.

"What do you mean?"

"Why are you so nervous? You were so sure of yourself at the club and on the phone. And now you're acting like...I'm not some damsel. If you're trying to prove you're a big, bad protector or whatever, it's not necessary."

"I—" Didn't know how to finish the sentence. I didn't know what the hell I was doing or what had gotten into me. This wasn't the first woman I'd been interested in. But it was the first person I'd ever had the desire to fully integrate into my life in a permanent way. She was the first person I'd ever felt the ache in my gums as the need to leave my mark on her grew.

"Is it my pack? Is this too much at once?"

"No," I said quickly, shaking my head. "It's not that at all."

"Then...what is it?" Her dark brows furrowed, and she sucked her bottom lip between her teeth as she watched me.

"I don't know. I've never been nervous like this. I just...want you. Badly. In a way that doesn't make sense to me."

She released her lip and a slow smile stretched across her beautiful face. "If I told you I wanted you just as badly, would you relax?"

I blinked. Then blinked again. Could she possibly be feeling the same unexplainable pull I was feeling?

"Yes," I finally said.

"Yes, you'll relax?"

Inhaling deeply, I nodded. "I'm sorry. I just wanted the night to go perfectly."

She lifted onto her toes and wrapped a hand around the back of my neck, pulling my face down to hers. The moment our lips touched the world stopped spinning. Or maybe it sped up. All I knew was everything had changed in that first touch.

I'd heard her moans, had had my hands on her bare ass, but this was the first time I'd had the opportunity to taste her, to explore the velvety softness of her mouth, to drown in the sweetness of cranberries mixed with something warm, like brown sugar.

I was a lost man. I was lost to this sassy, strong, sexy beta who had consumed my every waking thought and every wet dream since the first night I'd found her cornered by the man I'd been contracted to kill for the exact same type of crimes he would have no doubt committed against her had I not come along.

Wrapping my arms around her back, I dragged her closer until I could feel the softness of her breasts against me, trapping my rock hard cock between us. The smallest moan escaped her, causing my dick to twitch and my knot to begin to inflate.

Fuck I wanted her. I wanted her in my life permanently, but in this moment, I wanted to feel her wet heat wrapped around my shaft, to have her straddling my lap and riding me until she fell apart in my arms, to have her bent over the bed while I pounded into her hard and fast.

My balls tightened when her hands smoothed from my neck, down my chest and abs, then fumbled with the button and zipper of my jeans until her warm, soft fingers wrapped around my shaft and gave it a slow stroke.

Pulling my mouth from hers, I stared down into her eyes. "We don't have to do anything other than enjoy each other's company, lyubov. I don't want you to think I only want you for—"

Words left my mind as she lowered to her knees, eyes on my face, and took my length into her mouth, swirling her tongue around the head before swallowing my cock as far as she could take without involving my knot.

My beta's body wasn't meant to take a knot. And that was fine with me. Because right now, with my dick in her mouth, I was sure I would never want anyone the way I wanted her.

Her eyes stayed on my face as she bobbed her head on my length, slowly at first, her tongue gliding along the underside. Her hand lifted to toy with my balls and lightly squeeze my knot. And then I saw fucking stars.

"Lyubov. I won't last if you keep that up."

Apparently, all I did was spur her on. She continued fondling my sac and knot and increased the speed with which she bobbed on me and sucked hard.

It felt like she'd sucked my very soul from the head of my cock as I spilled onto her tongue and down her throat. She moaned as she swallowed, not missing a single drop.

When she was finished, she smiled up at me as she tucked my cock away and buttoned and zipped my pants.

"There," she said as she stood. "You should be relaxed now."

"Holy fuck, lyubov," I muttered. My brain was mush, my bones felt like jelly, and I felt as though I'd drank an entire bottle of vodka.

Lifting a hand, she swiped her fingers along her smiling lips. "You're sweeter than I thought you would be," she admitted. "Now that we got that out of the way, will you relax and just…enjoy our time together? This doesn't have to be awkward. You don't have to impress me or my pack."

I nodded numbly and let her take me by the hand and guide me from the room. ·

All eyes turned to us and matching smiles stretched on Wolf's and Spencer's faces. They might not know exactly what had gone on in my room, but they would smell the increased pheromones rolling from me and would see the utter satisfaction on my face.

She'd just blown me in the middle of what was supposed to be a getting to know you dinner. And now…I wanted more.

CHAPTER 12

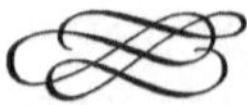

<u>Kennedy</u>

I might have used Alexei's obvious discomfort to get him alone for a moment. What could I say? I'd been fantasizing about the man for weeks. And now I was finally in his house and could have a moment with him where there were no cameras, no mics, no security, and no additional eyes on us.

His kiss had curled my toes and sent lava coursing through my veins. The feeling of his cock pressing against me had sent that same heat straight to my core and my libido had taken over. I hadn't really planned on blowing him. It had just...happened. And he'd tasted amazing. So sweet and crisp.

Was it possible to become addicted to the taste of a man's...

Get your mind out of the gutter, Kennedy. It was just a blow job.

Yet it had felt like so much more, like we'd connected on a stronger level, even though I'd remained fully clothed the entire time. The moment his taste had coated my tongue, it felt as though something had clicked into place, as though we'd formed some kind of bond without his teeth sinking into my flesh.

I wouldn't admit it to anyone – yet – but I wanted his mark. I wanted his mark on the shoulder opposite of where I carried Rey's. I wanted to be his on a deeper level, on a permanent basis.

And wasn't that fucked up being as I knew next to nothing about him.

My dad wasn't completely wrong, though. I rarely did anything I wasn't completely sure about. I followed my gut, and, thus far, my instincts had yet to fail me.

"So are you two hired assassins or hitmen or whatever the technical term is?" Spencer blurted out.

I damned near choked on my eggroll.

"Seriously, Spence?" Rey muttered under her breath.

Once Alexei and I left his bedroom, Alexei had suggested moving the collection of food to the living room so we could watch movies while eating and chatting. Apparently, sucking my Russian alpha off was a surefire way to help him relax. Something I needed to keep in the back of my mind for future reference.

Alexei and Wolf exchanged a meaningful look, and I glanced in Rey's direction. No way she hadn't figured it out from what I'd told her about the night Alexei and I had met. But assuming a thing and hearing it straight from the horse's mouth were two different things.

"Of the sort," Wolf finally answered.

"Explain. If you plan on spending time with my beta and my omega, I want to know they're both safe," Rey said.

Was it me, or had she glared at Wolf nonstop since the moment we'd stepped through the elevator doors?

"It means, we're hired by private parties to…eliminate specific people," Wolf said.

"You're paid to kill people."

"Yes," Alexei said, his eyes on Rey. "We are employed to kill people. But there are contracts we will not accept. We will not hurt children or innocent people."

"Define innocent," Rey said, draping a protective arm around Spencer and tugging him closer. Not that she could do a damn thing to protect either of us if these two men wished any of us harm.

"We have received contracts to off someone's mate or pack rival. We investigate the reason. If it's because the person hiring us simply wishes to get out of a romantic situation or is attempting to steal away a member of someone's pack, we refuse the contract," Alexei answered. "We're not murderers."

"You're just paid to kill," Rey said again.

"It's no different than the court system sentencing someone to death. We just happen to get paid to kill pedophiles, murderers, and rapists," Alexei said, his eyes landing on me.

Rey looked at me then turned her eyes down to Spencer. Was she gauging our comfort level? Because I wasn't a good choice for a moral compass. The fact the two alphas would turn down large sums of money when they deemed someone innocent...it was similar to the rules my dad had put into place when he'd first taken over as president for the club. No home attacks, no old ladies, and no kids were to ever be harmed, regardless of what rival or enemy they might be warring with.

Now I felt a little guilty for never fully divulging my past with my own pack. They knew my dad rode, knew he was a few states over, but that was as far as I'd ever really gone with them. I figured the club's business wasn't mine to share. The whole snitches bull shit still ran deep in my veins.

"Why do you keep looking at me?" Spence asked Rey.

"Because it's my job to protect you. And I need to know if you're comfortable. I need to know for sure that you and Kennedy are safe."

"We would never do anything to endanger any of you. You have my word we are not a threat to you," Alexei said.

"There you go. Now...can we talk about important things like babies and shit?"

"Spencer, for fuck's sake," Rey said. But she couldn't fully hide the smile on her lips, even as she sucked them into my mouth.

"What? Either of our houses have plenty of room for a bunch of kids. Seems like a waste of space otherwise."

"Wait…you two don't think we're going to uproot our lives and move in here, do you?" Rey asked.

Damn good question. The place was gorgeous, but the three of us were not the urban type and liked the quiet of our slightly secluded house and quiet neighborhood. Fighting traffic and dealing with a doorman was way outside the norm for us.

"It's something we can discuss in the future," Wolf said.

"Or we can go ahead and get it out of the way for now. Pretty sure I speak for all three of us when I say we don't want to live downtown," I said, glancing at Spencer and Rey for confirmation.

They nodded. Although Spencer looked a little more hesitant. Our omega liked pretty shit. He liked designer labels and chic crap. This type of home was probably perfect for him, but I was more than willing to remind him of the school districts and lack of playgrounds for his fantasy children if he fought me on it.

It was the alphas' turn to exchange looks as they had a silent conversation. As much as I wanted Alexei in my life, I couldn't expect them to uproot their entire existence for me, for us, any more than they could expect the same from us.

"A compromise?" Wolf suggested to Alexei with raised brows.

"We purchase a larger home with better security. That would keep us from worrying about your safety and give Spencer the extra rooms for the two of you to fill with babies," Alexei said to me.

I raised both hands and shook my head. "Nope. Don't look at me. I have never had the desire to get pregnant. Any kids that join our little family will be carried by our omega."

"Is this where I yell *I volunteer as tribute?*" Spencer teased.

"You're getting way ahead of yourselves," Rey said, always the voice of reason. "We know next to nothing about each other and the four of you are already planning a new pack house and filling it with pups."

"Ask anything," Wolf said.

Rey's mouth opened then closed. Apparently, now that we were all in one room and open to getting to know each other on a more real level, none of us could come up with a single question. At least not after they'd been so open about their career path.

"This is stupid. We're not on some game show where we ask silly questions to get to know each other. How about we just go back to having fun, watching TV, and talking. You know, like normal fucking people," Spencer said.

Wolf chuckled. Rey smiled and hugged him tighter to her side.

Me? I took a chance and stood from where I sat so I could plop my ass right down onto Alexei's lap. I might not have been as needy of touch as an omega, but my pack had spoiled me when it came to snuggling and cuddling. I liked to be held. And who better to be held by than the man whose gaze felt like a physical touch any time he looked in my direction.

His arms immediately wrapped around me as I leaned back against his chest. His lips found my cheek, my temple, before pressing a soft, promising kiss to my exposed shoulder directly over Rey's mark, sending the most delicious tingles throughout my body.

Spencer winked in my direction then glanced over at Wolf. "Plenty of room for a pack cuddle," he offered, patting the spot beside him.

A soft growl rattled from Rey and surprised both Spence and me. It was rare for our alpha to growl and even more rare for her to show even an ounce of jealousy. Hard to be possessive of your packmates when one of them tended to work in a fetish club.

Our omega nudged her with his elbow and frowned up at her, his dark russet brows drawing together in confusion.

The growl cut off, but she still glared at Wolf as he closed the space between them and lowered beside Spencer. Rey made a show of tightening her hold on her omega, leaving no room for Wolf to hold him.

That didn't stop the big, sexy alpha. He simply raised an arm to rest over the top of the couch and toyed with Rey's hair.

A chuckle shook Alexei's body as he watched the scenario play out.

"They both might have met their match," he whispered in my ear.

The thought of the two alphas in a power play was sexy in my head. And I really hoped they would either come to a comfortable compromise or fuck. Because one way or another, I was determined to turn our pack of three into a pack of five.

CHAPTER 13

<u>Rey</u>

I wasn't a fool. It was obvious Wolf was interested in my omega. And since Spencer wanted something I couldn't give him – babies – it would be damned near impossible to talk Spence out of wanting Wolf.

Oh, who the fuck was I kidding? I might have been feeling more than a bit of jealousy over the alpha so close to my omega, but I wanted Wolf, too. I had never felt such a bone deep desire for another alpha the way I had the moment I'd laid eyes on him at Kennedy's table that night.

When he and Alexei had paid a buttload of money for time with my beta in the VIP room, his eyes had almost solely been on me, as though he was picturing me being the one restrained, spread wide for him the way Kennedy had been.

He looked at Spencer with a softness. Me? It was like he saw me as prey. And fuck…I wanted that. I wanted him to dominate me. Or at least try to dominate me. It was something I couldn't get from my beta or omega. Not that they wouldn't try if I asked. But I was bigger and stronger than both and it would be far harder – if not impossible – for either of them to hold me down and fuck me until I felt boneless and lust drunk.

There was something about Wolf that told me he might just like the pain my lock would cause around his knot, that he would allow me to top him, to make him cry out, to pin him the way I wanted to be pinned.

But this situation wasn't about my sexual fantasies or even gratification. It was about ensuring the two alphas were right for my pack, that my beta and omega would remain safe if they were to be bonded into our family.

We'd all finally grown comfortable on the leather wrap around couch. Alexei laid on his side on one end, Kennedy pressed against his chest, his arm over her waist, both asleep as the movie came to an end.

My omega currently rested his head on my lap, his hand curled over my thigh, while Wolf laid behind him and used his hip as a pillow.

I was the only one awake. We hadn't discussed spending the night in the penthouse. None of us had brought overnight bags, but everyone looked so comfortable I hated to wake them. But sleeping sitting up was going to wreak havoc on my neck and back and I'd end up stiff in the morning.

Stretching to the side, I gently tapped Wolf on the shoulder, then quickly sat up when he shot straight up, instantly on alert. The man was almost intimidating. Almost.

"What's wrong?" he asked, looking around the room as though to check on each person in the house and to make sure there were no intruders.

I nodded my head down at Spencer. "We can't sleep like this. And it's late. I don't want to drive us home and fall asleep behind the wheel."

Wolf glanced up at the clock on the mantle above the fireplace as the arm clicked over to three fifteen in the morning.

"Shit. How long have we been asleep?" he whispered.

"Two movies. I've been sitting here thinking one of you would eventually wake up."

He huffed a soft laugh then pushed his hand through his shaggy hair. Fuck, he was sexy in a broody, bad boy kind of way.

"Sorry about that."

He carefully scooted out from behind Spencer's legs, then touched his shoulder to wake him.

"That won't work. He sleeps like the dead. We're used to sleeping through Kennedy getting home late at night."

Grabbing my omega's shoulder, I shook him a few times until he groaned in frustration and turned his head to look up at me.

"You fell asleep. Wolf's going to show us to a room for the night."

His brows drew together, and he looked around sleepily, trying to get his bearings as the sleep haze began to fall away.

"Damn. We all fell asleep?" he asked.

"Not me. But my legs are asleep, and I can't sleep sitting up. Get up so we can find a bed."

Wolf stretched out his hand and helped Spencer to his feet, eliciting another of those rare possessive growls from deep within my chest. Until he did the same with me and helped pull me to my feet, wrapping an arm around my waist until the feeling came back and I was able to walk without the pins and needles feeling.

"I'm fine," I said, shrugging away from his arm.

But I fought the urge to yank him away when he wrapped a hand around Spencer's and led him down the long hall toward the room where we would bunk for the night. If we were going to entertain the idea of becoming a pack of five, I had to accept the fact one or both of the alphas would be as interested in my omega as I was.

Wolf stopped at the fourth door on the right and pushed it open, reaching around the doorframe to flip on a light. "The sheets and bedding are clean. Towels are in the bathroom along with any toiletries you might need. Extra toothbrushes are under the sink. We can lend you all some clothes to sleep in if you don't want to sleep naked."

He winked down at Spencer and my alpha surged forward as a growl ripped from me and I could no longer hold my tongue.

"Can I speak with you alone, please?" I demanded rather than asked, wrapping a hand around Wolf's bicep and dragging him from the room just as Spencer shoved his jeans down his legs and dropped face first onto the mattress.

I pulled the door shut behind us and looked up and down the hall, unsure of where exactly we could go without either waking Alexei and Kennedy or letting Spencer listen in to my suspicions.

He took the initiative and led me to his bedroom, kicking clothes out of the way, making a path for me to enter without tripping.

"You're a fucking slob."

"That's what you wanted to talk to me about?" he asked, his brows pulled up.

"Spencer is my omega. He's my responsibility. It's my job to protect him. If all you're doing is–"

"I thought we were all trying to get to know each other. I thought this was a first date. Last I heard, all three of you agreed to letting Alexei and I court the whole pack."

"Yet you seem overly interested in Spencer."

"You've been practically wrapped around him since the moment you walked through the door and haven't stopped glaring at me," he accused.

Or maybe he was simply stating the truth. Because yeah, I was doing everything I could to keep him at a distance from my beautiful omega and watching for the slightest tell that the killer alphas might be full of shit or a risk to my pack.

He began to stalk toward me; I kept my feet glued in place. If he thought for one second I would back away out of fear, he was fucking with the wrong woman. I was a fucking alpha, just like him. I might not be as big, but I could fight and had no problem knocking him on his ass if he thought to use his size to intimidate me.

"If you had stepped away from him for one second, you would have realized I want *you*. Not your omega. Or as much as your omega. You're the one I've been staring at. You're the one I've jerked off to so many fucking times I'm surprised I'm not blind. You're the one I couldn't peel my eyes from in that fucking back room at the club. Spencer happens to be a beautiful bonus."

My mouth opened then closed. Opened then closed again. Shit. I had no idea what to say to that.

He saved me from having to say a word when he grabbed me by the back of my neck and jerked me forward hard enough I lost my footing and slammed into his chest as his lips claimed mine in a bruising kiss.

His tongue swept into my mouth and I kissed him back with as much ferocity.

Then shoved him away.

"The fuck are you doing?" I asked, touching my fingertips to my lips.

His chest rose and fell as his eyes darted from my eyes to my lips, down my body, then up again. With almost a foot between us, his gaze felt as though he'd run his hands along every inch of me and I grew wet between my thighs as need coursed through me.

Lunging at him, I nearly took him to the ground as I threw my arms around his neck and claimed his mouth the way he had mine. And then we were in a battle for control.

I was turned, then walked backward until my back hit a wall. His hands were rough as they smoothed up the hem of my shirt until he could slide them under my shirt and cup my tits through my bra. A moan tore from my lips but he swallowed it down.

Grabbing his wrists, I pulled them away and pushed my weight against him until he stumbled backward and fell over a pile of clothes, landing on his back with a thud and a huff as the wind was knocked from his lips.

While he watched me from his position, I tore my shirt over my head and reached around to unclasp my bra.

Then I lowered onto him, straddling his hips and leaning forward to kiss him again, gripping his hair tightly in my hands.

He grunted and struggled to undo his belt, button, and zipper. Then he went to work on my pants.

When he couldn't remove them from my position, he quickly sat up and flipped me onto my back, holding me down with a hand in the center of my chest while he dragged my pants down my legs until I wore nothing but a pair of panties while his cock jutted free from his pants.

Two alphas vying for control. And as much as I wanted to submit, to be fucked senselessly...he would have to prove he was strong enough to take what he wanted, to give me what I needed.

Sitting up on my elbow, I gripped his cock in my hand and squeezed, giving it a slow stroke and smiling at the way his hips bucked as though trying for more.

Instead, I released him and grabbed the sides of his jeans and shoved them, trying to get them off his hips.

Wolf had other ideas.

He swatted my hands away, grabbed the side of my panties, and ripped the seam until my pussy was exposed. He immediately dove face first into my cunt, his tongue swiping through the folds before sucking my clit between his lips.

Tossing my head back, I moaned, gripping his hair hard enough I felt a few strands pull loose as I tugged hard.

"Fuck," he breathed against my core.

He pulled away and his hands were rough as he grabbed me and flipped me onto my stomach, my body cushioned by the clothes littering his floor. The entire space smelled of autumn, of fallen leaves and warmth and the scent soaked into my very pores.

His body was heavy as he settled himself over my back, his legs straddling my thighs. One hand circled around to lightly grab my throat while the other gripped his shaft to position himself to my entrance.

I couldn't spread my legs far in this position, but that didn't seem to matter to him. He slid the head of his cock along my wetness, preparing himself, then thrust forward hard and fast, tearing a scream from my lips.

"I'm going to fuck you hard. And when I get you off, I want to feel that lock clamp down on my cock. I want my name to fall from your lips when you come. Do you understand me?"

He squeezed his hand tight enough I could barely croak out, "Yes."

And then he slammed his hips into me over and over, the sound of his hips slapping against my ass mixing with the wetness of my pussy.

He'd given as much as he'd taken. Was still taking. He'd let me fight him for dominance but had topped me.

Yet...he wanted me to lock him. He and I both knew that would cause him pain. It would lock us together for a period of time. He needed to be controlled as much as he needed to control.

We were both switches. And wasn't that the hottest thing in the fucking world.

Wolf finally released his hold on my throat and leaned forward, giving me more of his weight as he pressed kisses along my shoulder blades and the back of my neck.

"If I feel teeth back there, I'll do more than lock your cock," I promised.

Although...a tingling sensation tickled my heart at the thought of Wolf marking me as his, claiming me permanently. Never in my life had I thought I would like the thought of another alpha leaving his or her mark on me.

But never in my life had I hated *and* wanted another alpha the way I did Wolf.

Not hate. I didn't hate him. I just wasn't sure I trusted him to not bring danger to my omega and beta.

He chuckled at my threat, the sound rumbling against my back. There was no risk of getting pregnant being as we were both alphas, but neither of us had had the forethought to seek a condom, something we definitely needed to discuss later. Just because I couldn't get knocked up didn't mean I wasn't susceptible to the same diseases as any other human being, for fuck's sake.

For now, though, all I could focus on was the building pressure low in my belly.

"You better be sure about my lock, Wolf," I said as the pressure grew.

"Come on my dick, alpha. Lock me."

The moment he referred to me by my designation, fireworks exploded behind my closed lids and my body felt as though it had burst into flames as I came hard.

He grunted loudly as I locked around him, preventing him from doing more than making shallow thrusts until I felt the heat of his jets of cum filling me.

Moments later, he collapsed onto my back, holding the brunt off me on his elbows that bracketed either side of my head.

"Do you need more convincing of my intentions?" he said, his breath warm against the side of my neck as he pressed soft kisses to my cheek and temple.

I laughed and shoved at him until he rolled us to our sides so we could be more comfortable while we waited for my body to release its hold on him.

"Was I too rough?" he asked, his deep voice acting like both an aphrodisiac and a sedative. I wanted to straddle him and ride him again to release, but also wanted to relax into his hold and let sleep drag me under.

But not on the floor surrounded by, *hopefully*, clean clothes that were scattered everywhere.

"Not at all. Was I?"

He huffed out a surprised laugh. "Not at all," he said, repeating my phrase before pressing a tender kiss to the side of my neck. "But no way are we sleeping on the floor."

"You really are a slob," I teased.

"Do you three tend to sleep together? I don't want to keep you from your omega."

He tugged, but my lock was still in place, keeping him deep inside my core.

"Sorry, alpha. You have at least another twenty minutes before you're free to run away."

Another of his deep chuckles made a smile bloom on my lips.

He wasn't out of the woods as far as whether or not I fully trusted him with my pack just yet. But...I couldn't deny the chemistry between us, nor could I deny I wanted him for more than one night.

Maybe Kennedy had been right when she'd touted that fate had brought Alexei into her life that night. It had also brought Wolf into my life, into our life.

And, honestly, as sleep began to make my lids grow heavy and my thoughts fuzzy, I couldn't make myself think of any concrete reason as to why we needed to stay away from the two alpha hitmen.

CHAPTER 14

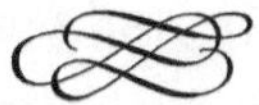

<u>Kennedy</u>

Alexei's crisp, wintery scent wrapped around me, warming me as much as his body curled around mine. It struck me as somewhat funny that each of the alphas smelled like a season, Alexei like winter, Wolf like autumn. Yet they complimented each other, creating a mouthwatering while calming combination.

A smile quirked up my lips at the memories from last night. I wasn't sure whether Wolf and Rey were aware, but nearly every sound they'd made behind closed doors had made it through the walls and straight to my ears.

Alexei had slept through the entire thing.

Had Spencer heard? Hell, had Spencer been present? Had he participated? Neither of the latter would have surprised me. My omega loved sex and was definitely attracted to the two new alphas. And apparently, had already started naming the children he would carry by them if his line of questions and conversation last night was anything to go by.

"Good morning," Alexei said, his voice deeper and huskier from sleep. I didn't think his voice could be yummier, but yep, I'd been wrong.

"Morning," I said, hugging his arm tighter to me.

I supposed I should have felt more awkward waking up on his couch after spending the night when all we'd planned was a dinner to get to know each other better. We'd talked, but not really. Most of it had been Rey giving the guys the third degree and Spencer practically demanding one of them knock him up as soon as possible.

Nope. We still didn't know each other, yet I felt completely at ease here in Alexei's arms, as though we'd woken in the exact same way dozens, even hundreds of times before.

"Since I was stopped from making you dinner last night, will you at least allow me to make you all breakfast?" he asked, nuzzling his face in my hair and pressing kisses to the back of my neck and the shell of my ear.

My stomach grumbled and I giggled. "Yes, please," I said, rolling onto my back to look into his pretty eyes. "Is it weird that we stayed the night?"

"Not at all. I would have suggested it instead of a simple dinner but didn't want to scare your alpha."

A surprised laugh burst from me. "I'm pretty sure she's officially fine with the two of you courting us."

He sat up and rested his weight on one elbow, staring into my face with a confused smile. "What makes you think that?"

It really wasn't my business, but he should probably know our packs were officially getting to know each other.

Before I could give him the details, a door opened from down the hall and several pairs of steps slapped against the hardwood floor.

Spencer's auburn hair was ruffled, his jeans were open and hanging on his hips, and his shirt was nowhere to be found.

Rey...was wearing a shirt that she definitely had not worn when we'd arrived at the penthouse last night, and there was a pep to Wolf's steps. Both had damp hair.

"You're lucky I didn't hear shit last night," Spencer grumbled as he stepped into the kitchen then turned with the most disgruntled look on his face. "No coffee?"

I wasn't sure whether Wolf and Alexei realized exactly how high maintenance our omega could be, but it looked like they were going to get their first experience.

"Sorry about that," Alexei said, lifting and swinging a leg over me so I wouldn't have to actually sit up for him to climb out from behind me.

"You needed to be awake for me to shower?" Rey said, positioning herself behind Spencer and wrapping her arms around his waist so she could rest her chin on his shoulder.

"Oh, please. You didn't exactly use scent blockers. You're covered in each other's scents. The least you could have done is let me watch if I wasn't invited to join."

Wolf snorted as he tried to hold in his laugh while Alexei turned to wink at me over his shoulder before refocusing his attention on making coffee.

"So does that mean I'm the only one who hasn't fucked either of you?" Spence asked.

"Excuse me, I haven't technically fucked either of them, either."

This time, Alexei turned around fully with raised brows as the coffee began to drip into the carafe.

Lifting a hand, I pointed a finger at him. "A blowie is not fucking."

"I *knew* you two fooled around," Spencer said, and yep, he sounded as though his feelings were hurt like he'd been rejected.

Oh shit. "Where did you two sleep last night?" I asked Wolf and Rey.

They both looked guilty as hell as Rey turned apologetic eyes to our omega. "Fuck, Spence. I didn't...I'm sorry." Rey turned Spence and tilted his head back so she could press a sweet kiss to his lips. "Next time, just barge in. You know I don't mind."

Spencer turned raised brows to Wolf.

"If you're waiting for me to say I don't like an audience, you'll be waiting a while. In case you don't remember the first time we actually met." He winked at Spence and caused my sweet omega to blush a bright pink.

"Duly noted," he said, resting his head against the crook of Rey's shoulder and neck and rubbing along her scent glands. I wasn't sure whether it was to mark himself, mark her, or simply reassuring himself that nothing had changed.

But hadn't it?

Last night was supposed to be nothing more than a dinner, a couple hours for us all to get to know each other a little better. And yeah, sure, we'd talked some, had delved further into the grittier side of what Wolf and Alexei did for money. But mostly, we'd ended up in a puppy pile on the couch after I'd sucked Alexei off enough to make him relax and be himself.

And, apparently, while the two of us had slept, Rey and Wolf had really gotten acquainted with each other. Well, while everyone else slept. I wasn't ashamed to say the sounds of my alpha with Wolf had been a major turn on.

Wolf and Alexei moved around their kitchen with ease, preparing breakfast for all of us. And Rey never stopped touching Spencer. Our omega might never come out and say it, but he needed touch, needed the constant reassurance from his pack. Even when I came home long after the two had gone to bed, I always crawled in with them.

And he had been alone in bed last night in a completely unfamiliar house. Well, *pent*house. But still. I would have been surprised if he'd been able to sleep more than a few hours at a time alone in the bed.

I hadn't exactly planned to fall asleep in Alexei's arms, but I still felt guilty. Rey and I would have to dote on him more than usual, maybe take him shopping or something. New goodies always made him feel better.

"Feel free to use the shower while we're cooking," Alexei said. "You're all welcome to any of my clothing. Sweats and tees are in the drawers of the dresser."

I crept up behind him, feeling oddly comfortable in his kitchen and in his presence after such a short period of time together, and wrapped my arms around his waist. "Will I find anything kinky?

Maybe your ex's panties?" I slid one hand down his stomach and snuck a little fondle of his cock, smiling when it twitched and instantly began to thicken under my touch.

"No panties. And nothing kinky…in my dresser." He looked at me over his shoulder and winked with the sexiest smirk on his soft lips.

After a quick squeeze, I pulled Spencer away from Rey and led him to the room Alexei had shown us last night, pushing in and rifling through the drawers for two clean pairs of sweats and t-shirts. I would need a sweatshirt or hoodie, as well. It wasn't quite warm enough to be running around without that extra cozy layer.

And I knew Spencer would absolutely be craving a little extra coziness after being alone last night. He was unusually subdued, even after the apology and snuggles from Rey.

"Holy crap," Spence said as he stepped into the bathroom and flipped on the light.

Our house wasn't exactly small, but I was pretty sure our shared bedroom could fit inside Alexei's ensuite bathroom. It was sleek and modern without being cold with warm brushed gold or brass and wood accents along with the plush towels and fuzzy robe on display.

Alexei either had amazing taste or he'd hired a professional. Either way, I could spend all day in here, just soaking in the humongous garden tub.

Actually, the longer I stared at it, the more I realized all five of us could spend hours soaking or playing in a steamy bubble bath.

"Okay, I'm so not opposed to moving in here if we all decide to pack up," Spence muttered to himself.

"Do I need to remind you of the fact you're gung-ho about popping out a bunch of kids. We'll have to enroll them in a private school. And there's not exactly any parks nearby—"

He waved his hand in the air, brushing off every single argument.

"Honey, with a place this big, we can build them a playroom. I have no problem with private schools. And I'll drive them to the damn park. This place is amazing. And safe. We wouldn't have to worry about something happening to our babies."

Our babies. I loved him for things like that. Even though I had made it known from day one with my pack that I had zero intention of ever getting pregnant, he acted as though I would be just as much a parent to any child born from him as the alpha who knocked him up.

"I think we have plenty of time to talk about all that," I said, stripping and folding my clothes into a pile before setting them on the vanity.

They weren't technically dirty, but the thought of wearing something that smelled so heavily of Alexei did something funny to my heart. His scent warmed me all over and increased the feeling that he was meant to be in my life.

They were both meant to be in our lives.

I just wasn't sure exactly how that would look or how it would work.

I needed to fully entrust my pack with my background. Though I'd have to keep some things to myself, the things that could incriminate the family who'd raised me, incriminate my own damn dad.

But they should probably know exactly why I wasn't freaked out by what Alexei and Wolf did for a living or why I wasn't still suffering the mental or emotional effects of the night Alexei and I had met.

Spencer turned on the spray and waited for it to warm. He stepped in ahead of me, but then turned wide eyes on me as his brows shot up his forehead.

"Seriously?" he said, reaching over and turning another spigot.

Two heads started and then more water rained down on us from another overhead.

"We could all shower at once and no one would get cold," he said, twirling like he was dancing in the rain. "I'm so turning on music next time and acting out my own freaking music video in here." He started dancing like he was in an Usher video…if Usher danced with his cock swinging around.

I chuckled and leaned my head back, letting the water plaster my coal black hair down my back. My muscles were a little stiff from sleeping on the couch, but they were quickly easing.

Okay. So maybe living in a place like this wouldn't be so bad. And

Wolf had offered to find or build something bigger in the right area if we were to combine our little packs and become a family.

Maybe Spence wasn't the only one getting ahead of himself. Hell. I'd already admitted to myself that Alexei belonged in my life right beside my alpha and my omega. What was the point of thinking of so many what ifs when I could do like my omega and simply enjoy what we were building together?

Once I'd washed using the stuff sitting on the tiled coves of the shower, I turned to watch as Spencer simply stood under the spray, his head tilted back, eyes closed.

"Sorry about last night," I said, moving forward to wrap my arms around his waist and press my cheek against his chest.

He hugged me tightly and rested his cheek on the top of my head. "It's not a big deal. I'm sorry I'm so fucking needy all the time."

"You're an omega. You're supposed to be needy."

He swatted my ass, earning a surprised squeal, then went right back to hugging me under the spray. It was like we were in a romance movie where the characters made out in the rain. Except we weren't making out, simply holding each other as we'd done hundreds, even thousands of times through the years.

"Since you and Alexei fooled around and Wolf and Rey obviously fucked, I think it's only fair I get my dick wet while we're in this ridiculously fancy penthouse."

"Technically, your dick *is* wet."

Any other jokes froze in my throat when he dropped to his knees and buried his face between my thighs before taking me hard and fast against the tiled shower wall, the sounds of my cries echoing throughout the space.

CHAPTER 15

Alexei

Kennedy, Rey, and Spencer had only spent that one night at our place in the past two weeks. In fact, I'd only seen my beta a few times after work. Wolf and I had been accepting back-to-back contracts.

What could I say? The prospect of adding not just one, but three more members to our family made us want to raise as much money as possible. Especially when it was obvious Kennedy and Rey had no interest in living downtown. But neither Wolf nor I would be willing to leave our omega or beta unsecured when we weren't home, meaning we needed to ensure any house we built had top of the line security including tall gates, cameras, and alarms. Maybe even some armed guards.

We had plenty of money now. And would make even more when we sold the three floors of the building where we lived. But...I wanted to make sure our omega had everything he wanted. I wanted to make sure Kennedy could quit performing if she decided that wasn't what she wanted for her future.

I, for one, had zero issues with her performing, but I had noticed a green fog slithered through my gut when she entered the back hallway for a private meeting with a VIP client on a night I arrived too late to get to her first.

Did she allow any others to touch her the way I had? Did any others bring her to the brink the way I had? Did she allow others to watch as her pack had when Wolf and I had played with her while restraining her spread out and completely at our mercy?

The thought of her restrained like that for any other alpha sent a red-hot rage coursing through me. Not because I felt she was solely for me, but because there were too many fuckers out there who could hurt her before security was able to get through the fucking door and stop them.

I was currently two floors below our penthouse, loading up a bag of my favored tools for the job lined up for the night. Wolf was across the room doing the same. We rarely worked together, but this was a two-man job. Actually, we probably would have been better with more than two of us, but we'd yet to come across anything the two of us couldn't handle, even when there were possible witnesses.

Before I had a chance to question the sanity of what I was planning, I inserted my ear pod into my ear and hit Kennedy's number, listening as it rang three times.

She was slightly breathless when she finally answered.

"Are you okay?" I asked.

"Fine. I left my phone in the bedroom and had to run to grab it. What's up?"

Even over the line, I could hear the smile in her voice. Just like any other time we talked. Most of the past two weeks had been mostly phone conversations, yet I was finding myself more and more obsessed with the raven-haired beauty. And...I found myself missing the omega and their alpha. Which was odd being I hadn't spent nearly as much time with either of them.

From that first night in our penthouse, it had felt as though they'd belonged there, as though that wasn't the first time we'd all slept under the same roof. And I badly wanted that again. Fuck, I wanted that on a nightly basis. I wanted to find a pack bed big enough to fit the five of us so we could fuck and snuggle through the night.

"Do others restrain you the way I do?" I blurted out.

Wolf turned and frowned at me as he shoved a few extra magazines into a duffel.

"In the VIP room?" she asked. And just like that, the smile was no longer in her voice. "On fetish night, it's common to be restrained."

"Do they restrain you in such a vulnerable position?"

"You know there are cameras, Alexei. You're not going to become one of those alphaholes and demand my body is solely for your eyes and all that shit, are you?"

Alphaholes. Clever. "I only worry about your safety. I'm aware there are cameras, but there are a lot of ways to injure someone in a short amount of time."

"I'm not a helpless damsel, lubova…or whatever you call me."

A chuckle rumbled from my chest at her attempt at Russian. "Lyubov. Perhaps it's time to teach you my native language. Take you home to meet the parents."

"Right. We'll just hop on a plane and head overseas so you can introduce your family to the beta you're courting."

I *was* courting her. But whether she knew it or was willing to accept it, I had no intention of letting her go any time soon. She was mine. I would share her with her pack and my packmate. I would even share her with those who paid thousands of dollars with an hour of private time with her. But she was mine and I would cut the hands off anyone who touched her in any way she didn't give explicit permission.

The thought of another man coating her round ass with cum sent another wave of possessive rage through my system. I couldn't stand the thought of another man leaving his scent on her or touching her in any way. But I would have to keep that to myself. At least for now.

"Is my job going to be an issue going forward?" she asked.

"My first instinct is to say no. I'm just worried about your safety."

"Let me put this out there right now because I know you're not saying what's got you twisted – no one else has ever done...I've never let anyone else put their hands on me and I sure as fuck have never let any other client jizz on me. So if that's part of your issue, consider it squashed."

Fuck me. The fact she practically read my mind was nearly as big a turn on as the memory of her ass cheeks shimmering with my cum or the way her skin had felt under my hands when I'd rubbed it into her flesh to leave her covered in my scent.

I had covered her in my seed, had spilled down her throat, but I'd yet to feel that beautiful body or sweet-smelling cunt wrapped around my cock. And the more time we spent apart, the more desperate I was to have her at my side day in and day out.

"And I don't think I'm ready for a fifteen-hour flight to meet your mommy and daddy just yet," she said, as though trying to lighten the moment.

It worked.

"When will I meet your family?"

"Actually, about that. My dad has been asking about meeting you and Wolf. But I think there are a few things we need to discuss before that happens."

"Then discuss."

"Nah. Not over the phone. Next time I see you. Which will be...?"

I sighed. "Wolf and I are working tonight, but I'm hoping to be there before the end of your shift."

She was waiting tables during drag month, so I wouldn't get to see her hanging from silk ropes or being tickled or spanked. But with as late as I often worked, it seemed I saw her only when she was at her place of work. I wanted time alone with her. And I knew Wolf was craving the same. If we were going to become a family, we both needed to ensure we spent time alone with each of my beta's pack.

"You said Spencer enjoys expensive things?" I said as a thought hit me.

"Oh, hell yes," she said with a soft huff of laughter.

"When is your next day off? I would like to take the two of you shopping."

"Take Spence. I'm not really into the same things he is. Besides, I think he's actually starting to get a little jealous. Like he feels like he's being left out of all of this and thinks he should be the center of attention."

Of course he would feel that way. He was an omega. And omegas tended to be the center of attention and sought like the rare gems they were. Spencer was even more rare, as rare as the beautiful alpha Rey. And I was spending all my energy on Kennedy.

But she was the one who had first caught my attention and made me feel as though my life had been empty before her, or as though I had been merely existing while waiting until she came into my life.

And I didn't give a fuck how sappy that sounded.

"You're right. I'll contact him and ask him on a solo date. Is there a restaurant or store he would prefer? I want him to feel special. We want him a part of our family as much as I want you."

Wolf cocked a brow at me and nodded slowly and I had to wonder if my packmate had already spent some time with the omega without bothering to let me in on all the sordid details.

"He'll love that. And my next day off is this weekend. We're actually switching over to burlesque so I'm not back on until…Tuesday," she said as though either thinking or looking at her calendar. "But he's home. Right now."

"We're preparing for work. But I'll text him and arrange a date with him."

Wolf's hand shot out and took the phone from me before I had a chance to respond. "Hey, beta, it's Wolf. Does your alpha like pretty stuff? Or sparkly stuff?" There was a beat of quiet where I could barely hear the soft murmurs of Kennedy's voice on the other line before Wolf thanked her and handed the phone back to me.

"He's got it bad for Rey," she teased. "I guess that's a good thing. I was kind of worried. You know, about adding two male alphas to our pack when we already have Rey. I would never let anyone make her feel as though she was no longer important or needed by us. I love her."

"Of course you do." But I had no idea whether the two were merely packmates like Wolf and I or whether the three enjoyed each other's bodies on a regular basis. As the image of Kennedy's face buried between Rey's strong thighs flashed through my mind, my dick grew almost painfully hard, and I had to adjust my boner to move it away from the back of my zipper.

I had to get my head in the game. The last thing I needed was to arrive on the scene of our hit with my dick tenting my pants.

"I'll try to meet you at the club before you're off. But make sure—"

"Someone walks me out. Yep. That one night was literally the only night I've ever stepped foot into the parking lot without a member of security. But thanks, dad," she teased, eliciting a smile.

"Is there any chance I can coax you into spending the night in my bed tonight?" I asked, and barely avoided holding my breath as I waited.

There was a beat of silence before she answered. "I'm always up to a little coaxing." And there was definitely a double meaning behind that answer.

"If I don't make it before you leave, call me when you wake up tomorrow. I want to see you."

"Maybe the two of you can join us at our house for dinner tomorrow? And we'll even cook for you. Or, you know, order out again."

"How about we make that a plan either way? I want to spend time with you, lyubov. But I'm also courting your alpha and omega and have neglected them. It's time to rectify that little problem."

"I don't know why, but that sounded so deliciously dirty. I've got to get going. Got to get ready for work. I'll see you tonight or tomorrow. And please be careful tonight."

A smile grew on my face at her concern. I'd teased her about meeting my parents, but they'd been gone for years. Something else we had never discussed. We knew only surface things about each other.

But she'd said her father wanted to meet me, to meet us both. That was a step closer to forming a bond with my beautiful beta and her pack.

CHAPTER 16

<u>Wolf</u>

Rage sizzled through my veins like gunpowder lit by a match. *That mother fucking cocksucker.*

We'd received a contract on a repeat offender of the worst kind. The piece of shit was trafficking not just women but kids. And we'd caught him red fucking handed as he stuck a needle in the arm of a thirteen-year-old girl. The child was already loopy as hell and incoherent. He was keeping her docile so she wouldn't fight when he sold her off.

The contract had simply stated a quick kill, to make it appear as an accident. That fucker deserved nothing less than what I'd delivered to him.

The intel we'd received had been wrong. Alexei and I had been warned there could be upward of ten others, mainly security types. But there had only been two on guard and they'd looked high as a kite. We were on them and cutting their throats before they knew they were no longer alone.

Anyone who stumbled upon the scene would know without a doubt there hadn't been an accident. The trafficking rapist's head laid a few feet from his body when we'd left. More than likely, if for some reason the police were to stumble upon the scene, they would think it was a rival of some form. Alexei and I had done this long enough there was never any evidence of our presence. Not even a fucking hair from our heads would have been left at the scene let alone a fingerprint or our faces on a security camera.

Even now as I stood under the spray, the blood speckles rinsing from my face, neck, and hands, I couldn't erase the scene we'd wandered upon, couldn't erase the urge to go back and kill that mother fucker over and over again.

This was what people didn't understand. They didn't understand how it was so easy for me to kill, for Alexei and me to take lives. We didn't prey on innocents. We didn't hurt children. We'd even killed those who'd hired us when we realized they were the monsters who needed to be eliminated. The money was always wired to an untraceable account beforehand, anyway. So...either way, we got paid.

Scrubbing at my skin, I hissed at the four grooves that had been scratched into my skin by the coward. He'd literally scratched me as I'd stabbed him over and over as though that slight discomfort would be enough for me to walk away and let him live another day.

To hurt another child.

We'd bundled up the barely teenaged girl, left her at the hospital, and headed home.

By now, Kennedy would be ending her shift and Alexei would be waiting outside, watching over her as he had every night since that first night. He would beg her to come stay at our penthouse. Maybe tonight she would agree.

Then what? He often returned carrying her scent, but not enough to tell me they fooled around. How the hell was he able to keep his dick in his pants when it came to the beta?

I sure as fuck hadn't after the first night I'd been buried inside Rey. She and I had come to ... an arrangement of sorts. I had no idea whether her other two packmates were aware or not, but if Alexei knew or suspected, he'd said nothing.

Tonight was looking to be one of those nights when I needed the fellow alpha to help ease the rage and emotional agony burning through my veins until I feared I might go feral and hurt someone who didn't quite deserve it.

After turning off the spray and drying off, I shot off a text to Rey's phone and pulled on a pair of sweats.

A chime filled the quiet of my chaotic space as I grabbed socks and shoes. After a quick glance at her reply, I pulled a sweatshirt over my head, shoved my feet into my shoes, and grabbed the keys to my Audi as I passed my dresser on my way to the bedroom door.

It would take close to twenty minutes to get to Rey, to where she would be waiting in the backyard for me. She and I had similar tastes. We enjoyed the give and take, the fight for dominance.

And she understood on nights like tonight I needed something... different. I needed a safe outlet for the rage that would otherwise either keep me up all night or send me out looking for a fight with some asshole alpha.

Killing the headlights, I silently pulled along the curb a few houses down and turned off the engine. I didn't bother locking the door as I silently pushed it closed, then began to jog toward the privacy fence lining the pack's spacious backyard.

Their property butted up and opened to woods, making it a perfect location for the hunt. And my beautiful alpha was more than willing to be my prey, even putting up enough of a fight to leave marks on me in the morning.

I caught sight of her white tank top fleeing toward the woods as I climbed over the top of the wooden fence and instantly started sprinting toward her the moment my feet hit the ground.

For a brief moment, I lost sight of her, but her scent was like a beacon, leading me straight to her. I'd noted during these sessions together that her red wine signature turned a bit sweeter with her arousal. And my dick reacted accordingly, hardening to the point it was growing more difficult to run at full speed.

I never called out to her. She never made any sound to lure me to where she was heading or where she hid. This was all part of the game. It was a way for us to both get what we needed while feeding the desire to hunt and destroy in a safe way with a consenting partner.

A partner who was quickly wiggling her way into the deepest crevices and darkest corners of my heart.

Leaves and twigs cracked underfoot ahead. I was gaining on her. At no point had she ever held back, had she ever slowed or pulled her punches when I caught her.

But I did. I might dominate her, pin her, even wrap my hands around her throat, but I had never left anything more than fading red marks on her soft flesh.

Her scent grew stronger as I drew closer. *There.* A flash of her white tank moved between trees. The air was crisp and cold and she must have been freezing. But we'd learned after the first few times of our little game her clothes rarely survived.

A smile twitched on my lips. I didn't think the perfect woman existed, yet here I was, chasing after her, a fucking female alpha willing to let me stalk her, chase her, pin her, and dominate her while she fought me in earnest.

The moment I was close enough, I lunged, tackling her to the ground, while using my arm to shield her head from hitting the cold, hard forest floor.

She immediately whirled on me, swinging her fist and punching me in the jaw. The ache throbbed from my face and straight to my cock as I wrestled with her wrists, pinning them over her head while she bucked and writhed below me.

A white tank top and sleep shorts. She must have been freezing while she'd waited for me to arrive. Unless she'd been watching through the window for my car to creep past then snuck out back.

Had she told Kennedy or Spencer about our late-night endeavors yet? Would they be pissed if they found out?

With her wrists clutched in one hand, I reached down and yanked her shirt up until her perky tits were exposed to the cool air, sucking in a breath at the way they pebbled and begged to be sucked between my lips.

"Use Kennedy's color system tonight," I growled out as I shoved myself between her thighs and widened her legs with my knees.

She continued to fight me, thrusting her hips as though to buck me off. All that did was rub her core against my cock encased in nothing but the cotton of my sweats.

"Green," she muttered when I stopped a moment and looked her directly in the eye.

The fact she allowed this, the fact she allowed me to hold her down and take what I needed to quell the beast raging inside of me told me she had come to trust me. At least she trusted me with her body. She trusted me to stop at her word, to refrain from injuring her in any way.

I released her wrists and grabbed the sides of her shorts, yanking them down her legs as she sat up quickly and shoved at me, swinging a fist and almost busting me in my mouth before I could dodge to the side.

Her shorts to her knees, I used the leverage of one foot to shove them to her ankles, then settled my weight on her again, holding her upper half down with my chest, slamming her arms to her sides with more force than I'd intended.

Stopping for the briefest moment, I looked into her eyes, almost blowing my load at the way her lips were parted and her pupils were dilated.

She knew what I needed.

"Green," she ground out as she continued to struggle, not because she truly needed to get free, but because she knew I needed this, I needed to be in complete and total control at the moment.

With one free hand, I shoved the front of my sweats down enough to free my cock, gripped it by the base, then positioned myself at her entrance. I would fuck her right here on the ground. She would continue to pretend to struggle.

Then the glorious tightness and spine-tingling pain of her lock would clamp down onto my dick as she came around me.

But not yet. I wasn't done with her yet. I should have tasted her first. Because now that I was buried in her tight heat, I wasn't sure I could pull away.

Her hands lifted, her fingers tangled in my hair, then she pulled hard enough to sting as strands popped loose from their root. Fuck…yes.

From that first night together, it was like we were perfectly in sync, as though we knew what the other needed without saying a word.

I'd even let her top me, let her strangle me as she'd ridden me to completion and demanded I not come without her permission during one of our times together out here in the dark woods. Because she knew that was what I needed that night.

But not tonight.

Rey's tits bounced with the force of my hips slamming forward, my dick burying as far as I could without pushing my knot into her.

Alphas weren't made to take knots.

We also weren't made to be locked, yet I craved that squeeze as much as I craved the wet heat of her cunt.

As her hands continued to tug at my hair until my neck started to be wrenched to the side, I grabbed one of them and slammed it to the ground and held it over her head. Nothing I could do about the other unless I was willing to either crush her fully with my weight or pull back and allow her to sit up.

Fuck it.

Pushing my torso against hers, I struggled to pull her fingers from my hair, then clasped it in my hand with the other wrist.

Locking eyes with her, I checked in again, making sure I wasn't cutting off her air supply. "Green, alpha. I'm not some weak fucking omega," she growled out.

Ohhh. My little pet was spurring me on, encouraging me to fully release it all on her tonight.

Pulling back too quickly for her to catch on, I gripped her hips and flipped her onto her stomach, then yanked her hips up into the air while keeping a hand against her head so her face was forced into the dirt.

There was no resistance when I shoved my dick back inside of her. No. She wasn't an omega. But she was sure wet enough for me I would have wondered if her pussy had produced slick just for me.

Grunts tore from my mouth as my hips slapped against her ass, the wet sounds of my dick sliding into her pussy like music to my fucking ears.

Knot. I needed to fucking knot her. I needed to bite her, to mark her, to make her mine. But I couldn't hurt her. Not once had we discussed either of those scenarios and I never took what wasn't offered.

"Can you take my knot, alpha?" I growled out, never losing my pace as my engorged knot pushed against her opening.

"I can take anything you give me," she said, no longer fighting as her needy cunt grew wetter at my words.

She liked the thought of the stretch as much as I loved the pain of her locking onto me.

It would hurt worse. If my knot stretched into her, she would either have to control her own biology or lock around the swell. And fuck me…I wanted to know that exquisite pain.

"I'm going to knot you like my good little toy. Then I want to feel you come. I want my name on those dick sucking lips. Then I want to feel your lock around my knot. Do you understand me?"

"You have to earn my lock, alpha," she goaded.

Oh yeah. I was going to fucking earn it.

With the one hand still holding her head down, I reached the other around to toy with her clit, pinching it until she grunted. Slowing my thrusts, I pushed forward a little more each time, my eyes almost crossing as her pussy began to swallow my knot.

Her breathing grew faster and the inner walls of her cunt began to flutter. My sexy as fuck alpha was going to come.

"Color?"

"Green. Green!" she almost screamed as I pushed until the widest part of my knot was stretching her.

And then she took me fully, a cry falling from her lips as her legs shook and her lock clamped around me.

Throwing my head back, I couldn't hold back the bellow as I came harder than I ever had in my life, the line between intense pain and pleasure completely blurred and becoming the same thing.

Fuck. We were so fucked. Both in the good way and bad way. Because now we had both locked onto each other, she was practically naked, and it was cold out here.

Yanking my sweatshirt over my head, I helped her so we could roll onto our sides, then tugged the shirt over her head, keeping her arms inside to help warm her as the adrenaline and dopamine began to wear off.

"You okay?" I asked, brushing my fingers through her hair to remove some of the leaves and twigs. I would check her over with the light of my phone when we were able to pull apart.

"I have to tell my pack about…us," she said.

Scooting one arm under her head to use as a pillow, I draped the other around her waist and hugged her tightly to my chest.

"I mean, I know Spencer smells you on me. But they need to know. Everything. That we're…"

"We're…what?" I asked.

She turned and looked up at me, her brows furrowed.

"If you're waiting for me to say you're mine, you don't have to wait. It took everything in me tonight to not mark you. I wasn't sure how you would feel about another alpha biting your shoulder," I said with a smirk.

She huffed a laugh, causing her pussy to clench and pulling a hiss from between my teeth.

With her face turned toward me, I pressed a tender kiss to her lips, then pulled back so I could rest my forehead against hers. "You're mine, Rey. I have never wanted another living soul the way I want you. I'm sorry I haven't been able to, you know, properly court you and shit. I've been working a lot. We both have. We want to make sure we have plenty of cash set aside for all the pups Spencer is planning for us."

She barked out a laugh and I grunted. "You got to stop laughing," I said, but was unable to hold back my own chuckle.

Pulling back a little, I tested the connection, but we were still firmly locked together.

"It would be easier if we were all under the same roof. That way, I could still climb in bed with the three of you even after a job," I said.

"Then I guess I need to talk to my pack about giving you a key. Because we're not moving just yet. But...I wouldn't have a problem with a sexy alpha sneaking into my bedroom late at night. *After* you wash off the blood," she said, jabbing a finger against my chest. "And you really need to spend more time with Spencer. I think he feels left out."

"Yeah. Alexei already texted him to invite him on a date, just the two of them. I'll do the same."

Then a dirtier thought occurred to me and I blurted it before I had a chance to actually think about it. "How does he feel about being tag teamed by two alphas?"

She slapped my arm but couldn't stop another chuckle as she snuggled in while we waited. "He's used to two women using him. I'm sure he wouldn't mind the two of you getting him off. But you can't... not like this," she said, looking at me over her shoulder. "This is for you and me only. He might like it a little rougher, but not like this."

Kissing the tip of her nose, I smiled into her face. "Excuse me, but this is a you and me only thing. I better not find out you're letting anyone else dominate that pretty pussy."

CHAPTER 17

<u>Spencer</u>

"*Y*ou're just going shopping and out to eat," Kennedy teased me as she watched me get ready.

She only had a couple more days off before she went back to the club to wait tables for drag show month. And I was taking one of those nights with her alpha.

"I just feel like it should be your night with him. You guys barely see each other," I said, tugging off the shirt I'd donned and rifling through my closet for another choice.

"And the two of you haven't spent any time together since that one night at their place. And Rey brought something up that I want to pass by you. Although I'm sure you won't have a problem with it."

I pulled a light gray Alexander McQueen button up that Kennedy had spent way too much money on from the closet and held it up.

"That one makes your eyes look amazing," she said with a nod when I turned for her approval.

Tugging it on, I stepped from the closet with her close on my heels.

117

"Is this a conversation where I need to sit? Do we need to have a pack meeting?"

"Well, being as Rey and I already know, I don't think we technically need a pack meeting. She suggested giving the guys a key to the house so they can come and go after their…jobs. That way, we can at least snuggle in the pack bed together even if we can't hang out as often as we'd like."

"They're going to have to cut back their workload when they become daddies," I said, trying to keep the conversation light. But my beta knew me probably better than I knew myself. She knew I was nervous as hell.

With my head lowered, I focused on buttoning my shirt without missing any holes before raising my eyes to her face.

"Of course I'm okay with them having a key. You and Rey really need to stop treating me like I'm made of glass."

As I made my way to the bathroom to check my hair for the tenth time, Kennedy stopped me, her hand gripping mine tightly and pulling me back to her. Not that I required a whole lot of urging.

"We know you're not made of glass. But we love you. And we want you happy. And safe. You're the most important thing in the world to us. You mean everything to both of us. So we want to run any and every pack decision by you. We'll never decide anything for you, Spence."

Well, shit. I was acting like a brat, sulking and pouting, and all this time they were simply making sure the two hitmen weren't trying to hurt me or lure me away from them. I mean, that wasn't exactly what she'd said, but I'd caught the meaning of her words.

"I want you happy, too. Both of you. And if Alexei and Wolf decide they're only interested in the two of you, that's fine with me. I mean, as long as I still have you two ladies…and they buy me presents to keep me happy."

"Brat," she said with a swat on my ass. "Alexei's going to be here soon so hurry up."

She left me alone in the room with my thoughts. I was so fucking nervous and it was stupid. We were doing exactly as Kennedy had said, going shopping and out for dinner.

But what if…

That was what had me nervous was the *what if*. As in what if after the date we happened to come back here? What if we happened to come back to the bedroom? What if my beautiful beta grew jealous over Alexei's attention being split with me?

What if I wanted him but he didn't want me?

It was fine. I had Rey and I had Kennedy. If a time came when I desperately wanted pups I could either find a willing alpha donor or go to one of those insemination clinics.

Or I could simply be happy with the life my little pack had built for ourselves.

But Kennedy couldn't work at the club forever. She was gorgeous and built like a real life goddess, but we all aged. Her body would eventually grow weak, or she would simply grow tired of being tied down and ogled.

At that point, I would be more than happy to contact that center, Omega Change, and seek a job safe for my designation. I knew Rey would be more than willing to get a job to provide for both of us if the time came.

You're overthinking everything again.

I always did. I always got ahead of myself and tried to think of all the worst- and best-case scenarios. Maybe this time, I would just enjoy a night with Alexei and see what happened next instead of dwelling on anything but the moment.

"He's here!" Rey called from the front of the house.

"You couldn't just go get him?" Kennedy said with a chuckle.

Checking myself in the mirror one last time, I took a deep breath and stepped from the room to find Alexei holding a bouquet of red roses and a gift box.

"You just earned your very first brownie point," I teased, stepping forward and pressing a kiss to his lips. He tasted…sweet but crisp. Juniper. Winter. And my dirty ass mind immediately wondered if every part of him would taste as good.

"You haven't even opened it, Spence," Rey teased.

Alexei handed the box and flowers to me. Kennedy took the flowers from my hand and sought a vase, water running in the kitchen a minute before she returned and set the vase containing the roses on the coffee table.

Setting the box beside the vase, I pulled at the bow and peeked inside, my eyes flying wide as I perused the contents.

"Um...I guess we don't need to go shopping anymore," I said as I pulled out my very own not yet released men's version of the Chanel coat. "You have to tell me how the hell you get your hands on stuff like this before the rest of the public."

"Just because I stay under the radar doesn't mean I don't have my own connections," Alexei said with a wink, that deep, Russian accent sending all the blood rushing from my brain and straight to my dick.

"Thank you so much," I breathed out as I pulled it free and held it up. "You really don't have to take me shopping now. This is...thank you." Words were escaping me as I stared at it. It was the most beautiful piece of art, the fabric so soft, the seam work absolute perfection.

That was where Kennedy and Rey didn't understand my desire for higher end labels – they were made better. They were made to last. And yeah...they were pretty.

"Oh, we're still going shopping. I'm officially courting you, my beautiful omega. And that means doting on you. And since Kennedy won't let me buy her things," he said, narrowing his eyes in a playful way at my beta, "I'm more than happy to buy you anything you want."

A smile stretched across my face, and I barely held back the excited giggles.

My beautiful omega. Did that mean he already thought of me as pack, or was he simply trying to woo me? Because, yeah, it was totally working.

"You boys have fun tonight," Kennedy said, kissing me before turning to Alexei and pressing a kiss to his lips, as well.

"What about you? Do you two have plans?" I asked.

She glanced back at Rey. "Wolf is coming over later. We're going to watch some movies and eat greasy takeout," Kennedy answered.

"Mmhm. Movies and greasy takeout."

Both my girls rolled their eyes and shook their heads.

Lifting the coat – because I was absolutely wearing my new gift tonight – I started to pull the sleeves up my arms. But Alexei stilled me, taking it from my hands and holding it up, waiting for me to turn and slide my arms in before he tugged it onto my shoulders like a gentleman, something I had done for my alpha and beta on numerous occasions.

"Thank you," I said as heat touched my cheeks.

"You boys have fun," Kennedy called after me as I led the way to the front door.

I let Alexei step out first and glanced back at my little pack. Kennedy waggled her brows up and down at me with a grin and all I could do was smile back with a shake of my head.

What exactly did she think was going to happen when we were at a mall or restaurant?

Alexei waited at his car…a fucking Bentley. Maybe I shouldn't feel so bad about him buying me the coat because with each time we were around the two alphas, it was obvious they were loaded. Which meant if we did officially form a pack and they bonded me and Kennedy, my sweet beta wouldn't have to work so damn much or so damn hard and I wouldn't have to share her attention with the strangers at the club.

Selfish? Hell yeah it was. I loved my beta. I loved my alpha. And I hated when we weren't all together, when Kennedy had to leave the pack house to dance or perform for people who would more than likely go home and spank their monkey to fantasies about her.

Eh. I couldn't blame them for that last part. Even though I had access to her on a nightly basis, even I stroked my cock to thoughts of her tight body at times when I showered alone.

Opening the door for me, Alexei gave me a warm smile as I settled into my seat and pulled my belt into place. The alpha might have only had Wolf as a packmate all these years, but he sure knew how to spoil an omega.

"Where to first?" I asked as he started the engine with a barely audible purr. I was no car expert, but I knew something like this had to cost upwards of a hundred grand and I was dying to get behind the wheel of it, especially since Kennedy still refused to let me drive her new Escalade.

"I promised my omega a shopping trip. And since you're the only one willing to allow me to spoil you, we're heading downtown. I thought maybe a little Prada? Chanel? Or did you have somewhere else in mind?"

I swallowed. Cleared my throat. Prada? Chanel? Holy shit. "Either?" I said, wincing when my voice came out in a bit of a squeak.

Alexei smiled over at me, a warmth I'd only seen him aim at Kennedy thus far in his eyes, and squeezed my thigh. "How about we hit a few places, see if anything jumps out at you. I made reservations for dinner at seven."

"At *Plumes et Fouets?*" I asked.

He shook his head, returning his attention to the road. "Tonight is about you and me. I don't want anyone stealing my attention from you."

My body warmed, my heart thumped in my chest, and my cock twitched in my pants.

Chewing on my bottom lip, I stared at his profile, studied the straight line of his nose, the perfectly blended fade of his hair cut, the softness of his lips. And suspicion began to rise unbidden.

"Did Kennedy put you up to this?" I asked.

He turned a confused frown on me, then pulled up to a red light where he focused his full attention on me for a few moments.

"Put me up to what?"

A hint of disappointment touched my heart. "I know you wanted her originally, and Rey and I were...well, we're kind of a package deal. If you don't...if you really only wanted Kennedy, you have my blessing."

Alexei lifted a hand and touched his fingertips to my cheek, his smile reaching his eyes and causing the sexiest crinkles at the edges.

"I want you, too, Spence. Yes, I met your beta first. But I am just as interested in pursuing a deeper relationship with you as I am your beta. I'm sorry I haven't been around much, but–"

"Duty calls," I teased. He and Wolf had been working nonstop lately, just like my beta. It had been almost primarily me and Rey for the past couple weeks and I'd grown...well, lonely.

"Yes. We've been taking on more contracts in the hopes of your pack accepting us. I understand you three don't wish to live downtown, but I would much rather you and Kennedy live in a more secured home. So, Wolf and I have begun shopping for contractors we trust to design and build something more...appropriate for our new omega and beta."

"I'm your omega?"

His smile was so sweet as he leaned forward and barely brushed his lips against mine. "Only if you'll have me."

A horn blared from behind us, breaking the magical moment. *Asshole.* I would have preferred we stayed parked right here so I could hear all the ways the sexy Russian alpha planned to win me over.

Even if he'd technically won me over the moment he'd saved Kennedy's life.

CHAPTER 18

<u>Alexei</u>

$\mathcal{I}$ was an ass. I had managed to make the sweet omega feel as though he would be nothing more to me than an extra member of the pack, as though I didn't feel the need to protect him, as though his witty and sexy personality didn't appeal to me.

That would change today. I would spend as much time and money as needed to convince him that I wanted him to be a part of my life as much as I wanted Kennedy. I'd just happened to meet the sexy beta first, had been able to spend time with her before I'd known of Spencer's existence.

Now I was glad Kennedy had suggested asking him on a solo date. This way, we could talk without the others distracting me or stealing my attention away from him.

He had to know how attractive he was. He wasn't petite or overly thin, his auburn hair had hints of gold when the sun shone on it, and his eyes were the color of clover in the summer. The dusting of freckles across his nose lent him an air of innocence that his strong, lithe body nearly contradicted.

"Do you have a preference of which store we stop at first? Is there anything you've been eying or something you're in need of?" I asked as I pulled into a secured garage. I could have easily parallel parked but didn't want to risk some asshole dinging or scratching my car when they were distracted by their phones.

He turned his face toward me, his dark auburn brows high up his forehead. "I really want to say you don't have to do this but...can we start with Prada?"

My heart did a little flip in my chest at the hopeful and excited look on his face. Kennedy was uncomfortable with extravagant gifts, but my omega apparently loved them. At least one member of the pack would let me lavish them with gifts.

Once my Bentley was parked and locked up, I extended my elbow and waited for him to slide his hand through the crook before escorting him toward the private elevator. His energy was practically palpable, and his apple pie scent filled the small space of the metal box.

Inhaling deeply, I pulled that sweet warmth into my lungs and swore I could taste it on my tongue. Fuck me. His scent was as tantalizing and as addictive as Kennedy's and I couldn't wait to see if he tasted as sweet.

The bell dinged and the doors smoothly slid open revealing the first floor of Prada. Apple pie exploded around me until I felt dizzy as all the blood left my brain and rushed to my cock.

Damn. This was going to be more difficult that I'd thought. I'd only meant to take him shopping, spoil the shit out of him, and make him realize I cared for him, too.

Now...I wanted to close the elevator doors, pin him to the mirrored walls, and take him hard and fast.

As inconspicuously as possible, I adjusted my raging boner and guided him forward until we were met by a sales associate.

"Mr. Potrov. What a pleasure. We weren't expecting you today," a young beta welcomed us.

"Gretchen," I said with a nod of my head and a smile. "This is my omega, Spencer. I would like you to spoil him rotten today."

"Would you like to wait by the fitting room and I'll bring a rack, or would you prefer to browse a while?" Gretchen asked Spencer.

His eyes were wide and he looked mildly overwhelmed. Gently gripping his shoulders, I turned him to look at me, placing my knuckles under his chin to tilt his face toward mine. "Why don't we have a seat and let Gretchen bring you a few choices first. If there's something in particular you've been eying, let her know and she'll include that, as well."

I rarely walked around the store. Gretchen had been my personal shopper for as long as I'd known her and was fully aware of my style. Not that I shopped for clothing often. But her taste was impeccable. All she needed was a size and a few ideas to get her started.

"Okay," he said with a nod, his apple pie scent increasing as he looked into my eyes.

Gretchen circled Spencer slowly, eying him up and down, and actually guessed his size correctly. She then studied his face, his eyes, his hair and skin color, then asked a few questions about his personal style before darting off into the store.

Another associate guided us to comfortable and plush couches while offering glasses of champagne.

"I didn't think this stuff really happened," Spencer whispered before taking a sip of his champagne then moaning his approval. And yes, that small sound made my dick harder.

"What stuff?"

He raised his champagne flute then waved a hand around as though motioning toward the entire store. "Personal shoppers, champagne while we shop, the whole thing. I thought that only happened in the movies. Or in places like New York City."

I chuckled and wrapped an arm around his shoulders, slightly surprised by how natural and comfortable he felt in my arms. It felt as natural as holding Kennedy, as though that night had fated not only the beta into my life but Spencer, as well.

"Alexei?" a familiar voice called out.

I tensed and turned to glance over my shoulder as Mikhail and a few of his crew approached, a forced smile on his face, his eyes narrowing on Spencer.

Fuck.

"Mikhail," I ground out, climbing to my feet and moving to intercept him before he could get too close to my omega. The last thing I wanted was for him to catch Spencer's scent or to say too much in front of the omega.

"What are you doing here?" Mikhail asked.

Tilting my head, I raised my brows. "What does one generally do in a store?"

His eyes moved over my shoulder then back to my eyes. "You're adding to your pack, I see."

I said nothing, simply stared him in the eye and watched his three buddies in my periphery. I didn't believe the four thugs would attempt anything in such a public place with so many security cameras. But after all the years I'd known these men, I would put nothing past them.

"My father has been trying to contact you," Mikhail said, lowering his voice.

"I'm aware. And the answer is and will always be no."

A muscle ticked in my former friend's jaw, and something flashed through his eyes. Since we were children, Mikhail's father believed I would join his crew, that I would become his hired assassin.

I had my own plans and goals, and killing indiscriminately was not one of them. Mikhail and the entirety of the Gusev Bratva were dishonorable men. Evil. The same kind of fuckers Wolf and I executed on a regular basis.

"I suggest you answer his call. And reconsider."

Turning toward Spencer, he took a step closer, extending his hand. "Forgive me. I am an old friend of Alexei. I am Mikhail Gusev."

Spencer frowned at me then crossed his arms over his chest, refusing to shake hands with the Russian gangster. It was a complete and utter show of disrespect toward the asshole and made me want to drag the omega into my arms and kiss him breathless right there in the middle of the store.

Mikhail's smile faltered then fell.

"We'll be in touch. Answer your phone, Alexei."

He jerked his head and the others filed away with him. I didn't relax until I watched them walk through the front door and disappear down the sidewalk.

Had they followed me in here? None of them carried bags. And Mikhail had never had any sense of style. The fact I had been unaware I'd gained a tail unsettled me and I had a sudden urge to drag Spencer back to my Bentley and to my penthouse. It was safe there. Their house was not. If somehow the Gusevs were able to follow us back to Spencer's house, if they were to discover where my omega, my beta, and their alpha lived, they could and would use them as a bargaining chip to get me to do anything and everything they demanded.

"I take it those weren't friends?" Spencer asked when I turned back to face him.

"They were not."

"Feel like talking about it?" He raised a brow, but it was more out of curiosity rather than suspicion. Now I was happy Rey hadn't come. Wolf and I were having a hard time earning the alpha's trust. And that little interaction would have done nothing to help our case.

"Not yet. But I might need to have a discussion with the pack at a later date."

He nodded a few times then sighed. "I understand." His eyes darted past my shoulder and a smile stretched on his face the same time I heard the faint squeak of wheels.

Gretchen was already back.

"Holy shit," Spence breathed out under his breath.

Gretchen had filled the cart to brimming. "I wanted to make sure I got you a little of everything so we can narrow your style down more. But I think I might have you pegged as..." She pulled out a crisp, hunter green button down and charcoal pinwale corduroy pants. "Something along these lines. I also gathered a few accessories in case you really wanted to jazz up your look for a pack date."

The hunter green would look amazing with Spencer's eyes and red hair. And from what I'd seen him wear so far, she'd pretty much nailed his personal style.

"Everything is so beautiful," he said as he moved forward to run his hands over various pieces.

"I'll leave a few pieces in the pack changing room for you. Once you've made your way through this selection or if you would like something different, there is a bell that will ring directly to my earpiece and I'll be here immediately. Can I get the two of you more champagne?"

"I'm fine, thank you," I answered.

"Yes, please," Spencer said, his eyes on a leather shoulder bag that hung from a hanger near the end of the selection.

This was going to be so fun. Kennedy had behaved as though the gifts made her uncomfortable. That was so not going to be a problem with Spencer. He was like a kid in a candy store as he watched Gretchen heft the first selection into the room that would be big enough for our pack to join while he tried on clothes.

Turning to follow her, he stopped and turned wide eyes on me. "Are you sure about this?"

I huffed a laugh as warmth touched my heart at the hopeful and excited look on his face. "Absolutely. Choose anything and everything you love. If Kennedy and Rey won't let me spoil them, that means you get their share, too."

His hand moved as though he was going to fist pump the air, but stopped himself and looked around quickly, then turned and disappeared around the corner into the changing area.

Pulling my phone free, I hit Wolf's number, then leaned back and got comfortable. If Spence was anything like me, he would end up trying on nearly every item on the rack. And we had all day. He could take his time, enjoy himself. I would buy him every fucking thing in the store if it made him happy.

"Yes?" Wolf answered on the third ring.

"I had a visitor," I said without preamble.

There was a beat of silence. "Are you with the omega?"

I ran down our arrival at Prada and how Mikhail and his syco-phants just happened to appear in the same store yet hadn't bought a single item.

"They were tailing you."

"That's my suspicion."

"Did he catch sight of Spencer?"

I crossed an ankle over my knee and dragged my free hand down my face. "Unfortunately. But he refused to shake Mikhail's hand and glared at him."

Wolf's deep chuckle rumbled over the line. "He might be a spoiled brat, but he's got an alpha's heart."

That he did.

"Want me to follow you back to the house?"

"I thought you were heading over to hang out with Kennedy and Rey," I said with a frown.

"I am later. But I'm sure they'll forgive my lateness if it's to keep their omega safe."

Raising my eyes as Spencer stepped out of the fitting room to check himself in the three-way mirror, I lowered my voice. "No. I'll pay closer attention. If any problems arise, I'll let you know."

"Fucking Gusev. Can't take a fucking hint. Let me know if you need me." And with that, Wolf ended the call.

"This is so beautiful," Spencer said as he turned this way and that, admiring the first outfit Gretchen had pointed out to him. The fit was perfect, too, as though it had been tailored specifically for his body.

"That is definitely a keeper."

Gretchen swept forward without either of us so much as raising a finger. "Just place the items you wish to keep to the side, and I'll have everything ready for you once you've finished. Don't bother with the hangers for those you don't like. That's my job." She winked at Spencer, and the omega gave her a flirty smile.

From what I'd seen so far, the omega tended to flirt with just about anyone, so I didn't give it much thought. Not that I would have a problem with him getting a blowjob between changes of clothes. I'd felt Gretchen's mouth on more than one occasion and knew she was a hell of a talented beta.

"We can stop with this one," Spencer said when he had the gall to glance at the price tag with wide eyes.

Pushing to my feet, I crowded him until he had to crane his neck to look into my face and put my full alpha bark into my words. "Do not look at the price tags again. You will get anything and everything you want. Do you understand me, omega?"

He wasn't mine. Not technically. And I was pretty sure Rey might have punched me in the mouth for bossing Spencer around. But I wanted him to enjoy himself. I wanted to spend my money on the people I cared about, and that absolutely included the omega whose pupils were now blown and whose perfume floated on the air and tempted me far too much.

"Yes, alpha," he breathed out, a soft whimper to his words.

"That's my good omega," I said, tilting his chin up and pressing my lips to his before turning him and guiding him back to the dressing room.

This time, I joined him in the room and took a seat in the corner of the room. "Is this okay?" I asked as he started to unbutton the shirt.

He looked at me in the mirror and nodded, his perfume growing stronger as he reached for the button and zipper on the corduroy pants and shoved them down his legs.

His tight ass was encased in a pair of cotton boxer briefs and perfectly outlined his hard length.

Fuck me. This was supposed to be about spoiling him.

Perhaps joining him in the room to ensure he didn't take a peek at any more price tags had been a bad idea.

CHAPTER 19

<u>Spencer</u>

Could shopping be considered foreplay? Because Alexei's eyes on me as I stood in front of the mirrors made me horny as hell.

Now, he was sitting in a chair in the corner of the pack dressing room, his legs splayed, his arms loose on the rests, his eyes on me, roaming me from head to toe as I stood in nothing but boxers while rifling through the selection for the next thing to try on.

If it were up to me, I would get one of each in my size. But it wasn't my money. And there was no guarantee they would all look good on me, either.

But from the look in Alexei's eyes, it didn't matter what I wore. He was watching me with the same hunger I'd seen in his eyes when it came to our beta.

And here I'd thought I would be the extra wheel. It was beyond obvious Rey and Wolf were hot for each other. And I knew they were having middle of the night hookups, even if she thought she was being sneaky. I knew she would disappear from our bed and sneak into our backyard. A while later, she would return covered in Wolf's warm fallen leaves scent.

Then there was the original attraction between Alexei and Kennedy. While I would have been satisfied with my girls and being doted on by the alphas, I wanted to be...well, shit. I wanted to be desired. I wanted to be cherished as the omega of the pack. And I really didn't give two fucks how self-centered that sounded.

Alexei was watching me like an alpha who wanted to breed his omega. And fuck me...I wanted to be his omega. I wanted both alphas to join our pack, to bite me and mark me and sleep beside me every night. I wanted both of them to join the three of us in our home, to join our family.

I wanted to build a family with them, to carry their children, to watch as Kennedy and Rey became mothers to our future babies.

Biting my lip, I tried to keep my thoughts and my eyes to myself as I pulled a shirt from the hanger and tugged it up my arms, then chose a pair of jeans. They were soft as butter and felt amazing against my oversensitive skin as though the brand had developed a line specifi-cally for my designation.

And who knew? They very well might have.

"Those, too," Alexei said, pulling my eyes to his in the mirror. "Put those in the keep pile."

He'd used his bark to forbid me from looking at the price of any of the clothing, but I'd online shopped more than enough to know the four pieces alone would be close to five grand. I might have to pretend I wasn't interested in any other selections to avoid feeling guilty later about the amount of money he was spending on me.

The sexy Russian shifted in his chair, his legs widening a touch as though making room for the obvious bulge in his pants.

Fuck. I knew my girls thought I was insatiable, but with someone like Alexei sitting there looking like a fuck toy come to life and watching me like he wanted to take me right there in the room, how the hell was I not supposed to be horny as hell?

I supposed I could always blame it on my biology. We omegas did tend to be aroused easier and more often, after all.

Yep. That was my excuse and I was sticking to it.

Especially when I turned, crossed the room, and lowered to my knees between his thighs, running my hands up his legs until I cupped him through his pants.

"If you're doing this because of the clothes…"

"I'm doing this because I want you. I'm doing this because you should be my alpha, too. I'm doing this because I want to fucking taste you," I said as I undid his belt, popped the button, and freed his thick, hard cock.

His eyes stayed on my face as I lowered my head and lapped at the bead of precum glistening at the slit of his cock, then took him into my mouth slowly, running my tongue along the raised ridge along the underside.

Alexei's hand was gentle as it landed on my head and began to guide me to the pace he wanted, and I was more than happy to oblige. Without anyone touching me, I was ready to blow my load in my boxers and these ridiculously expensive jeans merely at the crisp snowy and juniper taste of Alexei's dick.

His knot was swollen and bumped against my nose and chin each time I swallowed him down. Raising a hand, I toyed with his sac, then squeezed his knot, hollowing my cheeks and increasing the suction of my mouth while bobbing on him faster. I needed to taste him coating my tongue. I needed to feel the heat hitting the back of my throat.

Alexei had other ideas.

With a hand in my hair, he tugged me off him and forced me to stand, yanking me forward and freeing my cock before wrapping his lips around my shaft and taking me until I hit the back of his throat.

I bit my lip to keep from moaning too loudly and giving away our actions in the fitting room. Although, with as much money as Alexei was about to put out, I doubted they would have a problem with anything we did back here as long as it wasn't on the showroom floor.

It was my turn to fist his hair as he took my cock and sucked it like he was trying to suck my soul from the tip.

"Fuck. Alexei. I'm going to…"

He increased his tempo until my balls tightened and I blew in his mouth. I had never been sucked off by a male alpha. Fuck. I'd never been with a male alpha at all. Rey had been my first and only alpha. And now…I couldn't wait to have them both at once. I wanted Alexei to knot me while Rey's lock clamped around my cock.

My next heat was looking to be amazing.

Pulling away, Alexei stood as he swiped his fingers along his lips, sucking any drop he might have missed from his fingers, then turned me and bent me over the chair, jerking the jeans and my boxers down my legs and exposing me to him.

My entrance was slick and ready for him. The stretch was exquisite as he pushed into me slowly and the mirrors around the room gave me the most erotic and beautiful view as his eyes locked on mine.

He started out slowly, as though he was making sure I was okay with what we were doing. My only hard stop was to be knotted in here. I wasn't really prepared to be stuck together in a dressing room for the next thirty minutes.

But I was still flying high from the world-shattering orgasm he'd sucked from me and was more than willing to let him fuck me and fill me as much as he wanted.

Alexei's hands were tight on my hips, his fingers biting into the flesh as he began to fuck me faster, harder, his knot stretching my hole before he pulled away again.

"Fuck," he gritted out between clenched teeth.

Reaching around, he gripped my still hard cock and began to squeeze and stroke me to the same rhythm his hips were slapping against my ass.

With only a few strokes, I spilled all over the jeans pooled around my ankles the same time a soft grunt sounded from him and heat filled me.

Once our breathing and heartrates slowed, he gently pulled from me and closed up his pants.

"We'll definitely be buying those now," he teased before helping me redress.

Alexei stepped from the room, winking at me before he closed the door.

"Yes, sir?" I heard Gretchen say from outside the fitting area.

"We'll take it all, including the bag, the hat, and those scarves."

I stared at my reflection in the mirror, the glow on my cheeks from two amazing orgasms, glanced down at the jizz covered thousand-dollar jeans, then around the room at the clothes I'd yet to try on.

The man had just sucked me off, fucked me, and was now purchasing half the damn store.

Oh…he was absolutely going to be my alpha. Even if I had to fight my own damn pack to make that happen.

CHAPTER 20

<u>Kennedy</u>

I laid on my side on my bed, watching Alexei towel off. He'd finished his contract barely in time to meet me after work but hadn't been able to come inside…because he'd been covered in blood.

What had scared the shit out of me was the tear in his shirt near his shoulder. I'd shoved him into the shower and washed him myself so I could inspect the new wound. Thankfully, it was superficial.

"What if something happens to you? How the hell would I find out? You and Wolf don't always work together," I said as tears burned the backs of my eyes.

He wrapped the fluffy terry cloth around his waist and crossed the room to kneel on the floor in front of me.

"Nothing will happen to me, lyubov." His fingers were so gentle as he pushed them through my hair.

"You can't guarantee that. Look at your fucking shoulder. You got stabbed, for fuck's sake."

I pushed to a sitting position, pulling the blanket over my lap so at least my lower half wasn't distracting him, though his eyes repeatedly dipped to my bared breasts.

"I was cut. Not stabbed. I've been doing this a long time–"

"And have a shit load of scars. Meaning you've been cut or shot or whatever on several occasions."

He sighed and lowered his head until his chin rested on my knee, glancing up at me with those gorgeous hazel eyes of his.

"Don't give me the puppy dog eyes, Alexei. I'm serious."

"Am I allowed to say that I love that you worry about me?"

Throwing my hands in the air, I released a frustrated growl. "Of course I worry about you. It's not like you work a desk job. At any point, someone could take you away from me. Do you realize what that would do to my heart? What would happen to me if you were to be killed?"

I couldn't stop the tears from spilling over my lashes at the thought of Alexei being taken away when I'd barely just found him.

In the short time since he'd come into my life, he'd become so important to me. And I knew he was as important to Spencer.

"Do you know what would happen to Spence if you were killed?"

If I couldn't sway him, maybe using our omega would.

Pushing to his feet, he leaned forward until I had no choice but to lean away as he caged me between his arms. "Nothing will happen to me. I will always return to you, Kennedy. I will always be here. Even when you grow tired of me, you can't get rid of me."

A watery smile pulled up the corners of my lips at his attempt at a tease.

I raised both hands and cupped his face, staring intently into his eyes as he did the same with me.

"Alexei…" And then I couldn't force any more words from my mouth, couldn't force my lips to voice what I wanted.

And that was him. All of him. I wanted him to officially be mine, to officially be his. I wanted to carry his mark on my shoulder, to feel him deep inside my chest, to be able to follow that invisible thread that would tie us together and know without a doubt that he was safe and still breathing when we weren't together.

He closed the space between us and pressed his lips to mine, the kiss barely more than a caress as he raised a hand to cup the back of my head.

When he pulled away, he spoke against my lips. "Tell me, lyubov. Tell me how I can make you feel better. How can I put your mind at ease?"

"Mark me," I whispered in the silence of the room as my heart began to pound in my chest and my breathing grew shallow.

I was as nervous as I was turned on by the notion of my alpha making love to me and sinking his teeth into my shoulder, of forging an unbreakable bond, of tying me to himself permanently.

Once we were united, only death would be able to tear us apart. It was the only way to break a bond.

And yeah…that scared the shit out of me. What would happen to my heart and mind if I were to fully let him in only to lose him? I would still have Rey and Spence, but there would be a piece of my heart that would forever be missing, a hole in my chest that could never truly be filled if I were to lose my sexy Russian assassin.

"I need you to be sure, my love," he said, for once, using English for his term of endearment for me. "I can wait as long as you need. I'm not going anywhere. I have never wanted someone as badly as I want you. I have never longed to belong to a pack as I do with yours. I want all of you. I want your heart, mind, and body. I want you as my beta. I want Spencer to be my omega and one day carry my pup. I want Rey to fight alongside us to protect what is ours. I want every single part of you and every single part of your life."

Fresh tears welled in my eyes as he spoke each word and my heart felt as though it would explode in my chest.

"Take me, Alexei. Make love to me then make me yours. I *am* yours. You have all of me."

His lips crashed down on mine and pushed me back onto the mattress as he lowered on top of me. He urged my legs apart so he could settle between them, the damn towel and blanket separating us.

But it appeared Alexei had plans for my body before he marked me.

With a deep growl, his lips left my mouth and he began to nip at my jaw, my throat, licking and sucking over my pulse point, then lowered until he kissed between the valley of my breasts. That growl continued to rattle up his chest and I swore it was like a vibrator to my clit as he pressed his weight onto me and sucked one nipple into his mouth, teasing it with teeth and tongue before lowering his head further.

"Spread your legs for me, lyubov. I want to taste that sweet cunt."

A very omega sounding whimper tore from my lips as I did as he ordered and spread my legs further, nearly in the splits so he had as much access as he could possibly want. I hadn't lied when I said he could have all of me. There was very little I would deny him of, very little I would ever refuse him.

I had never been a hopeless romantic, but Alexei had made me begin to believe in love at first sight. Or perhaps second sight. Because since that night he'd paid to be alone at my table to watch as I was tied and teased, I had felt something warm growing in my chest. I had felt something deep growing for him and I refused to ignore it. My instincts had never steered me wrong so there was no point in disregarding them now.

His tongue swiped from my folds to my ass and back before he sucked my clit between his lips, teasing the bundle of nerves with his tongue.

My hands fisted in his hair as I arched from the bed, moans pouring from my mouth. I didn't bother keeping quiet. Wasn't sure I could when so many emotions were swirling through my heart and mind and Alexei was pushing me closer and closer to release with each swipe of his tongue.

A thick finger slowly eased into my entrance and I released a throaty sound as he bent that finger, rubbing all the right places as he continued to devour my pussy.

Heat built and built and I felt like I would burst into flames if he didn't...

"Alexei," I cried out when he added a second finger. I tensed as my inner walls clamped and fluttered and imploded from the inside out.

He didn't stop his relentless assault on my cunt, chasing my aftershocks as my legs shook and I grew oversensitive.

"So fucking sweet," he purred, his breath warm against my folds.

Pushing onto his haunches, he yanked the towel away from his waist, his cock bobbing, glistening at the tip as precum dripped and all I wanted was to lunge forward and lap up the moisture, to suck him deep into my throat, to taste him on my tongue.

I didn't get the chance.

He used one hand to grip his cock and guided it to my entrance, slowly pushing into me and giving my body time to adjust to the intrusion. My eyes rolled shut as I once again arched off the bed.

"I love the way your needy cunt squeezes my cock, lyubov. I want to feel you come all over me. I want to hear that beautiful voice call out my name."

"Yes. Fuck me, Alexei. Make me come again," I begged, raising my hips to urge him to move, to take him deeper.

He purred as he began to thrust into me, harder, faster, his hands gripping my thighs to hold me open as his intense gaze stayed on my face.

"You are so beautiful," he said, his purr soothing and arousing me.

I wanted to thank him. Or tell him how gorgeous he was. But the only sounds that would come from my mouth were the moans and begging for more.

"Can you take my knot, my love?"

"All of you. I want all of you, Alexei," I said, my words beginning to run together into almost unintelligible words.

His eyes lowered to where we were connected and his fingers began to toy with my clit as he pushed forward, a burning stretch growing where his knot was trying to enter me.

It burned…but fuck me, it felt amazing.

I had never been ashamed to admit a little pain turned me on. And why wouldn't that be the same when Alexei pushed my body past what a beta should be able to handle?

The rumbling purr turned into a deep, primal growl as his fingers worked my clit faster and he shoved forward until his knot fully entered me, locking behind my pubic bone and rubbing places I hadn't known existed.

I came with a scream and for the first time, wished I'd been born an omega. They got to enjoy a knot any time they wanted. Alexei was the first and only alpha I had wanted to lock me around him, the first I ever wanted to stretch me to my limit.

The first male alpha I ever wanted to fill my cunt with his hot come and maybe one day join Spencer in growing a round belly filled with Alexei's pup.

"Holy shit," I cried out as the waves of my release increased with each jet of cum his cock shot into me.

Alexei dropped forward as my body continued to tense, my inner walls continuing to flutter around his knot, and sank his teeth into my left breast.

Like fireworks, the bond opened between us, his cool wintery scent translating through the bond into something warm and cozy. I could feel him as distinctly as I could Rey and Spencer.

He was mine. I was his. Forever. No one could take me from Alexei, no one could ever tear us apart.

All I could do as the two of us came down from our orgasm high was hope my pack wouldn't be angry that I'd allowed the bond without discussing it with them.

But seriously – they had to know where this was going. They'd seen us together. They'd known from the first day he'd sent that ridiculous coat there was no way either of us would willingly walk away from the other.

Fate had brought us together. And I just happened to give fate a little push by begging for his bite.

CHAPTER 21

<u>Kennedy</u>

As I sat at my makeup table in the back of the club, using dark shadow to create a smokey appearance around my eyes, I was having a hell of a time erasing the smile from my lips.

Taking a second, I searched for Alexei in my chest and found the same full, content, loving feeling that mirrored my own. He felt my presence and flooded me with affection.

I now carried my big Russian alpha's mark. Unfortunately, he'd left that mark on my breast, meaning I would have to choose one of my newer outfits that would camouflage the healing wound now that we were switching over to fetish month.

High-collar bustier that showed off my belly with a sheer thong and I was ready for the stage. I still looked the part for my performance, but I would also still look as though I was available, something that aided in getting requested in the VIP room and earned fatter tips.

I'd told Alexei I had no intention of quitting my job. But would it be so bad to quit this side? To simply perform on stage during burlesque and do as I did during drag month and wait tables?

Or you could let him do as he truly wants and provide for you.

It was something to consider. Maybe not right away, but something we could all discuss in the future. Alpha biology demanded they take care of their omegas, to comfort and provide. But I wasn't an omega. And I had been raised to be independent, to never rely on anyone else.

But it wasn't just me. I had Rey and Spencer to think about. And if Wolf and Alexei truly wanted to…

Damn it. To continue making the level of income they made, they would have to continue with their career path. And every time they left for a contract, I feared they wouldn't return. I might not have been marked by Wolf yet, or even forged as close of a relationship with him, but I already thought of him as pack. The loss of any single member would tear my heart to shreds.

A pulse of concern plucked at that thread in my chest, so I flooded it with nothing short of love. He was picking up on my worries but didn't realize it was purely for his safety and had nothing to do with my own.

"You almost ready?" Milo asked.

He was my partner for the night, and held a mask in his hands that would cover his eyes. Milo looked as though he'd been cut from stone with his broad chest and shoulders and rippling abs. He wore a pair of leather pants that hugged his cock that he would fluff a little to enhance the appearance before we stepped out onto stage.

"Yep. Lipstick and I'm ready to play."

He shook his head. "I don't know how I let you rope me into this again."

"Because my pack keeps showing up and the alphas trust you. If it puts them at ease, then it's worth it."

He huffed out a breath. "I guess that was a compliment?" he asked more than said.

"It was a compliment, big guy," I said, winking at him in the mirror as I coated my lips with a deep, shimmery red.

It had grown more common than not to see at least one of my pack at my table lately. And as much as I appreciated their support, that meant no one else could sit there and leave tips when I was finished. Translation – I relied on the VIP room for the big bucks on the nights they came out to watch.

"So…spanking tonight?" Milo asked, shifting his weight from one foot to the other.

"Dude. You're not using your bare hand. Stop acting like a teenaged boy seeing his first tit."

He stuck his tongue out at me and pulled his mask over his eyes as I stood, slipping my hand into his.

"Just…don't be surprised if I get a boner," he teased.

"I'd be offended if you didn't," I shot back.

The room was full as all us performers stepped out of the back-room then were escorted up the few stairs and into our places.

And yep, all four of my packmates were currently crowded around my table. I knew damn well they were paying the hostess under the table to make sure they were up close and personal every time I performed. If Anais was aware, she hadn't said anything yet.

But *I* might have to later. Again…loved their support. But I missed the tips I got after.

Low, sultry music began to fill the room, quiet enough diners could still converse if they chose, but loud enough to put everyone in the mood.

Milo gently led me to the prop centered on the stage and eased my shoulders forward until my chest was pressed to the leather seat and my ass was bared to my pack, nothing but a thin strap covering my asshole and pussy.

My hands were restrained to the contraption to keep me from moving, then Milo made a show of kicking my feet wider so he could wrap the leather cuffs around my ankles.

I couldn't see my pack from this angle, but I could feel their eyes on me, could feel Spencer's and Alexei's arousal peaking. I could even swear I smelled Spencer's perfume past the filtration system as Milo stepped away and a sting spread from my ass cheeks to the rest of my nerve endings as he cracked a leather strap across my backside.

Whether anyone heard the moan over the music, I didn't know. But I couldn't hold it back, especially when the next hit was against the backs of my thighs and my mind went back to that first night in the back room with Alexei, when he'd paddled me, then used his bare hands to spank my thighs, my ass, and my pussy until I came hard.

My eyes raised to find someone at another table watching me closely, his eyes almost as piercing as Alexei's. I let a sexy smirk pull up one side of my lips and winked then grunted when Milo swatted my left cheek with the strap, my lips popping open as I began to breathe heavier.

Until Alexei, I had let the audience blur into nothing, faceless people who were enjoying my performance. But the man resting his elbows on the table, ignoring his own performer while keeping his eyes locked on mine was anything but a blur. I was nearly hyper focused on him, superimposing Alexei's face over his, pretending the friends sitting on either side of him were my pack.

I needed to force my mind back into performance mode or I would orgasm on the stage. Not that it was against the rules, but I didn't want to make Milo any more uncomfortable being my partner than he already was.

At least if I got off, my pack would be the ones with the front row seat to my release soaking my sheer thong and showcasing the smooth lips of my pussy.

The man watching me raised a hand, then leaned over to speak into the attendant's ear, gesturing in my direction.

Uh oh. If Alexei or my pack hadn't already reserved the back room, looked like they would either be second in line or would have to wait until we were all home to be alone with me. And yeah, the fact my performances were nothing short of foreplay for my omega and my new alpha was a major turn on for me.

Look at me having a great night. Top dollar from a stranger plus tips, then getting fucked by Alexei and my omega.

And Wolf? Maybe Rey, too. Why not just throw us all together in one big cum covered pile of arms and legs to finish the night off right. It was, after all, bound to happen eventually.

Swat after swat, my core grew wetter, and the warm scent of apple pie grew stronger. I definitely wasn't imagining Spencer's perfume. I really shouldn't have been able to smell him so strongly through the scent cancellers. Which meant my omega was getting closer to his heat way sooner than we'd anticipated.

Then again, we had added two more alphas to the mix. Their hormones were enough to send me into fucking heat and I was only a beta.

Thankfully, the performance ended without me causing poor Milo any lasting emotional trauma by coming from his attentions.

His hands were gentle as he released my wrists and ankles, then slowly and carefully helped me stand, waiting while the blood redistributed through my body so I wouldn't pass out.

The patrons clapped politely as we were each led from the stages and either guided to a private room or returned to the back room to change for the night.

"Raven," one of the attendant's said as she stopped me at the mouth of the dark hallway. "Room two."

I smiled and thanked her and headed to the room, taking my seat in the wing back chair while I waited for my visitors. And waited. And waited.

I was about to give up and leave after waiting fifteen minutes when the door opened and three men stepped in. My smile faltered slightly as disappointment hit me that the man who'd watched me so intently had, indeed, put in his reservation with me before Alexei could.

"Hello," I said, staying seated as I always did, and motioning toward the couch. "Is this your first time in the VIP rooms?"

"It is," the man who'd been watching me said. Was it me, or was his voice colored with a hint of an accent like Alexei's?

His hair was a dark, sandy blonde, his eyes a piercing, yet cold blue. His buddies looked as though they could have been Alexei's brothers with the same black hair, though they had brown eyes. And the same cold, dark look in the depths of their eyes as the blonde.

"Then let's go over the rules." I ran over everything from the fact I was in control at all times and held the right to stop the play with no refund if it went too far. I reminded them there was to be no penetration and no skin-on-skin touch, though they were welcome to masturbate or fuck each other.

That last comment drew a grimace from the dark-haired man on the left.

"There are cameras and microphones, so we will have an audience. It is as much for your protection as mine–"

"How much to turn off the cameras?" the leader asked.

Tilting my head, I glanced up at the camera near the door as something felt off about these three.

"The cameras remain on at all times and are monitored by our security team. As I was saying, it's just as much for your protection as it is for mine. You cannot be accused of anything you haven't done."

"I would prefer we have time together without an audience."

"Then I'm sorry that you have wasted your time and money. Because at no point will I agree to a session without being monitored."

He glanced back at his buddies and sighed. "Very well. I would rather have an audience than miss out on time with you, lyubov."

My hackles raised. That was the word Alexei called me. And I had so been right about his accent. What was the chance these were friends of Alexei?

No. He would have introduced me or let me know to expect one of his friends. Mere coincidence. Had to be.

"I use a color system. Green means I'm good to continue, yellow means you're toeing the line, red is stop. No questions asked. Everything halts immediately if you hear me say red at any point. Do you have any boundaries you wish to discuss?"

"We're not fucking each other," the man who'd grimaced growled out.

I lifted one shoulder in a shrug. "It's not required, obviously. I just wanted to let you know it's an option and something packs often do during or at the end of a session with any of us. But at no point are any bodily fluids allowed to touch me, and you may not touch me with your hands."

"Understood," the leader said with a smile. But...I still felt a sense of apprehension as he nodded at the table and gripped me by the hips, gently lifting me and helping me onto my stomach.

One of the men went to work attaching the leather straps around my ankles while another restrained my wrists.

I was spread out on the bench, my face hanging over the edge, and completely immobilized.

The two friends stepped away and I heard the squeak of the springs as they lowered onto the couch.

"So many options," the leader said as he perused the implements hanging from the wall, running his fingers along a crop, the leather flogger, before settling on the bamboo cane.

And my anxiety began to rise.

I could feel Alexei pushing through the bond, but I tried to send reassurances. I was under constant supervision. If I said my code word and these men didn't cease immediately, Milo or one of the others would burst into the room and put a stop to the action and throw these assholes out on the street. They would be barred from ever reentering *Plumes et Fouets*.

"How are you now, lyubov?"

"Raven. Please call me Raven."

His fingers ran through my hair and he lowered to press his face into the strands he held, inhaling deeply. "A beta," he purred. "Raven it is."

"Green. I'm green." For now.

The first slap of the cane was against the back of my thighs and sent nothing more than the lightest sting through my skin.

"Raven?"

"Green," I muttered, my eyes on the floor as I waited.

Another slap of the cane across the backs of my thighs, but this was a little harder and stung more. Yellow was on the tip of my tongue, but not because I was in pain. Something was off. I didn't feel as though this man was playing out a kinky fantasy but was preparing to inflict injury for no other reason than to watch someone writhe in pain.

He didn't check again, just swatted the cane across my ass, causing me to jump with the sharp bite. Unlike with Alexei, the pain wasn't sending wetness to my core. It was only causing my anxiety to climb, especially when I tugged on the restraints a little and realized how tightly they'd bound my wrists and ankles.

The cuffs were more for the illusion of sub play, the illusion that I was fully under their control. But these men had made damn sure I couldn't move away.

The next hit against my ass actually made me cry out in pain.

"Yellow," I bit out between clenched teeth.

"My apologies, Raven," the man said over the chuckles of the asshats watching.

And then he began to whip me in earnest, the backs of my thighs, my ass, then my back.

"Yellow," I said louder as the stings were turning to aches.

"Yellow?"

"Yellow," I repeated, attempting to turn my head to look him in the face.

And felt bile rise up my throat at the evil grin on his face as he raised the cane high and slammed it across my back. He hit me three times before I was able to scream out, "Red! Fucking red!"

But he didn't stop. He continued to beat me with the thin bamboo cane as I screamed red three more times, then yelled for help.

From my lower shoulder blades to my upper thighs felt as though they were on fire and tender.

The door slammed open and bodies filed in. Curses rose, threats were made. And then I was alone with Milo.

"Holy shit, girl," he muttered, rage filling his voice. He undid the wrist straps and ankle straps, then looked toward the cameras. "Send in her pack," he told the security watching.

"It hurts," I whimpered.

I liked pain. I liked the burn of Alexei's knot stretching me. I'd liked when he'd spanked my pussy and ass.

But this…this was agony. This hadn't been sexual. It had been full of nothing short of malice. Those men…they'd paid extra to hurt me, to cause physical injuries, to hear me cry out.

Milo's hands were gentle as he turned me then hissed through his teeth.

"Call for an ambulance," he said to the cameras.

"What? I don't need an ambulance," I protested, and tried to push off the table and to my feet.

But my thoughts grew fuzzy and the room swayed.

"I need you to sit down and wait for your pack. And you are absolutely getting checked out before I can let you leave," Milo ordered, guiding me to the couch and helping me to lie on my side on the soft cushions.

Anais rushed in, her eyes wide. She guided me forward so she could examine my back then a slew of French words that sounded an awful lot like she was cursing flew from her mouth.

Alexei was the first into the room with Rey, Spence, then Wolf right on his heels.

"Lyubov," he breathed out as panic filled his pretty hazel eyes.

"He called me that," I forced out as I struggled to keep my thoughts straight. I knew Anais had more than likely called the police. I had to remember as much as possible, as many details as I could recall.

"What?" Alexei said, kneeling in front of the couch as he brushed my hair from my face.

"That man called me that. And he–"

"Beat the shit out of her with a bamboo cane," Milo finished for me.

Alexei did as Anais had and rolled me forward, examining my backside. Curses filled the air from every person in the room as the full extent of my injuries were visible.

It had hurt, but I hadn't thought it warranted so much attention and surely not a fucking ambulance.

Alexei glanced up at Wolf and both men began to growl, the sound deep and scary. But not aimed at me.

Rey pushed Alexei out of the way and she and Spencer knelt in front of me. Tears streamed down Spencer's face as he turned toward Anais. "She quits. Right now. She's done with fetish night or the VIP room or whatever. No more. She's done."

"Spence—"

"No," he said, cutting me off. My sweet omega sounded as though he was trying to use an alpha bark on me. "You have no idea how your back looks right now. What if those cameras weren't there? What if the security hadn't gotten in here? Fuck, Kennedy," he said, his words choked with emotion.

It only took a few minutes for the paramedics to show up and order everyone out of the room so they could check me over and clean what, apparently, were open cuts from the cane. But I refused to go to the hospital. All I wanted was to be in bed with my pack around me.

And contemplate Spencer's words and Alexei's offer – tonight might very well have been my last night in the back room.

CHAPTER 22

<u>Rey</u>

Rage unlike anything I'd ever felt burned through my veins as concern for my beta caused my heart to hurt.

Some asshole had paid to beat the shit out of her. He hadn't taken her into the VIP room to fulfill some fantasy. No. His sole intent had been to hurt her, to injure her, to cause actual physical harm.

And now that cocksucker was nowhere to be found.

Why the hell hadn't security held him and called the cops? Great. They'd been barred from reentry into the club. But that wasn't enough. I wanted him and his buddies to hurt as badly as my beautiful Kennedy hurt. I wanted to take my pound of flesh.

Wolf and Alexei stood off to the side, their heads close, whispering as Spencer lingered near the door and watched the paramedics cleaning Kennedy's wounds and doing their best to talk her into at least having a doctor check her out at the ER.

I knew my beta, knew how stubborn she could be. No chance in hell would she allow anyone to bully her into taking a ride in an ambulance to have doctors poke and prod at her. Hell, I wasn't sure she was fully aware of the extent of her injuries, how ripped and bruised her skin from her shoulders to the backs of her thighs really was.

And why the fuck had it taken so long for security to burst into that room and put a stop to it? It was their motherfucking job.

When Wolf glanced in my direction and went back to whispering with Alexei, my temper boiled over. Stomping in their direction, I jabbed a finger in Alexei's chest hard enough to make him stumble back a step.

"You know who it was. How do we find him?"

Wolf put a hand on my shoulder, but I shrugged him off.

"Don't fucking touch me. You two know who it was. Do you know how to find him? And what the fuck are you going to do about…this?" I said, barely keeping my voice level as I waved in the direction of where Kennedy was still being tended to.

"I think I know who it is," Alexei answered. "But I can't be sure without seeing the footage. I need to see his face to be sure."

"Best guess," I growled out.

"An old…acquaintance," he said, dragging a hand roughly down his face, his eyes darting to the room then back. "A ghost from my past."

"Rey," Spencer said. I glanced back in time to see him hooking Kennedy's arm over his shoulders and helping her toward the dressing room.

"We'll talk about this later," I said, shoving a finger in Alexei's face.

"Take them to the penthouse. I want them secured tonight," Alexei said as he turned on his heel.

"Where the fuck are you going?"

"To hunt ghosts," he said as he knocked on the door that led to the room holding the security footage to every inch of the club.

He disappeared inside, so I hurried to join Spencer and Milo as they helped Kennedy through the door and began to carefully peel away the high collared bustier she'd worn during her performance.

Milo did everything in his power to keep his eyes averted, but that didn't stop Wolf from growling.

"No," I said, glaring at him. "Tonight, neither you nor Alexei get to play possessive alpha. If this ghost is a buddy of yours…" *Then it was their fault.*

I didn't need to voice the words. I could see the guilt and torment in his brown eyes. I'd seen the same thing in Alexei's hazel eyes when he'd mentioned it.

Spencer gasped, his eyes shooting up to my face.

"What?" I said, stepping around to face Kennedy.

On her left breast were two crescent wounds. An alpha's mark. My eyes raised to Wolf, but he held up his hands and shook his head.

Alexei had marked my beta. She'd allowed him to leave a mark on her flesh, tied him to her, to us, permanently. And hadn't mentioned it to either Spence or me.

Mixed emotions warred within me, but those were for another time. For now, we needed to get our beta changed out of her costume and, apparently, to the penthouse.

Did that mean the alphas feared this fucker knew where we lived? Did he know where to find my beta? My omega?

This was exactly what I had feared when Kennedy had broached the subject of courting them, of entertaining the idea of adding them to our little pack.

A whimper escaped Kennedy when Spencer carefully pulled a t-shirt over her head. No way could she handle a pair of pants. But I sure as fuck wouldn't let her leave this place with so much skin showing, either.

"Is there a blanket we can wrap around her?" I asked Milo.

"No. But the towels are big." He hurried away and came back with an armful.

Alexei entered the room and jerked his head for Wolf to follow. *Oh hell no.*

This was my pack. Kennedy was my beta. And these two might have led one of their enemies right to her.

"Well?" I asked after pulling the dressing room door closed.

Alexei looked gutted. As he should if this had something to do with him.

"The man's name is Mikhail Gusev. And that was a message specifically for me."

"Did you see him in the club?" Wolf asked.

"My attention was elsewhere," he admitted. As he turned, I noted a shimmer to his eyes that he was doing his best to hide.

And, for a brief moment, I felt like an asshole for blaming him for the abuse Kennedy had just suffered.

"Do you know where to find him?" I asked.

"No. But I will find him. I want the three of you at the penthouse until I track the mother fucker down. And then I'll end this."

"Why?"

"Why what?" he asked me.

"Why did he hurt her? What did you do to piss him off enough to..." Emotion clogged my throat, and I was unable to put words to the utter horror that was now Kennedy's back.

"Long story. That I promise to tell later," he said quickly, holding up his hands when I opened my mouth to berate him or force him to tell me everything. "For now, let's get her home and comfortable. Try to talk her into getting more medical attention. Some of those gashes...she could get an infection."

When a tear trailed down his stubbled cheek, he didn't bother swiping it away. The same rage and concern I felt in my chest was mirrored in his eyes.

He cared about Kennedy.

Nah. He loved her. I was pretty sure he'd fallen in love with her before either of them knew each other's name. And he'd marked her, bonded her for life. She was his beta as much as she was mine. And someone had hurt our girl.

"I'll go pack our bags and meet you all back at the apartment," I said, moving away from the alphas.

"Not alone, you're not," Wolf said, wrapping a hand tightly around my bicep.

I might let him dominate me when he had some steam to blow off, but at the moment, I was about to blow my top. And it would be far too easy to take my aggression out on his face if he didn't let go of my arm.

"I'm a fucking alpha. Just like you," I said, yanking away.

"And the man who did this doesn't work alone. If they see you pull up, they won't bother asking for consent before...I'll go with you, and we'll meet everyone back at the penthouse."

"Fine," I said after a few seconds of a stare down.

Stepping into the dressing room, I swallowed back the lump at the pain etched into every line of Kennedy's face as Milo helped her across the room with Spencer carrying her personal belongings.

We couldn't even carry her without hurting her further, not unless one of us wanted to toss her over our shoulder like a caveman.

"Lyubov," Alexei said as he pushed forward until he was walking beside Spencer. "I am so sorry."

"Don't be sorry. Find the fucker and kill him," she said through clenched teeth.

Milo snorted with a nod.

Wolf and I split away from the group and climbed into his Audi. From the outside, it seemed far too small for his big body, but it was actually spacious and extremely comfortable inside.

Neither of us spoke the entire drive back to the house. I had too many things to say and no energy to say them. I was pissed. I was afraid. I was worried for my beta.

But yeah...rage was the number one emotion currently taking up residence in my heart and mind. I wasn't sure it would go away even after Wolf and Alexei tracked that Mikhail fucker down and executed him.

"I want to be there when you kill him," I said as he pulled the vehicle into our driveway.

"Not a good idea. Killing someone...it changes you. You can't take it back," Wolf said before pushing from the driver's seat and looking around the yard.

"Why the fuck would I want to take it back?"

I led the way into the house, using my key to get through the door, then made my way into Kennedy's room first to find the most comfortable and loose-fitting clothes she owned.

Spencer would need some comfort items, too. His omega instincts would be on overdrive with one of his pack injured. And his perfume had been uncontrollable through the night, indicating an early heat because of all the new alpha hormones.

After shoving as much as I could into Kennedy's duffel, I tugged the straps over my shoulder and brushed past Wolf to start on Spencer's stuff.

"Rey," Wolf said, but I shook my head.

"I don't want to talk," I said, a nonstop growl rattling from my chest.

He jerked the straps from my shoulder and tossed it to the ground. "Then get it out."

"What?" I asked with narrowed eyes.

He pulled his shirt over his head and held his arms out to his side. "Take it out on me until we find the mother fucker. I won't fight back unless that's what you want."

My chest began to rise and fall as the rage built and built. This was his fault. This was Alexei's fault. They'd brought that asshole into our lives. And now Kennedy had been hurt.

Raising a hand, I smacked Wolf across the face. He dropped his arms back to his side as his face whipped to the side but didn't make a single move to defend himself.

It wasn't enough. The slight sting in my hand only spurred me on.

With another swing, I hit him with my other hand, this time, curling my fingers into a fist and clocking him in the jaw.

And again, his head jerked to the side, but he did nothing to stop me, didn't raise his arms, didn't even take a step away.

Tears blurred my vision as I lunged at him, swinging and smacking the side of his head.

Still wasn't enough. Hurting Wolf wasn't enough. I needed to find the culprit. I needed to punish the person responsible. And no matter how much my mind wanted to blame these two alphas, my heart refused to agree.

The tears were hot as they streaked down my cheeks and I continued to punch Wolf in the chest, shoving at him until he stumbled, then finally threw myself at him...

And wrapped my arms around his neck as sobs wracked my body.

His hands were gentle as he smoothed them up and down my back, but he said nothing, simply let me take what I needed. And in that moment, I needed to be held until I could cry the anger out of my body.

"I swear to you, Rey. Alexei and I will punish him. We'll punish anyone who had a hand in this. And as much as I would rather you not be anywhere near, if it's what you need, I'll let you be the one to pull the trigger and put a bullet between the mother fucker's eyes."

Sagging against him, I didn't bother trying to hold back the salty tears as they soaked my cheeks and his shoulder. Even when he lifted me into his arms and carried me until he sat on the side of the pack bed, I continued to cry, continued to release the maelstrom of emotions.

I should have protected my beta. I should have been the one who made enough money to support my pack so she wouldn't have been in that position.

I'd failed my pack. I'd failed my sweet Kennedy. And now, I would do anything and everything it took to keep her and Spencer safe, even if it meant moving in with the alphas temporarily to keep the two loves of my life safe from our new packmates' enemies.

CHAPTER 23

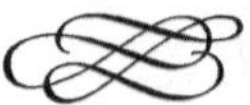

<u>Spencer</u>

*K*ennedy continuously tried to make light of the situation, over and over assuring me she was fine.

She was so not fine. Her back looked as though someone had whipped her until her skin was broken in several places. And it was obvious she was in pain yet refused to allow Alexei or me to take her to the ER.

"They can give you some really good pain killers," I said as I dabbed a cool, wet cloth across the cuts that still seeped blood.

"I took some ibuprofen," she said, rolling her head on her folded hands to look at me from the corner of her eye.

"So not the same thing."

"I agree with Spencer," Alexei said.

He sat at her feet, and I released a growl I wasn't aware I was possible of making. He might not have been directly responsible for this, but apparently, it was that same asshole we'd run into at the Prada store that had beat my beta until he'd broken her skin, until she'd screamed for help.

I hadn't seen the security footage. I didn't want to. Especially after seeing the look on Alexei's face when he stepped out of the locked room when he'd watched to see if he recognized Kennedy's abuser.

And that's exactly what that fucking alpha was, an abuser.

Bull shit. He was a fucking monster.

To get at Alexei, he'd attacked someone half his size. And not like he'd waited for her outside the club or the house. Nope. He'd paid to have her in a private room and restrained her so she couldn't fight back like the fucking coward he was.

Alexei sighed, a sad look in his hazel eyes, and pushed to his feet, taking a seat in a chair across the room from the bed where he'd laid her down. His bed. He hadn't even taken her to a guest room in the penthouse or a pack bed. If there was a pack bed here.

Nope. He'd guided her into his unbelievably spotless room and urged her to lie on her stomach on top of his white duvet.

Was it petty that I'd hoped she would bleed on the no doubt over-priced comforter?

Pushing my fingers through Kennedy's long, inky black hair and making sure it stayed away from the open gashes, I glanced back up at Alexei again and felt like a total asshole.

He was leaning forward, his elbows on his knees, his hands gripped together in front of his mouth as he stared at our beta. The same beta he'd marked. The same beta he'd sworn he would protect.

Fuck. "It's not your fault," I blurted out, waiting for him to meet my gaze. "There's no way you could have known this would happen. Security should have gotten to her faster."

"Why didn't they?" Alexei said, his voice mildly muffled behind his fisted hands.

"Did you use the color code?" I asked Kennedy.

"Several times," she said. Her voice was sleepy. She definitely needed rest. But I was terrified to let her sleep before she was fully checked out by a doctor. Which, of course, was stupid. She hadn't endured any head injuries. She might not be able to sleep on her back or, you know, sit on her ass for a few days, but as long as the open wounds were kept clean, she would heal fine.

But I still hated that she'd had to go through anything at all.

"Why the fuck didn't they intervene sooner?" I asked no one in particular.

"Did you see anyone other than Mikhail?" Alexei asked her.

She raised her head and propped her chin in her hands. "There were two other guys. I didn't get any names. And they were...I don't know. They just looked like regular alphas. Big. Brown hair. I didn't note any tattoos or anything to identify them if that's what you're asking."

"You're wondering if someone was outside the door," I said to Alexei.

He nodded.

That would make sense. The security at *Plumes et Fouets* was top notch. The moment Kennedy said red, the session should have not only ended, but security should have been through the door and using their own bodies to protect her. So...why hadn't they gotten there sooner?

"You watched the security footage. Did you see anyone stop the guards outside her door?"

"I only watched the footage from inside the room," he said, his eyes on her.

"Stop staring at me like you're waiting for me to fall to pieces. I'm fine," Kennedy said.

"You're not fine," Alexei and I said at the same time.

"Fuck, lyubov. I'm so–"

"Do not say you're sorry. You didn't have anything to do with this. If they attacked me to get to you, that's on them. Not you."

She was making excuses for him. And...fuck. I hated to admit that she was right. *He* didn't hurt her. He would never hurt her. He hadn't even bothered to hide the tears that had streamed down his cheeks as he'd driven us back to the penthouse.

"Are you hungry?" I asked Kennedy instead of continuing to dwell on who was at fault.

"Not really."

"I'll get you some water. Or would you rather something stronger?" Alexei asked as he pushed to his feet.

"Something stronger sounds amazing," she said with a wink.

Kennedy was in pain, her back, thighs, and even ass ravaged by that fucking bamboo cane, and she was still trying to put everyone at ease.

"Do you have a preference?" he asked, lowering and balancing on the balls of his feet so they were eye level.

"Hmm. Something with alcohol in it."

I couldn't help the huff of surprised laughter that burst from my lips at her comment.

Alexei's fingers were so gentle as he ran them over her cheek, then leaned forward to press his lips to her forehead.

"Make it a double," she said when he straightened, her body tense beneath my hand.

"I'll take something, too," I said before he could leave the room.

"It's not his fault," Kennedy said, grunting as she rolled onto her side, raised up on one elbow, and rested her cheek on her hand.

"I know."

"So stop treating him like it is. All four of you were there tonight. None of you were any the wiser to what was happening. What I want to know is why it took security so long. The moment I called out red, someone should have been through that door. Which means either someone was paid off or Alexei was on to something and there was someone blocking their entrance."

"Why are you so calm about this, Kennedy? Do you need me to take a picture of your back so you'll realize how serious it is?"

She blinked at me as her dark brows pulled together. "I was there, Spence. I know how bad it was."

Well, fuck me. Now I felt like a complete and total douche insinuating that she couldn't tell merely by the pain, acting as though *I* was the victim.

Now it was my turn to blink away tears. Yeah, I was the omega, but I was bigger than Kennedy. Stronger. I should have protected her.

"I was serious about you quitting, Kennedy. At least the VIP rooms. No more. I can't…they could have done so much worse. They could have killed you. Or taken you from us. I can't lose you." Tears flowed freely now and I didn't care to wipe them away.

Kennedy made the softest sound of distress as she pushed to a sitting position, swatting my hands away when I tried to stop her.

"I'm done with the VIP rooms. And everyone needs to stop blaming themselves. I'll be fine. It's nothing but some cuts and bruises. Not the first time I've been hurt in my life."

Narrowing my eyes at her, I tilted my head. "Maybe we should go stay with your dad for a while. Just disappear until Alexei and Wolf find that asshole and kill him."

I couldn't believe how cavalier we were all being about the fact our new alphas were paid to kill people and were actually cheering on this particular execution. If I had my choice, they would drag out the cock sucker's pain, make him feel every moment of agony my beta had experienced.

When she fully sat up and threw her legs over the side of the bed, I nearly burst into tears at the sight of my beta swaying on her feet.

"Fuck, Kennedy."

I'd been feeling symptoms of preheat for a few days. Not surprising with the addition of two new alphas. But my emotions were already on a rollercoaster. Seeing my beautiful beta in so much pain was doing nothing to ease the damn rush of fear, anger, and heartache. I would do anything to take it away. Hell. I would rather it have been me than her. At least my omega would have healed me faster. My sweet girl didn't have the accelerated healing of the omega or alpha hormones so would have to suffer for days or even weeks.

"Will you take a picture?" she said, handing me her phone and turning her back on me.

"Are you sure?"

"Spence. Remember how pissed you were when you thought we were treating you like glass? I'm not fragile. I'm not a damsel. I grew up…differently than you and Rey. I want to see what that dickwad did to me."

My hands shook as I took the phone from her and moved back far enough to get the full view in the screen. "Are you sure?" I asked before touching the red button on her phone.

"Take the picture, Spence," she said.

After a deep breath, I clicked a few times, then moved closer so she could get a close up of the deeper gashes left by the cane.

She took the phone and gingerly lowered back onto the bed.

For a few moments, she said nothing, simply scrolled through the pics. "That's why my ass hurts. There are mostly bruises. The worst of it is there, across my shoulder blades."

Tears blurred my vision as she stared at the pictures and talked as though she were viewing the abuse of a complete stranger, her tone clinical and detached.

"Kennedy," I started, lowering to sit beside her as Alexei reentered with two glasses with ice and a bottle of vodka. I wasn't a big vodka drinker, but anything to take the edge off the emotion sounded perfect right about now.

"Kind of stereotypical there, alpha," Kennedy teased him as he handed her a glass then poured some vodka in it before doing the same with me.

He huffed a forced laugh but there was no smile on his lips.

My beta sipped at hers, but I downed my first serving like a shot then shook the ice at Alexei for a refill.

He didn't bother with a glass, simply drank from the bottle as he retook his seat in the chair across the room.

"It's not as bad as you guys are making out," Kennedy said, looking through the pictures again. "I was expecting to see exposed muscle or some shit. It's just some cuts and bruises. It'll heal up in a few days."

Alexei was quiet a few moments, watching her as he took pulls from the bottle.

Then he pushed to his feet, handed me the bottle, and stormed out, his wintry smell holding a smokey scent as he battled his own emotions.

"You were perfuming during my show," Kennedy said between sips.

She sat on the side of the bed naked, not even bothering to cover her lap or drape a sheet around her shoulders.

"Yeah," I said, refilling my glass after downing the second serving.

"Your heat is coming soon. If we're going to stay here, we need to make sure the nest is ready. Get some supplies and shit. I might not be able to..." She inhaled deeply and blew it out in a rush. "I might only be there for emotional support, but you know I would never leave you during your cycle. I'll make sure there's plenty of water and food and even give you sponge baths."

She'd said the last part with a wink, trying – and failing – to make me smile. The last thing I cared about was my fucking heat. Yeah, it was going to suck. I would go through pain and endure high ass fevers. But I hadn't been beaten by complete strangers as some kind of punishment against our alphas.

Deciding it was best to change the subject, I raised a hand and gently ran my fingertips over the marks on her breast. "When did this happen?" I asked.

She lowered her chin and followed the path of my fingers then smiled at me. "Last night. Sorry I didn't tell you guys yet. I planned on telling you tonight after my show. Your perfume was driving me crazy and I'd worked up this beautiful fantasy of the five of us crowding into the nest and playing and then showing you the mark."

Yeah. That would have been a much better night.

"Where the fuck are Rey and Wolf? Shouldn't they be back by now?" Kennedy asked, lifting her phone and checking the time.

"They went to pack up some clothes for us. I'm sure Rey is reading Wolf the riot act and probably kicking his ass."

A smile bisected her face. "And he's loving every minute of it. I swear the two of them are–"

"Kennedy. For fuck's sake. Why are you acting like this is no big deal?"

I hadn't meant to raise my voice, but she was acting like nothing of importance had happened. I mean, yeah, I'd intended to change the subject by mentioning the mark on her breast, but I hated that she refused to acknowledge the fact she'd been assaulted in a place where she should have been safe, especially when her pack was in only yards away. We hadn't even heard her screaming through the damn soundproofed walls.

She took my hands in hers. "Spence, listen to me. I know this was scary. I know it looks like shit. But I'll be okay. It wasn't Alexei's or Wolf's fault. No one failed me. The only person responsible is that cocksucker."

"That doesn't answer my question." I narrowed my eyes at her as something turned my stomach. "Were you abused in the past, Kennedy?" I hated the thought of anyone hurting her. I'd met her dad and members of her family pack. They all appeared to adore her. But looks could be deceiving.

Her chest rose and fell as she took a deep breath. "Could we table this until I get some sleep and everyone is together? I really don't feel like telling the same story over and over."

I shot to my legs as the urge to hunt someone – anyone – down and beat the piss out of them chased away the tears. "Someone fucking hurt you before? Your dad? Another alpha?"

"Spence," she said, reaching for me.

And like a dick, I jerked away from her.

Until she struggled to her feet and I was right back to feeling like the biggest asshole in the world. She was trying to comfort me when it should have been the other way around.

Stupid fucking omega hormones.

"Not my dad. And I promise to tell you guys everything. I've kept a few secrets from you guys, but only because they weren't my secrets to tell. I need to call my dad in the morning. And then we'll all sit down and have a big ol' pack meeting. But...can you just hold me? Please?"

Tears shimmered in her eyes, the first moment of any form of weakness I'd seen from her since we'd gotten her into the car and Alexei had hauled ass to get her back to the penthouse.

"Fuck," I ground out, moving forward and pressing kisses to her cheeks, her nose, her forehead, and her lips. "I'm not sure how I can hold you without hurting you. Tell me what you need. I'll give you any part of me if it'll make you feel better."

She lowered back onto the bed, lying on her side. "You could be the little spoon."

A smile twitched at the corners of her lips and another wave of overwhelming emotion washed over me.

"Little spoon it is," I said, carefully lying down with her and rolling so she could drape her arm over my waist and chuckled when she wedged a knee between mine.

Her breath was warm against my neck as she sighed. "We'll talk tomorrow. We'll make plans. But I promise no more VIP rooms. I think…I might take a break from the club. At least for a while."

"The alphas make more than enough," I said, tugging her arms tighter around me. "We'll all do what we have to to take care of you, Kennedy. I love you. I love you so much."

"I love you, too," she whispered.

Within minutes, her breathing grew slow and steady as the night caught up with her and she fell asleep.

CHAPTER 24

<u>Alexei</u>

My phone dinged with a notification of entry into the penthouse. Glancing at the screen, I made sure it was only Wolf before I went back to beating the shit out of the punching bag hanging on the level below where my pack was now gathered.

Fucking Mikhail Gusev. That piece of shit had dared to touch my beta. He'd followed me or somehow discovered where my beta worked. He'd managed to blend into the crowd while I was too distracted by Kennedy's bared ass being spanked and then reserved time with her in that back fucking room.

And I hadn't had a clue she was in danger.

How the fuck had it gotten so far? Why the fuck hadn't security gotten to her faster?

I needed to see the rest of the footage. I needed to watch every minute of footage they had from the moment they opened their doors until we left. I needed to see how long Mikhail and his men had been there, how long they had watched my beta, and confirm whether he had ensured the bouncers couldn't stop the assault on Kennedy.

For Anais's sake, I sure as hoped that had been the case. Because if any member of the staff had been paid to stay away, to allow him to hurt her, they would be on the top of my hit list. And it wouldn't be a simple bullet to the brain. I would take my time, use the skills I had learned through the years to inflict as much damage to their bodies before taking their lives.

My knuckles bled as I continued to pummel the bag, forgoing the gloves or even tape. I deserved the burn. I deserved the torn flesh. I deserved far more.

He had gotten close to her because I had been distracted. Mikhail had gotten close to Kennedy because, instead of ending the threat, I'd simply ignored his and his father's demands I step in line and join the Gusev Bratva.

I saw the incrimination in Spencer's eyes. It was mirrored in Rey's. Not Kennedy's.

But it didn't matter how many times my mate reassured me this wasn't my fault. Had she never met me, she would have never been in Mikhail's sights.

My shirt sat on the floor where I'd dropped it as my body grew warm, as sweat ran down my face, my neck, my chest. My muscles burned and my hands protested, yet I couldn't stop.

I needed to expel this anger, this influx of energy. But I was also looking for a way to punish myself for my failure.

Because I *had* failed. I'd failed my mate. I'd sworn she and her pack was safe with me, with us. Had sworn to keep them safe. To protect them.

And I failed the day after she'd accepted my knot and my bite.

Opening the bond, I sought her. She was either shutting me out or sleeping. Hopefully the latter. I wasn't sure I could handle if she were to shut me out completely.

I fucking loved her. And I hadn't bothered to tell her. I didn't give a shit that it was early to feel such strong emotions. She carried my mark. She owned my heart.

She owned *me*.

"Fuck!" I bellowed, the sound echoing off the bare walls and floors.

My alpha needed to dole out more punishment. But I also needed to tend to my beta, to watch over her, to see with my own eyes that she truly was okay.

I knew the injuries would heal. And she'd proven from the first time she'd met me she was strong as fuck.

But none of that lessened my urge to draw blood.

The bell to the elevator filled the space then the doors opened almost silently.

I caught Wolf's autumn scent before the sound of his sneakers on the hardwood floor made it to my ears.

"The fuck you doing down here?" he asked, moving further into the room before leaning against a wall to watch me pace like a caged animal.

"How the fuck did I not see him, Wolf? How the fuck did I not know he was there? How the fuck did he get so close to her?"

Wolf didn't answer. Because he knew I wasn't truly asking him for answers, rather purging the same shit that repeated on loop in my brain.

He crossed his arms and watched me, only moving his eyes as I ranted and paced.

Then he pushed from the wall and yanked his shirt over his head.

There were red marks and bruising developing on his chest. Upon closer inspection, there was some swelling on both sides of his face and it looked like he was going to be sporting one hell of a black eye by morning.

"What the fuck happened to you?"

He shrugged. "Rey."

Rey. Her alpha had needed to expel the same angry energy as me. Kennedy had been her beta first. And then I'd come crashing into their lives and brought chaos right along with me.

Without another word, Wolf lunged at me, swinging his fist and barely grazing the side of my head when I ducked to the side.

Fuck...yes. This was what I needed. Someone who would fight

back. Someone who could do more damage than simply tear open the skin over my knuckles.

We went at each other, ducking, lunging, swinging fists. He would clock me in the chin and knock me back a few paces before I rebounded and attacked him.

By the time we began to slow, my breath sawed in and out of my lungs, my heart beat a painful cadence behind my ribs, and sweat glimmered across every inch of my exposed flesh.

We both sported injuries, but no broken bones, nothing that wouldn't heal within days. Nothing that either of us would have so much as batted an eye about on any normal day.

"Better?" Wolf asked, leaning over with his hands braced on his knees as he struggled to catch his breath.

"No. But it's a start." Moving to the wall, I lowered until I was sitting and drew up one knee, draping an arm over it. "Is she asleep?"

"Yeah," Wolf said, taking a seat beside me, his shoulder pressed against mine.

As alphas, we weren't as needy of touch as omegas. But that didn't mean we didn't enjoy the touch of our packmates. It settled the beasts that raged within us, especially when someone hurt a member of our family.

"She's spooning Spencer. Rey's pacing the living room. She wanted to climb into bed with them, but she's scared of touching Kennedy's back."

A growl built in my chest and I let it loose rather than holding back. None of us would truly be able to hold our beta for days. Or longer.

"You marked her," Wolf said, turning his head to look at me.

"Last night," I said with a nod. A smile quirked up my lips as the memory of last night began to play out in my head like a movie.

"What?" he asked. "What's the smile for?"

This really wasn't his business, but… "She took my knot."

"Fuuuck," Wolf growled out, a matching smile gracing his lips. "Rey takes mine, too. And fucking locks me."

A few moments of silence passed between us as we both pondered on the life we were building around the little pack of three.

"We're lucky fucking bastards," Wolf said.

I grunted. "Wait until you feel Spencer wrapped around your cock."

Wolf rolled his head to smirk at me.

"Seriously? When did that happen?"

"Hey. You were at work. He got horny. And Rey and I just happened to be in the mood."

This was what I needed, even for just a few moments. A way to get my mind off the urge to find and kill someone. Anyone. Just to ease the blood lust burning through my veins.

"You got a plan?" Wolf asked after a while.

"Find Mikhail. Torture Mikhail. Kill Mikhail. And anyone who helped him."

Wolf snorted and pushed to his feet, stretching his arms over his head with a grunt. "I'm getting too old for this shit."

"Or maybe you should stop sneaking out into the woods and playing Little Red Riding Hood with Rey." I grinned at him when he shot me a look. "Yeah. Everyone knows. You two aren't nearly as sneaky as you think."

I hadn't fucked Rey. Not that I didn't find her smoking hot. But being as we'd only had a few moments here and there together over the past couple months, it felt like most of my time had been spent obsessing over Kennedy, convincing Rey I wasn't a threat to her pack, and courting Spencer.

All that time trying to convince Rey and look where that got me. Fuck.

"I don't want them leaving the penthouse until we find and neutralize Mikhail, his fuck buddies, even his father," I said as I pushed to my feet and followed him to the door.

"Agreed."

While I would never make decisions for Wolf, I had no intention of accepting another contract until I knew one hundred percent Mikhail was no longer a threat to my beta, to my omega, or even Rey.

Until further notice, my entire existence would revolve around being their personal bodyguards while hunting the mother fucker who'd dared to touch what belonged to me.

"Oh. And heads up," Wolf said as we rode the elevator up one floor to the penthouse. "Rey said she thinks Spence is going into heat early."

Well fuck.

CHAPTER 25

<u>Kennedy</u>

I swore I'd been sleeping off and on for two days. There wasn't much else for me to do being as my pack refused to let me out of bed for anything more than using the bathroom or a quick shower.

Boredom and I were never very good friends and right about now, that bitch was annoying me.

Voices rumbled from the other parts of the penthouse. This place was huge and beautiful, but still unfamiliar to me. I missed my bed. I missed my furniture and belongings and collected décor I'd found in various places such as estate sales, thrift stores, and the like. Not that I couldn't afford to buy new stuff, I'd just always preferred more unique items, antiques, vintage goodies.

Wolf and Alexei's place was chic and just this side of compulsively clean. As I laid on my stomach, staring at the stupid TV that had been playing nonstop, I was half tempted to pull some clothes from my duffel and toss them around for no other reason than to give the room a lived-in feeling.

Yep. Absolutely bored out of my mind. I mean, if they were going to make me stay put, the least they could all do was stay in here and keep me company. The worst gashes on my back didn't even hurt that bad. It was the bruises that ached, the places where the cane hadn't broken the skin but had caused perfect stripes of blue, purple, and black to crisscross and line my back, ass, and upper thighs.

Technically, I could move around just fine. But sitting or lying on my back for more than a few minutes at a time hurt like a bitch. Which did not translate to being unable to walk. Yet all four of my pack members demanded I rest. How much freaking rest did they think I needed?

With a groan, I rolled from the bed and pushed to my feet, stretching my arms over my head as I stood on my toes. It stretched and strained the healing skin, but damn it felt amazing on my joints and muscles.

If we were at home, I could have snuck down to the basement and used the barre to stretch further, sit on the mats that I used to protect myself when trying out a new routine and limbered up.

Just walking around would be enough for now, as long as I was no longer lying in bed.

Screw it. I was so done being horizontal. And my neck was getting sore from turning it at a weird angle or propping it on my chin to watch the boob tube.

After scouring the room, I found one of Wolf's discarded shirts near the bed and tugged it over my head. It was big enough it didn't chafe the more tender wounds and long enough it stretched almost to mid-thigh, covering my booty and the rest of my naughty bits. Not that any of the pack would care if I walked around naked, but there was no reason to give them a glimpse of my back side and have them ordering me back to the bedroom.

A pair of tall, thick, fuzzy socks and I was on my way to get a little exercise and see what my pack was up to. I'd been promised a conversation, yet no one had told me shit. They were treating me like I would shatter like crystal, and it was getting on my damn nerves.

Thing was, I'd also promised to tell my pack more about my past, but Dad had yet to call me back. I needed to make sure he was cool with me giving away a few club secrets. Not that I would give them details that could incriminate anyone. I knew no one in my pack would hold my past or my family pack against me, nor would anyone run to the police and tell them they had knowledge of a not so on the up and up club. Didn't mean I had free reign to spill Kingsmen secrets.

Fallen leaves, red wine, and warm apple pie acted like a beacon as I shuffled silently through the long hallways until I found them around a table, cards in their hands, their conversation low.

"You know I wasn't sleeping. Why are you all whispering like you'll disturb me?" I complained as I made my way to the kitchen for a snack.

"Because you should be resting," Spencer said, pushing to his feet and hurrying over to me, his arms outstretched as though waiting for me to fall.

"Unless you're hoping to cop a feel, I suggest withdrawing your hands before I break them."

He stilled, his brows raising up his brow. "So…if I grab your boob, it's fine. But if I try to catch you if you fall…then you'll break my hand? You sure you didn't suffer a head injury?" To show he was teasing, he actually reached both hands up and squeezed my boobs, complete with a honking sound before stepping away.

"Much better," I said, fondling his junk before returning to my search of something super bad for me and full of salt and sugar.

"Are you doing okay? Do you need more pain killers?" Rey asked, joining Spence and me in the open and humongous kitchen.

"Seriously. How do you find anything in this place? It's like searching through a jigsaw puzzle," I said as I opened and closed drawers and cabinets in my search.

"Snacks are in the pantry," Rey said, passing me and opening a door that practically blended in with the wall to expose a room that could easily swallow one of our bathrooms back at the house. "Kennedy–"

"I'm fine. Don't need any pain killers. What I really need is a big ol' bowl of salsa and some salty as hell chips," I said, my back to my alpha as I perused the selection.

And then something clicked in my brain.

Turning to face Rey, I stepped out of the pantry and turned my head toward the table where Wolf still sat, his head turned in our direction. "Where's Alexei?"

He had only checked in on me a few times but hadn't stayed any longer than it took to bring me pills, clean my wounds, or to make sure I had food. He hadn't snuggled with me the way Rey and Spence had. Hadn't slept on the couch the way Wolf had when the three of us took up too much space for him to join us without rubbing against my wounds.

Rey and Spence exchanged a look before turning to Wolf as though they refused to answer. And that alone made me anxious.

"Where is he?"

"So, they own three floors," Spence said with a shrug. "He's been spending a lot of time downstairs."

"Doing what?" I asked, looking from one alpha to the next and even checking in with my omega.

"Don't look at me. I've been up here taking care of you," Spence said with a shrug.

When Wolf didn't answer my question, I crossed the space separating us and crossed my arms. "Take me to him. I want to see him."

Part of me wondered whether he was hiding from me out of guilt. But a terrified part of me wondered if he was making plans of going after that Mikhail guy on his own. Depending on how many people his Russian buddy had working for him, there was no way I would ever allow my alpha to walk into a fight outmanned and outgunned.

"He said–"

"I don't care what he said," I growled out, cutting off any excuse Wolf might make. He was an alpha in our pack but wasn't technically my alpha yet. I didn't carry his mark the way I carried Rey's and Alexei's.

And…well, I had never been the best at following rules or being overly affected by an alpha's bark, anyway.

"Either take me to him or I'll just start wandering the building in search of him."

Spencer snorted a laugh that he tried and failed to hide. My beautiful Rey smirked and shook her head.

"What? You didn't fall for me because I was weak and easily persuaded," I said with a shrug.

I fought against the pinch of pain that small movement caused. The last thing I needed was for any of the three to see an ounce of my pain and demand I return to bed. Bruised and scabbed or not, I would throw an ever loving fit if I had to lie down for one more minute. Especially since they were leaving me alone. Might not be an omega, but I still needed the touch and scents of my pack.

"Fine," Wolf said after a few minutes of studying my face as though trying to decide whether or not I would do as I threatened.

Of the two alphas, I knew Wolf the least. We hadn't really spent much time together alone, but I adored the way he treated Spencer and Rey, adored the absolute love and affection that practically oozed from him whenever his eyes landed on my beautiful alpha. That alone earned my respect and loyalty.

"You're lucky it's your rear end that hurts or I'd end up carrying you," he said as he gently took my hand in his and led me from the kitchen.

"Or end up spanking her for being a brat," I heard Spencer mutter, and was answered with a tinkling laugh from Rey.

Hm. That almost sounded like my two original packmates had some experience with Wolf's particular form of brat taming.

Wolf glanced down at my knee-high socks and huffed a soft laugh.

"What?" I said, tilting my chin down as he hit a button on the panel and used a keycard to make the doors close and get the elevator moving. "I like unicorns."

The bell chimed and the doors slid open soundlessly, revealing a foyer similar to the one upstairs. But the further in we moved, the more I realized that, while this floor was obviously meant to be another apartment, Wolf and Alexei had turned it into their own personal training room.

Grunts and growls mixed with the sound of something being hit. I almost took off at a sprint, ready to throw myself at somebody flying monkey style for hurting my alpha, but Wolf tightened his hold on my hand and nodded toward a corner of a wall.

And then he released my hand and took a step back, following me at a distance. And I had no idea whether it was to watch over me in case my injured body gave out…or to protect me from my alpha.

My heart stuttered to a stop when my eyes fell on Alexei.

He was shirtless and wore a pair of shorts that looked as though they'd started out as sweatpants before they'd been cut. He glistened with sweat and was beating the crap out of a punching bag.

What squeezed my heart was his bloody fists and the smears that splotched the bag in various places.

"Alexei?" I said softly.

He didn't stop. Simply continued punching and punching, a nearly nonstop growl mixing with the grunts from his efforts and the *thump thump thump* of his fists hitting the bag.

"Alexei," I said a little louder.

He stopped mid-swing and turned wild eyes on me. His nostrils flared with his deep breaths, his pupils were blown, and the longer I stood there, the stronger his juniper and crisp winter sweetness grew until it was tinged with something…different. Something foreign to my gentle, romantic alpha.

My heart began to thunder behind my ribs as his eyes fell on Wolf standing at my back and that growl grew louder as he stalked forward.

"Alexei!" I said louder, moving to step in his way.

What the fuck was going on?

"Brother, stop," Wolf said, holding his hands out, even when Alexei stepped around me and swung at him.

Wolf ducked and blocked blow after blow.

Alexei had gone feral. My beautiful Russian alpha had gone feral.

And there wasn't a way in hell I would sit here and watch him take out what happened to me on his own packmate.

"Damn it, Alexei!" I yelled, launching myself until I was clinging to his back and my bare ass was met with the cool air.

"Get off him, Kennedy. You're going to hurt yourself," Wolf barked as he kept blocking blows from Alexei.

"Kennedy," Alexei growled.

Tightening my hold on his throat, I did the first thing that came to mind. I lowered my face, opened my mouth, and bit him hard on the shoulder, clenching my jaw until the coppery taste of his blood coated my tongue.

He shuddered and stopped trying to attack Wolf.

"That's your mate, Lex. She's claiming you. You're going to hurt her if you keep fighting me."

Damn right he was, because no way was I releasing my hold on him until he chilled the fuck out.

I'd seen plenty of alphas go feral through my life, but usually when their mates were either in imminent danger or after they'd died. Never because they'd simply been injured.

He blamed himself. My alpha blamed himself for something someone else did. And nothing I said had made a difference.

Finally releasing my jaw, I pulled my teeth from Alexei's now ruined flesh and slowly slid down his back, my body becoming slicked with his sweat and scent.

The action also irritated my injuries but not a chance in hell would I say a word. My luck, there would be no more reeling Alexei back in and Wolf would have to hurt his own pack brother to stop the feral onslaught. And then I would be pissed at them both.

"I need to check your mate," Wolf said, keeping his hands out in front of him.

"I'm fine."

"I'm not leaving you with him like this," Wolf said, his eyes staying on Alexei even as he talked to me.

"He won't hurt me. He attacked you because of me. We'll be fine."

"He's feral right now. He could go into rut," Wolf argued, finally daring to turn his eyes to my face.

"And if he does, I'll ride him until my legs go out." Wouldn't be the first time I'd take his knot. And hopefully not the last.

Alexei had turned and was running his fingers through my hair, pushing it from my face. But the look on his face was nothing short of intense. There was a mixture of agony, fear, pain, and lust burning in his pretty hazel eyes.

And blood seeped slowly from where I'd latched onto him. I couldn't believe I'd marked an alpha. Not that it was completely unheard of, but not something I had ever really thought of doing.

But when I'd chomped down, I hadn't been thinking. I'd only reacted. Did the first thing I could think of to snap him out of his rampage.

Once I got him calmed down and somehow found a way for him to snap out of this, I needed to clean his knuckles. They were so damaged and blood was dripping onto the mats below our feet.

"Kennedy–"

I glanced around the room, pointing at various cameras. "You can watch us, right? Make sure I'm okay?"

"Yeah. But it'll take me time to get to you."

"He won't hurt me. But the three of you can hover around a phone or tablet to watch if it'll make you feel better. He won't calm down as long as another alpha is near me, not when he's like this."

Wolf dragged a hand down his face. Just because we hadn't made love and I didn't carry his mark didn't mean he didn't care about me. I just assumed he cared about me in the same manner he cared for Alexei. And that was completely fine with me as long as he continued to treat Rey and Spence like royalty.

It took a few more moments before Wolf sighed a sound that was more growl than an exhale of breath, then began to back away, his eyes on Alexei before glancing once more at me. "Please be careful."

"Always," I said, keeping my eyes on Alexei so as not to send him flying off the handle again.

I waited until I heard the soft whoosh of the elevator doors open and close before I gripped Alexei's wrists and held his hands to my face.

"I need you to come back to me, alpha," I said softly as that growl morphed into a purr.

He stepped close enough his body lined against mine and I could feel the hardness of his cock through his sweats and my borrowed t-shirt.

Oh shit. The shirt I'd borrowed from Wolf.

He seemed to catch the scent of another alpha on me the same time I remembered. He reached down and ripped it down the center before tossing it across the room so that I was standing there naked.

His eyes roamed my body from head to toe and that purr increased as his nostrils flared, scenting my arousal that spiked at his sound.

"Mate," he growled out, his arms wrapping around me and tugging me closer.

And effectively putting entirely too much pressure on the lashes and bruises across my back.

No matter how hard I tried, I couldn't bite back the whimper his embrace elicited.

Alexei instantly tensed and yanked his arms away as though only just remembering my injuries.

And the few seconds I'd successfully calmed him blew up in an instant.

CHAPTER 26

Kennedy

For a moment, it looked as though Alexei was looking for the threat. Or a target for his rage. He turned toward the punching bags with both hands in tight fists, then toward the elevator doors.

Nope. That wasn't happening. Whether he went up or down, he would end up hurting someone who didn't deserve it.

"Alexei, stay with me," I pleaded, putting myself in front of him even as he continued to try to stalk forward.

It was creepy, as though he no longer realized I was there, like he couldn't see a butt ass naked beta right in front of him.

Fuck it.

Reaching down, I grabbed as much of his junk as I could fit in my hand and squeezed...hard.

He flinched, baring his teeth, and growled down at me.

"Either calm down, or I'm going to do some real damage. And then

I'll be pissed off because I won't have access to your dick until you heal."

Alexei's nostrils flared as he scented me, his intense gaze leveling on me.

And like a switch had been flipped, he lowered his head until he could slant his mouth over mine while lifting me to wrap my legs around his hips. I felt the pain of his hands on the bruises, but the sensation of his cock straining against my core through the sweats overrode everything else.

"I want my alpha on his back," I ordered against his lips and hoped he wasn't so far gone that he would slam me against the wall and rut into me hard and fast. There was no way I could hide that amount of pain, not with a concrete wall biting into so many damn lashes.

His knees buckled and down we went with me wrapped around his waist, my arms clutching tightly around his neck to keep from falling backward.

His mouth found mine again as both of his hands moved to my head, one tangling in my long hair while the other smoothed down the side of my face, my throat, over my shoulder, then to the breast where he'd left his mark.

It was still healing but that didn't stop the erotic shivers that tingled through my body and sent heat straight to my core.

I needed my alpha. My alpha needed his beta. And there was nothing and no one that could stop us.

For the briefest of moments, I wondered if the pack was still watching, if they were being pervy and watching as I reached below me to yank the front of Alexei's pants down to free his cock, if they were smiling to themselves as I gripped his shaft and lowered myself onto him.

Or if they were watching in fear that Alexei would hurt me. Part of me wondered if Wolf was waiting by the elevator door to come rushing downstairs at the slightest hint of danger.

But like I'd told him, I didn't fear Alexei hurting me. He was feral, yes. He was going into rut, absolutely. But it wasn't because of me. It was because of what had happened to me. His alpha side wanted to punish someone while punishing himself for his ill perceived failure.

Lowering until I was seated as far as his knot would allow, I stilled my hips, and pulled away, cupping his face and staring into his eyes.

"Look at me, alpha," I said, putting as much force behind my words as I could.

He opened his eyes and stared at me, the lust haze competing with his alpha's need for violence.

"I'm going to fuck you. Hard. I'm going to milk your cock of every drop of cum in your balls. Then I'm going to take your knot. And you're going to come back to me. Do you understand me?"

He nodded once, his Adam's apple bobbing as he swallowed hard.

"I need to hear the words, alpha."

"I understand, mate."

A smile quirked at the edges of my lips.

"That's right. I'm your mate. You're mine. No one here will hurt you. And they sure as hell won't hurt me."

A growl began to rumble up his chest again as his fingertips grazed over my back.

Nope. No way would I let him sink back into that.

Pulling his arms away, I gripped his hands and pressed them to my tits, his big palms instantly gripping and massaging.

"Stay. With. Me."

And then I began to ride him, slowly at first, my gaze on his face, staring intently into his eyes to make sure I didn't lose his attention, that he didn't begin to sink back into his violent state.

Not that he would hurt me...on purpose. But if his alpha went fully into rut and flipped me onto my back, it would hurt like a mother fucker. If he flipped me onto my hands and knees, he would see the full extent of my injuries and we'd be back at square one.

I'd never had to be so careful while fucking someone.

As his hands toyed with my tits, his fingers rolling and pinching my nipples, I began to ride him faster, pushing down harder with each thrust as pressure built low in my belly, the need for release building and building until I was ready to cry if I didn't come soon.

When his arms twitched as though he wanted to wrap them around me and hold me against him, I tightened my hold on his wrists to keep them to my chest.

"*I'm* fucking *you*, alpha. And this is where I want you."

In hopes of avoiding him once more trying to reach for my back, I shoved at his shoulders until he was fully lying down and I was able to take him faster, harder, deeper.

"Mate," he growled out, that purr mixing with the rumbling in his chest.

"Yes, alpha. I'm yours," I said as the first wave squeezed my lower half, and I threw my head back and cried out.

"*Mine*," he growled loudly as his hips thrust up, slamming his knot into me without giving my body time to adjust to the invasion.

And I welcomed the stretch and burn. He practically howled with his release as hot jets filled me, his dick twitching and his knot throbbing in time with each spurt inside of me.

Dropping onto his chest, I pressed soft kisses to his pectorals, to his collarbone, then to his lips. "Are you with me?"

His eyes still held a hint of the feral alpha wanting to break through, but he looked more focused as he stared into my face. His hands rose and cupped my cheeks, drawing me forward so he could sip at my lips.

"I'm so fucking sorry," he choked out between gentle kisses. "Fuck, Kennedy. I'm so sorry."

I should have stopped his apologies. Reminded him he wasn't responsible for what had happened. But at least he was coherent enough to actually form complete sentences and not try to beat something or someone to a pulp.

As our breathing began to slow and our heart rates returned to normal, I draped myself over him, resting my cheek on his shoulder.

"Are you with me?"

"I'm here," he said, his voice still sounding as though emotion was clogging his throat.

"Will you come upstairs? Can you come upstairs without attacking Wolf?"

He huffed a sardonic laugh. "Is he pissed?"

"Nah," I answered for the other alpha. "He knew there was a risk coming down here, but I didn't give him much of a choice."

"I would never hurt you," he said, his fingers brushing through my hair, his fingertips barely grazing along the bruises on my back.

"I know."

"But I will fucking kill Mikhail. I can promise you that."

Maybe his words should have concerned me. But I knew the moment my dad called and found out what had happened, I would have a hell of a time keeping the Kingsmen in their territory instead of racing here to exact revenge on some Russian mobsters.

That's exactly what this town needed – a big ol' showdown between a rag tag group of bikers and Russian hitmen. Or at least I assumed that was what Alexei's enemy did, you know, since that was my mate's job and all.

Showdown. I could have barked out a laugh at the mundane word for exactly what would happen once my dad and family pack found out about my assault, especially if I couldn't keep them all back at home.

Maybe a visit was in order. That would keep them from rushing to my aid and give us some time away from town while I healed.

"I need a shower. If I ask you to come help me wash, are you going to freak out again when you get a glimpse of my back?" I teased.

Alexei sat up, pulling me back with a hand in my hair so he could look into my face, his eyes bouncing between mine.

"Why are you being so dismissive about this? You were assaulted. Badly. You might have scars because I was so distracted I didn't notice my enemy was within touching distance of my mate, of my fucking pack."

"Okay. One – no more blaming yourself. Kind of getting on my nerves. Got it? Two – I hadn't planned on talking about this shit until we were all in the same room so I didn't have to say it more than once, but this isn't the worst I've been hurt by an alpha." His mouth popped open as his brows slammed together, but I slapped my hand over his lips to stop him. "I'll tell you everything when we're all in the same room. And you and Wolf will tell us everything. I think there might have been a few things you left out when you promised us your job wouldn't be a danger to any of us. And no– " I shook my head when he started talking against my hand that was still firmly pressed against his lips. "I still don't blame you. You can't control another person's actions."

Finally pulling my hand free, I replaced it with my lips, then pulled back. "Any chance you have a shirt down here since you ruined Wolf's?"

A sheepish look crossed his face as he glanced down at my naked body, lingering where we were locked together by his knot. I might be sore down there later, but fuck me, it was so worth it.

"I don't. But the elevator is private, so no one will see you but the pack. And we've all seen that beautiful body before."

Except it wasn't covered with marks that made everyone look at me with a mixture of rage and pity. The rage, I was fine with. I felt the same emotion. The pity was getting on my nerves. Everyone tiptoeing around me and demanding I rest was driving me nuts. I just wanted to go back to normal.

"I promised Spence I was done with the VIP room. And I think I might be done with fetish nights all together." Just because violence wasn't something new to me didn't mean I wouldn't experience a level of PTSD any time I heard the sound of something hitting flesh.

"Wolf and I make more than enough to keep all of us comfortable. And if you get bored sitting around the house or taking Spence shopping, you could find a part time job to occupy yourself. I'm just saying you don't have to work. Unless you want."

He was rambling. And it was so fucking cute.

Pressing a kiss to his lips, I shimmied and was relieved when I was able to lift from his deflating knot. But now we were both covered in cum.

"Okay. No clothes. How about a towel to clean up before we head back upstairs?"

CHAPTER 27

<u>Wolf</u>

Eventually, there was going to be a path worn into the marble of the foyer. I'd started watching the camera feed on my phone the moment the doors had closed behind me when I'd left Kennedy and Alexei, making sure Alexei was at least aware Kennedy wasn't a threat.

And then I'd continued to watch like a fucking voyeur when Kennedy had straddled his lap, telling myself I was just making sure Alexei wouldn't lose himself and slam her onto her back and settle between her thighs.

Once they began to talk and Alexei started up the apologies, I turned off my phone and resumed the pacing.

As much time as I'd spent with Rey and even Spencer, I hadn't spent nearly enough with Kennedy. I adored the little beta.

Yet I'd neglected her because I'd become so addicted to Rey's tendency to allow me to dominate her or to switch when I needed to release control.

Spencer was the perfect snuggle partner and gave one hell of a blowjob.

Kennedy…I'd been treating her as though she was nothing more than my buddy's girlfriend, almost like she was nothing more than an afterthought. And yeah, I felt as though I was just as much to blame for the injuries she was sporting as Alexei felt he was.

I hadn't paid enough attention to the alphas in the club. I hadn't paid attention to who was making their way down the hallway for time in the VIP room.

Because I'd been too busy ogling Kennedy and whispering promises into Rey's ear of what I planned to do to her later.

It could have been so much worse.

Alexei had made a trip back to the club while we'd forced Kennedy to rest so she could heal. As a beta, she didn't have the increased healing alphas and omegas did. It was literally the only reason I wished she had a different designation – I wanted my sweet girl to heal. I hated seeing her in pain, no matter how hard she tried to hide it.

"Instead of hovering like a weirdo, why don't you make some lunch for them? Or run a bath. Or just, you know, sit down and pretend you didn't just watch them fuck on the gym floor," Spencer teased as he snuggled into Rey's side.

My cheeks burned and I turned my back on him.

Couldn't run a bath. Her wounds that were beginning to heal shouldn't be soaked in oils or salts or whatever women used in their baths. But I could definitely get some clean clothes ready for Kennedy and make them some lunch.

It was good to see Alexei returning to his normal, calm, and steady self. I'd sparred with him last night. And by sparred, I'd deflected his blows when he'd attacked me for entering the gym as another alpha in his space. Or maybe it was because I'd carried Kennedy's scent after checking on her and making sure she was comfortable.

Alexei had barely spent more than a few seconds at a time with her since we'd brought her home a couple nights ago. And I knew it had everything to do with his wrongly placed sense of guilt.

Had Kennedy been an omega, she would have been an emotional mess with Alexei's distance. But not only was our girl a beta, she was strong as hell and stubborn.

Pulling ingredients from the fridge and cabinets, I made some warm soup and garlic bread, then hurried into the bedroom to lay out clean clothes for both Kennedy and Alexei.

I stepped back into the kitchen to pull the garlic bread from the oven just as the elevator doors slid open and the two stepped into the foyer, Kennedy's cheeks pink as she shuffled naked through the house.

"You should definitely run like that more," Spencer said, leaning over the side of the couch to watch her. "I love watching your ass jiggle."

"For fuck's sake, Spence," Rey said around a giggle.

"What? She's got an amazing ass."

That she did. Sure, I'd noticed the beta's beautiful body. And of course I'd noticed how pretty she was. But I'd kept my distance for Alexei's sake when he'd shown obvious signs of obsession. And yeah… I'd been just as obsessed with the beautiful female alpha who was watching my every move, who winked at me when she caught me watching.

Her brows raised and I frowned in confusion.

Rey jerked her head toward the hallway.

With a tilt of my head, I turned off the burner and set the tray of bread on the stovetop before moving closer to Rey.

"Go check on them. I can tell your alpha is all over the place. You need to make sure you're level, too. Can't have two of you going all feral with only me, Spence, and Kennedy to keep you calm."

My frown grew deeper. "How the hell are you so calm?"

She shrugged and kissed the top of Spencer's head. "My omega ate me out while you were downstairs with Kennedy and Lex. Took the edge off."

A burst of perfume exploded from the omega at the mere mention of tasting his alpha.

Yep. Our omega was getting close to his cycle. And Kennedy was far from ready to be involved in a heat induced orgy.

Adjusting my boner at the mere thought of both Spencer's head buried between Rey's thighs and fucking Spencer from behind while Rey locked his cock, I inhaled deeply through my nose and blew it out in a rush.

"He's going to fucking attack me again," I grumbled.

But she was right. I needed to check on them to keep my alpha instincts in check. Sure, I could always ask Spence for the same favor, but that would only last so long before the need to protect and provide for my pack overrode everything else.

It was so different with Rey. She was an alpha, too. And Spence was practically glued to her side, so I rarely felt the need to protect him, as though my alpha knew he always had a protective bubble around him.

But with Kennedy, she not only worked to provide for the pack – before Alexei and I came along – but tended to end up behind closed doors with strangers, with alphas whose appetites could run on the darker side. And had been severely injured because of that.

I'd heard her promise Spence she was done with that side of the job. But I wanted her to be home with Spence. I wanted to be the one to provide for my pack, to provide for my omega and beta. Well, me *and* Alexei.

And I preferred the idea of Rey staying home with them so my alpha was always reassured there was another who could keep them safe while Alexei and I were out playing judge, jury, and executioner.

Fuck. What the hell was going on with me? It was like between Spencer's approaching heat and Kennedy's assault, my alpha was reverting to a more primal state.

"Hey," I said as I stepped into the room.

For the briefest moment, Alexei stepped between me and Kennedy, but her small hand landed on his arm and shoved him to the side. Well, he *allowed* her to shove him, being as he was nearly twice her size.

"We're not doing that, mate," she said, rubbing her cheek along his arm and earning a rusty sounding purr from Alexei.

"I made you guys some lunch. And, uh, set out some clean clothes." I jerked my chin toward the clothing sitting on the bed.

Although now that I was looking at what I'd chosen, I realized she might not be able to wear the underwear or leggings yet. And since Alexei had destroyed the shirt she'd been wearing – *my* shirt – she would have to borrow another of ours if she wanted something big enough to cover her naked body without flashing the room her ass.

Kennedy lifted the clothes and wrinkled her nose, setting them back down and pulling a blanket around her shoulders instead.

"Sorry. I didn't think about…that. But I made soup. And garlic bread. I'll keep it simmering if you two want to shower first."

Her ebony brows drew together and her eyes narrowed. "What's going on with you? Why are you acting so weird?"

Alexei's arms were crossed over his chest as he watched me as though I was a threat to his beta.

To *our* beta. She didn't carry my mark. We hadn't been intimate. Yet she was still my packmate.

"My alpha is…"

"Going crazy?" she offered with a smirk. "At least you didn't try to kill the punching bag downstairs."

Huffing out a laugh, I shrugged and shoved my hands into my pockets.

A growl began to rattle up Alexei's chest the longer I stood there staring at Kennedy.

But that was better than him full on attacking me like he had downstairs. One step at a time and all that.

"Anyway. Shower or dress or whatever. Then come out and eat."

"Yeah. We all need to have a pack meeting. You two have some shit to discuss and so do I."

With a nod, I walked backward, my attention on Alexei. Part of me worried he might attack me from behind if I gave him my back. The dude wasn't in his right mind, not since Kennedy's assault.

I got it. I really did. I wasn't nearly as close to the beta and even I was feeling murderous.

Pulling the door closed behind me, I stood with my hands on my hips and stared at the door. What the fuck was going on with me? I got the whole protective, possessive issue with my alpha, but I felt unsteady.

I was never unsteady. I didn't get nervous. Or at least I didn't allow anyone else to see my nerves. Or any emotion, for that matter.

Except Rey. She saw me at my worst several times and fully accepted me.

At least we had the full pack in the penthouse and could ensure their safety while they were here. And neither Alexei nor I were joking when we'd brought up having a house built specifically for the pack with top-of-the-line security including a tall enough fence surrounding the property to deter anyone who might think about attacking our home.

The low murmurs of Kennedy and Alexei talking made their way through the door followed by the sound of the shower starting.

And I was still standing outside the door like a fucking weirdo.

"Do you want to fuck her?" Spencer asked from behind me and actually startled me.

How the fuck had the omega crept up on me without me noticing?

"It's not that," I said. Or at least it wasn't completely that. I felt this need to solidify the bond with her, to prove to her and my alpha that we could keep her safe.

Moving away from the door, I returned to the kitchen and turned the burner on low to keep the soup warm, then joined Rey on the couch. She patted her leg. With a smile, I laid down, resting my head in her lap and purred as she ran her fingers through my hair, her nails scraping my scalp.

"It's because of the assault. Our alphas have all become more possessive over another alpha hurting her. It might be time to mark her," she said, staring down into my face.

"That doesn't piss you off? Or make you jealous?"

"Oh, please. Like she has any right to be jealous over sharing either of us," Spencer said, helping himself to a bowl of soup before the rest of us even made it to the table.

I'd been banging Rey for months and had only recently begun to play with Spencer when he joined me and Rey.

And honestly, I had no idea whether I'd kept my distance from Kennedy for Alexei's sake, for fear of pissing off or hurting Rey, or because I feared Kennedy might reject me.

But marking her didn't exactly mean I needed to spear her with my dick.

I could wait. I could wait until Spencer's heat, wait until she was lost to the pheromones of her omega to sink my teeth into her flesh.

"No. It wouldn't piss me off or make me jealous. We're pack. She's just as much your packmate as Spence or me." Although I hadn't marked either of them, either.

What the fuck was I waiting for? Why did I keep waiting for the other shoe to drop?

Oh. Right. Because of shit like what happened at the club. Because of the fear of fully attaching myself to this pack then having them ripped away from me.

We needed to end this threat. And I needed to find a way to form a closer bond to Kennedy and finally mark Spence and Rey.

But first, I needed to convince myself and my alpha that I could and would protect this pack, even if I had to sacrifice my own life to do it.

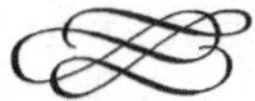

Alexei

Kennedy had pulled on one of my t-shirts after our shower together. I'd rubbed my cheek along her face, her neck, even her torso to cover her with my scent.

It wasn't enough. My alpha was fucking unstable.

I'd made a trip to *Plumes et Fouets* and gained access to the security footage throughout the club from the moment they opened until the moment we all hurried Kennedy from the club.

I saw the moment Mikhail and his asshole buddies showed up about thirty minutes before us. He hadn't done as I had and slipped the hostess money under the table to be seated at Kennedy's table. Did that mean he hadn't truly known about my connection with Kennedy until he'd seen me practically drooling over her during her performance? Had I been the one to put the fucking bull's eye on her?

I'd watched from various camera angles as Mikhail kept his face turned away from my table and noted the moment he'd zeroed in on

Kennedy. I watched as he beckoned over a member of the staff to reserve time with her in the VIP room.

I watched as my mate was escorted from the stage and down the dark hallway, and watched as Mikhail and his buddies leaned their heads toward each other before stepping through the door.

The security split the camera views for me and I watched with horror as two others stationed themselves outside the door while Mikhail and two men I recognized from my time with the Gusevs stayed inside with Kennedy.

My stomach turned and my vision blurred with a red hue as I forced my eyes to stay glued to my mate being beat over and over with the cane. The sounds of her screams would stay with me until the day I died.

This was where we'd all been leery of whether Mikhail or his father had people in position in the club. But security had tried to get inside and had been blocked by the Bratva members long enough that Kennedy had endured skin tearing lashes.

I had spent a few moments here and there checking on my mate, but I feared staying too near her for too long. I feared being too near our omega, either. I bordered on feral at all times and didn't want to rut Spencer or my beautiful beta simply because my alpha was losing control and blood lust was overwhelming every other thought and emotion coursing through me.

Because of the separation, my alpha had attacked Wolf simply because he'd been close to Kennedy, because she'd been wearing his shirt and covered in his scent.

Mine. She was mine.

Even now as she sat curled on her side with her head in my lap, and her feet on Rey's, I fought the urge to growl at the female alpha for touching my beta.

She wasn't only mine. She was *ours*. Wolf and I had joined *her* pack. We had been welcomed into *her* life. I had to remind both sides of myself of that little fact over and over until I could get my shit under control.

Kennedy held the phone to her ear, listening to something her father said on the other line. He'd finally called her back. And it wasn't lost on any of us that she hadn't bothered to mention what had happened to her at work.

"I'm aware of that. But we have our own little issue that has risen here, and I need to—no Dad, I don't need you to send anyone. I just want your permission to give them enough background to explain a few aspects of, uh, my personality," she said, shrugging her shoulders at Rey when she shook her head.

Personally, I felt she should tell her dad everything. Since he didn't live in the area, she might be safer with him until we could neutralize the threat of the fucking Gusev Bratva. No matter how much my heart would ache with the distance.

As I watched her struggle to explain her situation without giving away too much, my patience was ground to nothing.

Reaching down, I snatched the phone from her hand and put it to my ear. "This is Alexei Potrov. I am one of Kennedy's alphas," I said as an introduction.

"You're the alpha who saved my baby's life," a gruff voice said over the line.

"Yes, sir," I said, assuming he meant the night we met. Which meant she'd told him some of the details and he hadn't demanded she keep her distance from me. "What your daughter isn't telling you is someone from my past assaulted her at her place of employment. Her omega and first alpha are confused as to why she's not–"

Kennedy yanked the phone from my hand and released a growl that could have rivaled Rey's.

"Sorry about that, Dad," she said, frowning at me as she pushed to a seated position, lines of pain etched into her beautiful face. "I just need your permission to give them – I'm fine. I promise. Nothing close to what I experienced in the past…that's what I mean. I haven't really told Rey and Spence anything about our past. But I need your permission in case the club comes up…I said I'm fine. I mean, I'll probably have some interesting scars, but nothing is broken and I didn't need any stitches…actually, we might. I'll talk to you about that later. And we might be making a road trip to come visit soon."

At least she'd come up with that on her own so I didn't have to request she leave the state in case I started a fucking gang war in the middle of downtown.

"No. We're at the alphas' penthouse for now. They felt it was more secure...some Russian asshole. Assholes. But only one of them...Dad!" Her eyes flicked to mine, and her frown increased. Now I was beginning to understand why she'd tried to avoid telling him that little tidbit. "I have three alphas and my omega here to take care of me. I don't think Ghost or Poe will have any interest in bringing me breakfast in bed or cleaning my booboos."

My alpha bristled at the thought of anyone else coming near her just yet.

"I will. I promise. I love you, Dad."

A second later, she ended the call and turned a glare on me.

"I did not want him to know about that, Lex," she said, using Wolf's nickname for me. "Now he's going to be freaking out. Don't be surprised if the doorman lets you know a dozen long-haired bikers have filled the fucking lobby in a couple hours."

Pushing to her feet, she began to pace, her scent turning from sweet to tart as her anxiety and anger spiked.

"Well? Can you tell us whatever secret you've kept from us for the past couple years?" Spence teased.

Actually, when I turned to look at him, his expression didn't match his teasing tone. He looked...pissed? Hurt? I wasn't sure.

And now I was torn between calming my beta and calming whatever was causing my omega's sweet apple pie perfume to change to a sour fruit smell.

Rumbling tore from my chest unbidden, and Kennedy whirled on me, her finger pointed directly at me.

"Knock it off. I get it. You blame yourself. Your alpha is trying to go feral again. Blah, blah, blah. We've all had a few bad days. Get over it."

For a few tense seconds, it felt as though no one so much as breathed.

And then a loud guffaw exploded from Spencer. Within seconds, Rey and Wolf were chuckling right along with him.

"Fuck. Sorry," I said, rubbing the back of my neck.

No one else in this room had seen the videos. They hadn't heard Kennedy's screams of pain. And if it were up to me, they never would. The echoes of those screams constantly playing in my head was part of what kept my alpha on the edge of rut.

But I had to find a way to keep my shit together. Because Kennedy was right. I had heard and seen that shit, but she'd been the one to suffer the pain. She still suffered, even if she didn't let any of us see it. I was making all this about me like a total fucking asshole.

"Would a blowjob calm you down? It worked that first night," Spencer said, earning another round of chuckles and finally a smile from me.

"Not right now. Maybe later."

"There he is," Spencer said. "Missed you, alpha."

I huffed a laugh and rolled my eyes. I had been in and out of the penthouse, but he was right – I'd not only been physically absent but mentally and emotionally, as well.

Spreading my knees, I patted my leg and held out my arms. "Would it hurt too much to let me hold you?" I asked.

She crossed the room and gingerly lowered onto my lap, shifting until she was comfortable. "Just don't squeeze," she said, leaning forward and pressing a kiss to the tip of my nose.

"Okay. So tell us the secret. And then the two of you have a lot of shit to spill," Spencer said, wagging a finger between Wolf and me. "I've been as patient as possible for the past two days," Spencer said.

Rey snorted. "You've been anything but patient."

Wolf stood and left the room, returning with arms full of blankets. He draped a fuzzy one over Kennedy's exposed legs, and I forced a thankful smile on my face instead of growling at him like my alpha wanted to.

Another was draped over Spence while the rest was set aside in case they were needed. I'd never seen Wolf act as though he wasn't sure what to do with himself, as though he was lost.

Put a gun in the alpha's hand and the fucker was a cyborg. But we now had three packmates to protect, one of whom had already been injured simply because she was acquainted to us. He might not be going feral, but he was obviously feeling out of sorts.

Rey had been reluctant to give Kennedy her blessing to court us. We'd given her our guarantee that we weren't a risk to the pack.

And we had fucking lied.

Not we. *Me.* Kennedy was in pain, had been brutally assaulted simply because she was connected to me.

And I would find a way to eliminate the threat, and then spend the rest of my life proving to the pack I could protect them. I would keep them safe, no matter how much money I had to spend, no matter how many guards I needed to hire, no matter how many alarms and cameras I needed to put in place to ensure no one ever got close to my beta or any of my packmates ever again.

CHAPTER 29

<u>Kennedy</u>

I was still livid that Alexei had taken it upon himself to give my dad the details of what happened. No matter how much I tried to ease my dad's concerns, I wouldn't be surprised if they all made a trip this way instead of waiting for us to visit them.

"Spill," Spencer said, shifting so he could lean against Alexei's side and run his fingers along my exposed legs.

As much as I loved my omega's touch, I knew he was soothing himself. Were I in better shape, I would have turned onto my side and let him line himself along my back, let him hold me as much and for as long as he needed.

"There's not much to tell. I grew up as the daughter of the president of Inland Kingsmen. It's a biker club."

"You're the daughter of a one percenter?" Wolf said, his brows drawn together.

Raising a hand, I stopped him. "No. At least never say that to anyone or in front of my dad." I chuckled. Sure, they might have done a lot of the same shady shit as some of the more well-known clubs, but my dad had made sure they stayed under the cops' radar from the beginning.

"Do you ride?" Rey asked.

"I can. I haven't in a long damn time, but I can still ride, yeah."

"That's kind of hot," Spencer said, his fingertips raising to skim the inside of my thighs.

Lowering my chin, I raised a brow at him.

With an unrepented smirk, he shrugged and continued teasing my upper thighs so close to my sex that I had to struggle to keep my thoughts straight.

"What? I can smell you this close. And I haven't had sex in–"

"An hour?" Rey teased.

"Excuse me. *You* got off. *I* didn't."

I huffed a laugh and rolled my eyes.

"Anyway," I said with a shake of my head. "The shit that happened the night I met Alexei didn't emotionally scar me because I've seen worse. Although I've never witnessed it that close. And this," I said, pointing over my shoulder, "isn't freaking me out because I stupidly thought I was in love with a prospect who beat the shit out of me on a regular basis."

"Your father didn't kill that mother fucker?" Alexei said as a growl rumbled from his chest.

"Only after he found out. Charger and I lived off the compounds in a mobile home. When I stopped coming around, he would make excuses that I wasn't feeling well or was out shopping or whatever. But my dad sent a couple enforcers over to check on me when I stopped answering my phone. I couldn't answer because my cock-sucker boyfriend destroyed it during one of his rages," I explained when Spencer frowned up at me. "Two of my dad's guys had grown up in the club with me and found me barely conscious on the bedroom floor. I was taken to the hospital. When I was taken back to the trailer to pack my shit, there was a lot of blood in the house but no more Charger."

"I hope your dad tore him to fucking pieces," Wolf said, his growl matching Alexei's.

I was mildly surprised Rey wasn't growling right along the other two alphas, but she looked more concerned than enraged.

"He never gave me the details, but there was a new grave deep in the woods surrounding the club's property. And I watched with nothing short of joy as several of my dad's men set fire to the trailer. It felt like watching the hell I'd gone through burned to the ground. And I decided that day to leave all my fear, all the PTSD, all of it in the ashes along with everything else that burned."

"How the hell–" Spencer started but cut himself off, his fingers no longer teasing the seam of my closed thighs. Tears shimmered in his eyes.

With my beautiful omega so close to his cycle, his emotions had been on a rollercoaster. I was sure finding out his beta had been beat nearly to death by someone who was supposed to love her so soon after finding me a sobbing, painful mess at work wasn't doing him any favors.

"Seriously. I'm fine. Yeah, it took me years to be able to trust any alpha who wasn't family. But my dad made sure I went through therapy. He didn't give a shit that some might think there was a stigma around it. My dad…he's fucking amazing."

"Your mom?" Wolf asked.

"Momma died when I was pretty young. She was a beta, too. He never sought another mate. I was raised by my dad and the club."

"Explains why you're such a bad ass," Spencer said, his sweet scent back to normal as his fingers were once more teasing my thighs.

"I'm not sure about bad ass. But I've been through hell and survived. I've always figured as long as I didn't die, I could survive just about anything."

Except losing any of my packmates. I was pretty sure that would kill me. Or at least render me emotionally dead.

"So that's it. That's my big secret. It was never that I didn't trust you two with it," I said, locking eyes first with Spence then Rey. "But it wasn't solely my secret to tell. My dad likes to stay as far under the radar as possible. He has never wanted the Kingsmen to be some big, famous club. All that does is put a spotlight on their less…savory activities."

Wolf huffed a laugh and shook his head. "You said they're out of town?"

"Yeah. They're based in Iowa."

"You're a cornfed girl?" Spencer teased as his fingers slid between my thighs a little more.

I clamped them together hard enough he gasped. It wasn't that I wouldn't have loved to spread myself on the couch and let my omega help me forget about the past few days, but there was still more conversation to be had. As in, our two new alphas needed to tell us exactly what kind of bullshit we were up against.

Well, that, and it still hurt to lie on my back or even sit for prolonged periods.

"Cock blocker," Spencer grumbled before removing his hand and sitting up, still keeping a hand on my shin.

"Alright, boys. Your turn."

"Can we talk about your dad for another second?" Alexei asked, dipping his chin to look into my face.

"Is this your way of avoiding the subject?"

His head wagged side to side. "I promise to tell you everything. But…there might come a time when it would be safer for the three of you to spend some time with your family."

"Bull shit," Spencer said.

My brows shot up my forehead as I glanced at him.

"He's trying to send us away so he can fight the Russian mob alone. Not happening. We're pack now. Even if two of you haven't bothered to mark me. Oh, and one of you is avoiding our beta for some unknown reason." He cut his eyes to Wolf, who blushed a bright pink and shifted in his seat.

There was so much in that accusation that would need to be addressed later.

But for now…

"I'm with Spence. We're not leaving the two of you to take on a bunch of mobsters or whatever Russian mafia guys are called."

Wolf snorted as he tried to hold in a laugh.

"Bratva," Alexei said. "The Russian Bratva. Similar to the Italian Mafia."

"Except they're usually military trained," Wolf muttered.

My eyes widened as I turned my face up to Alexei for confirmation. My alpha was too busy glaring at Wolf to look at me.

"What the fuck does that mean?" Rey asked, sitting up straight and turning her head to look from Alexei to Wolf then back again. "What the fuck are we up against?"

We. She was absolutely correct to use that term. Because we were a pack. I might only carry Rey's and Alexei's marks, but Wolf was as much my packmate as the rest. And if someone fucked with one of us, they got all of us.

And no, I wasn't above calling my dad for help. I knew he would have zero issue with either all five of us spending some time there while we came up with a plan or sending in some reinforcements. But no way would I leave Wolf and Alexei to fight this battle on their own.

Alexei inhaled deeply and started talking.

"I was raised in Russia–"

"Duh," Spencer said. I poked him in the side to shut him up.

"My parents died when I was a child." His eyes landed on mine.

"So…no going to meet mommy and daddy," I said. We'd joked about that early on and he hadn't bothered to reveal the tiny fact that he was technically an orphan.

And I couldn't say I was overly thrilled he'd hidden that fact, but I hadn't exactly been open with any of them about my past, either.

"I was taken in by Dima Gusev. Raised as brother to Mikhail since I was twelve. I was trained by Dima's men, trained to be a member of his crew. My first kill was at his order. My first dollar was earned by working for him. And then I watched in horror as his Bratva set fire to the house of an enemy. An entire family, the enemy, his wife, and three young children screamed in terror and burned to death."

My heart began to pound painfully in my chest. Pushing to a more seated position, I shifted onto my hip and leaned back against Spencer so I could look into Alexei's face as he spoke.

It wasn't that I didn't want to touch him. It was that I feared my own changing scent and rising emotion would affect him all over again. And the last thing we needed at the moment was any single member of this pack losing their shit when we all needed to come together.

"When everyone loaded into the SUVs, I couldn't see anything but the house in flames. The screams of those kids...just fucking babies." His gaze looked far away as though the memories were coming to life right there in the fancy penthouse living room.

"What happened after?"

"I waited until everyone turned in for the night or went out partying. Packed my shit. Bought a plane ticket to the states. Caught Wolf waiting in my motel room to kill me."

"What?!" Rey, Spence, and I all barked out at once.

Wolf chuckled. "Yeah. All I had was a name and location. Knew nothing about him."

"How...you didn't kill him," I said, nothing short of gratitude and relief coursing through my system.

"He put up a hell of a fight. After we wore ourselves out, we actually took a few minutes to talk and I learned the Bratva put a hit on him for being a traitor and walking away. Wasn't quite enough of a reason for me to take a life. I only kill monsters," Wolf explained.

"Thank fuck for that," Spencer muttered.

"So how the hell did that dude find you?" Rey asked, leaning forward and resting her elbows on her knees.

She'd been calm when Alexei and I had returned from the downstairs. Now...she looked as though she was fighting her own alpha's need for blood.

"That I don't know. But they tracked me. A few of them moved here, I assume to set up operations in the state on behalf of Dima. Mikhail has been texting me on behalf of his father, demanding I return to the family. We ran into him at Prada," he said, jerking his chin toward Spencer.

I only knew bits and pieces of that day, including running into an old acquaintance of Alexei's and how Spence had immediately picked up on the bad mojo. But I'd all but forgotten about it after finding out about the two finally connecting in an extremely erotic way in the dressing room.

"I'm used to the threats. Mikhail and I were both trained through blood and pain. Threats were the only love language Dima Gusev knew. We fell in line, or we were beat to a pulp on a regular basis."

I was only a beta and now I wanted to hunt down this Dima asshole and shove my foot so far up his ass he would taste the rubber of my soles.

"I don't know how they ended up at *Plumes et Fouet*. But I think he had intended to go after Spencer until he noticed my interest in you, realized it would be easier to get to you than my omega," he said, turning to look me in the eye. "And I'm so fucking–"

"Ugh!" I growled out. "Stop. Seriously. How the hell were you supposed to know that would happen?"

"Because he'd said more than once he would destroy anything and anyone I loved. And since he knew he didn't have a chance in hell of taking out Wolf, he went after you."

"Better me than Spencer," I blurted out.

My omega sat up straight, his auburn brows pulled together so tightly I worried the crease between them would be permanently etched into his beautiful face.

"The fuck is that supposed to mean?"

"It means I'm just a beta. And you're the one who's going to give our pack babies. And I'm used to...well, violence. Yes. It hurt. Still hurts. And it scared me when the security didn't get through those doors, but–"

Spencer waved his hands in the air, that frown still in place. "Are you seriously trying to pretend I'm more important than you because of my designation? Do you not hear how fucked up that sounds? Like, at any point when that thought ran through your mind, did you think 'huh, that's kind of fucked up'?"

Well, shit. The last thing I'd intended was to piss off my omega.

Although…the longer I looked into his glassy eyes, the more I realized he was hurt. Scared. And maybe a touch betrayed.

Pushing past the pain, I moved closer to him until I could press myself into his side. "I'm not saying you're weak. I'm just saying…shit. I don't know. Can you say you would change things and been the one in that room instead of me?"

"Well, yeah. You're my fucking girl. I love you."

"And you're my love. I'm glad it was me. And I'm glad it's over."

"For now," Rey pointed out. "Until they either figure out we're here and find a way into the building or they wait us out. Because face it, we can't hide out here for the rest of our lives."

Tears still glimmered in Spencer's eyes, but he hugged me tightly and I bit the inside of my cheek against the pain. Honestly, I needed his touch as much as he needed to hold me.

Alexei and Wolf stared at each other as though they were having a silent conversation. And it was grating my already frayed nerves.

"Do you have a plan or not?" Spence said.

I turned my face up and noted the pinched expression.

"You okay?" I whispered.

He nodded but didn't say anything. But his perfume had definitely grown stronger over the past few days.

It was selfish of me, but I kept hoping his biology would hold off just a little longer so I could actually be there for him when his heat hit. But it didn't look like we had much time left.

"We're working on it," Wolf said, but he looked about as convinced that everything was under control as I felt.

"How about we talk about the immediate future? As in, the next few weeks. Spence is close to his cycle. Is the nest ready?" Rey asked, ever the prepared and dutiful alpha.

"It's stocked with pillows and blankets," Alexei said.

"I can head back to your house for more of his personal items to put in there to keep his omega as steady as possible," Wolf offered.

"Clothes," Spence said, moving beneath me as though he couldn't get comfortable.

"You want me to get some of your clothes?" Wolf asked with a confused frown.

"Your clothes."

Shit. His eyes were a little unfocused and he was growing warm under my touch.

"You want our clothes in there? Our scents?"

"Yes," Spence said, dragging me closer until I couldn't hold back the whimper of pain when his arms banded around the more tender wounds across my back. He loosened his hold and tears welled in his eyes again.

"Is there a TV in the nest? I think Spencer and I should go hang out in the dark and binge some rom coms for a while."

A soft whimper tore from his lips.

"I'll bring one in," Alexei said, pushing to his feet. "And grab some of our clothes to add to the blankets."

"I'll head to your house and grab some of his stuff from the nest," Wolf offered, immediately moving toward the door and slipping his feet into shoes.

"You're not going alone," Rey said, following closely behind him.

I wanted Rey to stay here. And I knew Spencer would feel better with his alpha here, as well. But, like Rey, I didn't like the idea of anyone leaving the penthouse alone.

Pulling from Spencer's arms, I pushed to my feet and offered him a hand. "Let's go snuggle while we wait for everyone to join us."

His hand clenched his lower abdomen as he stood and let me lead him down the hallway in search of the nest. Alexei ended up having to show us which room since we'd only seen the space once. He set up the TV and started the streaming services, then headed out again.

By the time he returned with arms full of dirty clothes from each of us, I was lying on my side beside Spencer, my fist wrapped around his cock and slowly stroking him as the first small wave of heat began to hit him.

He wasn't fully in heat yet. It would be a few more hours before he would require either Rey, Wolf, or Alexei. But for now, at least I was able to bring one of the loves of my life a little relief.

CHAPTER 30

As much as I wanted to beat the shit out of Wolf and Alexei for keeping all this from us, I supposed I could understand. Besides, my own beta had been keeping secrets, too.

I guess they were all trying to protect us, all of us, in their own ways.

I'd grabbed the biggest duffel bags I could find, and Wolf and I shoved as much as would fit into them before hurrying back to the SUV.

It wasn't lost on me the way Wolf constantly checked his mirrors, like he was watching to ensure we weren't being followed to or from the penthouse.

"How did Mikhail know to find Alexei at the club?" I asked.

"He'd been spending nearly every night there since he killed that guy. Rookie fucking move. He became a stalker's wet dream the moment he laid eyes on Kennedy."

He chuckled, but the sound was humorless and there was no smile on his face.

"So then there's a chance he knows where you two live. Which means he'll know where to find Kennedy and Spence."

"And you," Wolf pointed out.

Turning a glare his way, I let a growl rumble up my chest. "How is it you constantly forget I'm an alpha, too?"

"An alpha who hasn't spent her life taking the lives of other people. I know you want to protect Kennedy and Spence, but I need you safe, too."

He reached over and laid a hand on my thigh, squeezing hard enough to hurt while sending heat coursing through me. I swore this asshole knew exactly how to distract me.

But this wasn't the time for distractions. I was still pissed. And now I was a little irked that he saw me as someone else he needed to protect.

Peeling his hand from my leg, I turned as much as my seatbelt would allow and ground my teeth as I struggled with my temper.

"You realize I protected my beta and omega long before you two big, bad men came into our lives."

"From other asshole alphas. Not from men who willingly kill anyone and everyone who get in their way and brush it off as nothing more than collateral damage."

Maybe he was trying to give me an out, make me feel better about his and Alexei's insistence that they be the main shields between my little pack and the rest of the world.

Opening my mouth to lambast him, Wolf held up a hand. "I'm not saying you're not an alpha. What I'm trying to say is those fuckers won't hesitate to put a bullet in your brain for no other reason to get to Alexei. They won't hesitate to take me out if they can get me alone. They'll rape you, Kennedy, even Spence as a way to torture Alexei. They're monsters. Evil fucks. And I would rather cut my own throat right here in the vehicle than let anyone hurt any of you."

"I get your protective instincts with me, even Spence. You barely talk to Kennedy. You only just stopped getting squirmy when either Spence or I brought up marking or fucking her."

A muscle feathered in his cheek and a vein bulged on his forehead.

"Do you not want her?"

"I didn't say that."

Staring at his profile, I noticed the way he refused to even glance in my direction.

"Then what is it? I already told you I wouldn't be jealous. And I know it wouldn't change anything between us."

I couldn't voice the words, but I was so fucking in love with Wolf it scared the shit out of me. Other than Spence and Rey, I didn't think I'd ever loved someone so much.

That muscle continued to jump in his cheek. His knuckles were white where he gripped the steering wheel.

"You're in love with her," I said as the pieces clicked into place.

His head whipped in my direction, his eyes slightly wide. "What?"

"You never touch her. You barely spend any time alone with her. But the moment she was hurt, you went all protective, possessive alpha. And trust me, I understand the feeling."

"I'm not…" He trailed and blinked a few times.

"You didn't even realize it. You've been putting so much distance between you and her for Alexei and, I assume, me, that you didn't realize how deeply you felt for her."

"You a shrink now or something?" he teased, glancing at me from the corner of his eye.

"I told you – I won't be jealous. We're pack. Don't you think if I'm okay sharing Spencer with you that I'd be okay if you're falling for my beta, as well? Besides, I don't blame you. She's fucking amazing."

I'd fallen for her quickly. She was so strong, so funny, and sexy as hell. But I tended to spend so much of my time and energy on our omega that even I had neglected her at times. Yet she never complained. She never whined about needing to be touched or held. She went to work over and over, exerted so much energy either on the silk ropes or tied down. She allowed strange men to play out dark fantasies for the extra money she made in the VIP room.

Fuck. At least she'd agreed to give up part of her job. I would rather she be home with Spence and me and let Wolf and Alexei bring home the paychecks.

I had no need to be a kept woman, but I preferred someone be home with my little pack. Especially now that we knew there was some evil, sick, twisted fucks out there who would harm them simply because they wanted Alexei to pledge fealty or some stupid shit.

"She's going to be down the next few days," I muttered barely above a whisper.

"We'll make sure she doesn't feel left out," Wolf said. "Even if she's only able to be there for Spencer, that should make them both feel better."

An omega tended to become overly emotional and extra clingy during their heat. My Spence would want all of us in the nest until it was over. So, even if Kennedy wasn't healed enough to be fucked silly by the omega or any of us, she could at least still be there, her scent would still combine with ours and keep his biology from sending him into a blubbering mess.

Wolf hoisted the duffels over his shoulder once we were parked in their reserved spot. After swiping his keycard and hitting the button for the penthouse, his eyes scoured the parking lot until the doors closed.

The moment the doors slid open to our temporary home, my alpha pushed to the surface and my core clenched at the heavy cloud of perfume saturating every inch of the penthouse.

"Holy fuck, he smells amazing," Wolf said, leading the way down the hallway and pushing through the door that led to a dimly lit space with a padded floor and walls.

Wolf froze in the doorway and I had to push around him. My body didn't create slick, but my pussy was instantly wet as I watched as Spencer slowly rose up and down on Alexei's cock, his hands cupping and fondling Kennedy's tits while she sat on Alexei's face.

And here Wolf and I were worried she wouldn't be able to enjoy the pleasure that came with an omega's cycle.

Spencer's sounds of pleasure tightened my core. When he picked up our scents, he turned his head and whimpered.

"Alpha," he begged, even as he continued to ride Alexei's stiff cock.

"I'm here, omega."

Dropping what was in my hands, I immediately began to remove my clothes. Perhaps we should have taken the time to bring a crap load of water bottles and snacks in with us, but Spencer's fucking perfume was like a damn tether tied straight to my pussy and reeled me in. For some reason, there were some who didn't realize a female alpha's need to breed her omega was as strong as a male's, even if we couldn't actually impregnate them.

Wolf upended the duffel bags and dumped the contents onto the floor near Spencer. He didn't appear to need any of that right now, but at least they would be close for when his omega needed soft and cozy.

Lowering to kneel between Alexei's knees, I pressed against Spencer's back, reached around, and wrapped my hand around his shaft, stroking him to the same rhythm that he rode Alexei.

His moans were like music to my ears.

When his head dropped back to rest against my shoulder, I got a perfect view of Kennedy's full tits and glimpses of Alexei's tongue as he lapped at her clit, her moans mixing with Spencer's.

This would be our first time through one of Spencer's heats as a new pack. And already, we'd fallen into a dance as though we'd rehearsed.

Within moments of taking Spence with my hand, he tensed, a long moan drawing from his lips as he spilled over my fist and onto Alexei's stomach. Alexei's hips began to thrust up faster before he finally grabbed our omega around the waist and pulled him down as he pushed up, locking Spencer onto his knot and filling him with his cum.

Kennedy fell over the ledge seconds later, crying out the sweetest, softest sound, her head thrown back, her long hair nearly brushing the top of Alexei's head.

"Wow," Wolf whispered as he lowered to the floor, his hand outstretched, his fingers combing through Kennedy's midnight black hair.

Yeah. Our beta was stunning when she came.

CHAPTER 31

<u>Wolf</u>

"**Y**ou're in love with her," Rey said.

Shock and confusion sped up my heartrate. "What?"

"You never touch her. You barely spend any time alone with her. But the moment she was hurt, you went all protective, possessive alpha. And trust me, I understand the feeling."

"I'm not..."

"You didn't even realize it. You've been putting so much distance between you and her for Alexei and, I assume, me, that you didn't realize how deeply you felt for her."

"You a shrink now or something?"

A small smile quirked up Rey's lips as she looked at me from the passenger seat. "I told you – I won't be jealous. We're pack. Don't you think if I'm okay sharing Spencer with you that I'd be okay if you're falling for my beta, as well? Besides, I don't blame you. She's fucking amazing."

· · ·

As Spencer dozed on the floor of the nest, his head cradled on Rey's boobs and Kennedy wrapped around his back, the conversation played in my mind.

Was I in love with Kennedy? I had been so focused on my obsession with Rey, with building a relationship with my omega, that I hadn't really even considered it. Besides, Alexei squandered nearly every minute of her free time when he wasn't on a job. The only time I'd spent with her had been as a pack or with Rey when Alexei and Spence had their first date.

The fact I felt something beyond unadulterated lust and respect for Rey had hit me like a fucking brick. Even after such a short time with her, I would never have imagined I was capable of feeling so strongly for someone as I did for Rey. Spencer had been a pleasant bonus and practically unavoidable when it came to feelings. The omega had a way of forcing himself into your life and your heart.

And then there was the beautiful beta with horrific bruising and healing lashes on her back.

Alexei was currently downstairs grabbing bottles of water and easy to eat snacks to get us through the day. But we all knew we would need far more than that once Spencer's cycle was in full swing. The past hour had only been a taste of what was to come. His temperature was only just rising, and the cramping had started a few hours ago.

The reprieve would be short. We all knew that. Which was why I had no intention of waking anyone up, even if I wanted to have a real conversation with Kennedy, to check on her wounds, to ask if she needed any painkillers.

The beta was probably one of the strongest women I'd ever met. No matter how much she wanted to pretend otherwise, I knew she was in pain, had noted every wince, every line of pain on her face when she'd joined us in the living room, when she'd demanded to see Alexei, when one of our pack tried to hold her.

Leaning onto my elbow, I reached forward and carefully lifted the curtain of coal black hair from her back and peered at Kennedy's injuries in the dim light. It had only been a few days, but already, some of the bruising had green and yellow shading around the edges as her body struggled to heal. Some of them were dark purple and black. Others were raised and an angry red in color from where the cane had ripped her soft flesh.

Breezing my fingertips over the raised ridges, a rush of rage burned through my veins. Guilt followed directly after.

Alexei blamed himself. But I was there, too. I knew who Mikhail was. I knew what he looked like and hadn't noticed him. I'd been whispering dirty promises of what I planned to do later into Rey's ear as I watched Kennedy bent over the table and spanked, her body twitching, her breathing heavy as the swats to her ass turned her on.

Either that or she was an amazing actress.

Even through the filtration system, Spencer's perfume wafted on the air and made my dick feel as though it would stab a hole directly through the crotch of my slacks. I was a lucky fucker who'd managed to land a pack with three of the sexiest creatures to exist.

Kennedy sighed and rolled slightly, glancing at me over her shoulder. "You okay?" she asked.

That fucking guilt grew. She had been injured because Alexei and I had been too distracted to notice the enemy was in the wire and she was checking on me.

Could Rey have been right? Could I have been falling in love with her and ignoring all the signs, refusing to acknowledge the feelings for fear of hurting Rey or Spence or pissing off Alexei?

"I'm fine. I was just checking your back."

She pulled her arms over her head and stretched, wincing slightly when the skin on her back pulled taut.

"We're going to find him. And we're going to kill him," I promised her, looking her directly in her beautiful blue eyes.

"I know," she said, giving me the softest smile. "Why aren't you resting?"

"You three put in the work. I haven't done anything yet."

She huffed a soft laugh, then turned to make sure she hadn't woken Spencer.

Carefully and slowly, she inched away from the omega's back until she could sit up. The worst of the damage had been on her back, but I knew her ass and thighs had to ache, too. Yet…she didn't bitch and complain, didn't demand we all wait on her hand and foot so she could lie around. In fact, she'd grown bored and wandered from the bedroom in one of my shirts.

And fuck me…she'd looked sexy as hell. I knew part of what had set Alexei off downstairs was the fact she was covered in my scent. He'd already been teetering on the edge and my alpha hormones on his beta had simply been the icing on the cake.

"He's going to need you three, though. You should rest while you can." Her dark brows drew together as she glanced at Rey and Spence then back up at me. "Where's Alexei?"

"Gathering supplies."

She nodded. "I guess that'll be my job this week."

She smiled and sounded as though she was trying to make light of the situation, but I could see the disappointment and sorrow in her crystalline eyes.

"Nah. He'll need you."

"Not much I can do, though. Besides, I'm the beta. My job is to take care of you guys and make sure everyone is calm." She rolled her shoulders and huffed a sardonic laugh. "Haven't been doing the greatest job of that lately."

"That has nothing to do with you," I said, reaching over and brushing my fingers through her hair, tucking it behind her ear so I could see her face clearly. "And your job is to simply be here. You know he'll be a mess if any of us are missing when his cycle fully hits."

She shrugged up her narrow shoulders, then drew her knees up to her chest, wrapping her arms around her shins. Laying her cheek on her knees, she looked me in the eyes.

"You're blaming yourself, too, aren't you?"

It was my turn to shrug.

"I only have so many ways of saying *it wasn't your fucking fault. Neither of you*," she said, lifting her head and widening her eyes as she enunciated each word as though I didn't speak the same language.

"Our job is to protect our pack. And neither of us noticed that cock sucker was mere feet from you and Spence. We failed."

"Oh, for fuck's sake," she grumbled, struggling onto her knees so she could crawl to me where she leaned forward and cupped my face in her small, warm hands. "There were half naked people all around the room, including your beta who happened to be within touching distance. Anyone would have been distracted by that. And there is strong security in place that failed because they obviously planned...something."

"Alexei watched the security footage. I don't think they were originally there for you. It appeared they were simply following Alexei. Maybe watching for a moment when they could get to Spencer."

She shuddered. "See? It could have been so much worse."

My mouth popped open. "How the fuck could it have been worse than you getting beat to a pulp by a fucking bamboo cane, Kennedy?"

Her shoulders rose and fell. "They could have taken our omega. They could have raped him. Impregnated him. Hell, they could have killed him simply to fuck with Alexei. And those are way worse than some bruises and scratches that will be completely gone in a week or two."

My gaze bounced between her eyes as her chest rose and fell with her anger. She downplayed what she'd gone through. In her eyes, she would have rather gone through the abuse than risk someone she loved.

As my eyes roamed her face and down to her bare breasts, I realized...Rey was right. I was falling in love with our beta. But I wasn't sure what to do with that. I would never step on Alexei's toes. And she didn't appear as though she was attracted to me. I could love her from a distance, as long as she was still in my life in some capacity.

I would continue to work my ass off to ensure she never had to step foot in that fucking club again. Alexei and I would build an impenetrable fortress of a house for our pack. And then, Spencer would eventually get his wish of filling every room with pups.

"What?" she asked after a few moments. "What's wrong?"

Shaking my head, I forced a smile as my hands tingled with the urge to reach forward and touch her. There was no doubt my hands – or mouth or cock – would be on her at some point over the next few days, but for now, I decided to clasp them in my lap.

"Just thinking."

She shivered lightly. The room was fairly warm, but she was still naked from the first mini round of Spencer's heat.

Reaching beside me, I grabbed a blanket and wrapped it around her shoulders. "Go back to sleep. Get some rest."

"Nah. I'm so tired of lying around. I'm going to see if Alexei needs some help."

When she swayed a little as she tried to stand, I lunged to my feet and helped her make her way over the cushioned floor, wrapping an arm gently around her back. I told myself it was merely to keep her from falling. But it was one way I could touch her without the hormones being in control.

Fuck. Would Alexei and I be able to control ourselves when it came to our beta when our alphas pushed to the forefront, when our hindbrains were in charge of our actions? I would rather take a punch to the junk than risk hurting the sweet beta.

A soft whimper tore from Spencer's mouth, but his eyes were still closed. He curled closer to Rey, his hips slowly moving forward as though his body was seeking relief even in his sleep.

This was going to be a hell of a week.

CHAPTER 32

<u>Kennedy</u>

By the time I'd caught up with Alexei, he was balancing a case of bottled water under one arm and a butt load of snacks in the other. He'd mainly grabbed bags of chips and pretzels, but we would need more than that within the next few days. My omega would need fruit or at least food with some nutrients to sustain his energy until the cycle broke.

"You and Wolf are getting on my nerves," I said as I grabbed some of the bags from his arms.

I'd kept the blanket wrapped around my shoulders when I went to help him gather stuff, but it was slipping when I wasn't holding on to the sides.

"What did I do now?"

I raised a brow at him. "You're both blaming yourselves for something that had nothing to do with you. Wolf told me it didn't look like I was the target. I was nothing but bait. How the hell were you supposed to know he'd do…all that," I said, waving a hand toward the general direction of my back.

"We should have been more observant. We'd had zero situational awareness. Had I been paying attention, I would have seen the son of a bitch sitting just a few tables away from you, away from my omega, away from my fucking pack. We both promised we weren't a danger to any of you and I delivered you straight to my biggest enemy's hands."

Releasing a growl of frustration, I tossed the bags to the ground and whirled on him. "Do I need to kick your ass to make you understand?"

He blinked a few times as his brows shot high up his forehead. "Excuse me?" The corners of his lips twitched as he fought a smile.

"Hey, I might be smaller than you, but I grew up around a lot of men – bikers, in case you forgot – and know exactly how to disarm a man of any size. And I know how to inflict enough damage to put your ass out of commission for days. Is that what you want? You want me to hurt you badly enough you'll have no choice but to sit and watch the rest of us take care of our omega?"

Alexei's body shook as a deep rumbling chuckle bubbled up his chest. "I love you so fucking much."

My heart stuttered in my chest as I stared up into his face wide-eyed. "What?" I whispered.

It was obvious we'd both grown strong feelings for each other fairly quickly. I might have said love at first sight, except I'd felt something for him before I'd even seen his eyes.

But neither of us had voiced those three huge words.

It took a second for Alexei to realize what he'd said. Then he blinked and his eyes grew nearly as wide as mine.

"Shit. I'd meant to say it in a more romantic way."

"You love me?"

"I'm so fucking in love with you, Kennedy. How do you not know that by now?"

I mean, I think I did know that. But…

"I love you, too," I whispered.

Alexei bent at the knees and lowered the case of water to the ground. As he straightened, he cupped the back of my head and tugged me closer so he could slant his mouth over mine, his tongue instantly dipping into my mouth to taste and tease.

His fingers tangled in my hair and tilted my head, deepening the kiss. I was so close to lunging at him like a flying monkey so I could wrap my legs around his naked waist and take him deep into my core.

Until a loud whine broke through the air.

We pulled apart at the same time, our breaths coming in short pants.

"Shit. Spencer," I said, bending to grab my abandoned load as Alexei did the same.

We hurried through the penthouse and down the hall to the nest. The door was open; Spencer's perfume was like a cloud of fucking temptation luring us inside.

A deep purr rattled from Alexei's chest as he stepped through the door, dropping the case on the ground near the entrance without hesitation.

Rey straddled Spencer's hips, slowly rising and falling on his cock, leaning forward and kissing him deeply. His whimpers were soft and needy. His fingers clutched at Rey, clutching her hips in a grip that would leave bruises, and tried to force himself up into her harder and faster. He wanted her lock. Needed it.

Only the alphas could give his body what it truly needed to chase away the worst of the heat symptoms.

"Alpha," Spencer moaned against Rey's lips.

"You want my lock?"

"Please, alpha. Please."

Setting my chips beside the water, I took a spot beside Wolf against the wall. He hadn't moved forward, wasn't intervening as Rey took this round. Depending on how much Spencer's hindbrain was in control, we would have another short reprieve, or one of the other alphas would need to take over and knot him, giving Rey a break.

I had always done what I could when it was the three of us, bringing him to release with my hands and mouth, letting him fuck me when Rey needed a break. There was something so addictive about the sweetness of my omega's cum on my tongue, though. And omegas tended to come a lot, especially during this time.

By the end of the week, Alexei or Wolf would need to call in professional cleaners to clear the cushions, pillows, and blankets of drying cum, sweat, and pheromones. As far as I knew, betas were the only designation who were able to run those types of companies without losing their ever-loving minds to their biology.

Spencer rolled them until he was settled between Rey's thighs and began to thrust his hips hard and fast, causing my beautiful alpha's perky tits to bounce. It had been so long since the two of us had simply enjoyed each other, both of us always doting on Spencer. But Rey was…

My alpha was a work of art. Stunning. Beautiful inside and out.

As I watched my first two packmates make love, I became overly aware of the heat from Wolf's body beside me. Leaning over, I pressed my shoulder against his and rested my head against his arm. He lifted his arm and gently draped it across my shoulders.

"Is this okay? Am I hurting you?" he asked.

A wistful smile was on my lips as I kept my gaze on my alpha and omega. "Aren't they perfect?" I said.

Wolf surprised me when he lowered his head and pressed a kiss to the top of my head. That was probably the most affection he'd shown me other than taking care of me the first couple days after the incident.

And that was how I preferred to refer to it instead of what my pack insisted on calling *the assault*.

Rey's moans grew louder until she threw her head back and cried out. The moment she locked around Spencer's cock, he practically howled, his hips now only making small movements as he continued to thrust through his own orgasm, spilling inside of his alpha.

After a few more seconds, he dropped onto her, holding his weight on his elbows and began to press kisses to her shoulders, her breasts, her lips.

He wasn't done. He'd just come inside of Rey and another wave was chasing the first.

This was it. Preheat was over and we were going headlong into our first heat as a full pack of five. And for the first time in years, Rey wouldn't have to carry the full brunt of it. She wouldn't be wrung out, exhausted and sore for at least a week after being the only true way of helping Spence through his pain.

His hips started rocking again, but he was locked into place until Rey's body released him.

"Alpha," Rey said, looking over Spencer's shoulder at Wolf.

He pressed another kiss to the top of my head, then pulled away from me, moving to settle himself behind Spencer.

My omega's whimpers grew louder when he couldn't get the relief he needed as waves of pain wracked his lower half. Even if he could stroke himself, it would bring him comfort, but a female's alpha lock was exactly that – a fucking lock. There was no way for him to pull away from her without hurting one or both of them.

Wolf tested Spencer's opening, sliding a finger through the slick coating his ass and thighs. Using the slick on his hand, he lubed the head of his cock to prepare himself to enter, then slowly pushed forward, breaching Spencer's ass slowly.

A long, guttural moan tore from my omega's mouth as Wolf pushed forward, filling and stretching him.

"You're taking your alpha so well, Spence," I said, crawling closer and running my fingers gently through his hair.

In the short time since I'd left him asleep to help Alexei carry supplies from the kitchen, Spencer's temperature had risen to feverish, and he was covered in a sheen of sweat. I hated how much he suffered during his cycles, but there was something so erotically beautiful about him in such a primal state when his body and mind wanted nothing more than to breed with his pack.

"You're so fucking beautiful," I said, pressing kisses to his temple and neck as Wolf began to push into him, slowly filling him before pulling back.

Sitting back on my haunches, I followed the line across Spencer's back to where he and Wolf were connected, then raised my eyes to find Wolf watching me, a look I couldn't decipher in his warm brown eyes.

Hormones. Alpha hormones were spurring him on, sending him into rut. And I was a naked woman. It was hunger in his eyes.

At least I assumed that was all I saw.

Spencer began to push back against Wolf as Rey's lock loosened, successfully fucking himself on Wolf's cock while sinking into Rey below him.

The chorus of grunts and moans heated my blood and made my pussy wet. I so badly wanted to join him, to sit on Rey's face, to beg Alexei to bend me over and take me hard and fast, to ease the pressure that was building from simply watching the carnal scene inches from my face.

But this was about taking care of our omega. Eventually, I would get a chance to ride Spencer. When my alphas needed a break, I would straddle his hips and take his dick deep inside of me. I would fuck him until I felt the heat of his release deep inside of me, until it spilled out to mix with the rest of the pack's that would eventually coat nearly every surface of the nest.

For now, I lowered a hand and pressed my fingers through my folds, toying with my clit to relieve some of the pressure. My eyes rose back to Wolf's face. His gaze was intent on my hand, zeroed in on where I stroked and fondled myself.

The two of us hadn't spent a single moment alone together. We'd forged a sort of roommate type relationship. He was in love with Rey. I was in love with Alexei. Well, and Spence and Rey.

But now, watching how loving and gentle he was with my original pack, something warmed in my chest for him. I was grateful for his presence, grateful that he wasn't simply pounding into Spencer as he chased his own release.

He was taking care of an omega the way an alpha was intended to do.

A gasp tore from my lips when his hand wrapped around the back of my neck and tugged me forward until his lips were pressed against mine in a bruising kiss, his tongue forcing itself into my mouth until I was practically melting against his chest.

My hands roamed his chest and abs, the feeling of his muscles bunching and releasing as he made love to my alpha doing nothing to calm the inferno building inside of me.

Hands gently trailed up my sides to cup my breasts. A warm body lined against my back.

Wolf tore his mouth from mine. "Careful," he said, his eyes over my chest.

Alexei. My Russian alpha was joining us instead of waiting on the sidelines. And I more than welcomed what I knew he could do to my body. Sure, he might have to be careful of my back, but he could easily take me from behind without hurting me.

One of his hands left my breast and trailed down my stomach to join my fingers in toying with my folds, my clit, before he inserted a finger into my entrance.

Wolf pulled me back so he could resume claiming my mouth. And that was exactly how it felt, as though he was placing his claim with his tongue, branding himself on me with nothing more than his kiss.

The blunt head of Alexei's engorged cock slid through my folds before pushing in, pulling a moan from my lips that Wolf happily swallowed.

As Alexei began to thrust into me, he pushed me further against Wolf and Spencer until my breasts were grazing my omega's back.

"Shit. Oh fuck!" Spencer cried out as Wolf began to pump into him faster, pushing Spencer's cock into Rey.

The scents of my pack built and combined and became a drug, making me feel as though I was having an out of body experience.

Or maybe it was simply the way Alexei knew exactly how to play my body like a fine-tuned instrument.

As the first waves of orgasm rippled through me, I tore my lips from Wolf's and threw my head back, crying out as my inner walls fluttered and clamped around Alexei. I wanted his knot. A beta's body wasn't made for an alpha's knot, but I'd grown addicted to the burning stretch of Alexei.

But he needed to save that for Spencer. Because once he locked himself inside of me, he couldn't help my omega, couldn't ease his suffering as each wave of his cycle crashed over him like a tidal wave.

"You're so fucking beautiful," Wolf muttered, his hand still gripping the back of my neck as Alexei took me from behind.

"Alpha. Please!" Spencer cried out.

I had no idea whether he was begging Rey or Wolf, but they both began to move, Rey's hips lifting as Wolf pounded hard and fast into Spencer.

Lowering my eyes, I watched as Wolf pushed forward, watched with nothing short of awe as Spencer's body stretched to accommodate the alpha's knot until his ass swallowed it and locked Wolf inside of him.

Wolf's hand dropped to my breast as he gritted his teeth, squeezed his eyes shut, and grunted, his muscles going tense and taut as he filled Spencer.

Rey followed seconds later, crying out Spencer's name as she fell over the edge, locking Spencer inside of her.

The three would be locked together for no less than ten minutes. At least their bodies released each other faster during heat cycles. Nature's way of ensuring successful breeding. It allowed the alphas to fuck their omegas over and over without having to wait the longer periods for their knots to deflate or their locks to release.

Alexei's hand tangled in my hair and began to pull until my back was against his front, his hips slapping against my ass.

"I want to knot you so badly," he whispered in my ear.

"Save it for Spence," I whispered back. "And you can knot me as many times as you want next week."

I winked at him over my shoulder and began to push back against him, urging him on, spurring his hips to slam into me so hard his knot actually stretched my opening with each push forward.

His hand tightened in my hair as he barked out his release, his teeth skimming over my unmarked shoulder as though tempted to bite me again. And I knew I wouldn't have voiced a single protest.

CHAPTER 33

<u>Alexei</u>

olf, Spencer, and Rey had rolled onto their sides the moment the omega began to relax and his eyes drooped. The three should no longer have been locked together, but no one had pulled apart, leaving Spencer inside of Rey and Wolf inside of Spencer.

I'd covered them with a couple of soft blankets, then pulled Kennedy until she was splayed across my chest, her legs straddling on either side of me while she used my shoulder as a pillow. Her breaths came in slow, steady pulls as she slept.

The TV was still on, colors flickering around the room, but the sound had been silenced at some point. I knew I sure as hell would much rather hear the sounds of pleasure that came from my pack-mates than any dumb ass TV show or movie.

Gently cupping the back of Kennedy's head, I craned my neck to check on the threesome. Something was different; something between Wolf and Kennedy seemed to have shifted.

And to be honest, I wasn't sure how I felt about it.

When I'd broached the subject of courting the pack, I'd meant it. I had truly been intent to combine our tiny packs, for all of us to truly become connected.

And then I'd watched as Wolf took Kennedy's mouth in what could be described as nothing short of a sensual as hell kiss. It wasn't alpha hormones that drove him. I'd seen him watching her, even before she'd crawled over to dote on her omega. I'd seen his eyes on her as he'd pushed his dick into Spencer.

Did my first packmate want my beta? Had he wanted her all this time but kept his distance out of respect for me?

And I was right back to that first question – was I okay with that?

I was completely fine with sharing Spencer. And I hadn't found myself wanting to feel Rey wrapped around my cock. Not that the alpha wasn't sexy as fuck. She was strong, quick witted, and had a tongue sharp enough to cut.

But it was Kennedy who had successfully carved out a piece of my heart and crawled right into the hole. It was Kennedy who made me want a full pack. And it was Kennedy who made me actually wonder about fatherhood.

Although she'd already shot that down. If our pack were to ever grow, if we were to ever decide to fill our lives with pups, it would be Spencer who carried our children. And the omega was more than willing – almost downright demanding, in fact – to carry as many babies as we could fill him with.

Kennedy had opened her arms and her life to Wolf and me. She willingly shared her alpha and her omega with us. She was determined to convince us both that the injuries that littered her soft flesh weren't our fault.

So how the hell could I deny her if she and Wolf were to develop feelings?

Didn't mean I had to like it. But if she found herself pulled toward my darkly handsome packmate, I wouldn't stand in her way. I would share her the same way I already shared her with her original pack.

For some reason, I hadn't felt an ounce of jealousy over the fact she'd already had an alpha. It could have been because Rey was a woman. Or maybe it was because I'd yet to see the two women engage in any form of sexual activity. I'd caught her blowing Spence. Had witnessed the two having sex in the shower and hadn't felt any need to step in or join them.

But Wolf was not just an alpha but a male. Meaning he had a dick. Meaning he could breed my beta.

Fuck me. I was getting way ahead of myself. And, honestly, my thoughts were out of control and just this side of feral.

Neither Wolf nor I had any desire to force Kennedy to carry our offspring. Neither of us had any desire to breed her. Fuck her? Absolutely. At least I did. And would every second of every day if I had the chance. I was pretty sure I would never tire of the way she felt wrapped around my cock, of the sweet moans that escaped her lips when I drew out her pleasure, of the way she squirmed and squeezed her thighs when I sucked her clit and drew out the aftershocks of her orgasms.

And those were all things Wolf would experience if I were to step out of the way and allow the two to explore...whatever it was that I'd witnessed not fifteen minutes ago.

If that was what she wanted. Anything and everything I did since the moment I'd laid eyes on her in the club's back lot had been with her in mind. Every dollar I made on contracts was in hopes of her leaving her job and allowing me to lavish her with gifts the way only Spence allowed. Every decision I made from that moment was based on a future with Kennedy.

And how fucked up was that? After so many years on this planet, all it took was one small, feisty beta to knock my world off its axis.

Rey shifted, rolling onto her other side and pressing her back against Spencer's chest. Her eyes fluttered, closed, then opened and locked on mine.

"You should sleep while you have the chance. His waves tend to be close together," she whispered barely above a breath.

I nodded, Kennedy's hair tickling my chin and catching in the whiskers that had begun to grow along my cheeks and jaw.

She followed my gaze, looking over her shoulder at Wolf. "He's in love with her," she whispered.

My brows drew together, both in confusion and a touch of jealousy.

"He's refusing to admit it to himself and he's keeping his distance from her. And I'm pretty sure it's because of the two of us."

Fuck. That was the last thing I wanted. All I wanted was for my beta to be happy.

Not true. I wanted all my pack to be happy. I wanted everyone to feel as though they could truly be themselves, as though we could be open with each other, trust each other implicitly.

Denying feelings because Wolf was worried either Rey or I would be jealous would prohibit Wolf from being fully happy. And, as much as I hated to admit it, could keep Kennedy from truly being happy.

Yep. I was a selfish dick. I wanted to be all she wanted and all she needed.

But was I willing to no longer allow Spencer to take my dick into his mouth when the mood hit him? Was I no longer willing to press him against a wall and fuck him senseless when his perfume caused my dick to become painfully engorged? Those scenarios hadn't exactly happened on a recurring basis, but definitely something I wanted again.

And again. And again.

Memories of our time in the dressing room at Prada had my cock waking again until the tip brushed Kennedy's core that rested over my groin.

If that wasn't a prime example of why it wasn't right for me to decide for Kennedy whether she and Wolf should form a relationship outside of simple packmates…

"I had a feeling," I whispered back after a few minutes.

"Try to sleep. He'll be awake and hurting soon," Rey said, closing her eyes and tugging the blanket further up her shoulders.

None of us were dressed. What was the point of redressing when we would have to strip down again when Spencer's omega woke him and arousal and pain overrode any logical thought.

Fighting the urge to wrap my arms around Kennedy's back and hug her tightly to me, I made sure she was covered and closed my eyes, struggling to keep my swirling thoughts under control long enough for the exhaustion to take me under.

The next time sound touched my ears, it was the breathy moan of my beta. She was no longer sprawled over me, but instead, sat on Spencer's face while sucking his cock in the world's sexiest fucking sixty-nine.

"Fuck me," I muttered, palming myself under the blanket as I watched Kennedy's head bob up and down the omega's length.

I'd tasted Spencer's release, tasted the sweet warmth of apples, ginger, cloves, and something else. It was like the world's sexiest apple pie. And fucking addictive.

My eyes found first Rey who laid on her side, her head propped in her hand as she watched her packmates at play. Then I found Wolf. His eyes were glued to Kennedy's ass and pussy, his hand fisted around his dick as he stroked himself slowly, his pupils blown, his scent stronger, smokier in the air.

From where I laid, I couldn't fully see her ruined flesh, but I'd seen plenty of it when I'd taken her from behind earlier. Anger had bubbled up in my veins, but my alpha took over as my hindbrain kicked in, the need to breed stronger than any other emotion. And who better to fuck than my biggest obsession.

From the look of hunger and desire in Wolf's eyes, he had been fighting his own obsession.

When he glanced at me, I nodded my head toward Kennedy, as though giving him permission to take her without voicing the words.

I wasn't sure I could. Not yet.

Wolf tilted his head and frowned.

"I told him," Rey said to Wolf after glancing between us.

"Brother–"

I lifted a hand. "She's our beta. We agreed we'd both court them. I won't make the decision for her."

The words tasted like ash in my mouth. But I would have to get over it. I would learn to accept that my packmate loved Kennedy. How the hell could he not? I'd fallen in love within moments of laying eyes on her. I couldn't imagine anyone who spent more than a few minutes with her wouldn't see how incredible she was, and not just because of her physical beauty.

Wolf slowly pushed to his knees to move forward, his brows raised as though waiting for me to stop him.

"Do not fucking hurt her," I growled out as my alpha grew more possessive.

I was fully aware of Wolf's appetite, of the primal play he and Rey liked to enjoy. My sweet girl might not have been made of glass, but she was still healing from a serious assault. I'd rip my friend to pieces before I allowed him to inflict a single ounce of pain on her.

"I would never hurt her," Wolf said, hesitating within touching distance of her.

"You won't hurt her," Rey said, lifting to a sitting position, her hand smoothing over Kennedy's round ass gently, lovingly. "Kennedy, do you want your other alpha to fuck you?"

She moaned and wiggled a little like a cat in heat. For a beta, my girl's libido was as active as our omega's.

All three of us alphas huffed a laugh at her wanton display of acceptance. It looked as though she was begging for more attention back there yet didn't want to pull her mouth from Spencer.

Wolf purred, the sound deep and rumbling as he moved closer until I could no longer see where he pushed the head of his cock against Kennedy.

But I knew from the sounds coming from her when he pushed into her, when his dick speared her and stretched her.

Rey's eyes roamed across where Wolf was taking Kennedy, to where the beta's mouth was wrapped around Spencer, reached down to fondle Spencer's sac, then threaded her fingers through Kennedy's hair.

So far, we'd only received minutes of a break between the few waves of the first day of Spencer's heat. How the hell had only Rey and Kennedy managed to take care of him without ending up in the hospital from dehydration and exhaustion?

Wolf's jaw was clenched so tight a muscle jumped in his cheek. A smile spread across my face. I knew the feeling. Kennedy was so tight and warm. The way her body squeezed a cock was nothing short of miraculous. And more than once, I'd had to fight my own urge to pound into her to chase after my release, always determined to hear her throaty moans before allowing myself to get off.

"Oh shit," Wolf moaned.

I frowned until Rey chuckled.

"You're perfect, omega. You look so beautiful right now with your beta straddling your face, your cock in her mouth, while you suck your alpha's balls."

Ah. Wolf was a goner. I knew firsthand the kind of magic Spencer was capable of with his mouth and add to it the feeling of pure ecstasy wrapped around his cock, he'd be lucky if he could hold out much longer.

Rey continued to praise Spencer, giving his omega exactly what it needed while Kennedy drew him to the edge, sucking him into her mouth and bobbing faster.

A long, keening sound pulled from the omega's lips and I watched in awe as Kennedy swallowed, her throat bobbing as she tried to keep up with the onslaught coating her tongue and the back of her throat.

Wolf began to pump into her faster, his hands on her hips, fingers digging into the sides to leave the sexiest divots from his grip.

When Kennedy pulled her mouth from Spence and lifted her head, a shimmer from the drops she'd missed glistened on her lips as she cried out, her hair swaying each time Wolf's hips slapped against her.

"Wolf," Kennedy panted.

I crawled closer and pushed her hair away from her face. I wanted to see her. I wanted to see all of her.

Those sapphire eyes turned to me and the sexiest smile pulled the corners of those full lips up. I kissed her, savoring in the mixture of Spencer and her unique taste on her tongue and lingering on her mouth.

I had fought the jealousy when I'd realized Wolf saw my beta as more than simply a packmate.

But seeing them together, seeing the entire pack entwined like this...

There could never be anything more perfect.

CHAPTER 34

<u>Kennedy</u>

Four days. Four days and Spencer was finally sleeping soundly. We'd all urged him into the shower to wash off the sweat and cum, then the five of us lingered in a hot, bubble bath, easing our sore muscles and joints.

I'd been a little down that I wouldn't be able to participate in our first heat with Spencer as a new pack, but none of them allowed me to stay on the sidelines.

And Wolf had spent a lot of time with me. He'd held me, kissed me, gently worked knots out of my hair with his fingers, and made love to me. Several times.

Honestly, that had surprised me being as he tended to keep me at arm's length most days. Sure, we snuggled on the couch periodically, but as a pack with Spencer and Rey wedged between us. He and I had even hung out with Rey and watched movies while binging junk food when Alexei had taken Spencer out for a shopping date.

I supposed it could have been his alpha hormones, the fact his omega was in heat or the fact his beta was injured. Maybe a combination of both.

His beta. I absolutely thought of Wolf as one of my alphas, as a member of the pack. But he hadn't left his mark on either me or Spence. Then again, Alexei hadn't bothered sinking his teeth into any part of Spence, either, and that didn't make the two of them any less packmates.

Currently, the alphas were damned near comatose as they lounged on the pack bed with Spence slumbering between them. Sure, I had been included, but the three had done the most work, knotting and locking Spencer over and over every time another wave of his heat threatened to drag him under and sent pain and fever coursing through his system.

His perfume still hung heavy in the air, coating every surface of the penthouse. And this place wasn't exactly small. My omega simply had the most delicious pheromones.

Dressed in one of Alexei's long-sleeved tees and nothing else, I padded barefoot into the kitchen to start some coffee. Eventually, someone would amble from the pack room in search of caffeine. And since I was currently the only one vertical, I figured it was the least I could do.

Memories of the last four days had a perma-smile on my lips as I moved around the open kitchen, setting up and starting the fancy ass coffee maker that looked as though it would cost as much as a car payment. These two alphas sure as hell loved their luxury. Although if I had to guess, I would assume it was Alexei who'd chosen this particular piece of kitchenware.

Wolf was more like me in his tastes. He was more about comfort. And, unlike Alexei's bedroom, his room was far from spotless. I hadn't ventured into his room in days, but the last I saw, it still looked as though his dresser had exploded, leaving clothes laying on the floor, the furniture, even the bed.

As the coffee dripped into the carafe, I raised my hand and touched my fingertips to my lips. When he'd kissed me as he'd made love to Spencer, something inside my chest...shifted. I didn't know how else to describe it.

Of course, I'd always thought Wolf was attractive. Anyone with eyes could see that. And he obviously adored Rey and Spence.

I'd just assumed he saw me as a member of the pack, as Alexei's mate, as Rey's and Spencer's beta.

Something had definitely changed over this past week. And I wasn't mad about it.

It was amazing how big a heart could grow to include someone, how much love we held in our hearts for so many people. And...for the first time since meeting Wolf, I felt a glimmer of something beyond platonic affection. It was as though the moment our lips met, my heart and soul recognized yet another piece I hadn't known was missing.

The smile never faded, even as I began to pull easy to make ingredients from the fridge and pantry. I definitely wasn't the chef of the pack, but I could make something simple, something to fill all our bellies and give us all a little energy.

As I set a skillet on the stove, the bell rang from the doorman.

Craning my neck, I looked down the hall, waiting for either Alexei or Wolf to hurry in and answer. I had had very little contact with the doorman since we hadn't left at all after we'd arrived here from the club. And I'd only been to the penthouse a handful of times since the day I agreed to allow Alexei and Wolf to court us.

When no one appeared, I jogged to the phone on the wall and lifted it to my ear.

"Hello?" I asked, unsure of how exactly I was supposed to interact with the staff of the building.

"Is this a member of Pack Cillian?" a male asked.

My brows rose. I couldn't remember ever hearing either of the alphas refer to themselves as pack anything. But I wasn't going to argue since it was Wolf's last name.

"Yes, sir. This is their beta." I cringed a little, feeling as though I was pretending since I had never really had to put on such an air of professionalism.

"A package has been left for your pack. Would you like to retrieve it or should I send it up?"

"Um…can I get back to you on that?" I asked, leaning to the side to look down the hallway again.

I didn't know their protocol and didn't want to assume anything. This was their house, their home. We were just staying here for our protection. Or at least that was what they'd told me over and over when I'd asked to home the first then second then third night since arriving here.

"Yes, ma'am. We'll hold it here until we hear from your alphas."

I couldn't help but bristle at that a little. Yeah, I'd had an alpha before meeting the guys. But I was the breadwinner of the pack. I was the one who made sure we had a roof over our heads, that all our bills were paid, that my beautifully spoiled omega had the designer crap he loved.

The call ended and I set the phone back in the cradle.

After pouring myself a cup of coffee and doctoring it to perfection, I hurried to where my pack was still lying unmoving on the pack bed. At least the alphas' eyes were all open. They just didn't look as though they had another ounce of energy to commit to anything more than breathing.

"Hey," I whispered. Three sets of eyes turned to me. "The guy downstairs called and said a package had been delivered. He asked if I wanted to come down and get it or if we wanted it sent up. I didn't know what you guys normally do about that kind of stuff."

Alexei and Wolf both frowned, their bodies tensing. Each rolled from the side of the bed and my thoughts grew a little fuzzy the same time my mouth went dry at the absolute perfection of my two new alphas.

Their bodies looked as though they'd been carved from stone and their thick, heavy cocks swung as they hurried to their bedrooms to get dressed.

"Fuck, they're gorgeous," Rey muttered. But she didn't bother climbing from the bed, simply stayed nuzzled against Spence, her fingers lazily trailing through his auburn hair while he slept.

It would be another few days before his body recuperated from the last four days. I hadn't been fucked half as much as he had and I was sore. Everywhere.

Not that I was complaining. It was the most delicious soreness in all the right places.

Leaving my two original packmates in bed, I hurried down the hall and waited in the living room until Alexei and Wolf emerged from their bedrooms, fully dressed all the way to shoes. And, if I wasn't mistaken, there were bulges under their shirts as though they'd holstered pistols to their hips.

"It's a package, guys. Not an army."

"We don't get packages. We don't order shit online. And no one other than the three of you know where we live," Wolf said, gripping my shoulders and turning me toward the bedroom where Rey and Spence remained. "Go into the bedroom and lock the door. There's a Glock under the bed. It's loaded, but you'll have to chamber a round if anyone gets in here."

"Wait…the guy just said a package. He didn't say there was anyone waiting with the package. Why would I need to shoot–"

"Go," Alexei barked. And even though I was a beta and shouldn't have been swayed by that sound, my body tensed and demanded I obey.

"Damn it," I grumbled. "Don't shoot the doorman." I turned on my heel and stomped back to the room, my mug still in my hand as my coffee gradually cooled.

Rey's brows drew together when she spotted me closing and locking the door behind me.

A Glock under the bed. Why the hell did the alphas keep guns hidden all around the penthouse if it was supposed to be so much safer than our house? We could have easily stashed weapons every-where if that was all it took to make them feel level-headed.

My alpha sat up and threw her legs over the side of the bed, her wide eyes moving from my face to the gun in my hand and back.

"What the fuck is going on?"

She reached over and shook Spence a few times until the omega finally opened his eyes.

"Go into the nest," she barked.

Spencer tensed under her command and frowned. "The fuck? I was sleeping. Why do I need to–" His words cut off when he spotted me popping the magazine free to check the number of bullets, slamming it back into place, then pulling back the slide to chamber a round. "Okay. First of all, that was hot as fuck. Second…what's going on and why are you playing with a gun?"

"There's a package downstairs and Wolf and Alexei got all weirded out and told me to grab the gun and lock us in here. That's all I know."

"In the nest," Rey barked again.

The command finally made it to Spencer's omega hindbrain, and he was on his feet and stomping in that direction within seconds, grumbling under his breath the entire time.

"Are we in danger?" she asked when the nest door slammed shut.

"I don't see how. The doorman just said a package was left downstairs for us. Them. Whatever. Then they freaked out and said they don't get deliveries, and no one knows where they live and demanded I come lock us behind the door with the gun."

She lowered her head and searched the floor for any scrap of clothing. We had all crashed on the ginormous pack bed when Spencer's heat finally broke, but our clothes weren't in here. I had removed anything we'd been wearing when it all started and tossed it into the laundry.

"I really don't want to have to fight with my tits flopping everywhere," Rey said.

Her words and tone were serious. That didn't stop the burst of surprised laughter from escaping my lips.

"I really don't think we're in danger. Like I said…a package. He didn't say there was a gang or SWAT or anything like that. It's probably something Spencer ordered and forgot about."

Because our omega loved to online shop.

Minutes ticked by with me holding the gun at my side, my finger at the ready, resting off the trigger. Finally, there were a few rapid knocks on the door.

"Open up," Wolf said.

I popped the magazine and cleared the chamber before tucking the Glock back under the bed then unlocked and pulled open the door.

"Well? Was there a bomb waiting for you downstairs?" I teased.

Wolf didn't so much as crack a smile. "Everyone get dressed and meet in the living room."

"Does that mean I can come out now?" Spencer called through the nest door.

Wolf frowned at the door then glanced down at me. With a shrug, I nodded toward Rey. "She ordered him to hide in there until we knew what we were up against."

Another chuckle bubbled in my chest as she hurried past me to get dressed, her firm ass jiggling, and frowned at me over her shoulder.

"I think we need to start keeping a change of clothes for everyone in everyone's rooms," I said then shook my head when Wolf gave me a confused look. I wasn't sure he was interested in humor at the moment, not with a look that was nothing short of murderous in his brown eyes.

Putting on a serious face, I called for Spencer and escorted him to the room the three of us had claimed for our belongings and waited while he dressed. I still didn't relish the idea of pulling on pants of any form, but at least some of the worst of my injuries were healing well and I hadn't suffered from any infections.

Spencer's moves were jerky and stiff as he tugged on a pair of sweats and a t-shirt before snatching his favorite hoodie from the floor and pulling that over his head. Just because his body was no longer oversensitive didn't mean my omega didn't require comfort.

His eyes were puffy from lack of sleep, and he was paler than I would like, but at least I'd been able to get him to drink plenty of water and eat a little over the past few days. He just needed a few days of rest and some hot meals before he was back to his playful self.

Once he was dressed, I wrapped my arm around his waist and leaned into him, escorting him into the living room where Rey was already dressed and glaring at the huge basket sitting on the coffee table as though it contained a severed head.

From what I could tell at a distance, it looked like a gift.

"A heat gift for the new pack," Wolf said, lowering onto the couch.

Spence sat beside him and curled into his side, nestling his head into the crook of his shoulder when Wolf draped an arm around his shoulders.

"That's nice. From who…wait. You said no one knows where you live," I said. And I hadn't given my dad the address. "Oh shit."

"What's in there?" Spencer asked, lifting his head to peer inside.

The fact our omega wasn't tearing into the basket revealed exactly how tired he really was.

"We hadn't actually gone through it yet. But, uh…fuck," Wolf said, pushing a hand through his hair and tightening his hold on Spencer.

"What?" Rey asked, moving closer to look inside.

She began to rifle through until a growl rattled from deep inside her chest. The first thing she pulled out was a shirt that Alexei had bought for Spencer on their date. It had been shredded as though someone slashed at it with a knife. The next thing Rey pulled out was a piece of her clothes. I couldn't be sure, but it looked like her favorite pajama bottoms and the crotch had been cut out.

The last thing sent acid churning in my stomach. Several pairs of my panties were gripped in Rey's fist before she threw them across the room. Without getting close, I could smell something out of place, an alpha who didn't belong.

The alpha who'd beat the shit out of me in the backroom.

"He fucking jizzed all over them," Rey said, scrubbing her hand against her pants before hurrying to the kitchen to wash her hands.

Why had they only cum on my stuff? I was only a beta. If they really wanted to destroy our pack, they would go after Spencer. And Alexei had told us Mikhail was fully aware of Spencer's existence.

"It's a taunt," Wolf said, his voice deep and rumbly as a growl rattled nonstop.

"It's a fucking message. A warning. Not only do they know where your house is, but they let themselves in. They sent this as a warning to me. To let me know how easy it would be to get to you three," Alexei said, his words barely more than a growl.

"You said we were safe here," Rey said as she dried off her hands before kicking the panties in the direction of the kitchen trash can as though she couldn't stomach touching the soiled fabric with her hands.

"You are. You should be," Alexei said.

"Should be? That's not a fucking guarantee, Lex. I have to keep my pack safe."

"They're our pack, too," Wolf reminded her, his eyes bright with rage.

The alphas all growled and began to talk over each other while Spence all but curled into Wolf's side, as though trying to hide from the hormones exploding in the room.

Let them argue all they wanted. Let this asshole Russian think he had the upper hand.

Because as I listened to the raised voices, I began to make a plan of my own. Mikhail might think he could scare us, but he didn't know I had my own army at my beck and call, one who I knew would be more than happy to help even the score.

CHAPTER 35

Kennedy

Wolf sat on the edge of the bed as I shoved our belongings in the duffel bags. He'd followed me into the room but had yet to say a word.

After a few minutes, I stopped and lifted my head.

"Spit it out. I know you're pissed about this or have some kind of protest. Let's hear it."

Wolf didn't speak for a few heartbeats as his eyes bounced between mine.

"I need to tell you something," he said, his voice unusually soft.

My brows pulled together as a new wave of fear squeezed my heart.

"And just so you know, this was Rey's idea."

Oh shit. Were they going to ask me to leave? To go back to my family pack?

No. That was a stupid conclusion to jump to. It was my anxiety over the upcoming next few days – or weeks – that had me fearing every worst-case scenario.

Sitting beside him, I turned so I could sit crisscross and look him in the eye, steeling myself for whatever big secret he and Rey had been keeping from me.

"Tell me."

"I'm in love with you," he blurted, his voice barely above a whisper.

I blinked. Then blinked again.

"What?"

"I'm in love with you," he repeated without bothering to raise his voice or offer any form of explanation.

"Rey told you to tell me that? Why? If you're worried I'll get jealous or if there's someone you guys were interested in courting–"

"That's not it. And why would we want to court anyone else? We have the perfect pack." He actually looked confused by my statement. Maybe a touch pissed. Or hurt?

"Then…what? Spence's heat is the first time you've really touched me. Or kissed me."

"Because you were Alexei's. And because I didn't want Rey or Spence to think…fuck. I don't know. I just…I'm in love with you and want you to know that before we all split off. In case I don't come back."

My heart clenched at the thought of losing either alpha. I'd already wondered about the warm unfurling in my chest from the feeling of Wolf's lips on mine, of the way he'd touched me so gently and made love to me as though he cared about me and not simply because his hindbrain insisted he breed someone.

He'd been sweet, his hands soft when he'd touched me.

"You're coming back. Both of you. I refuse to believe otherwise," I said, pushing from the bed as my emotions became a fucking tornado inside of me and made me dizzy.

"Kennedy," he said, reaching out and grabbing my hand, pulling me until I was settled between his knees. "I need you to listen to me."

The backs of my eyes burned. It was hard enough to feel so strongly for Rey, Spence, and Alexei. And at least Rey and Spence would be with me and under complete and total supervision and protection. If I allowed Wolf into my heart, too, and lost one or both of them…

I wasn't sure I could survive it. I wasn't sure our little pack wouldn't fall to pieces if we lost the two newest members who'd became like shelter in a storm.

They had put their lives on hold, ignoring calls and contracts so they could stay with us and keep us safe.

Granted, we were only currently in danger because Alexei's ghosts had caught up with him, but that didn't make the care they showered us with any less appreciated.

Honestly, I had been just as much to blame that night Mikhail had assaulted me as they thought they were. I had been distracted by my pack, by my omega's scent, and had been giving googly eyes at the person who would turn out to be a monster since I couldn't see the people who meant more to me than the breath in my own fucking lungs.

"Alexei and I contacted our lawyer. If anything happens to us, all our assets transfer to the three of you. The penthouse, the two floors below, a couple safe houses, our vehicles, and the entire bulk of all our accounts."

I couldn't stop the tears from falling. "You sound like you're convinced you two won't survive."

"Because there's always a chance in our line of work. And this is… The paperwork has been left in a lockbox. The lawyer will contact you with details when he is alerted of our death. I want you three to sell this place and move as far off the grid as possible. Use every penny possible to find the safest place you can. Even if you have to install a drawbridge and moat stocked with crocodiles."

I knew he was attempting to make light of the situation. He could send in a whole troop of clowns juggling polka dotted unicorns and I still wouldn't be able to crack a smile.

"Why did you have to tell me that, Wolf," I squeaked out around my closing throat. "Now I can't deny it anymore. I can't ignore it. I can't lose either of you, asshole."

I shoved his shoulder. Then shoved him again. He barely moved. I was tempted to step back and slug him but knew that would do nothing but hurt my damn hand with as big as he was.

He finally grabbed my wrists and tugged me closer, his eyes on mine. And my heart hurt a little more when his beautiful brown eyes grew glassy with unshed tears.

"I don't want you to ignore it. And I'm sorry I didn't tell you sooner. I'm sorry I didn't…I just didn't want to get in the way of you and Alexei."

"Does he know?"

He huffed a laugh, but his smile was sad. "Yeah. Apparently, Rey took it upon herself to fill him in on what she knew before I was even willing to admit it to myself. That was why I was so fucking out of sorts when you were hurt. I wanted to take care of you, to hold you, to hunt down the fucker who hurt you. But I felt like it wasn't my place. Or like I would be stepping on toes."

He pulled me closer until our bodies were nearly lined up, his thighs on either side of my hips.

"I promise you this – if we make it back to you, I'll do whatever it takes to prove to all three of you how important you are to me. I'll spend time with you. I'll hold you and whisper in your ear and …fuck. This is all coming out wrong. I sound stupid."

I pressed my lips to his to stop him. Words were no longer needed. I hated that he'd admitted his feelings. Because now I had no choice but to acknowledge my own. There were now four people living permanently in my heart, four people who owned every piece of me, four people who could destroy me so fucking easily.

Wolf's hands cupped my face so tenderly, his lips sipping at mine before his tongue teased the seam of my mouth.

As we deepened the kiss, his hands smoothed down my back to my thighs. "Am I hurting you?" he asked against my mouth.

"No," I said as I climbed onto his lap the same time he lifted me and pulled me closer.

There was nothing separating us but the sweats he wore and our shirts. And I wanted them all gone. I wanted to feel him pressed against me. I wanted to feel his skin on mine.

And I wanted to carry his mark before he left. I wanted our bond solidified so I could feel him in my chest, so I could trace the thread that linked us when we left each other's sides.

I could feel Rey, even now. I could trace the link that fed straight to Alexei. And I could feel the anxiety and fear from them both.

But I could feel them. I would know if something happened to Alexei or Wolf as long as they didn't shut down the bond while we were apart.

Reaching down, I tugged at the hem of his shirt and pulled up, tracing my fingers over his abs as I removed it. We broke our kiss only long enough to tug the shirt over his head, then remove my own, leaving me completely naked on his lap, his long, hard cock pressing against my core through the cotton.

"Will it hurt you if you lie on your back?" he asked, pushing the hair away from my face.

I shook my head slowly and let him turn us until he could settle me on the mattress while he pushed his sweats down his legs, his cock springing free, the tip glistening with what I knew would be a warm smokey flavor that would explode on my tongue. Just as it had in the nest.

He moved slowly, his hands smoothing up my calves, my thighs, his lips following the trail until his face was buried in my mound, his tongue sliding through my folds.

Head back, I arched off the mattress as his hands slid up my stomach to tease and pinch my nipples while he devoured my pussy, sucking my clit between his lips while flicking it with his tongue.

I wasn't going to last. The man was a maestro with his fucking mouth and was playing a fucking symphony with my body.

My mouth opened and a breathy moan escaped me as he slid a finger inside me, quirking it and rubbing the perfect spot, sending me spiraling over the edge.

He flattened his tongue and continued to lick and finger me

through my aftershocks. Until a sharp pinch on my right inner thigh stilled the breath in my lungs.

Lifting my head, I watched as he lapped at the blood that seeped from my ruined flesh, the crescents of his teeth causing an explosion within me as our bond snapped into place and everything he felt sang inside my chest.

Love. He did love me. It wasn't mere words. Wolf had felt so much for me for a while and had kept it to himself, denying himself to avoid getting in the way of Alexei or hurting Rey.

"Fuck. I love you, too," I said as tears began to stream down my temples to soak into my hair.

He slid up my body, leaving wet kisses along my stomach, my ribs, my breasts, before he settled between my thighs and hooked my legs over his arms, opening me more for him.

The bulbous head of his cock teased at my opening; he tilted his chin down to watch as he slowly pushed inside of me, giving my body time to stretch around him.

"I love you," he whispered, locking eyes with me as he began to pump his hips, gliding his dick in and out of me as his knot pressed against my opening and teased my clit.

I had to swallow the lump in my throat. His words felt more like a goodbye than a declaration of his emotions. And I still hadn't had a moment alone with Alexei.

For a moment, I wished he was in here with us, wished I could make love to them both, wished we could spend another four days locked together and pretend there weren't monsters out there waiting for us to step outside of the penthouse or waiting for us to let down our guard in any way.

Wolf leaned forward and pressed his lips to mine as his hips began a more frantic pace, his knot stretching me a little more each time. And, although I knew I would experience a moment of pain, the only reason I didn't beg him to knot me was because we would be locked together for twenty or more minutes. We had plans that were already in motion. The schedule had already been halted while we said goodbye in our own way.

Not goodbye. I had to push that thought away. This was not good-bye. This was simply a shared moment, time that we deserved yet had denied ourselves for weeks.

Pressure began to build again, the waves rolling over and into each other until everything from the neck down tingled and tightened and another cry tore from my lips, Wolf's name leaving my mouth.

He followed me seconds later, his hips jerking forward as his cock twitched over and over as he filled me, his knot nestled just enough to stretch my opening without locking behind my pubic bone.

Tears still trailed down my temples. And one dropped on my cheek from Wolf's eyes.

It was as I feared. This was him saying goodbye. This was the last moment he thought he would have with me.

And I refused to accept that.

One way or another, the five of us would be together again. We would find the ridiculously big and overly secured house Alexei and Wolf wanted us to have, and Spencer would pop out fifteen kids.

And we would all live happily ever after, damn it.

CHAPTER 36

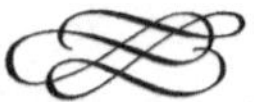

<u>Spencer</u>

Just because they'd all told me the plan didn't mean they actually asked whether I approved. Because they knew it would have been a big fuck no.

So now, Rey, Kennedy, and I were piled into the gifted Cadillac Escalade on our way to what was supposed to be a safe house owned by Alexei and Wolf.

The plan was to make sure we took our time loading the vehicle, took our time leaving the garage, even went through a fucking drive-thru for fast food that now sat cold and greasy on the floorboard of the SUV.

The three of us had zero appetite, but we were doing what we could to be seen...

And followed.

I didn't doubt Alexei's or Wolf's abilities. But the rest of the plan hinged on so many factors, so many things that could go wrong and end up causing me to lose one or all of my fucking packmates.

I hadn't even had time to recoup from my heat before I was being ordered around and told the fucking plans. *Told*. Not asked for input. Not asked for my opinion.

I was the fragile omega everyone wanted to protect when all I wanted was to keep the two beautiful women in my life safe.

What had really irked me was the performance we'd put on as we'd stepped out of the elevator. How Rey, Kennedy, and I had to tell the alphas they weren't worth the trouble, blame them for Kennedy's injuries, accuse them of bringing danger and trouble into our lives.

The tears that had flowed freely between all of us were real and made the acting all that much more believable.

So, as far as anyone who'd been watching would think was that the three of us had decided the two alphas weren't worth our time and were leaving. They would believe we were taking off.

I wasn't convinced whoever was watching wouldn't realize this was a ploy when we went to a house owned by the Russian alpha instead of our personal house, but Wolf was convinced they would believe we were simply too scared to return home after someone had let themselves inside and taken personal belongings.

And honestly? That wasn't all that far from the truth. We still had no idea what kind of condition our pack home had been left in, whether they simply stole a few things and left or whether they destroyed the place.

We might never know. As convinced as everyone else was that this whole fucking thing would end in a day or two, I wasn't convinced we would all survive it. And with the way the four were determined to use themselves as human shields between me and the world…

Nope. If they thought for one second they would wedge themselves into every crack in my heart then slip away, leaving me hollow, they were fucked in the head.

"You need to chill out," Rey said as she pulled the SUV onto a bumpy road that led to a secluded cabin surrounded by acres and acres of trees. Seclusion that was supposedly a part of the plan.

My scent would give my anxiety away without me speaking a word. Or maybe it was my bouncing knee rocking the vehicle.

"What if this—"

"Spence," Kennedy said, turning and shaking her head in the most imperceptible movement.

Nothing about this fucked up plan was to be discussed once we were on this driveway. We were supposed to commiserate about how the two alphas had ruined our lives. We could fuck and snuggle and cry.

We could lie and say Alexei and Wolf were the worst things to happen to our little pack.

I hadn't been a drama kid growing up. Before I'd perfumed and presented as an omega, I had been big into sports and hoped to one day go to college on a baseball scholarship. Maybe even play pro.

But the coaches refused to let me be in a room full of testosterone riddled alpha teens who could go into rut. As though it was my fault they couldn't control themselves.

The places my mind went when I was trying to keep from lashing out.

Well, at least if we got a day or two before anything happened, I could rest a little more. According to Wolf, the cabin was completely redone and had a huge garden tub where I could soak and a big, flat screen TV with a few streaming services.

I would guilt trip my girls into the tub with me for a nice, long soak, then we could snuggle in a puppy pile on the couch and binge watch some trashy reality TV or maybe some old school rom coms. The older ones were definitely my favorite, especially anything with Meg Ryan or Julia Roberts.

"I can't believe they would put us in this position," Kennedy said as Rey parked the SUV close to the porch wrapping around the log cabin.

It was rustic but beautiful with the setting sun sending dappled light through the trees. But it wasn't home. Not without my other two alphas.

. . .

"I don't want to do this. I think we're better together," I had begged Wolf as he'd ushered me to the door.

I didn't have his mark. I didn't have the bond to him or Alexei like Kennedy did. And I had no idea whether that was done on purpose to save me from the complete and utter agony of a shattered bond if the two didn't survive the next few days.

"Two days max," Wolf said.

Alexei took Kennedy's face in his hands and pressed a long, wet kiss to her lips. He then pulled me close and did the same, his fingers tight in the hair at the nape of my neck.

I couldn't stop the tears from trailing down my cheeks. I was still riding the emotional rollercoaster of my heat, still suffering from stiff muscles and soreness of the last four days, and now it felt as though someone had reached into my chest and ripped out a huge chunk of my heart.

There were duffel bags piled up near the front door. Almost everything we had at the penthouse was going with us so we could keep up the charade of leaving the alphas. And, while this whole thing might be nothing more than show, it felt far too real and permanent for me.

"Wouldn't it be better if we stayed together?" I tried again, all but begging as emotion lodged a lump in my throat.

"They have to think you've not only left us but are completely unguarded. It's the best way to smoke them out and lay a trap," Alexei said.

What really pissed me off was this whole plan had been my beta's idea. She'd been the one to bring it up, the one to make some phone calls, the one to offer the three of us as bait.

Not that I wouldn't have willingly handed myself over to keep my pack safe. But I didn't like the idea of my alphas and a bunch of people I had never met being out there against a bunch of pissed off Russians who, according to my alphas, were often trained by the fucking military. This wasn't a rag tag group of brawlers or wannabe gangsters. These men, the members of the Gusev Bratva, were the real deal.

And we were not only inviting them to attack the five of us, but doing so away from any peering eyes who might be able to call the cops if something went wrong.

. . .

"At least we have somewhere to stay until I find us another house. We'll put ours up for sale since they lured a bunch of assholes straight to our front door," Rey said.

I tried to form the words, tried to play along, but my heart ached, as though speaking poorly of my alphas made it all true, as though we really had left them, as though we would no longer be wrapped in each other's arms again.

"Come on, omega. Let's get you inside and in the tub," Rey said, opening my door and holding out a hand for me.

If the Bratva assholes knew we'd all been locked away while I was in heat, it wouldn't seem odd that I was acting emotional or subdued. Hell, even the fact we were supposedly walking away from the two alphas who were supposed to be courting us would have sent any omega into a bit of a tailspin.

Tears burned the backs of my eyes, but I blinked them away and let Rey guide me into the house while Kennedy grabbed a few of our bags.

Inside was as pretty as the outside but had been modernized like Wolf had promised. While the walls were still exposed lumber, the floors looked as though they'd been sanded down and restained. The floor plan was open with the kitchen and living room flowing together beautifully.

Rey flipped on lights as we moved further into the cabin, opening doors to check out the rooms, not that we would be sleeping separately. Both Kennedy and Rey currently had firearms hidden under their clothes just in case something went wrong or our backup was late.

They hadn't bothered to give me one. And yep, it rubbed me the wrong way.

But my alpha and beta had actually trained with firearms where I had never touched a gun in my life. I would probably end up shooting my own foot before actually helping in any way.

There were three bedrooms, two with ensuite bathrooms, then a separate bathroom with a toilet, vanity, and shower.

That was it. Just a big open space with a total of four doors. Didn't leave a whole lot of places to hide should the time arise.

But we knew something that, hopefully, the Bratva didn't. Wolf and Alexei alerted us to the nest hidden inside one of the bedroom's closets. By all appearances, it was a typical nest with padding and pillows and dim lighting.

But the walls and door had been reinforced to create a panic room for this very type of situation since this cabin was generally used as a safe house. If – or rather when – shit hit the fan, I was ordered to immediately retreat to the nest until one of my alphas gave the all safe. All three of my alphas used their fucking barks to boss me around.

So, yeah, I was feeling not just scared shitless over the safety of my packmates, but a little butthurt that I couldn't even help. I couldn't protect my girls, couldn't help my alphas. All I could do was hide in the nest and wait for the bad guys to be eliminated.

Kennedy hefted a few of the bags in and dropped them at the foot of the pack bed, then dropped heavily, raising her brows in silent communication.

I nodded and sighed heavily.

"I just want a bath, a blowjob, and a pack cuddle," I said, trying to behave as normally as possible.

If these assholes were either out there listening or had managed to somehow install some form of surveillance in the cabin without triggering Wolf's and Alexei's own security system, we had to behave as we would any other day. And asking for a blow job was more than normal for me.

Hell, I would live every moment of my life with my dick in my alpha's or beta's mouths if I had the choice.

"How about the two of you get the bath running while I grab the rest of the bags?" Rey said, raising one brow at Kennedy.

She sighed and nodded. No verbal communication whatsoever about anything other than the lies we planned.

"We'll be fine," Kennedy said. "We were fine before them, and we'll be amazing without them. I make plenty of money to keep my sexy ass omega in the lap of luxury," Kennedy said as she began to pull her clothing off, tossing them near the bags as she made her way into the pack bathroom with the biggest tub to fit all three of us.

My heart clenched and it took me a few tries and Kennedy's wide eyes before I could make the lies leave my tongue. "I think we should look for another alpha. Maybe a bigger pack. Someone who won't put us in danger. It's time for us to find someone who can actually protect the three of us." The words tasted bitter in my mouth.

Because I had a pack. I had my alphas. I loved all three of them and my heart ached from the distance.

I couldn't imagine how the hell Kennedy was being so calm when she could literally feel both Wolf and Alexei through their bond.

Or maybe that was exactly why she was so calm. She, unlike me, carried their marks and knew they were safe, could feel their love and affection, could feel the reassurances they would push down the little threads of their pack bonds.

My legs felt as though they were full of concrete as I shuffled behind my beta, tugging my shirt over my head with heavy arms.

She kept her eyes locked on mine, doing her best to convey so many emotions through just the look, as she popped the button and pulled down the zipper of my pants, then shoved my jeans down my hips.

I had made the comment about the blow job to keep up appearances in case someone was listening. But…who was I to deny my girl if she was in the mood to wrap her lips around my cock?

Once I was naked, she turned and started the water, her hand under the rush until she was satisfied with the temp before hitting the plug to let the tub fill. After adding some bubble bath she found sitting on the ledge, she removed her pants, then reached behind to unclasp her bra until she was as naked as me.

Even with the strain on my heart and the stress of what could or couldn't go wrong over the next couple of days, my dick still hardened at the sight of my beta's full beautiful tits, of her sweet and tart cranberry scent mixing with the floral fragrance of the bubbles lifting on the air with the steam.

A sad smile quirked up the corners of her lips. She jerked her head, beckoning forward.

"I love you," she said, grabbing my hips and drawing me closer. *Soon*, she mouthed. We would all be back together soon. This would all be over soon.

Our alphas would be back with us soon.

A tear fell over my lashes before I could stop it.

"Now, I believe my omega requested a blowjob, a hot bath, and a pack cuddle," she said loud enough to be heard by anyone listening in.

When her lips closed around the head of my cock, I forced all my fears away and focused only on the wet, hot velvety feel of her mouth and tongue on me and lost myself in sensation.

Soon. This would all be over soon. I trusted my beta. I trusted my alphas.

I had to trust in their plan and their promises that, in just a couple days, all the bull shit would be over and we could live our lives like the fairytale I'd always dreamed of.

CHAPTER 37

Alexei

No matter how many times they argued with me, no matter how many times I tried to convince myself otherwise, all this bullshit was my fault.

Thing was, even if I caved and joined Mikhail and his father, it wouldn't stop there. I would either become the slop man and receive the tasks that would more than likely end up getting me killed or incarcerated, or they would kill me and my pack anyway, if for no other reason than to teach others a lesson.

And that lesson being it was foolish to go up against the Gusev Bratva, to defy Dima Gusev.

Fuck them. Fuck Mikhail. Fuck the whole lot of them.

I might have been able to simply move on, to ignore the threats. But then they'd dared to touch my beta.

As if that wasn't bad enough, they'd broken into Kennedy's, Rey's, and Spencer's house, stolen items of clothing, and jacked off on

Kennedy's panties. That shit right there had earned anyone and everyone who'd been involved a death sentence.

Wolf and I were currently downstairs from the penthouse, packing up several duffel bags with any and every single weapon we might need for the upcoming hunt, including things that went boom. Explosives would be a last resort being as we didn't exactly want to bring too much attention to the area, to the safe house, or to the fight.

Had either of us been members of Omega Rescue and Extraction, we could have simply called in for backup. But being as we were hired killers working in the shadows with offshore accounts, we couldn't exactly call the local authorities and give them a heads up.

Nope. We had to get this done as quietly as possible, clean up the mess, then hope that no one ever got wind of the activities that were only a day or two away from going down at what we had always considered a safe house.

It would be abandoned after this was over. Neither of us had anything specifically under our name being as we worked under the radar, so maybe if we had more bodies than we could dispose of with stealth, we'd simply drag them into the house and burn the place to the ground.

"I fucking hate this," Wolf grumbled as he set a full bag near the door.

I grunted in response.

"I can feel Kennedy. I can't feel Rey or Spence. I should have fucking marked them both."

Neither of us had marked Spence. We should have left our mark on him during his heat, forged the bond between us all. But we hadn't exactly discussed it. All we knew was that he wanted one or both of us to one day fill his belly with pups. That didn't mean he wanted a permanent scar on his shoulder that would link us together until one or both of us died.

Kennedy...if Wolf or I fell during our little hunt she would feel it like someone reached in and ripped out a piece of her heart. It would be both physically and emotionally agonizing. Perhaps we should both be thankful we wouldn't be inflicting our omega with that same pain, just in case the worst happened.

It was hard to live the life we did without accepting the fact there might be someone who got the drop on us someday. Ours was a dangerous life. I'd accepted my own mortality a decade ago, accepted the fact there was a slim as fuck possibility I would ever make it to old age.

Kennedy would. Rey and Spencer would. They would be the most adorable elderly pack, their gray hair and wrinkles telling the stories of their lives.

Fuck…I truly hoped I would be there to see it.

"We'll mark Spencer as soon as he's safe. Fuck, Rey, too. Although you know that woman will demand she return the favor," I said, forcing a smile on my lips.

After a moment or two, a smirk crept across Wolf's face. "She's threatened a time or two," he said. "I can't believe you haven't fucked her."

I shrugged up my shoulders. She was gorgeous. No doubt about it. But I felt about her the same way I felt about Wolf and didn't really have the desire to sink my dick in either of them. Not that seeing her with our packmates didn't send heat coursing through my veins.

By the time we'd stuffed the duffel bags until they could barely be zipped closed, there were hardly any weapons left in the safe. All we could do was hope we'd planned this out well enough.

It wouldn't only be the two of us, although we hoped that Mikhail and his fucking asshole friends believed otherwise. That was the whole point of this charade, of allowing our three packmates to pack up and leave, to put on a show of leaving us.

Were they still keeping up the charade? We'd instructed them to keep any and all conversations as guarded as possible, to only discuss the lies we'd made up, the stories we'd fabricated. At no point were they to discuss the truth or the plan in case they were being monitored.

Which I assumed they were. If it were me and I was hunting someone, I would have them under twenty-four/seven surveillance. I would find a way to hang on their every word for any hint as to where my enemy was or what they had planned.

We were anticipating Mikhail and the Gusev Bratva attacking the safe house, to attempt to drag our packmates from the house or at least attempt to break in. The fact my omega and my beta were being used as bait filled my throat and mouth with bile, but this had been Kennedy's idea.

As much as I'd wanted to protest, to scream and demand they stay right there at the penthouse and let us handle it all, neither Wolf nor I could deny her plan was nearly foolproof.

Nearly. Nothing was ever one hundred percent guaranteed. And the lack of that guarantee was what would end up giving me a fucking stroke.

Wolf wasn't doing much better, no matter how hard he was trying to act as though this was nothing more than another contract, another mission. Another kill.

"Ready?" he asked, hoisting bags onto his shoulders.

With a nod, I grabbed the last of them and followed him to our private elevator, waving my key over the pad and hitting the *G* for garage.

Even if someone happened to see us heading to the SUV, nothing was visible. They would only see two alphas carrying bulky duffel bags. Maybe they would assume we were moving. Or that we were a couple going on a vacation.

How wonderful that would have been to have a mundane life.

Fuck it. After all this shit was done, that was exactly what we would do. We would plan a vacation for the five of us and do family fun crap like water slides or picnics or whatever.

And then, Wolf and I would take turns trying to knock Spencer up each heat, give him as many babies as he wanted, build a gigantic house for our growing family.

But we had to make it through the next couple days and pray that everyone arrived on time and were in position before it was too late.

Kennedy hadn't seemed a bit worried.

But Spencer...

Our poor omega was a fucking mess. It didn't help that his hormones were still all over the place after barely ending his cycle a couple days ago. He hadn't even been given enough time for his body to heal from the fever, the pain, and all the fucking that came with it. His body would be as big of a mess as his emotions.

Wolf and I had both tried to reassure him that we would all be safe, that we would be together in less than a week. I'd even promised him a shopping trip and at least one try for pregnancy during his next cycle.

Not that any of us had actually taken any precautions this round. I had no idea whether Spence or Kennedy was on any form of birth control, but simply assumed at least Kennedy was since she'd outright said she had no desire to carry a child.

I would literally give either of them the entire world to make them happy. Rey, too. I didn't need to have her in my bed or wrapped around my cock for her to be as fully embedded in my heart as Wolf. She was my packmate. I fucking loved her. I loved how she cared for Kennedy and Spence. I loved how protective she was of them both.

The elevator dinged on the basement level and Wolf stepped out before me, his eyes roaming the space as we both tensed and prepared for any and everything.

Just because the garage was supposedly secured didn't mean someone hadn't been able to make it inside as easily as Wolf and I had many times through the years when taking out a mark.

Before we opened the doors, we both took turns checking over the SUV for any signs of explosives or tampering. When we were as confident as we could be without fully dismantling the fucking thing, Wolf used the fob to pop the hatchback so we could load up our weapons and tools.

"They should be settled in by now," Wolf said as he steered the SUV out of the garage and onto the highway that would lead us to the safe house.

But we wouldn't be turning up the long driveway. Our plan was to park a few miles away where I would hike it through the surrounding acreage to stay under cover in hopes that the Bratva would take a more direct route and attack head on. Especially if they believed it was only the three in the cabin.

At some point, we should meet up with the backup that was called in, and fuck me, I prayed they were nearly as trained and bad ass as Kennedy assured us. I also hoped we weren't completely outnumbered or there would absolutely be use of some explosives or high caliber, long range rifles. And that would be noisy as fuck.

Instead of dwelling on every worst-case scenario, I leaned my head against the seat rest and let my mind wander. I tried to picture my packmates in the cabin, pictured them lounging in the tub or snuggling in the pack bed. I pictured Spencer choosing one of those romantic comedies he loved so much. Or maybe Kennedy would choose one of her favorite sitcoms to watch for the fifteenth time.

And Rey would smile and hold them both, not bothering to offer a single complaint over watching something they had all seen a dozen times.

I pictured Kennedy in one of my shirts, the hem nearly reaching her knees. Spencer and Rey would probably be naked. My omega would need the skin to skin contact to keep him leveled, to keep his emotions steady and nerves from fraying.

Focusing on the bond between Kennedy and me, I sent her all the love in my heart, and then smiled when I felt it returned down that invisible thread. Even with the distance between us, I felt her deep in my heart and soul, could feel her presence, could feel her as though she was right there in my arms.

Soon, lyubov. Soon, sweet omega.

Soon, this would all be over, and we could finally start to plan our lives together without the ghosts of my past fucking everything up.

CHAPTER 38

<u>Kennedy</u>

*D*ay two. This was it. At least we were assuming it would go down today. All we could do was listen to Alexei when it came to the Bratva. He believed we would be followed to this cabin, that our phones were more than likely being tracked, maybe even monitored.

So now…it was time to put on a show.

"Why can't we just call them and—"

"No, Spencer," Rey said, putting on a show of her life.

None of us would ever win an Oscar for our pitiful acting, but anyone who might be listening would have no idea that we were faking it. As long as we didn't slip and tell the truth, any eavesdroppers should take our words at face value.

"We could tell them we're willing to work it out. Maybe…I don't know. Tell them we'll all move to another state. That way, we won't have to worry about the Russians. Or what if we only allow Wolf to join the pack?"

I watched Spencer as he spoke, watched the way it looked as though he was choking on the words as they left his mouth. I got it. They were both ours. Both alphas were ours. Alexei and Wolf were our alphas as much as Rey.

Except…Spence still didn't carry their marks.

That was something we could use to our advantage. Or…something that could turn into a nightmare if the Bratva were able to infiltrate the house and the panic room and dark bond our omega. I wasn't sure there was anything we could do to break that bond if it was achieved. I'd only ever heard of the slave like bond, had never met anyone who'd suffered the bond.

I sure as fuck wouldn't let that happen to Spencer. I would use my own damn body as a shield before I let the enemy anywhere near my sweet omega.

"What if he demands Alexei join him?" Rey said.

We were all currently lounging on the couch with the TV on low. But our ears were tuned to any sound outside the cabin, our phones sitting on the coffee table in case they were somehow using them to either listen in or track us.

If this didn't work, I was out of ideas. According to Alexei, they were able to circumvent security systems, meaning they could very well have hacked into the one here and be watching us on the cameras, hanging on our every word. They could have somehow tapped our phones and locked onto our locations. They could be right outside at this very moment, just waiting to crash through the door.

Not yet. The cheese had to be set in the trap before we were ready for the rats to pour forward.

"Fine. But not the Russian. Text Wolf and ask if he's willing to walk away from Lex," Rey said.

My heart clenched, but a moment later, a wave of comfort trickled into my chest. They were out there. Even if I were to step outside and start wandering the woods, I knew I wouldn't find them. I wouldn't see any of them. That was the point, to become ghosts, hidden right in plain sight.

The hard metal of the Glock pressed against my spine settled me yet scared me. I really, truly hoped I wouldn't have to pull the thing free. Not that I would have a single problem putting a bullet between the eyes of anyone who dared touch any of my packmates. But if I had to pull the gun, that meant the enemy succeeded in getting past our line of defense. It could mean they'd executed our alphas and our backup.

It would mean it would be up to me and Rey to protect Spencer.

It would mean we would lose everything within a matter of minutes.

Spencer lifted his phone and tapped out the rehearsed message to Wolf, telling him we were willing to accept him as pack but not Alexei, inviting him to join us at the cabin, telling him that we were willing to forgive what had happened as long as we no longer had to deal with the Russians any further.

By the time Spencer set the phone back down, his face looked as though he'd sucked on a lemon. And I understood. Alexei was my fucking soul mate. They all were. Each of the four now owned a corner of my heart. They were literally what kept my heart beating, and I wasn't sure I would be the same if I lost any of them.

The answering ding sent butterflies and hornets fighting for space in my stomach and adrenaline burning through my veins. This was it. This was the trap. And the three of us had just become the cheese.

If Alexei had been right about the Bratva, they would have intercepted the text. They would be anticipating his arrival. They would converge upon the property of the cabin to lie in wait if they weren't already out there watching.

That thought creeped me out. It had been one thing when I'd felt Alexei's eyes on me when I would leave the club. I'd felt safe, felt as though I'd had a dark guardian angel watching my every move.

But I hated to think there could be people out there right now watching us through the windows, listening to our conversations, making plans with what they would do with us after they killed Wolf and Alexei.

I fought the shudder. They would dark bond Spencer. They would rape all three of us. They would probably either keep us as their own personal slaves or sell us off to the highest bidder.

Nope. I'd put the barrel of my gun into my mouth before I allowed that kind of shit to happen.

As the TV droned on, Rey, Spence, and I exchanged silent looks without turning our heads. If someone was out there, if someone was watching the camera feed, we couldn't give anything away.

Another wave of comfort trickled into my heart. This was distinctly from Wolf. It was amazing how easy if was to tell each of my three alphas apart, how their bond threads were as unique as their scents.

Alexei and our backup would be somewhere out there in the dark, sneaking among the trees, watching, waiting.

Wolf would be making his way toward us. Any time now, his vehicle would bounce up the uneven and cracking driveway that would lead him to the cabin. And all I could do was pray the Bratva wouldn't immediately open fire, that they wouldn't shoot my alpha in the head.

That would be stupid, right? Wouldn't it be better to have all four of us in one place to use against Alexei? Wouldn't it benefit the Gusevs to have the people Alexei cared about under one roof to truly use as bait? As a bargaining tool?

I'd been so sure of this plan when I'd approached everyone with it. Now?

Now I had so many doubts and fears. So many things could go wrong. People could get hurt. They could get killed. I could lose everyone I loved in a single night.

Leaning into Rey's side, I tensed as headlights shone through the window and bounced along the wall.

This was it. If this failed...fuck. I hadn't thought of a plan B and had no idea whether anyone else had, either.

The sound of the door swinging shut was loud, even from inside and over the TV. Wolf's heavy, booted steps echoed through the house, matching the pounding of my heart.

He didn't bother knocking, simply pushed his way inside. This was his place, after all.

His eyes roamed each of us silently, checking our location, before turning and closing the door.

I wanted to ask him how long he thought we would have to wait. Wanted to ask whether I should drag Spencer to the nest now, just in case. Wanted to throw myself into his arms, wrap my arms around his neck, and cover myself in his scent.

I wanted to ask if Alexei was in place, whether he'd seen the Kingsmen hiding among the trees, whether my dad had gone against my wishes and joined the enforcers I'd requested when I'd put in a call for help.

There hadn't been a moment of hesitation when he'd agreed to send as many men as I needed, both alphas and betas. They would all be armed to the teeth and would all be out for blood. After all, the former Pres of the Kingsmen had skin in this game. His daughter had been assaulted by a Russian mobster who was now out to hurt me and my pack again.

I wouldn't have been surprised if my dad had put in calls to clubs in surrounding states, as well. I might have never been a fully-fledged member, but I was a legacy. I had grown up with these bikers, had grown up with the men who now acted as enforcers, as hitmen, as the muscle who got things done.

As long as all went as planned, the fucking Gusev Bratva were about to have their minds blown…literally and figuratively.

CHAPTER 39

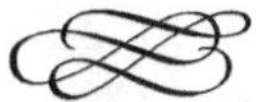

<u>Alexei</u>

It had been thirty-six hours since the last time I'd slept. Wolf had dozed in the SUV when we'd parked a few miles away, making sure we were out of sight of the enemy but close enough should our pack need us. He'd never been real hip on going long stretches without his beauty rest.

Me? I could go two or three days before my aim began to falter and my sight began to blur. Adrenaline was a hell of a thing, and something I had grown to rely on during shit like this.

Thing was, I might have lived in the states for a while and worked solo – or occasionally beside Wolf – as a hitman, but I had trained with the same motherfuckers who would be attacking my pack within hours. Or less.

I checked the time on my watch as I crept silently closer to the cabin. By now, Spencer would have suggested inviting Wolf over. They would have sent a text. As long as I was right, Mikhail would either have someone outside watching and reporting, or they would have hacked into our security system – something I did to this day when tracking marks and had learned from my time with the Gusevs – and would hear my pack's conversation.

How many would Mikhail send? Would he be brave enough to attack himself? Or would he send some low-level assholes to do the dirty work?

I really and truly hoped he showed his face. Because I had plans for him, plans that included a whole lot of fucking pain and ending with a bloody, painful death.

A twig cracked about twenty yards to my left. Halting my movement, I lowered to a crouch and peered around a tree in time to catch someone clad in black, a few patches visible through the thickets.

Whoever was moving forward needed to watch their fucking steps before they gave away their location. Shit. *My* location since I wasn't all that far from him.

Through the thick press of trees, I heard the telltale sound of our SUV. Wolf was on the move. As long as this shit went smoothly, we would only have moments. Moments before the Bratva arrived. Moments before they attempted to wrangle my pack. Moments before I could lose one or all of them.

Staying low, I crept closer, moving as quickly as I could while staying invisible in the moonlight filtering through the bare limbs. Had this gone down during the warmer months, I would have been swathed in complete darkness. But I would have also had a harder time finding my way forward without making too much noise.

I would also be sweating my balls off in my tactical vest and weighed down with so many weapons, pistols, the rifle strapped around my neck and shoulder, even the knives shoved into sheaths at my hip, leg, and ankle.

My girls had their pistols. Hopefully, they remembered to keep one in the chamber and had them hidden away in their pants. The only rooms in the cabin without cameras were the bathrooms. I'd made sure to remind them to only handle the firearms in there so Mikhail was unaware they were armed.

Shit. Now I wished we'd left more weapons in the cabin for backup. We'd just never really thought it was necessary, had never expected to use it for something like this. Had never really thought it would be necessary, period.

Within twenty minutes of Wolf arriving, the sounds of an engine rumbled from the distance, creeping closer. Then another. Whoever was coming wasn't alone. And they weren't doing the best job of hiding their approach either.

I was close enough now I could see the exterior of the cabin and the lights glowing from the windows. I could see movement inside, saw when Wolf stopped at the kitchen sink and made a show of getting a glass of water, his signal that all was secure inside.

So…why didn't that ease the anxiety burning a hole in my fucking stomach?

Oh. Right. Because there were military trained Russian assholes creeping toward the people who meant more to me than anything in this fucked up world. If I'd thought handing myself over to Mikhail or even his father would keep my pack safe, I would have done it in a heartbeat. But I knew they would use me as an example of what happened to those who don't bend the knee to the Gusev empire. They would slaughter my pack, in front of me, before ending my life. Or worse, they would take Spencer and Kennedy, rape and torture them in front of me before ending my misery with a bullet between my eyes or a blade across my throat.

The sounds of the engines cut off. In the distance, I barely caught the sounds of car doors being shut. And then silence.

Turning my head left to right, I sought the Kingsmen who would be hiding in wait alongside me. For a bunch of men who weren't trained for this kind of shit, they sure were good at being invisible. Other than the one biker I'd seen when Wolf had arrived, I hadn't caught a single sound nor the slightest hint of a scent since I'd begun my trek through the woods.

No voices met my ears, but a variety of scents carried on the wind. Alphas. A lot of them, though I couldn't pinpoint the exact number from signatures alone. It was hard to differentiate their scents past the pine trees and forest smell all around me.

Balancing my weight on the balls of my feet, I pressed my shoulder against a tree and watched around it, peering through the gaps in trees and bushes, watched for movement, waited for those mother fuckers to get close enough to my pack.

Kennedy had offered to use herself as the lone bait. She'd offered to head out on her own in a vehicle and wait for them to follow her.

We had all shot that one down before she'd even finished with the details of her plan.

This one…this plan had been a combination of Kennedy's and Wolf's plans. They were all being used as bait. The Kingsmen and I would attack from outside while Wolf would keep our pack safe from inside. And if anyone got through, there was a panic room for the three, although I had a hard time imagining Rey or Kennedy cowering in there. I could see them now, shoving Spence through the door, locking it, then standing sentry outside with the pistols in their hands.

And holy shit…the image gave me a fucking boner. Definitely not the time for my libido to take over. I had no desire to enter any kind of fight with my dick acting like a sword in my cargo pants.

Focus, asshole.

As much as I wanted to rush forward, to put my body between the enemy and my pack, I had to wait, bide my time, make sure they were in the right position. This was planned. And planned well. We had taken hours and hours to consider any and every outcome to ensure success.

But I'd been around long enough, had dealt with enough evil fucks in my lifetime to know there would always be circumstances for which I didn't plan.

I refused to entertain a single doubt. I had to trust in my pack, in my abilities, and the loyalty of Kennedy's family.

Low voices rumbled from thirty, maybe forty feet away. Why the hell were they making so much noise? Stealth was of the utmost importance for any assassin worth their salt.

A smirk crept across my face as their words began to form more clearly. They believed Wolf was the only one watching over two women and an omega. They believed this would be an easy crash and grab.

If that were the truth…why was I still seeing men dressed in various outfits from sweats and jeans to suits making their way to the cabin? Why bring so many for four people?

Raising my rifle, I closed one eye and peered through the scope, trying to count the number of men approaching. They didn't drive closer, but they were no longer remaining silent. And their heads turned side to side, their eyes squinted as they searched the woods as though they could feel so many sets of eyes on them.

As quickly as possible, I ran every single detail through my mind, recalled every single conversation we'd had, including when we'd ensured all of our phones were not only turned off, but in a room far from where we spoke. Sure, that might have seemed a tad paranoid, but I'd seen enough and committed enough of my own secret spy shit to know there wasn't nearly as much privacy as people liked to believe they had, even in their own homes.

There couldn't have been a single moment when Mikhail or his men would have been able to glean any information or detail of our plan. Unless one of the three inside that cabin had slipped in the time since they'd pulled into the driveway.

Eventually, the men stopped moving forward. I couldn't quite make out the exact number from my location but fuck if it didn't look like there were at least twenty cocksuckers lining up outside the cabin and gradually spreading until they completely closed off any exits or an escape route for my pack.

I had anticipated Mikhail wouldn't arrive alone. I hadn't anticipated *this* many. How many Kingsmen were currently hidden in the woods all around me? How many guns did the Bratva have?

And did they have anyone lurking downwind to bolster their numbers if needed?

Clenching my jaw, I shook my head. My heart began to pound so loudly in my chest I feared the enemy would hear it. I had never been nervous before taking out some evil son of a bitch. I had never been nervous while stalking my prey.

But my nerves weren't for myself. If I failed, I would lose my entire world in one night.

Fuck.

Pushing to my feet, I slowly made my way forward, my eyes moving constantly to keep as many of the soldiers in view as possible.

"Is this the part where I offer you safe passage for your omega?" one of them called out.

My feet halted, my eyes narrowed. Mikhail. He wasn't here for my omega. This was some kind of game.

With my rifle against my shoulder, I peered down the scope, the mark perfectly centered on Mikhail's temple. All I would have to do was pull the trigger and that mother fucker would no longer breathe the same air as my pack.

But then, his buddies would either start firing wildly into the woods, possibly hitting one of the bikers who'd volunteered as backup or attack the cabin with my pack inside.

Mikhail turned, looking from left to right into the pitch black woods. For a brief moment, his eyes grazed over me and I feared something had reflected off the glass of my scope and given away my location.

But he returned his attention to the front of the cabin.

"I hate to the bearer of bad news, but the only way anyone is leaving here tonight is once Alexei is dead at my feet. Although I would be willing to let your omega go if you toss that pretty beta out the door." There was a long beat of silence, presumably while Mikhail waited for a response.

He turned his back to the cabin, his eyes once more scanning the dark forest surrounding the cabin and switched from English to Russian.

"Brother, I can feel your eyes on me. End it now. Step out, put down your gun, and I'll let most of your pack go with their lives."

My heart thundered behind my ribs as my eyes turned toward the windows, the shape of Wolf backlit moving through the house, lights quickly flipping off, swathing the entire area in nothing but moonlight.

"I can't promise you anything about that little whore of yours. Although, it would be a shame to lose something so…delicious."

Rage burned through my veins, warring with the icy tendrils of fear for my pack. I had to trust in my beta's guarantees of her father's men, had to trust they would at least get Spencer, Kennedy, and Rey to safety if everything went to shit.

"Nothing to say, brother?" Mikhail asked, still speaking in Russian.

Wolf knew basic words, enough to know we were getting closer to exchanging gunfire. I could only hope that he caught on to the fact Mikhail was going to make a hell of an effort to get to Kennedy where he would either torture then kill her in front of me or add her to his disgusting harem of women he kept as slaves.

I swore I could feel Wolf watching me, could feel my packmate shaking his head, telling me to keep my ass in the woods.

But that wasn't the plan. I had to make an appearance and hope none of Gusev's men opened fire the moment their eyes landed on me.

Fuck. Rolling my head on my shoulders, I cracked my neck, took a few deep breaths, then stood from where I'd crouched and watched Mikhail and his men.

I didn't bother hiding my steps as I moved forward, my rifle aimed at Mikhail's head.

"Ah. There you are. Still as predictable as ever." He'd switched back to English, meaning he wanted my pack to know I was now exposed.

I was far from predictable. This was planned, no matter how much everyone had protested against my actions or the fact I was stepping directly in the line of fire. I could as easily be hit by friendly fire as I could by the enemy.

Deep chuckles rumbled around me as those who hoped to climb the ladder of the Bratva believed they had succeeded in drawing me out with threats to my pack, to my beta and my omega.

They better be in that fucking panic room. Otherwise, I was going to kick Wolf's ass myself when this was all over.

If I made it out of this alive.

Honestly, I would gladly lay my life down if it meant Kennedy and Spencer, and even Rey would make it through the night.

CHAPTER 40

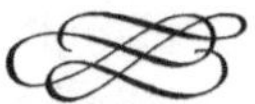

<u>Kennedy</u>

As planned, the moment the censors located along the driveway alerted us that someone had followed Wolf up the driveway, Rey and I ushered Spencer toward the back of the house, closer to the nest, aka the panic room.

If bullets started flying, our omega needed to be protected. And holy hell, he was still glaring holes in the side of my head because I was more than willing to sacrifice my own fucking life for his.

He believed his life was no more important than mine. And, sure, maybe he was theoretically correct. But he and Rey were both such rare designations, they would be dragged away from us if they weren't killed by a stray bullet. I didn't want to even consider the ways they would hurt my two loves, or the fact Spencer might be forced into one of those fucking compounds where he would end up being used as a breeder to some psycho alpha.

Wolf stayed far enough from the windows that he wasn't in direct line of anyone's sight, but close enough to keep an eye on the large number of men surrounding the house.

He looked at me over his shoulder when Mikhail began to taunt him, goad him into coming out with threats to me and Spencer.

Come on in here, asshole. I've got something for you.

Even now, I stood with my back to Spencer, the Glock I'd brought with me clenched in both hands, a round chambered and ready for the first motherfucker who stepped through that door.

I knew the plan. We'd gone over and over it back at the penthouse. Yet the moment Wolf nodded at me and began to flip off the lamps and turn off the lights throughout the cabin, the sign Alexei had stepped out of the woods and onto the driveway, my heart began to thunder painfully, the cadence too fast, too heavy.

Breathe. Just breathe, I repeated to myself, slamming the bond between us closed so Alexei wouldn't pick up on my fear or anxiety. He needed to focus and feeling anything from me would be a distraction that could cost him his life.

As I strained to hear through the closed doors and windows, I cursed in my head over the fact I hadn't bothered to learn any Russian other than the term of endearment Alexei had used for me since the beginning.

But I could easily guess that he was back to taunting Alexei, threatening him, maybe even offering to let him walk away alive if he… what? Handed me or Spence over like some kind of trophy? As if Wolf or Rey would ever allow that to happen. As though Alexei would ever even contemplate putting his life before ours.

"It's time," Wolf whispered barely above a breath.

Inching backward, I shoved at Spencer, moving him closer to the nest, to the room that would keep him safe.

"All three of you," Wolf said, glancing at us over his shoulder as he clutched his own firearm in his hands, the muzzle pointed toward the floor, his finger barely hovering over the trigger.

I could never hold a gun like that, not in such a high stress situation. I'd end up jumping at the slightest sound and shooting a hole in the floor or my own foot.

Rey growled softly, the sound barely a rumble in her chest, but began to inch closer to us until Spence and I were both standing in the entryway of the nest. All it would take was a step back and swinging the door shut, then we would be encapsulated inside a perpetual bomb shelter. Nothing short of a bazooka would be able to get inside.

With the cabin bathed in darkness, I could barely make out Wolf's silhouette as he moved away from us and crept closer to the front of the house, pressing his body to the wall and peering through the window. A sliver of moonlight cast the right side of his face in silver.

This couldn't be the last time my eyes drank in that face. This couldn't be the last night I heard Alexei's voice.

And then there were the men hidden among the trees, my father's men, Inland Kingsmen who were more than willing to hunt and kill the asshole who'd hurt me, who was threatening my pack.

Alexei blamed himself for my assault. But if any of the Kingsmen were hurt or killed, that would be on me. It had been my idea to put in the call, my idea to ask for their help, my idea for them to fight against alphas who might have been trained by the fucking Russian government to be killers.

"Wolf, you might as well come out and join the party," a man called out, presumably Mikhail. I'd only met him the one night and most of the memories of that night were of fear and pain. I would have thought their faces, Mikhail's face would have been burned in my memory until my last breath.

But alas, my beautiful brain decided to blur his and his buddies' faces out. I supposed that was a good thing. It would be even better if my brain could help me forget the feeling of my skin being torn, of the look of absolute devastation on the faces of my pack when they finally made it to my side.

"Don't you dare," I whispered to Wolf.

That wasn't part of the plan. He was supposed to stay inside until the very last minute, as a last resort to keep Spencer safe if someone were able to get through the door before we could get him safely enclosed in the nest.

You know what? Fuck it.

Shoving back with my shoulder, I forced Spencer inside and pulled the door closed, locking it from the outside. He could lock it from the inside, as well, but I knew if I didn't lock it out here, he would immediately yank the door open and demand I either come in or he come out with me.

The softest thuds sounded from behind me as Spencer pounded against the door. Damn. The alphas weren't kidding when they said the door was secured, that no one could get through without enough firepower to take out a bank vault door.

"Go in with him," Rey whispered, nudging me with her shoulder.

"Not yet," I said, my eyes glued to Wolf.

If that asshole made so much as a move to step through that door before time…

What? I couldn't exactly chase after him. I would be nothing but a pawn in the game Mikhail was attempting to play with my alphas.

But I could kick his ass when this was all over, when we were back at home, wherever that happened to be.

Making sure my bond to Wolf was wide open, I sent a warning. He glanced at me over his shoulder again and I swore I could see the faintest hint of a smirk in the light of the moon.

A sound near the rear of the house forced Rey and I both to turn. We crouched low, Rey moving toward the back door, her gun raised and pointed. I wanted to follow, but my need to stay close to my omega was stronger.

"You can come out and play or I could send in a few of my buddies to play with your pack, Wolf," Mikhail called out.

Play. I knew exactly what that asshole was threatening, and anyone who stepped foot through the door would be met with three guns pointed at their heads.

"Back door," Rey whispered so low I barely caught it.

Someone was trying to sneak in through the back.

Making a soft whispering sound with my lips, I caught Wolf's attention and pointed toward the door Rey was watching over.

We'd planned for this, as well. Someone thought they were being sneaky, not knowing there were pissed off bikers watching them in the shadows, simply waiting for either Alexei or Wolf to give the sign to release fire and brimstone, to mow these fuckers down. Although… did any one of them really deserve such a quick death?

I had never been one to enjoy the more violent aspects of my father's club or their businesses. I sure as hell hadn't enjoyed being coated in a man's blood.

But these men, these mobsters were threatening the people I loved. They were threatening my soul mates.

And that earned them nothing short of death.

CHAPTER 41

<u>Wolf</u>

This was not what I did. This was not how I operated. I was not a fucking bodyguard and was anything but patient.

Yet I was holed up in the house with all but one of my packmates, waiting for a signal from Alexei, waiting for the moment when someone fired a shot or made a move.

Someone was attempting to sneak in through the back. Rey was currently watching that door and there should be a few leather clad bikers keeping an eye on that side of the house to make sure entry wasn't gained.

They weren't to move forward unless absolutely necessary. Because the moment Mikhail and his sycophants learned the five of us weren't alone, bullets would begin to fly. I'd been in enough firefights to know how fucking easy it was for the wrong person to get shot, for a stray bullet to take the life of the wrong person, to end up getting shot by someone on your own fucking team.

Which, of course, was why I preferred to work alone.

Alexei had shot down every plan I'd come up with, including hunting Mikhail and his men on their own turf and taking them out there. It wouldn't have been all that hard to manipulate their security systems, to sneak in, cut a few throats, then sneak back out.

The biggest issue with that plan was daddy dearest was rarely seen in public with his son. And he sure as fuck didn't go clubbing. Either we would risk splitting up to take out Dima and Mikhail, or risk Dima Gusev sending his entire fucking crew after us for executing his son.

The knob on the back door shimmied lightly. Did these fuckers not realize or remember that sound carried? They were making a racket trying to break in.

Turning my head in that direction, something felt...off. Wrong. Why were they making too much noise? If these men worked for the Gusev Bratva, they had to have had some kind of training. They would know to remain silent. Stealth was a bad guy's best friend.

Distraction. From what? Why were they drawing our attention to the back door? There were plenty of people on all sides that there was no way for the five of us – four since Spencer was safely locked away – to keep track. So...why draw our attention to the back door?

Glass shattered a second later and flames erupted in the kitchen.

A startled squeak escaped Kennedy's mouth, but she hurried to what was burning and attempted to stomp it out, putting her right in front of the fucking window.

"Get your ass down," I growled out, not bothering to whisper.

She no more dropped to her knees that a bullet whizzed inside, missing her head by mere inches. No loud pop from a firearm. They'd attached suppressors to the muzzles. Which wouldn't give us much warning when they fired.

Apparently, we were no longer waiting for Alexei's signal. Because I sure as fuck wouldn't stand there like a fucking statue while someone took a potshot at my beta.

Pushing from the wall, I hurried to where she was crawling on her hands and knees toward Rey and attempted to stomp out the fire myself while keeping my head below the firing range of the window.

Bullets whizzed overhead, but they would have to climb onto a stool to shoot any of us inside.

"You motherfucker," I heard a male yell from outside and had no idea who said it or whose team they were on.

Then...the woods sounded like the fourth of July as gunfire erupted all around. And all the while, that damn doorknob continued to jimmy and wiggle.

The crawl space. There was the smallest space below the structure of the house, not even big enough for Kennedy to crawl more than halfway before she would get wedged.

But it was big enough for items to be tossed beneath.

As though my fear came to life with the mere thought, smoke began to billow from the thin gaps of the hardwood floor. Why the fuck hadn't we spent money restructuring the floor, putting something more solid beneath like concrete or even a big, fortified basement.

"Shit. Get in the nest," I barked at both Rey and Kennedy, jabbing a finger in that direction.

"Are we going to fucking suffocate in there?" Rey asked, no longer whispering now that the quiet evening was filled with pops and cracks, loud enough I feared we might garner attention from any neighbors within a five-mile radius.

"No. Get your asses in there now!" I barked again, turning and shoving both women.

Rey slid the lock out of place and pulled the door open, Spencer's shouts cutting off the moment the sound from outside made it to his ears.

His arms shot out and he hugged both women to him, dragging them backward as I swung the door shut. They would lock the door from inside. Or at least that had been the plan and one they had better fucking stick to. Because if we didn't make it through the night, I needed to know my sweet packmates survived.

Now that the three were safe and secure, I darted toward the back door and ripped it open, pointing and firing at the asshole who'd successfully kept us distracted enough while his buddies threw a fucking Molotov cocktail through the window and another, apparently, set fire to something below our feet.

Even if the cabin burned to the ground, Spencer, Rey, and Kennedy would be safe inside that panic room. There was even enough oxygen pumping in there to last them a month if they were to get trapped. One way or another, the three loves of my life would make it to live a wonderful life, with or without me and Alexei.

Perhaps firing at the asshole at the back door hadn't been the best plan. Because now there were others moving around the back and firing at me, the bullets hitting the wood log siding and going through the door as I kicked it shut.

But the bikers had moved forward and were returning fire. I could hear them firing at the Bratva assholes who were cursing and yelling in Russian.

Fuck. How was Alexei faring? I didn't have a pack bond with him, wouldn't feel whether he fell, whether he died out there. I wouldn't know shit until I stepped out onto that porch. And with the sounds of so many bullets hitting the sides of the house, I worried I would be caught in the crossfire if I tried.

But I needed to get to my brother's side, needed to back him up.

Pressing my back to the wall, I peered through the back door again. No movement. No flashes from any muzzles. It might be my best shot at getting outside and to Alexei.

Pulling the door open, I kept my body hidden behind it and pressed against the wall, waiting for that whizzing sound to tell me whether or not this was a safe exit.

When nothing happened, I slowly peeked around the corner to find a few dead bodies littered around the porch and the clearing between the deck and the woods.

Pulling my backup pistol from the back of my pants, I gripped both firearms and crept out, staying low, my eyes darting around in search of movement while I tried to pick out any sounds past the firing of semiautomatic weapons.

Sounds of a struggle came from the west side of the house as I sprinted forward. Alexei and Mikhail were in hand-to-hand combat, knives wielded in their hands, while men in leather vests and jackets held a few remaining Bratva assholes at bay with guns pointed at their heads.

The gunshots that still rang out came from a distance. Had a few of these cocksuckers attempted to run? If so, that would explain why the Kingsmen gave chase. And I couldn't help but hope the Russians would be nothing but a pile of bodies by the end of the night.

Watching as my packmate dodged from the swipe of a knife was harder than I thought. I wanted to simply raise my pistol, aim, and drop Mikhail, end this whole thing here and now.

There was blood running down Alexei's side and an open gash over his left eye.

But Mikhail looked as though he was barely staying on his feet, swinging the blade wildly in an attempt to stab at Alexei.

"Move again and I'll fucking end you here and now," someone growled from my left.

I glanced over to see a biker with the muzzle of his firearm jammed against the temple of a man wearing a suit.

None of these fuckers would walk out of here tonight. I didn't see the point in prolonging their lives. There were only five of them left, not enough to truly be a danger to my pack. But that was five men who could run back to Daddy Gusev with the news of who exactly was behind the execution of his son and his men.

Don't worry. We're coming for you next.

As Alexei continued to dance with Mikhail, I sauntered over to the five kneeling on the ground, lifted one of my firearms, and fired a round directly between his eyes. I moved down the line, executing each of them until it was only Mikhail left, the only enemy still standing.

And I had zero doubt Alexei was toying with him, drawing this out, causing as much pain and drawing as much blood from him as he could before taking his life.

Personally, I would have rather tied the fuck down and tortured him to death, taken a pound of flesh for what he'd put our beta through.

This shit would end before the night was over. I didn't care if we had to catch a plane and track Dima Gusev down. My pack would have a peaceful life. We would build that house we talked about, fill it with pups, and live as happily as a mismatched family with rare gems, two assassins, and a fetish performer beta possibly could.

Turning back to the two men, I felt a smile stretch my lips as Mikhail swayed, his hand opening until the knife he'd clutched fell to the ground with a dull thud.

His knees gave out. He dropped to the ground, tilting his head back to stare into Alexei's face.

My packmate, even covered in splatters and streaks of blood, looked like nothing short of death itself as he glared down at his former friend with so much hate, so much rage. He lowered, balancing on the balls of his feet and began to speak lowly in Russian.

I only knew basic words, but I caught enough to know Alexei had just told Mikhail that we would be ending the entire Gusev bloodline. And fuck yes, that was a good plan. End any and every single mother fucker who carried Dima's blood through their veins, cut off the head of the snake then hunt down every single person who was loyal to that mother fucker.

Raising his hand, Alexei pressed the edge of his blade to Mikhail's throat and slowly dragged it across his flesh, opening the skin and severing arteries. Mikhail didn't try to stop him, didn't raise a hand to stem the rush of blood leaking from the gaping wound.

When his eyes closed and his body dropped backward, a puddle of blood creating a dark stain on the ground around him, the smile that had formed on my lips turned into a grin.

The war wasn't over. But we'd won our first battle.

CHAPTER 42

<u>Kennedy</u>

I wasn't sure who was holding who at this point. My arms were wrapped around Spencer's waist, his around my shoulders. Rey had her arms wrapped around both of us while we waited.

Taking a risk, I opened the bond and sought my alphas, relief nearly bringing me to tears when I found them both still alive, if not alight with rage.

Since we were safely behind these ridiculously fortified walls, I made the decision to keep the bond open as a way to keep at least an emotional eye on my alphas. I might not be able to be out there with them, to help them fight the bad guys, but I couldn't sit here and wait, couldn't twiddle my thumbs and count the minutes until either we were told it was safe to come out or the oxygen ran out when everyone was dead.

When a sense of purpose and triumphant trickled down the thread from Alexei, I sagged. Wolf's thread sparked with relief, love, and a bit of anger.

Was it over? Was it safe for us to leave?

I was too scared to open the door. When Wolf had ordered the three of us in here, smoke had been pouring in from under the house. What if the fucking cabin was on fire? Would we still be safe in here? Would they be able to get to us or would we be trapped in here for days? Weeks?

Sending a rush of urgency to Wolf, I felt his answer.

At least I hoped I felt the right answer. If they were to come knock on the door, we wouldn't hear it, not from inside.

Pulling from my alpha and omega, I crept forward and slowly pulled the lock out of place.

The moment it was unlocked, the door was ripped open from my hands, and I instinctually raised my weapon, my finger on the trigger and ready to fire.

"It's me, baby girl. Don't shoot."

"Dad? What the hell are you doing here?!"

Yeah, I'd asked for some help from the club, but really hadn't wanted my dad to get involved. Between his age and his deteriorating health, the last thing I wanted was for him to be running through the woods or taking gunfire like he was still in his twenties. I'd been a later in life baby and my dad was already in his early sixties. Add on a life full of booze, drugs, and crime, and he'd aged…well, like shit.

"Did you think I would send my men without coming and protecting my baby girl myself? Now get your ass out of there. The house is full of smoke."

I wrapped my hand around Spencer's bicep and shoved him toward my dad to be pulled out of the house, Rey and I right on his heels.

"Is the house on fire?" Rey asked between coughs.

We stayed hunched low, but that didn't help when the smoke was coming from below.

"Can't tell, but you're more likely to die from smoke inhalation than burning up. Get your asses moving," Dad said.

Once we were outside, we all took deep cleansing breaths…

Then froze.

There were dead bodies lying everywhere in the back yard of the cabin. It was hard to tell who was who in the dim light, but I could only pray there were no Kingsmen patches attached to any of those bodies. The thought of someone giving up their lives for me hurt my heart.

"Where are Wolf and Alexei?" Spencer asked, pulling from my dad to press himself to Rey, wrapping an arm around my shoulders to tug me closer as though to protect me from the corpses we had to step over.

"They're fine. Out front. They told me to come get you three. Time to hit the road."

As we moved toward the front of the house, moonlight cast a silver halo over my two alphas. From where we were, it was hard to make out details, but it sure as fuck looked like Alexei was bleeding.

"Alexei!" I screamed out, pulling from Spencer and sprinting to him.

He opened his arms and wrapped them around me when I crashed into him. It was a few moments before I allowed myself to pull away and noted the cool air brushing against something wet on my cheek.

Raising my fingers, I touched the damp splotch and held them up in the moonlight, my heart stuttering when I realized it was, indeed, blood.

"You're hurt," I said as tears burned the backs of my eyes.

"Not all mine, lyubov," he said, taking my face in his hands and pressing a bruising kiss to my lips.

"Is it over?" I asked when he pulled back.

"Not yet. Mikhail is no longer a threat. But we need to track down his father and cut the head off the snake," Wolf said.

"Hell no. You two are not leaving my side for at least a month," Spencer demanded, rushing forward and throwing himself into Wolf's arms, a whimper escaping his lips when Wolf cupped the back of his head and deepened the kiss until Spence was practically bent backward.

That should shut him up at least long enough for me to find out what the fuck had happened and what the hell they meant by hunting down the head of the Gusev Bratva.

* * *

I PACED the living room of the penthouse while my dad played doctor and stitched up a few deeper cuts on Alexei's arm, his side, and over his eyebrow. As much as I hated that my alpha had been injured, I had to admit he was going to carry some sexy ass scars.

Wolf and Rey had Spence wedged between them as he watched every single move my dad made.

"You didn't tell me you grew up with a bunch of sexy bikers. I feel like I'm living out a porn fantasy or something," Spence said as Ghost, Charm, and Poe leaned against the wall and waited for my dad.

"You saying we're not enough, brat?" Wolf muttered, bumping Spencer's thigh with his own.

"All I'm saying is there's nothing wrong with healthy fantasies… coming to life."

Charm winked at my omega, but the others looked mildly uncomfortable with the attention. Especially when growls erupted from both Alexei and Rey.

Rey, I understood. Alexei shocked me, though he was currently in a bit of pain.

What really surprised me was that Wolf didn't bat an eye at Spencer's antics. He must have grown as used to the omega's flirtatious and crass moods as Rey and me.

"PS," Spencer faux whispered, "feel free to call me brat tonight."

My dad shook his head. Charm huffed a laugh. Ghost actually blushed and averted his eyes, looking anywhere but at my omega.

When Dad finished with Alexei, I couldn't wait any longer and moved closer, pressing my forehead to his. We were all in one piece. Mikhail was no longer a threat.

But Alexei and Wolf were already making plans to track down his father and ending the threat of the Gusev Bratva for good. That scared the shit out of me.

For one, they would have to track Dima Gusev down, find him when he wasn't heavily guarded, then get away without getting caught. Too many unknowns for my taste.

It was something I would fight with them about later. Maybe I could find a way to bribe them, threaten them, something to keep their asses at home until a better plan was put in place.

Besides, there was no guarantee Dima would know for sure who'd killed his son. Although…who was I kidding? Being as he'd sent his son after us, after Alexei, who the hell else could it possibly have been?

A majority of my dad's men had stayed behind to clean up the mess, piling bodies into the cabin they planned to torch, picking up as many shells as they humanly could, and making sure there wasn't a single thing that could tie anything back to any of us if the authorities were alerted. And they would once the flames shot high enough for anyone nearby to see. At least it wasn't so dry out that the Kingsmen would start a forest fire while trying to hide the slaughter.

"You five need to come our way for a while," Dad said as he washed his hands and cleaned up all the bloody gauze and first aid supplies.

"Okay," Wolf said.

We all whipped our attention in his direction.

"What? Makes sense. We move closer to the Kingsmen, build our pack a safer house, and when we're out hunting, we'll know they're still guarded. Makes total fucking sense to me."

"I like that one," Dad said to me, pointing at Wolf.

Wolf grinned at me like the cat who got the fucking bird.

But…he did kind of have a point. And I didn't exactly have ties to this state other than my job at *Plumes et Fouets*. Being as I planned to quit, there was nothing keeping me here. As long as the entire pack agreed to the move.

"What kind of shopping do you have in Iowa?" Spencer asked.

"I doubt they have a Prada or Chanel store there, omega," Rey said before pressing a kiss to his temple.

"Online shopping," Wolf offered with a shrug.

I turned a raised brow to Alexei.

"Why are you looking at me? I go where you go, lyubov. I can work anywhere."

Of course he could. Because there would always be someone who needed to end up dead.

CHAPTER 43

Thirteen Months Later

<u>Rey</u>

I had never seen my beta more beautiful than I did right now. I lapped at her folds, running my tongue across her clit before sucking it between my lips while Wolf took me from behind.

All I'd intended was to wake Kennedy up and let her know breakfast was ready. But she'd become a hot sleeper and rarely wore anything at all to bed. When I'd opened the door and found her practically spread on the bed, waiting for some attention, I couldn't hold back.

It wasn't often I made love to my beta, but I had never grown any less addicted to her cranberry taste on my tongue.

Wolf...well, he'd come to find out what was taking so long and took advantage of my ass in the air and slid into me.

Kennedy's hands tightened in my hair as she cried out, her thighs clamping around my ears as she came on my tongue. I savored the sweetness of her release, lapped at her opening as her body tensed and shuddered.

"Fuck, you two are hot," Wolf said, his hips pumping into me harder until he pushed me toward my own release only seconds before he grunted and stilled, filling me with hot jets from the head of his cock.

He didn't knot me, nor did I lock him. We needed to get our beta down for breakfast and couldn't do that if the two of us were stuck together for the next thirty or more minutes.

And knowing Wolf, the moment we were loose from each other, he would want another round.

Since the moment Spencer's and Kennedy's pheromones had changed, everyone in the house had become overly protective and hypersensitive.

And downright fucking insatiable.

"I'm surprised Alexei hasn't come bursting in here demanding to know what's taking so long," Kennedy said through her pants as she came down from the high of her orgasm.

Wolf pulled from me and grabbed the towel I'd used from my shower this morning to clean himself than me. Then I helped Kennedy roll from the side of the bed and grabbed clean clothes from her.

By the time we made it to the table, Alexei was pulling his mouth from Spencer's cock. That explained why he hadn't come looking for us yet. My omega must have gotten lost to his hindbrain and Alexei had helped him out.

"About time," Spencer said as he tucked himself back in his sweats while Alexei pushed to his feet and pressed a kiss to his forehead.

Kennedy took a seat beside Spencer, and, as if on cue, they both reached over and stroked each other's swollen bellies.

Somehow, both our beta and omega had managed to get knocked

up during Spencer's last heat. Within a few weeks, we would have two sweet little babies in our pack.

"No one tells you how fucking horny you'll be when you get pregnant," Spencer said, rubbing his hand over his belly, his free one stroking Kennedy's.

Kennedy hadn't wanted to carry a pup. But within a week of that first positive test, she had become not only accepting of the fact she was carrying a life but seemed to be looking forward to it.

We still had the threat of Dima Gusev hanging over our heads but being as we'd not only moved to another state but currently lived on the same street as a fairly large gang of bikers who had already become more than protective of our two pregnant packmates, I wasn't concerned about the Russian. He would be dealt with eventually.

"I think it's the influx of hormones. Like during your heat," Kennedy said.

She withdrew her hand from Spencer's belly and dragged the plate Alexei sat in front of her closer. "Damn, I'm hungry."

"You're always hungry," I teased her, kissing her hair before bending and kissing her belly then Spencer's.

I could never carry a child. Female alphas weren't able to impregnate or get pregnant. But I still felt as though these two babies were mine. I might not give birth, but I was just as much their mother, just as much their parent.

In a way, I almost felt sorry for the poor kids. As if Wolf and Alexei weren't already going to be overbearing papas, they had a huge crew of patched bikers who would kill anyone for looking at them the wrong way. And if one of these babies happened to be a girl? Holy shit. Any boy who tried to date them was in for a crazy ride.

We'd all discussed our fears of either of them presenting as anything other than beta, but it really didn't matter to any of us. We only wanted them to be happy and healthy. Regardless of their designations, they would be loved, cherished, doted on the way a child should be.

"Why did I get an alert that another delivery was coming today?" Wolf asked, glancing at his phone with lowered brows.

"Baby clothes," Alexei said with a shrug.

All four of us raised our eyes to his face with our brows almost to our hairlines. "They both have plenty of clothes," I said.

"They need more. Babies grow fast. And since neither of you will find out what we're having, I decided we needed more variety than just green, yellow, and orange."

"I happen to like orange," Kennedy teased.

"Your favorite color is red. But no way was I ordering anything for my pups that reminded me of you on the silk ropes," Alexei said with a grimace.

I barked out a laugh, unable to hold it in.

"Milo is performing tonight if anyone is up for a road trip," Kennedy said.

She'd officially quit her job the day after Mikhail had been killed. Anais had cried and told Kennedy how much she would miss her, that she loved her like family, but she'd been understanding.

Milo had kept in touch and was scheduled to come visit as soon as the babies were born. He'd also finally gotten over his nerves and danced during burlesque months, doing a strip tease that made even my blood hot when he'd sent us a video of his first performance.

"They really need to change the no sex in the club rule," Spencer muttered between bites.

Wolf chuckled. He was probably thinking the same thing I was, that Spencer would try to fuck one of us or beg for a blow job the moment Milo took the stage and started wiggling his hips.

"I'd rather neither of you travel for a while. You're too close to your delivery date," Alexei said, ever the protective papa.

"We've got weeks," Kennedy pouted. "And I'm going to get this out there now, I'm a one and done. How can something so small feel so freaking heavy?" She put her hand on her lower back and stretched.

"I want at least three more," Spencer said, shoveling a bite of pancakes into his mouth and chewing with glee.

"Yeah. Let's wait and see if you still feel that way once the contractions start," Kennedy teased.

EPILOGUE

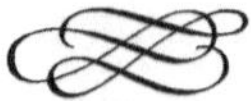

<u>Kennedy</u>

*S*pencer and I laid in the pack bed, snuggling into each other's side with Rey wrapped around his back. He was still sleeping, but I watched through sleepy eyes as Wolf cuddled our daughter that I had delivered, and Alexei stared down at our son in his arms.

Labor had sucked as badly as I'd thought it would. But at least I didn't have to be cut open like Spence. He would need more time to recoup. Good thing we had so much backup…and I didn't mean only our pack.

My dad and several of the Kingsmen had come by several times a day, making sure we had hot meals, the house was clean, the nursery was ready, and the laundry was caught up. Seriously, there weren't many things that felt odder than watching someone as big as Ghost folding pink, blue, and green onesies while wearing his leather cut.

Little Mable looked so much like Alexei while Wolfram Alexei looked…well, like Wolf. That had been a nice coincidence since none of us could sway Spencer from his choice of names. We'd taken to calling him Alex. Except the club. They called him Wolfie, something I was sure our son would grow to hate.

For now, though, it was too stinking cute.

"Have you two gotten any sleep at all?" I whispered, hoping not to wake up my omega or Rey.

Alexei's hazel eyes rose to mine. "They woke up. So we woke up. You both need your rest. Your dad said he always made sure your mom slept while you slept."

"But…I'm awake and so are they."

Wolf waved me off. "Go back to sleep. We've got them."

"Are they still awake?"

Both men shook their heads and continued to stare down at the babies. After a few minutes, they exchanged a look then traded babies as though they both wanted equal time with both our children.

THE NEXT TIME I opened my eyes, it was only Spencer and me in the bed and his hand had strayed south, toying with the seam of my panties.

"How can you be horny when you were cut open a couple days ago?" I teased, opening my thighs to give him better access.

"Have you seen yourself? I swear you're even more beautiful. Like motherhood unlocked some love potion in you or something. I really think you should reconsider your one and done thing."

"Hey," Rey said as she stepped in. "Hands to yourselves. Doctors both said no hanky panky for a few weeks. Too many stitches and risk of infection."

Rey had taken on a caregiver role for not just the babies, but Spence and me, as well. Not that I was complaining.

"Weeks my ass," Spencer grumbled, pulling his hand away and slowly pushing to a sitting position.

Rey raised both brows and smirked. "You can barely sit up and you thought, what, that you were going to bump uglies with my beta?"

"Hey. She's mine, too."

"You two can fight over me when everyone is healed up."

"Where are the alphas and the babies?" Spencer asked, craning his neck to look around Rey.

A wistful look crossed over Rey's face. "Downstairs with your dad. Grandpa demanded some baby time. He's been here a few hours, holding one baby then the other then back again. I'm surprised Wolf or Alexei hasn't had a stroke. This might be the longest they've gone without cuddling Mable or Alex."

That was an exaggeration being as the babies slept in bassinets beside the pack bed. But only a *mild* exaggeration. The moment either our son or daughter so much as whimpered, one of the alphas was wide awake and holding them in their arms.

Had someone told me I would not only fall in love with two assassins for hire, but that they would turn out to be the most doting, caring, gentle fathers, I might have laughed in their face.

Yet, here we were, living our dream life only a few houses down from my dad.

My life was complete.

"I think I want to try for another one during my next heat," Spencer said as he nestled down into the blankets.

Apparently, though, other members of my pack wanted an even fuller, more chaotic life. And...I didn't hate the sound of that.